THE IMPOSTER

Life Is Not Easy In The Big Easy

Also by Judith Lucci

Alex Destephano Novels
Chaos at Crescent City Medical Center
Viral Intent
Toxic New Year
Evil: Finding St. Germaine
RUN For Your Life
Demons Among Us-Coming in 2020

Michaela McPherson Mysteries
The Case of Dr. Dude
The Case of the Dead Dowager
The Case of the Man Overboard
The Case of the Very Dead Lawyer
The Case of the Missing Parts

Dr. Sonia Amon Medical Thrillers
Shatter Proof
Delusion proof
Fool Proof
Tamper Proof
Obsession Proof-Coming in 2020

Artzy Chicks Cozy Mysteries
The Golden Rings of Christmas
Almighty and the Corn
The Jewel Heist
Death on the Slopes

Other Books
Beach Traffic: The Ocean Can Be Deadly
Ebola: What You Must Know to Stay Safe
Meandering, Musing & Inspiration for the Soul

THE IMPOSTER

Life Is Not Easy In The Big Easy

A NOVEL BY

DR. JUDITH LUCCI

Bluestone Valley Publishing

Harrisonburg, Virginia

Copyright © 2013 by Judith Lucci
ISBN: 9781512271591
2nd Edition

Judith Lucci

Acknowledgements

Once again, it has taken a village for me to write this book! Many thanks to Dr. Julie Sanford and Dr. Donna Trimm for their beta reading and editing of *The Imposter* as well as Alice Tutwiler for her review of the book prior to publication. I would especially like to thank Jennifer Mandell of Bluestone Valley Publishing for her excellent input and final editing of the manuscript. Also, as always, I wish to think Eric Blumensen for his assistance with the final preparation of the book.

Dedication

This book is dedicated to my son, Eric and my daughter Tracey. Thanks for being there for me!

About the Author

Dr. Judith Lucci is a Wall Street Journal, USA Today and Amazon best-selling author. She is the award-winning author of the Alexandra Destephano Medical Thriller and the Michaela McPherson "Two Sleuth's and a Dog" Crime fiction series. Her newest series, Artsy Chicks Mysteries, features a group of eccentric and talented but zany artists in their Art Gallery at a Mountain Resort.

In 2017, 'Viral Intent' (Book 3) Alexandra Destephano Series) was awarded a Gold Medal by Readers' Favorites for 'Best Political Thriller' as was her crime thriller 'The Case of Dr. Dude' (Michaela McPherson #1) for a Gold Medal for 'Best Amateur Sleuth of 2017. 'The Most Wonderful Crime of the Year' won an additional gold medal for 'Best Holiday Read' of 2017.

Her favorite things are reading, writing, art and animals. In her spare time, she teaches painting, and raises money for needy causes. Judith lives with her family and her dogs in the Shenandoah Valley of Virginia. She loves to connect with her readers and is available at judithlucciwrites@gmail.com. Check out her website at www.judithlucci.com and sign-up to her newsletter for a free book.

Chapter 1

"Holy Crap, Mary, Mother of God! What the hell is wrong with people? Are they crazy, stupid, or just nuts," hollered Jack Françoise to no one in particular, even though he was sure his rants could be heard through the bullpen of the 8th Police District. "Honest to God, two tourists with their throats torn out in the deepest, darkest part of the Quarter. What is *wrong* with these idiots? I don't even go in that part of the French Quarter. No one needs to go down there; no one in their right mind *wants* to go down there, not even NOPD's swat team in full combat gear. Holy Shit, can anybody be that stupid or that drunk?! I just don't get it."

Newly-minted New Orleans Police Commander, Jack Françoise, sat behind his massive, but deeply scarred, walnut desk at 334 Royal Street glaring at two crime reports placed in his in-basket for review. A big, burly man who tended towards overweight, Jack looked distinguished in his commander uniform and his polished medals matched the glint of silver in his hair. A man's man, Jack commanded the respect of almost everyone he met. He stared out of his tall office windows, already heating up in the August sun, but saw nothing. His attention returned to the crime sheets, and as he reached for his coffee cup, his administrative assistant and PR guy knocked at his doorframe.

"What's up, Jason? Did I wake everybody up yelling?"

Jason Aldridge grinned at his boss. "Well, maybe a few left over from the night beat, but they were due to go home anyway," Jason joked.

Jack shook his head. "Did you check out these murders in the Quarter last night? What the hell?"

"Yeah, pretty bad. Young people, too, from what I heard. Kind of similar to that woman they found in that abandoned warehouse near Canal over in the First District several years ago. By the way, the coroner's office just called and they want you over there ASAP. It's about this new case, the one they are investigating in the Quarter now."

"Yeah, I just bet it is," Jack muttered sarcastically. "Who's working the scene in the Quarter? Think I'll go over there on my way to see the M.E."

"I think Bridges caught the case, but he's probably gone now. Don't know who the head of the forensic team is. I can check for you."

"Never mind, I don't care. If the M.E. calls back tell her I'm coming, but am stopping by the scene first."

"Will do, Capt'n! Whoops, Commander." Jason stumbled over his boss's title and smiled apologetically.

"Just call me Jack. Skip the title. I don't act like a commander anyway. Didn't even want to be one. I was and am happy in the trenches and on the street. But, as you know," Jack said wryly, "I never planned to leave them."

Jason nodded. "Yeah, I know that. I'm sure you'll always be a beat cop, no matter the title. You've never left the streets before, and you're too damned old and stubborn to start at this late date," Jason acknowledged, waving his boss out of the office. His heart swelled with pride, watching the big guy leave the 8th district office.

Jason loved being Jack's right hand man, a job he had just formally assumed several months ago when Jack had risen in the ranks. Jason had more respect for Jack Françoise than he'd ever had for any one man. Françoise could come across as a total police asshole, but deep inside, he was kind and generous and a true advocate for the citizens, particularly the victims of murder and violent crimes in New Orleans. Jack was also tenacious, bull-headed, and hard to work with, but

2

Jason was used to this as well. Sometimes, Jack's dark moods surfaced when he reached a dead end in the crimes he sought to solve. In Jason's mind, Jack was a hero and always would be even though Jack would never claim fame or recognition for the cases he solved.

Jason smiled while considering that magical way Jack disappeared from press conferences and the media. He was sure Jack planned to keep it that way, even as a commander. He was as humble as he was caring and altruistic and Jack flat out hated the press. Jason smiled to himself as he reflected on his years with Jack Françoise. *An honorable man,* Jason thought, closing the commander's door quietly as he left the office.

Chapter 2

Jack hated the blast of August heat that momentarily blinded him while exiting the 8th District office. He jumped into his vintage, police-retrofitted silver Cadillac parked in a no parking zone on the side of the building, and headed down towards the Canal crime scene on Burgundy. He parked, illegally of course, at the corner of Toulouse, knowing that all NOPD in the area knew his car and would never ticket him. He trudged down towards the scene, wiping the sweat off his brow with a white linen handkerchief.

Jack, as hardened as he was to street scenes, turned his head away from a man with a needle in his arm and a guy lighting up his crack pipe while sitting in a doorway. He was convinced that neither man had seen the inside of a house or had a meal or shower in days. He quickly glanced inside a vacant, burned-out building on Canal noting several other vagrants boldly smoking crack, not caring who or what could see them. The bottom of the barrel, the dregs of humanity, hung out in this part of the Vieux Carre. The commander hurried his pace towards the crime scene. He could see the yellow tape several blocks away and thought what a bitch it would be to climb back up the hill in this August heat. He hailed the CSI team's chief processing the scene.

"Yo, Vern, what's your ornery ass doing up so early in the morning?" Jack asked, slapping the forensic chief on the back. "I thought you were working nights!"

Detective Vernon Bridges stood up, turned, and faced Jack smiling broadly. "Why, Commander, what in the world are you doing down here in this hell hole so early? With your big promotion and all, I never expected you'd leave your air-conditioned office on Royal Street," Vern joshed, pumping the commander's hand.

Jack returned the grin, happy to see his old friend. "Vern, you know me better than that. I get the hell out of there every chance I get so I don't have to write reports and go to meetings. I hate all of those damned meetings." Jack shook his head and sighed. "These bureaucrats are crazy. They even meet to decide where to place the water fountains." Jack rolled his eyes and Vern laughed heartily.

"Well, then, who writes the reports and goes to the meetings? Isn't that why you got the big pay raise?" Vern teased his old buddy.

"Jason goes. He likes meetings and, as my assistant, it's his job to make me happy. So, he goes to the meetings and writes the reports, and that makes me happy. Besides, he's glad to get me out of there so he can do his own thing. So, what do we have here?" Françoise questioned, gesturing towards the crime scene.

Vern pointed to the two chalk-etched bodies on the ground and groaned, "The meat wagon took the bodies away an hour or so ago. Two kids, probably late teens or early twenties. Most likely tourists. They were pretty tatted up, lots of body piercings. Looked Goth, if you ask me, but then what the hell do I know? Black clothes, black hair, black nail polish and lipstick on the female vic, lots of metal."

Françoise shook his head. "Geez, not again. The report said their throats were torn out, sort of like an animal had attacked them. Anything else?"

Vern searched out his digital camera and flipped to a couple of shots. "They also had their wrists slit."

"Not much blood around here," Jack said. "Has anyone hosed down the streets? Had city maintenance been through here before they were found?"

"No, I don't think so, although they often come through before dawn. We waved off one truck when we got here a little after 5."

5

"Who called it in?" Jack asked.

"Anonymous. Someone dialed 911," Vern said, shrugging his shoulders. "Figures, doesn't it? Probably the sick SOB that did it. I got a funny feeling that he's sitting somewhere close, watching us work the scene. Been thinking that all morning," Vern ended, looking around the area at the rundown buildings and dark alleys.

"Could be. It's happened before. Any possibility they could have been killed somewhere else and dropped here? Any witnesses?"

"Shit, Françoise, you think we got a fairy godmother hanging out down here in no man's land? Nobody saw anything, nobody heard anything, and, the truth is, everybody we've seen is smoking a crack pipe, shooting up, or is drunk or drugged out of their mind."

"Yeah, got'cha. Figures. Get the troops to canvass the neighborhood. You may get lucky. Keep me posted. I am off to the coroner's office. The M.E. sent for me to talk about these two vics."

"Will do. See you, Jack. Hey, by the way, looks like the male may have been upside down on that wrought-iron fence at one point. See the blood on the concrete? Stay out of trouble and meetings," Vern joked as he turned back to the scene.

"Upside down, what the hell?" Jack muttered to himself as he began his hike back to his car. "Damn, it's hotter than the gates of hell already."

Chapter 3

When Jack reached his car, he was sweating like a pig. He opened the door of his silver Cadillac and sat down relishing the plush seats. He turned the AC on full blast, aimed all the vents towards himself, and sat there for a good three minutes taking pleasure in the cold air. Finally, he started the short distance towards the M.E.'s office on Rampart, praying for a decent parking place, even if it was illegal. He spied one. Bingo! It looked promising as he viewed the street parking. And the parking spot was legal. The day was looking a bit brighter as he slid into the metered spot. Of course, he would never put money in the meter.

Jack squinted from the fluorescent lights as he entered the temporary administrative offices of New Orleans Forensic Center. He was overcome by the smell of disinfectant and bleach. He high-fived the guard at the desk, signed-in, and continued down the back hall to the stark white autopsy room and morgue.

The NOLA Coroner's Office had been under considerable strain lately due to bad publicity in the media. The *Times Picayune* had run a whole series of articles about screw-ups at the coroner's office. The stories had focused on staff losing DNA evidence, filing incomplete reports, and misinterpreting autopsy findings that had never existed. Worst of all, the office had been accused of selling body parts. It was rumored the coroner had made thousands of dollars selling livers, corneas, and bone marrow. These accusations were providing a field day for defense lawyers. Jack clenched his jaw and gritted his teeth just thinking about it. Damn the liberal press!

The coroner's office employees, like most state offices in the many parts of the nation, were underpaid, understaffed, and under appreciated by most people who crossed their thresholds. The NOLA staff was demoralized and the office had experienced lots of turnover when, in fact, it was also home to some really fantastic forensic pathologists, dentists, and physicians. They were probably some of the best in the country, although you can bet the *Times Picayune* hadn't reported that little detail. He cursed the newspapers again under his breath.

The autopsy room was busy. Three physicians were autopsying recent victims, but he didn't see his favorite medical examiner. Nor did he find his two stiffs from this morning – at least, he didn't think he did, since the victims on the tables all looked pretty old.

"Yo, Fred," he hailed a morgue tech, "You seen Dr. Jeanfreau?"

"Yeah, she's in her office. Straight back, Commander," Fred gestured, giving the commander a big grin. Fred was a favorite of Jack Françoise because he always knew what was going on, never played dumb, and wasn't lazy, all traits which put Fred on his way to meeting most of Jack's criteria for earning praise.

"Thanks, man," Jack said, starting back down the hall, noticing the decrepit condition of the offices. Unlike the bright autopsy room, the temporary offices of the coroner were pretty shabby. Jack eyed the faded, dirty carpet as he wandered down the hall towards Maddy's office. He wondered when they were moving into their new building, although he hated the thought of them leaving his police district. It had been convenient having them so close. Now he'd probably have to hit I-10 to get there. What a pain. Traffic was always bad going out of New Orleans. As a matter of fact, traffic in New Orleans was always awful and he didn't know all of the illegal parking spots in that part of town.

Maddy's door was partially open. Since she wasn't dictating, Jack decided to knock and interrupt her.

"Yo, Maddy, you rang?"

Dr. Madeline Jeanfreau, Assistant Medical Examiner, stood and walked around her desk to greet Jack. She was a tiny woman. Even with high heels, she was only a little over five feet tall. She hugged Jack and kissed him on the cheek. Jack returned the hug.

"What the hell, Commander? You get promoted, have a party, and don't even invite your favorite M.E.? How do you expect to keep getting special treatment from me or my office?" the diminutive Dr. Jeanfreau queried, as she smiled and shook her short, highlighted hair.

"That wasn't a party; it was just a bureaucratic BS hour. I didn't want to go and you would have hated it. Think of who you would have had to hobnob with for an hour, all the while getting nothing but punch and cookies. It was grueling."

"Well, you owe me lunch then and it's going to cost you a bunch ... and drinks as well," Maddy insisted, giving Jack a grin. "Soon! I want my lunch soon."

"Anytime, Maddy. You're the busy one. You know I just sit around and eat chocolate éclairs all day," Jack commented sarcastically. "What's up? Jason said you wanted to see me."

"Yeah, about those two dead kids that came in a couple of hours ago. Have you got any ID or information on them?"

"No, nothing yet. I just talked to Bridges, the detective who caught the case. We're still looking for witnesses. There was no ID found with the bodies. The detective said they looked Goth and were tatted up. Not much blood at the scene, though probably enough for DNA. Why?"

Maddy shook her head and said, "It's pretty strange. We haven't finished the autopsies yet, but we started collecting body fluids when they first came in, before we put them in the chiller."

"Yeah, so? That's pretty normal, right?"

"Yes, it is," Maddy replied, looking straight at Jack. "Problem is, they didn't have any."

"Didn't have any what? Maddy, I am not getting this. What are you telling me? The stiffs didn't have any fluids?"

"That's right, Jack. They didn't have any blood. It's likely the C.O.D. will be death by exsanguination." Maddy stared at Jack.

Jack's shoulders slumped and stared back at his friend. He felt the fear crawling out of his pores. Maybe not fear, just uncertainty perhaps? *What The Fuck! Not again! Please, not again,* he thought to himself. Their eyes locked, each reading the meaning on the other's face.

Maddy finally broke the silence. "Yeah, Jack. Here we go again. Just like 2009, 1984, and 1933."

Jack was suddenly overcome with fatigue. He shook his head. The day really wasn't getting better after all. "Well, keep me in the loop. Hopefully, these are the only two. We'll know more when we ID them." His voice sounded worn and tired.

"If you ever do ID them," Maddy replied. "Remember, we never had an ID for the case in 2009. I'll handle the autopsies personally. There could be another cause of death, but it's unlikely with the two of them and the fact that they were young and healthy."

"Yeah, I know," Jack replied, while checking a text message that had just come in. "I've got to go. I just got a 911 from CCMC. I hope there's nothing major gone wrong over there." He groaned, hugged Maddy, and left her office. But, he knew better. He knew something bad had happened. Whenever he got called to Crescent City Medical Center, it was always something bad.

"Oh, Jack," Maddy called after him, "the vics had a receipt on them for $116. From *Howl*."

Jack turned around, looked at her, and shook his head. "Great, this day just keeps getting better," he said sarcastically.

Chapter 4

It was a little after midnight and Angela Richelieu was just finishing her nursing shift report when the red light went on in the corner of the nursing station at Crescent City Psychiatric Pavilion, signaling an All Staff Alert. "Damn!" she muttered under her breath. Flashing red meant all hell had broken out somewhere on the unit. Sadly, she knew what that meant for her and picking her daughter up on time. Her shift had ended at 11, but paperwork had taken her an hour after that. Now who knew when she would get out of there?

Cursing under her breath, she unlocked a small metal cabinet and took out a syringe filled with Vitamin G. She laughed a bit as she thought about the Vitamin G – a nickname for Geodon. A powerful anti-psychotic agent, it could settle down a horse almost immediately. G for goodnight! She placed the syringe in the pocket of her blue uniform top and cautiously opened the security door that led onto the Psych unit. Never knew who was hanging around, just waiting to get into the office.

The coast was clear and Angela saw everybody heading towards the east corridor. She heard an angry "Get the hell off of me! I'm a policeman!" coming from that hallway. *Big Jim!* she thought to herself.

She was surprised and not surprised at the same time. James McMurdie, the former NOPD cop, had been a model patient up until now, so she was surprised that he was involved. She was not surprised because she had almost seen something coming earlier in the evening.

It had been a great shift on the unit until that new administrator, Lester What's-his-name, had shown up. He wasn't even a real employee. Don Montgomery, the CEO, had contracted with him to run the Psych Pavilion. Lester was

12

weird, just as weird as some of the patients. The patients had been quiet until he came onto the unit. Once the patients saw him, a sort of agitation had set in like a wolf walking into a field of tasty sheep.

Plus, he was creepy. Angie shook off a chill when she thought about the way he'd looked at her. He was gross and struck her as a real letch. He'd stayed most of the evening on the unit. He was working in his office between the general psych and the prison units when he wasn't on the units talking with the patients. She remembered the other nurses saying how inappropriate it was that he talked so much with the patients. He'd spent a lot of time talking with Jim in the day room. A lot of time.

Angela hurried past the shuffling patients and when she turned the corner and looked down the corridor, she saw a sight that was both tragic and comical. Jason, the lone security guard, whose best asset was his enormous weight, was lying on top of Jim in the hallway. Ben, the orderly, had control of Jim's right arm and Amy, a petite Asian-American patient care assistant, was trying to control his left arm. Amy was wrapped around the arm like a python while he threw her up and down as if she were weightless and he tireless. Amy grunted each time Jim slammed her onto the dirty green tile floor.

Ben looked up as Angela ran down the hallway. "Hurry up! He's beating the hell out of Amy!"

Angela looked to Jim's left arm where Amy was clinging like a tired squirrel to a tree trunk, and saw that Jim's sleeve had ripped at the shoulder, exposing his taut deltoid muscle. Without hesitating, she sat down on top of Amy. Mercifully, their combined weight kept the flailing left arm pinned to the floor as Angela plunged the needle into the deltoid muscle and pushed the Vitamin G into Jim's body. She withdrew the needle and waited.

As she sat perched on the softening arm, Angela thought about what a joke the Psychiatric Pavilion was. The "Pavilion" was really an old three-story storage warehouse that CCMC had hastily renovated into three psychiatric units about eight years ago when psychiatric and substance abuse services had actually been moneymakers for the hospital. Now they weren't and the building had been sadly neglected. It was beginning to have the look of a "blighted" building that Angie remembered from her Community Health class at LSU where she had recently received her Bachelor's degree in Nursing. *Fat lot of good that did me*, she mused.

But Angie knew in her heart that her degree did matter. She chose to work at the Pavilion where the salary was at least fifty percent more than the medical units because the patients were so sick, scary, and dangerous. The Pavilion was actually three nursing units. Pavilion I was now the Prison Unit and housed some of the most dangerous, criminally insane inmates from the Deep South. Pavilion II was now general psychiatry where chronically psychotic patients were committed by temporary detaining orders. They were kept there "until they promised not to try to kill themselves or others again." Angie thought it was criminal that these sick patients were generally discharged in two days. Jim was one of the exceptions. Pavilion III was the substance abuse unit where patients were detoxed and "cured" in three days, and then discharged. The absolute worst was the CCMC Pavilion management. Don Montgomery, the CEO of CCMC, had contracted with the state hospital over in Mandeville to take their forensic psychiatric patients several years ago when a public outrage from the good citizens of Mandeville had succeeded and the hospital closed. Even though CCMC received a premium for housing and caring for the forensic patients, none of the money went back into the safety and security of staff and patients at CCMC. Angie shuddered and felt a chill when she thought about the patients she'd worked with over the past year. Some of them had nearly frightened her to death. She had thought Jim was one of the safe ones – until now.

While plunging the needle into Jim's shoulder, she had made the mistake of looking into his eyes. The eyes were there, but Jim wasn't. It was as if he were somewhere else. He hadn't recognized her. Recognition was the basis of human interaction, and is what separated friend from foe. Those empty eyes terrified her!

"What set him off tonight?" Angela asked Ben as she came back to the present. "He was one of the good ones – I thought."

"Louis and Jim were playing Battleship in the day room. Louis won and Jim said he was cheating. It was so strange. Normally Jim didn't care if he won or lost. Not this time. Next thing, Jim said Louis was sleeping with his wife. Crazy! Louis hasn't had a hard on in ten years. Next thing, Jim lunged at Louis and missed and Louis ran into the hallway yelling. Jim followed with murder in his eyes. Louis ducked under Jason's arm and Jim ran smack into that arm. Knocked him down and Jason got on top of him. I came out of the day room and jumped on Jim's arm."

"Thanks, Louis. Many thanks to you, Jason. And Amy – what you did was above the call of duty. I think you're going to be pretty sore. If you need to call off for your next shift, I'll vouch for you," Angie said as she looked at the poor battered Asian-American woman.

"Thank you, Miss Angie," replied Amy in broken English.

"Okay, let's get a stretcher and get Jim into the seclusion room. I've got to go back to the office and write up the report for this incident." Angie got up and hurried back to the office, carrying the capped syringe with her to deposit in the Sharps Container.

Chapter 5

It was after two a.m. when Angela finally stood in front of the first of two locked metal exit doors. This one bore the scars of countless chair and table strikes. The institutional grey paint was scratched and the graffiti had not been washed off for a week. She fumbled with her keys, finally got the key in the lock, and urged the heavy tumbler to turn. "Damn," she cursed glancing at her watch and noting the time. She wished she had called the childcare center in the main hospital to tell them how late she would be picking up Jessica. *Oh my God, I'm three hours late*, she thought. *They're going to kill me over there.* She felt her pulse race with anxiety as she considered how upset her sixteen-month-old daughter was going to be when she woke her up to take her home.

I've got to get a new job, she thought. *This psych unit is killing me.* She closed the door and heard the reassuring click as it locked. She walked down the short hallway to the second locked door. This one only bore a couple scars, but they were deep. She didn't remember who it was or when, but one of the patients had followed a staff member through the first door with a broken off chair leg in hand. Most of the blows had landed on the unlucky staff member. A few had landed on the door. The door had survived – the staff member had not.

I never get off on time, she thought. She glanced behind her just once to make sure nobody was in there with her then she unlocked the second door. Once through that door, there was a long hallway, then an exit door with a push bar. The second door closed behind her and she made sure it was locked before she walked down the long hallway. *Boy, it's dark out there*, she thought, peering through the glass windows

17

of the hallway. Sensing freedom, she pushed on the bar to open the door to the outside. The elation was short-lived.

The heat smacked Angie in the face as she walked into the August night. The air was close and heavy. A crimson-tinged bolt of lightning highlighted the sky for an instant then things went dark again. *Thunderstorms*, she thought. *I've got to get home soon. Jessica is scared of thunderstorms and and she will freak out if it happens in the car.* She walked quickly through the darkened path towards the parking lot. She looked around and told herself she was alone. *It's pretty spooky out here,* she thought. For a moment, she considered calling security and then she remembered that it would take at least thirty minutes for the guard to get over to the Pavilion. Besides, if he were busy, it could be twice that time.

With the cutbacks heralding the new health care act, there was only one security guard on the night shift now. There used to be three or more guards, even on weekends and now there was only one roaming guard and one – Jason – in the forensic psych unit where Angie worked. After all, it is New Orleans and even post Katrina, the crime rates were startling.

Angie continued to reflect on the Pavilion as she walked to her car. Now psychiatry was a money-loser, a liability to the bottom line – and CCMC, a world-class hospital, wasn't about to spend large sums of money to safeguard patients or staff. Managed care payment systems made it almost impossible for you to be crazy, have a breakdown, or recover from prescription or street drug abuse or alcohol. Reimbursement had all but disappeared and with health reform on the horizon, it would only get worse. The mental health system in the U.S. was sadly and severely broken, irretrievably so, perhaps. In fact, with everyone getting care under the new reformed system, it was predicted that mental health care would increase steadily with shorter-term admissions.

Angie shook her head when she considered just how awful the mental health system was in the U.S. Depressed, deranged, and addicted psychiatric patients could no longer come in for a few weeks of therapy, get their meds regulated, have a few art classes, and play some board games to learn to control their anger. Why, just last week they had discharged a newly diagnosed Bipolar II female patient who had attempted suicide and been in a coma for ten days with an aspiration pneumonia. She only stayed on the psych unit for two days, because the patient promised, "I'll never do it again. I don't know what came over me." Of course, her insurance didn't want to pay either, but the hospital would have been ethically bound to keep her if she had asked to stay. In Angie's mind, that bordered on gross negligence. Suppose that woman went home and "offed" herself with her small children in the home? Worse still, suppose in her psychosis, she killed herself and her family? It had happened before. What safeguards had been put in place? *Oh, I forgot*, Angie admonished herself. *She had two days of counseling and three days of Lithium.* At least that's what the attending shrink had told Angie when she questioned the discharge. That should do it. *Yeah, sure*, Angie thought. She was disgusted with the entire U.S. mental health system. How in the world could anyone get better in only several days? These poor, mentally sick, often physically ill patients were discharged back on the streets of NOLA or even to their homes with no regulated medicines or skills to fight back against the demons that endlessly plagued their minds.

Her walk in the black night seemed endless. Even this late, the Southern air was stifling and viscous. She was sweating, but she felt cold on the inside. Angie continued to think about the dangerous patient population at the Pavilion.

19

Many of CCMC's psychiatric admissions were initiated at the hands of the New Orleans Police and the local magistrate who had them committed after they had been picked up for a crime or some sort of outburst. Angie quivered again when she thought of some of the deeply psychotic patients trying to live on their own. They also had to medicate several of the most violent patients prior to bedtime. Angie had doled out six Thorazine Slurpees like they were health food drinks, but even then the brutality was awful. She thought about it and then deliberately pushed it from her mind.

When she was honest, Angie admitted to herself that she hated working in psychiatry. She hated it because she was afraid. And she knew the patients knew. It was almost as if they could smell it on her. She could see the recognition in their eyes when they realized it. They seemed to give her a secret smile. Many of their eyes seemed to have an evil glint. Besides, on the critical care units or in the emergency room, you could predict physiological changes in patients. You knew if a patient was going to "go bad" and have a heart attack or throw an embolus. You knew what to expect. But, in psych! You just couldn't tell. You couldn't anticipate the interworking and short circuitry in the minds of the profanely and criminally insane. They'd go off at the drop of a hat over nothing. You could hand them their fork the wrong way and they'd come after you. It was frightening. Many of the patients were violent criminals, who had committed heinous crimes, yet CCMC cared for them and she didn't mind caring for them. She just wanted to have enough staff to work in a safe place.

Angie continued her musings on the way to her car. Her background was critical care and emergency department but there'd been an opening on the psych unit where she could work just weekends and get paid for full time. This was ideal in many ways as it allowed her time with Jessica. She could be the kind of wife her husband wanted – at least most of the time. Besides, the money was good. Everybody at CCMC knew the Psychiatric Pavilion was the armpit of the hospital and that nurses were paid a premium to work there because it was dangerous. The Pavilion was also isolated, turbulent, and chronically understaffed, especially now because nobody really knew what health reform was going to do to psych care. Usually Angie didn't mind so much. But the past three nights had been particularly stressful for her, more so than usual. She had been on a different unit each night and besides, Jessica had a cold and she always felt bad leaving her baby in daycare when she was sick. Her Catholic guilt kicked in every time.

It was darker than the blackest of nights, as an ominous feeling of dread hung thick in the night air. Thunderstorms earlier in the evening had created a mass of low, overhanging clouds that completely obliterated the moon. Suddenly, Angie felt a chill come over her. She looked over her shoulder as a quiver ran up her spine. Her legs tingled. Did she hear someone breathing? She strained her ears. She couldn't hear anything strange. The hum of the cicadas and other night insects was deafening. Angela picked up her step, making a pact with herself never to walk to the parking lot alone again. Not ever. It was scary and unsafe. What in the world was wrong with her? Why had she made such a reckless decision? After another minute or so, she heard another noise. It sounded like a set of keys hitting the pavement or, perhaps, like metal hitting metal, she thought. Then, she heard a cough and a sigh of what seemed like satisfaction.

Angie's autonomic nervous system kicked in. Fight or flight! She started running for her life, but was no match for her assailant. He quickly overtook her, grabbed her by the hair, stuck a rag in her mouth, and pulled her over into a crop of trees to the right of the road. Her attacker seemed huge and had a large scarf tied over his face. His head was covered with a hat. Angie looked into her attacker's face as he leered over her. Her eyes widened in disbelief when they adjusted to the darkness. She knew this man! Her heart was firing erratically and she was dizzy and weak with fear. Her assailant looked at her and laughed.

"So, you recognize me, you little slut bitch. We can't have that now, can we?" Her assailant spat the words at her.

Angie was paralyzed with fear. Her hands were pinned down and her assailant's knee was in between her legs. Her captor outweighed her and was strong. She couldn't move, but struggled against him anyway, trying to overcome his strength.

He let one of her hands go for a second while he pushed one of the metal spikes into the soft ground.

Angela's hand ripped the hat off her assailant's head and she dug her nails into his hair, pulling as much hair out as she could. She had wanted to poke out his eyes, but had missed.

"You little bitch. I could kill you for that! How dare you touch *me*. You *are* one of them." The man slapped her, dislocating her jaw.

Angie felt the bone pop near her ear. The pain was overwhelming and she started to vomit. This further enraged her captor and he slammed her face into the dirt, ripping off her uniform pants. His intent was clear, but all Angie could do was lie there and focus on the smell of the rotting vegetation on the side of the road. She tried to detach herself from her surroundings. It didn't work.

She heard him grunting while he pushed three more stakes into the ground, singing quietly to himself as he moved methodically through his tasks, clearing old leaves and trash out of his way and away from her. It was like he was cleaning house. For a moment, she thought he had forgotten about her and she felt a bit of hope. But it was far-fetched. He turned to her, smiled sweetly, and bit her on her shoulder. Angie screamed and then her attacker hit her in the head with a piece of metal pipe.

Angela felt the searing pain rip through her head and down into her neck and shoulders with the first blow. The second blow didn't seem to hurt so much. Her last conscious thought was how pretty the twinkling lights looked in the intensive care unit in the main hospital building. She could see them clearly from where she was and she wished she were working a double shift up there where everything was predictable, where the patients were harmless and appreciative. Then, finally, blessedly, she lost consciousness.

Chapter 6

"Oh, no, no ... no ... oh, no ... it can't be. It just can't be. This has to be a joke and it isn't funny. Stop telling me these things. Angie's at home right now taking care of the baby. She worked last night; she only works on the weekends. Today is Monday," Bridgett insisted.

A short silence followed as Bridgett continued to listen to the voice on the other end of the phone. Her voice was confused, skeptical as she responded, "You've got to be kidding me. This is wrong, wrong, WRONG! It's not funny!" Bridgett's voice reached a fevered pitch as she continued to argue with the person on the other end of the phone for playing games with her about her sister. Finally, she slammed the phone down and marched into Alex's office, all legs, high heels, and long, blond hair.

Alex, the legal counsel for Crescent City Medical Center, looked up from her desk, startled to see her normally good-natured, fun-loving secretary glowering at her, full of rage. Bridgett could best be described as a blond bombshell. She was tall and beautiful. She wore bright colors and survived a full day in the highest stiletto heels Alex had ever seen.

Bridgett's big blue eyes flashed anger and her voice was clipped as she addressed her boss. "I'm so mad, in fact, I'm pissed. Somebody from the E.D. just called and told me Angie is all beaten up and a patient there. It really isn't funny and it's a sick joke. I know Angie's at home taking care of Jessica." Bridgett glanced down at her watch and added, "Besides, it's 10:00 in the morning, and she worked *last* night over at the Pavilion. I know, because I talked to her."

Alex stared at Bridgett, confused by the conversation. "Who called you, Bridge?" Alex asked, her voice soft and concerned.

24

"I've no clue. I didn't hear their name. I'm sure it's a mistake, but I am still pissed because they got the wrong person. They need to be more careful over there. Besides, I'm too busy for this stuff today. I love to have fun and cut-up, but not about sad stuff. This just isn't funny. It pisses me off." Bridgett fumed, her blue eyes stormy with anger.

Alex and Bridgett heard a knock in the outer office and stared as the door to Alex's private office slowly opened. Crossing the threshold into her office were Dr. Monique Desmonde, the chief of psychiatry at CCMC, Commander Jack Françoise of the New Orleans Police Department, and Alex's old nemesis, Bette Farve, the chief nursing executive at CCMC.

Alex felt a cold, numbing twinge in the pit of her stomach and the hair on her arms began to rise. She knew something was very wrong and surmised what was coming next.

Dr. Desmonde gave Alex a hard look, shook her head negatively and then turned her attention to Bridgett.

Jack moved into a position behind Bridgett and gently directed her towards the elegant sofa grouping in Alex's office.

Alex felt as though she were watching a perfectly choreographed production.

Bette Farve stood uselessly to the side of the group for a moment, studying her bright red manicure, and then took a seat in a Queen Anne chair.

Alex's heart was thudding as Monique motioned for her to join them on the sofa.

Bridgett seemed transfixed, unable to talk. She looked like a tall, beautiful Barbie doll.

Dr. Desmonde began slowly, "Bridgett, I'm afraid I've some bad news for you."

Bridgett's eyes were blank as she stared at Monique, a beautifully groomed, dark-haired woman in her forties.

Dr. Desmonde began gently, "Bridge, can you hear me? We must talk, now."

Bridgett nodded her head slowly.

Alex could feel fear and uncertainty crawling up her spine. Her knees began to shake and her heart was pounding madly. It was the same feeling she always had when something bad had happened. Alex felt her knees jerking so badly that she was sure they would cause her feet to jump out of her 4-inch heels.

Jack touched her knee, realizing Alex's discomfort and offering support.

Alex gave the police commander a small, tight smile.

Dr. Desmonde continued, her voice soft, her eyes meeting Bridgett's straight on. "Angela worked yesterday, Bridgett. She worked the 11a.m. to 11 p.m. shift on the psych unit."

Bridgett interrupted Dr. Desmonde. "Yeah, yeah, I know. I tried to call her last night. I called early in the evening, but she was working on the prison or forensic unit or wherever. We never spoke, at least last night," Bridgett continued, the irritation in her voice unmistakable. "The idiot from the E.D. said she was over there and had been beaten up or something, said she couldn't speak so I didn't believe them." Bridgett turned and noticed Commander Jack Françoise at her side and addressed him, her brilliant blue eyes full of anger. "Commander, can you do something about this? Someone is harassing me about Angie," Bridgett said as she started to rise from the sofa. "I've got to go. I have a ton of work to do." Bridgett rose from the sofa to leave, as if nothing real had just happened.

Jack looked over at Dr. Desmonde who gave him a thumbs-up sign. He took Bridgett's hands in his own and said, "Bridge, it's not a joke. Someone hurt Angie after she left work last night. She was attacked and we didn't find her until this morning and..."

Alex's heart lurched at the sight of Bridgett's big blue eyes. They were filled with terror and uncertainty. Her pupils were huge, surrounded by liquid pools of white. Her long blond hair created a halo around her head. Alex wasn't completely sure if Bridge understood what the police commander p had said.

Dr. Desmonde interrupted, "Angie's over in the E.D. They're going to take her up to surgery and I thought you might like to see her before she goes." Monique's voice trailed off, uncertain of Bridgett's level of comprehension.

"Yes, yes, I would. Is she okay?"

Monique continued, slowly as she shook her head, "No. Not really. She is very sick. In fact, she is in critical condition. She has a machine breathing for her, a ventilator, and she has some head injuries. She's lost a lot of blood. She also has some internal injuries and Dr. Goshette wants to do an exploratory to be sure she isn't bleeding on the inside."

"How'd she get hurt?" Bridgett asked in a dazed and child-like manner as she looked around the room. It was clear to all of them that Bridgett really wasn't getting it.

Alex couldn't help but be amazed at how good the brain was at screening out bad news.

Being the psychiatrist that she was, Monique tried hard to work through Bridgett's shock and denial. She started again, "Bridgett, Angie was attacked and beaten last night after work. She's very ill. Do you understand?"

Bridgett nodded impatiently. "Yes, you told me. I'd like to go see her now, if you don't mind. You said she was going to surgery, right?" Bridgett stared at Dr. Desmonde as if she was a moron for not understanding her.

"Yes," Monique sighed. "Bridgett, you must understand that she has bruises and cuts on her face and that ...," Monique stammered, searching for words, "You must understand that she looks very different. Someone beat her badly. Are you sure you're up to seeing her?"

Bridgett nodded her head impatiently. "Of course, Dr. Desmonde, of course I am. But it isn't all that bad, not nearly as bad as you say. Angie and I are twins. If she were hurting badly, I'd be hurting too. It's always been like that, since we were babies." Bridgett smiled and continued, "I'm really not worried, let's go." She looked around the group. "Hurry up! I just need to get my purse."

Alex, Jack, and Monique looked at each other while Bridgett went into her office.

Bette Farve had completely removed herself from the situation and was flipping through a copy of "Architectural Digest" she'd removed from Alex's coffee table.

What an uncaring bitch, Alex thought silently to herself.

Monique rolled her eyes at Bette, shrugged her shoulders and said, "Well, Bridgett doesn't really get it. Angela looks pretty bad, and believe me she's really hurting. The reason Bridgett isn't feeling any pain is because Angie is in a coma."

Alex was startled. "Oh no, is it really that bad?" She searched the faces of her good friends and colleagues. Her crystal blue eyes locked with Commander Françoise's dark ones. "Please say it isn't, Jack," she implored.

"Wish I could, Alex, but I can't. It's bad. It's real bad. I'll fill you in later. Let's get Bridge through this part first." Jack lifted his large, bulky frame from the chair and moved into the outer office to help Bridgett gather her things.

Dr. Desmonde added quickly to Alex, "Jack's right, Alex. Angie is pretty beat up. She may be bleeding internally. She has a skull fracture and some seriously broken bones. Her jaw is broken, as well. She was out there for hours before anyone found her. She lost a lot of blood and Lord knows how long she's been unconscious. Her crit, CBC are way down."

"Shsssst!" Monique put her finger to her lips as Bridgett and the commander returned to Alex's office. "We'll catch up later."

Bette looked up from her magazine and spoke for the first time. "My secretary called Bridgett's husband and he'll meet us in the E.D. They're looking for Angela's husband. He is supposedly on his way." Farve's voice was flip and tinged with sarcasm.

Alex immediately moved into Bette Farve's personal space to confront her, but Monique waved her away while she motioned for Jack and Bridgett to wait in the hall for them.

"Later, Alex," she cautioned, "We have enough going on here and you're not dying on the Bette Farve hill right now." Monique glared at Bette Farve. "See me later, Ms. Farve. I want to discuss the concept of empathy with you. And I *do* mean it."

Alex smiled to herself as she watched Bette bristle with anger and then felt ashamed for enjoying the exchange. Dr. Desmonde was probably the only person at the medical center who disliked Bette Farve as much as she did and this behavior was so unlike Monique it was a bit shocking. They both had Farve's number and supported each other when the nurse executive ran roughshod over the staff. Bette was uncaring, incompetent, inept, and not very smart. Unfortunately, the CEO, Don Montgomery, didn't share their opinion of Bette – most likely because they were very much alike. If you were to believe the hospital scuttlebutt, they were lovers. Gross, yuck, is all Alex could think about that rumor. It made her feel slightly sick.

As Monique and Alex joined Jack and Bridgett in the hallway, Alex began to feel angry about what had happened to Angie. For three years, Alex repeatedly asked the hospital executive committee to move the psych units closer to the main hospital, if not into the main medical complex itself. Of course, Don had a shit fit over that one. He would never tarnish his "world-class, prestigious medical center, soon to be a health sciences center" with the likes of the crazy lowlifes of New Orleans and criminals with HIV. He had even declared at the Board of Trustees' meeting that he would never turn CCMC into an insane asylum or increase the number of beds for the psychiatric community. Alex doubted if he ever knew how much he had appalled the board or that he had made an enemy of Monique Desmonde for life, which was probably not a good thing.

Needless to say, Alex had met massive resistance from both Farve and Montgomery, who had issued a joint press release suggesting that "psychiatry, while a necessary albatross to any hospital, was CCMC's gift to the sick, poor, and disenfranchised mental cases of New Orleans." Monique had seethed with anger and it had taken her and Alex several bottles of Virginia wine to settle both of them. Alex had always been afraid that an accident like Angie's would happen and that someone, whether a patient, visitor, or staff member, would be seriously attacked in or around the Pavilion. Now it had happened.

All four were silent as they waited for the elevator to reach the ground level E.D. The elevator seemed to take forever as it stopped on each and every floor. They were met at the nursing station by Sandy Pilsner, the nursing director of the emergency department.

Sandy eyed her friends for some nonverbal direction. She moved close to Bridgett, took her hand, and said, "Bridge, Angie looks bad. Her face is black and blue, her eyes are swollen shut, and she's hard to recognize. We have IVs and bags of blood hanging and she has a tube down her throat, hooked to a machine that is breathing for her. She'll be going up to surgery in a few minutes. We think she's bleeding internally because her lab results are so bad."

Bridgett smiled brightly at Sandy. "Is Angie talking you to death? I know how she is. She has never even been in the hospital, except for when Jessica was born. Do you think we can even count that?" Bridgett was totally out of it.

If Sandy was surprised at Bridgett's lack of understanding, she didn't let on. She said very clearly, "Angie is not talking. She's not breathing on her own and she cannot talk to you. Bridge, do you understand me? She is very sick. Maybe she can hear you, but she cannot talk to you. There's also a possibility her assailant raped her."

Bridgett didn't respond. Her expression showed no emotion and her affect was flat.

Sandy glanced at Alex and Dr. Desmonde, who shrugged her shoulders and nodded her head.

"Let's go, Sandy," Monique said gesturing forward with her hand. "We've got to break through this denial somehow."

Jack's face was impassive.

Alex knew him well enough to know that he was feeling phenomenal stress. She patted his hand for reassurance.

The sounds of the E.D., the newly renovated patients' rooms, and the spanking clean floors brought no comfort to Alex. As physicians and nurses glanced at her and offered tight smiles, she felt their pain. They all knew Angie and many had worked with her over the years at CCMC. They'd celebrated her graduations from nursing school – first from Delgado at Charity Hospital and then LSU. They'd celebrated her marriage and the birth of Jessica. They'd worked side by side with her every day. Angie was one of the team, one of their team. She was their friend. She was one of their own, one of CCMC's highly skilled and coveted nurses, and one of the millions of caregivers all over the world who gave endlessly and selflessly of their time, talents, and gifts every day.

Alex noticed that Monique was eyeing Sandy carefully. They both knew this was especially hard for her. Angie had worked in the E.D. prior to the birth of her baby and Sandy had hosted her baby shower. Sandy had already lost her good friend and mentor, Diane Bradley, during the tragic accident in the emergency department just before Mardi Gras earlier in the year. Sandy seemed to be holding up pretty well.

Nurses are tough creatures, Monique thought to herself. *Much tougher than we docs.*

As they entered the patient bay, they walked slowly towards the bed.

Bridgett looked hard at the patient in the bed and said angrily, "What in the world is going on? I don't know who this is, but it certainly isn't Angie. What kind of sick joke is this?" Bridgett's eyes flared with anger at Alex.

The next few seconds seemed like eons and finally Monique said gently, "Yes, Bridge, it is Angie. Look carefully. Her face is swollen, her jaw is broken, but it is Angie."

"It is not, it is *not!* Why are you all doing this to me? I thought you were my friends." Bridgett's enormous blue eyes brimmed over with tears as she stared at the faces of her friends around the bed.

Sandy reached to remove the O.R. cap from Angie's head.

When Bridgett saw the long, mussed up blond curly hair, just like her hair only matted with dark, dried blood, she knew and she began to scream, "Oh, no! Oh, no, no ... PLEASE, no, it can't be. Angie, Angie, talk to me, please, Angie, please answer me." Bridgett touched the long knife wounds extending from her sister's forehead all the way around her face. She looked at her friends around the bed. "Who did this? Who did this? It must be a monster. It looks

32

like someone tried to cut off her face!" When she noticed her sister's Mother's Ring with Jessica's birthstone, she began to sob. "Oh, no, she wanted that ring for so long and Johnny just gave it to her on Mother's Day." Her sobs became uncontrollable and could be heard throughout the E.D.

Sandy and Monique pulled the sobbing Bridgett away while Alex and Commander Françoise stayed by Angie's bedside, continuing to observe her injuries.

Alex, numb with shock, turned away, attempting to control her emotions.

Jack gently touched her on her shoulder, "Alright, Alex, we can go. You've seen enough."

"No, just give me a moment." Alex drew a deep breath and turned to face Angie again. As she worked hard to dissociate herself from the body of her friend, she noticed some funny shaped marks on Angie's left shoulder, visible where her hospital gown had fallen to the side. She eyed them curiously and looked at the commander. "Jack, what are these? They look weird."

Commander Françoise shuffled uncomfortably. "It's a damned bite mark, Alex. The SOB bit her at least three times. He's a sick son of a bitch. I'd like to kill him. I will kill him when I find him," Jack hissed, as he felt for his holstered gun under his coat.

Alex looked at Jack Françoise with alarm. He was working himself into a frenzy. *Not good*, she thought to herself. Ever since the spring, when Jack had finally gone to Dr. Robert Bonnet complaining of chest pain, Alex had been afraid that Jack's stress level and stressful job would cause him to have a heart attack or stroke. He'd done absolutely nothing Robert had recommended. Typical, stubborn Jack. He was still overweight, had high blood pressure, and had high cholesterol. He drank gallons of black coffee every day, and his diet was horrendous.

Jack had spent his life living on the edge. He had been a football star in high school and at Tulane University, where he had played linebacker. Shortly after graduation, Jack had joined the service and gone Army Spec Ops. Alex assumed Jack had been engaged in Black Ops, but didn't know for sure. Jack didn't talk about it much, but she knew that he had been everywhere in the world where there had been a skirmish in the last twenty-five years. He finally retired from the reserves about ten years ago.

Of course, now, he was a police commander in New Orleans, working in the city with the highest crime per capita of any city in the U.S. Plus, he now was commander over the district with the most crime. This was further complicated by the fact that Jack was an honest cop and still clung to his ideologies, even after all of his years of investigating murders, assaults, drugs, and abuse. Jack didn't even need to be in the trenches anymore. He was a commander, for God's sake! But, Alex knew that Jack would never leave the trenches. It wasn't in his genes. He didn't go to meetings, ever, if there was a way he could get out of them. He cared about the victims, and worked endlessly to avenge the dead and maimed. Besides, Jack liked to get even, and Jack liked to get back at the perpetrators. It was who Jack was and what had earned him the nickname of "Get Back Jack."

For a fleeting moment, Alex considered calling Dr. Robert Bonnet, the chief of surgery at CCMC. Robert and Alex were close to Jack and shared concerns about him. Six months earlier, Jack Françoise had saved both of their lives as they were being pursued through the French Quarter by an assailant intent on murdering them. Consequently, a short while later, after he'd been shot by that same man, Robert had overseen Jack's surgery. Robert had been injured as well, by a gunshot injury to the medial nerve in his right arm that could still cost him his career as a surgeon.

Robert couldn't operate. The verdict was still out on his injury. Additional surgery and physical therapy would render a determination of Robert's future in a few months. Hopefully, he would be able to operate again. If not, he'd be an excellent medical doctor, as Alex had told him repeatedly. Robert was a natural healer, but he was NOLA's most outstanding surgeon. The police commander, the surgeon, and the lawyer had become close at that time and forged a bond that would never be broken. The three had traveled to Alex's family home in Virginia with her grandfather, Congressman Adam Patrick Lee, and her grandmother, Kathryn Rosseau Lee, for a well-earned vacation and deserved respite. Alex and Robert had been married while attending the University of Virginia. They divorced later, but had begun to build a new relationship in New Orleans.

Alex's thoughts briefly returned to her relationship with Robert Bonnet, back when the two were still married. Alex had loved Robert without reservation. They met when Robert was a surgical resident and Alex was a doctoral student in clinical nursing. They dated for over a year, became engaged, and married at the University Chapel on the Lawn in Charlottesville in a very proper circumspect ceremony. The marriage had merged two of the most powerful political families in the South – the Bonnets of Louisiana and the Lees of Virginia. Robert's family had been prominent in the social, cultural, and political fabric of the state since the French had discovered Louisiana in 1769 and his ancestral grandfather had been the first governor of French Louisiana. Robert's father, a former governor, presently served as a United States Senator for the great State of Louisiana.

Alex's Virginia heritage was equally impressive. She could trace her ancestry to Richard Henry Lee, father of Robert E. Lee, Commander and Chief of the Confederate Army during the Civil War. Her uncle still owned the ancestral family home, Stratford Hall, in Westmoreland County. Another relative owned a historic plantation on the James River near Richmond. Alex's grandparents, Congressman Adam Patrick Lee and his wife, Kathryn Rosseau Lee, owned a large estate in Hanover County, Virginia – not far from Scotchtown, the home of Patrick Henry.

Congressman Lee, a diehard law and order politician, had been overwhelmed with respect for the then Captain Françoise's integrity, character, and investigative skills. He had tried unsuccessfully to lure Jack into a high-level position with the FBI in Washington, D.C., but Jack was resistant. He told the congressman quite bluntly, and on several occasions since then, that he "wasn't working for no damned bureaucrats," that he was not for sale. Congressman Lee had loved the response and had tried even harder to recruit the burly, fearless New Orleans policeman. In fact, the congressman was still trying to get Françoise to come to Washington and work on some special law enforcement projects, particularly anything related to terrorism, but Jack still refused. Alex knew Jack would never leave NOLA. Alex felt an arm on her shoulder that halted her daydreaming. She turned and looked at Jack Françoise.

Alex's mind returned to the grim situation at hand. She stared again at Angie's battered body. Alex noted how pale, almost waxen, Angie's face looked and turned to Jack. "Jack, she is so pale. She looks like a corpse. Feel how cool she is."

"Yes, I see." Jack was thinking back to the pale young corpse he had seen at Dr. Jeanfreau's morgue last week. She had looked just like Angie.

Alex continued to stare at Angie's face and said, "Most of these areas look like bruises, but they aren't discolored like I would have thought they should be. Bruises are generally discolored from blood perfusion. These slice marks look superficial, and there is little blood. Jack, it looks as if she has been cleaned up and prepared for burial. I guess her eyes are swollen from her brain swelling. We call those raccoon eyes," Alex exclaimed, remembering her own ICU nursing days, feeling more angry and agitated than before.

Just at that moment, Sandy re-entered Angie's room with the O.R. transport. "Gotta go, folks," Sandy said, as she helped the O.R. disconnect and reconnect Angie's tubes to portable equipment and push the bed out of the bay.

Alex and Jack watched respectfully as Angie was wheeled from the E.D. Alex shook her head and looked at Sandy. "She just looks awful – why, she already looks dead. She's so pale. How much blood did she lose?"

"I've no idea but there must have been a lot at the scene. Her head wound is a closed fracture, so no blood loss. Her blood values, specifically her H & H are 5 & 18, really low, almost incompatible with life. We're thinking there must have been a ton of blood at the scene because we frankly cannot explain the blood values. Several of the docs think the attacker thought she was dead when he left. Did you notice the rope burns on her wrists? They were bleeding a little. One of her wrists was slit."

Alex felt her poise and composure completely leave her. She knew she had to get out of the E.D. She looked at Jack, whose face was a mask of outrage and fury. "Sandy, I've got to get out of here before I lose it. Jack, let's go to the cafeteria, and grab a bite. We'll talk, and you, you can fill me in." Alex smiled at him and firmly, but gently, removed him from Angela's bedside. Sandy hugged Alex as she left the E.D.

"Yeah, I'd like that." Jack looked at his watch. It was almost noon. The thought of something sweet improved Jack's mood significantly. "Do you think they have any jelly donuts left? I didn't get one earlier. Maybe if I get my blood sugar up, I won't be so damned angry." Françoise looked at Alex sheepishly.

She laughed and said, "Yeah, maybe, but I doubt it. If they do have donuts, I may fight you for them. I need some comfort food." As they walked towards the cafeteria, the pair reminisced a little. It seemed like a good way to diffuse their incredible stress and anger.

Chapter 7

"I'll never forget the first time I met you, Jack Françoise. You were brutally interrogating a nurse and eating a jelly donut. Might I remind you how rude you were to me? I was not impressed!" Alex's voice was stern and emphatic, but her blue eyes were laughing.

"It's all in the past now, Miss Lawyer Lady. I had to check you out good, you know, and you finally earned your stripes!" Jack teased then turned his attention to the food line. Ahead he could spot the donut case. "Oh, good. This day's getting a little better – two jellies left."

Alex shook her head as she watched Jack help himself to the remaining two jelly donuts and a cup of black coffee. She helped herself to decaffeinated black currant tea and a bagel. She decided to spare the commander any lectures on his health. The day had been difficult enough, and it had barely started.

As they moved through the line towards the cashier, Commander Françoise said, "You pay, Alex. You make the big money. Besides, I don't get a hospital discount, although I should considering how much time I spend in this place."

Alex laughed and nodded in agreement, handing her CCMC ID badge to the cashier, who scanned the amount and charged it to Alex's account. The two selected a private table in the back of the physician's dining room. They munched in silence for a few minutes, each caught up in their own thoughts about Angie and Bridgett. Finally, Alex broached the inevitable topic, "Well, Jack, what you got?"

Jack shook his head. "Not a lot. These kinds of cases make me sick. Nurses should never be expected to walk that far alone at night. It's at least two blocks from the psych unit to the parking deck. It's unlit, heavily shrubbed, and unsafe.

It's a perfect setting for a brutal crime like this one. I'm surprised there haven't been more crimes over there."

Alex and Jack were interrupted by Dr. Desmonde who joined their table with a cup of tea. Her voice reflected Jack's anger, "I agree. You're right, Jack. I've been screaming at Montgomery and Farve for three years to do something about the location of the psych units, or at least the parking. I would have been satisfied with some lights, for God's sake."

Monique said, "Alex, you've known my concern about this for a couple of years! We both tried to get administration to move towards making the psych areas safer. This hospital doesn't give a rip about psych because it isn't a money maker." Monique slammed her teacup down on the table in frustration.

Alex eyed her friend carefully. Monique was a beautiful woman in her mid-forties. She was clearly distraught over Angie. The tall, thin psychiatrist was impeccably dressed as always, but her luxurious dark hair had fallen out of its neat chignon. Her normally pale, lovely face was flushed with anger and frustration. Her voice, usually low and controlled, was close to hysterical, or as close to hysterical as Monique would ever be.

Alex nodded. She knew Dr. Desmonde was right. She didn't challenge her at all. Monique Desmonde was uncharacteristically upset. She rarely wore her emotions on her sleeve and she was a master at controlling her feelings and behavior. After giving her friend a chance to recover and compose herself, she asked Dr. Desmonde how Bridgett was.

"Bridgett's gone home with her husband. I gave her a sedative and a prescription for later. They were going to get Angie's baby, who I might add was in the hospital nursery all night. Damn! Those nursery workers should become suspect if a nurse never shows to pick up her child. Damn, these people." Monique's deep voice was loud. Several physicians looked at her curiously from their tables in the private dining room.

Alex intervened and changed the subject. "What do we have as far as evidence? Did forensics get anything good?"

Jack answered, "Just the normal stuff – you know, pubic hair, oral, anal, vaginal, and rectal swabs, that kind of stuff. We also got some skin and blood that we found under her nails. She must have gotten one swipe at him before he beat her into submission." Jack paused for a few moments while Monique and Alex watched the emotions of hate and rage cross his face. He continued, his jaw clenched, "I'd like to kill the SOB." Neither Monique nor Alex doubted the intensity of Jack's desire for true justice.

"Is there any forensic evidence other than what you've just told us, Jack?" Alex looked at him, expectantly.

"Labs aren't back yet. We don't know if we're even going to get the PEPA and the PGM – you know, those semen tests – because too much time may have gone by." Jack shook his head. "I sure hope we can nail him with the forensics."

"You've got to catch him first, Françoise," Dr. Desmonde reminded the commander.

Jack raised his eyebrows and glared at the shrink. "Not to worry, Doc, not to worry. I'll get 'em. In fact, I plan to get him soon. You know me, Get Back Jack," the stocky police commander declared to the psychiatrist.

Alex was deep in thought. As a nurse and an attorney, she knew the proper collection of forensic evidence was critical for a court conviction of a rapist. She also knew that semen usually contains three genetic markers at levels adequate enough to allow for routine typing for evidence. Unfortunately, PEPA decreases within three hours after intercourse and PGM would not survive for more than six hours. Consequently, the early gathering, testing, and analysis of the semen specimen were pivotal to building a successful case. The semen genetic markers were ABO blood group antigens and testing was done by quantitative electrophoresis analysis. Since the genetic markers occur in variable amounts in different populations, their presence or absence in combination with each other often were used to arrive at a percentage or likelihood of whether the suspect is the rapist or not. Hopefully, the comparison of the crime scene evidence with blood and hair samples from the suspect would provide compelling evidence in court and would render a guilty verdict.

Alex continued to review her knowledge of forensic medicine and asked, "Jack, how do the experts handle the bite marks on her back and shoulder? Who did you call in to look at that?" She shuddered as she thought about Angie being bitten by her attacker.

"Damned bastard, a real animal. SOB must be crazy. Probably one of your patients, Monique! Have you thought about that possibility?" Jack turned towards the psychiatrist, flashing his angry, dark eyes.

"Yes." Monique practically hissed at him. "I've thought about it, Françoise! Do you think I'm an idiot? That's all I have been thinking about since this morning! I've got the team working on it now, looking at charts, and putting together a profile among the inpatients." Dr. Desmonde glared at the commander from across the table, barely able to conceal her anger.

Alex ordinarily would have interceded between the two, but knew Jack and Monique had been friends since childhood and were actually pretty close. Alex also knew that Jack was uncharacteristically affected by this rape because of his fondness for Bridgett and Angela. It would be difficult for the psychiatrist and the police commander to be completely objective on this one. *And, me as well,* Alex thought. *Angie and Bridgett have been my friends since I've been here.*

Alex asked again, "What about the bite marks, Jack? What do you make of them?"

"Don't know yet. The crime guys photographed them and were smart enough to include a reference scale this time." Jack rolled his eyes and told Alex and Monique about the time the NOPD crime team had forgotten to use a reference scale with the bite mark. "When we got to court, the evidence was useless because there was no reference scale with which to compare the size of the bite with the mouth and teeth of the suspect. As you can imagine, the evidence was inadmissible. It was a big loss to the prosecution. Lots of heads rolled on that one."

"I bet they did and they should have," Alex said. "A huge error of omission. I bet the prosecutor was enraged." Alex could imagine the colorful and politically astute Harry Connick Senior, the New Orleans prosecutor, being caught with his pants down. *The man just hates to lose, just like me,* Alex thought. *I do hate to lose.*

"Are you all sure you did everything right this time?" Alex inquired, with a hint of that old Virginia Southern drawl slipping passed her lips.

"Yeah. Best I can tell. We took the photos, included the scale, and called in a forensic dentist. The crime team also asked that casts be made to use later to identify the perp. I think we're covered. One thing the CSI team said is that one of the forensic nurses noticed some puncture wounds on each side of Angie's neck. She said they were hard to see because they were in the slice wounds going around her face."

The three sat in silence for a few moments, pondering the horrific attack on Angie. Finally, Alex said, "Puncture wounds. Why would she have puncture wounds? Have you ever seen that before, Jack?"

Jack thought for a few minutes and answered, "No, I haven't. I really didn't notice them in the E.D., but we'll crosscheck that with other similar injuries in the database. We may get a hit."

"Did they mention a lot of blood at the scene?"

"Nope. It didn't come up, but I haven't been to the scene yet. If there was, it'll show up in the crime scene photos," Jack replied, looking at both women.

After several minutes of silence, Dr. Desmonde asked Alex, "What do you think the liability of the hospital is on this?"

Alex shook her head. "I don't know yet, probably significant. Personally, I feel that we should provide a safe place for our staff to work and that we should provide security for them to get to and from their cars, which we do —"

Monique interrupted her angrily, her face flushed. "Dammit, Alex. You sound just like a Main Street lawyer! You know as well as I do that the location, staffing, and administrative management of the psych department are unsafe. It's a joke!"

"Unsafe to you and me, Monique, nevertheless, the standard of care." Alex sighed. This was getting difficult. She continued, hesitating a little and then continued, "Well, the nurses can choose to call security to escort them to their cars when they get off and —"

"Stop it, Alex. That's shit." The usually tranquil chief of psychiatry at CCMC was livid, her pale face colored with anger. Monique rarely used bad language. "You and I both know it! Escorting nurses to their cars during the off hours is the lowest security priority in the entire hospital. Last night Angie Richlieu stayed late. There was some sort of patient commotion. One of the patients attacked a woman in the day room. I don't have the details, yet. Anyway, the patient incident got the entire unit in an uproar. Angie stayed late to help the nightshift calm the unit down. She didn't have to.

She doesn't get paid for staying late anymore. In exchange for staying three hours overtime, she's told it'll be thirty to forty-five minutes before security can escort her to her car! Alex, for heaven's sake, give it up. You know it's wrong!" Monique's voice and hands were shaking.

Alex sat quietly and said nothing. She knew it was a losing conversation.

Commander Françoise placed his big, callused hand over the psychiatrist's small, manicured one. He said to her, "Monique, you've got to calm down some. Things are terrible, but for us to help Angie and her family, we've got to get ourselves together. You're an important player in this. Right, Alex?"

"Right, Jack." Alex looked at Monique. "I agree with everything you say, Monique. You're singing to the choir. Don't forget, I'm a nurse! I've been on your side the entire time about everything – about relocating the Pavilion, putting up lights, increasing staff. This will give us an opportunity to really address these things and make some changes. Let's take the lead on this for now. First things first."

Dr. Desmond retorted angrily, "Alex, don't give me any of that psychobabble. That's my job!" Monique hesitated for a moment, thinking. Then, she said to Jack and Alex, her voice uncharacteristically sarcastic, "So what did the esteemed leaders of the hospital do for the psychiatric service? They contracted it out and gave us to strangers to manage. People who have no knowledge of New Orleans, our culture, heritage, or diversity. Give me a break! We now have contract management in psychiatry, which is inadequate to say the very least, and the patient care conditions, safety, and units are less safe now than they were last year. This is totally pathetic and self-serving of hospital administration. The contract administrator has actually cut staffing."

Monique paused briefly and continued angrily, her voice becoming higher and higher, "I'm sure the bottom line has come up. The place is probably making money now, but what a dump. That contract administrator, Lester Whitset, looks like a patient. He even gives me the creeps. I'd like to give him a frontal lobotomy." Monique tossed her head angrily, her dark hair bobbing, her tone of voice acrimonious.

Alex and Jack sat quietly and watched the conflicting emotions trail across Monique's usually well-controlled face.

After several very long moments, Monique finally reached for Alex's hand and squeezed it. "I'm sorry and you're right, Alex. I'm overwhelmed and incredibly tired and I am being a total bitch. Angie shouldn't be fighting for her life and her husband shouldn't be wondering if their young daughter will ever have the mother that she once knew. The whole thing just stinks and I hate that it's happened. And even though I've got concerns about Lester and the contract management group that is handling CCMC's psychiatric services, they came well recommended and are leaders in Behavioral Health Services. Perhaps I am over-exaggerating, but it seems to me our administration and the contract management service is much more concerned with money than with patient and staff safety. I'm afraid that with our growing, acutely ill, psych population we could be in for more trouble, particularly with health reform coming onboard. The delivery system they've implemented is simply not safe for our patient population. We are the only inpatient facility in the state that houses such dangerous psychotics and the criminally insane. It is truly a dangerous place."

Alex nodded and said, "I couldn't agree more and I couldn't be more concerned. Let's meet soon and talk about it. I've been concerned about the Pavilion for several months. Plan on my office at 10 o'clock tomorrow, okay?"

"You've got it, Alex. If things settle down, I'll be there. Do you want to invite Farve? For what it's worth, I'm sure it will be a waste of our time, but a lot of the safety issues obviously concern the nursing staff."

Alex shook her head negatively and shrugged her shoulders. "When has she ever helped the nursing staff? Why would we even want to include her? Let's get Dr. Ashby." Alex stared at Monique strangely. "I am surprised you asked, Monique. Do you really want her at the meeting?"

"Hell, no! I don't want her," Monique retorted. "She's been a pain in my butt for years. I have loathed her from the first day I met her, but we should have her there. If we can get her on our side ..."

Jack grinned at Monique and said sheepishly, "Come on, Monique. Don't hold back. Tell us how you really feel!" Jack and Monique started to laugh and Alex joined them in their laughter.

"You're right, everything you say is correct, Monique. I guess we should invite her because it's politically correct and her role should concern the safety of all staff." Alex hesitated for a moment and continued, "We'll have to include her, it's the best thing to do. She'll be mad as a hornet if we don't and we *will* hear about it." Alex's tone of voice was almost apologetic as she looked at Monique, who was once again seething with anger at the very thought of Bette Farve.

"Invite the obstructionist bitch, I don't give a damn. I'm going over to the Pavilion. Call me if there's any change in Angie's condition." Monique grabbed her lunch tray and slammed it on the tray rack as she headed towards the door.

Alex and Jack looked at each other in amazement as Monique exited the cafeteria.

Jack spoke first, "Man, I've never seen Monique so blown away. This just isn't like her at all. I sure hope she gets it together."

"She will," Alex assured him. "This is Monique's worst nightmare. She has been waiting for something like this to happen for months and now it has and she feels responsible. Trust me, that's exactly what's going on here because that's the way she is. Jack, by any chance, did you check out that guy, Lester, who is managing the psych services? I've never seen him or met him, but I hear he's pretty weird. If you haven't, maybe you should question him."

"Not to worry, Alex. I'm questioning everyone and he is for sure on my list."

"Good," Alex said looking thoughtful and continued, "Let's see what the psych team puts together. There may be inpatients who have a history of rape or assault. We should know more about them later and we also need to do a historical chart review of former psychiatric patients who have been on the unit. What do you think?"

Françoise was slow to respond. He stared at his coffee and looked longingly at the plate that held his jelly donut.

Alex could tell by the look in his eye that he really, really wanted it.

"Well, I don't quite know what to make of this crime yet … this guy is a pervert who crosses the categories of defined rapist. If you've got a few minutes later on today, a representative from our sexual crimes division will be coming over to the Pavilion, sometime around lunch time. We're going to meet in the executive conference room. Why don't you join us if you can?"

Alex glanced down at her watch. "It's almost noon now. Would you be willing to meet in my office, since I don't have a secretary or administrative assistant today? I really need to get back to see what's going on."

Jack looked hesitant for several moments.

Knowing Jack as she did, Alex added, "I'll have lunch sent into my conference room. Does that help you make up your mind?" Alex asked, smiling.

"It absolutely does. You win. You know I'll never turn down a free CCMC lunch, particularly if Don Montgomery is footing the bill and won't be attending. I'm gonna make tracks over to the Pavilion and pick up Nadine. She's our sexpert – you know, our expert on sex crimes," Jack added hastily, noting the frown on Alex's face.

Alex's voice was frosty as she said, "Jack please don't use that word. Let's just refer to her as an expert on sexual crimes. In some way it sounds demeaning, the word 'sexpert.' To me, it sounds demeaning to both Nadine and Angie."

Jack looked forlorn. He hated it when Alex corrected him or seemed disappointed. "Okay, okay, okay, you got it. I didn't mean to sound disrespectful," Jack said quietly as he rose to leave.

Alex smiled at him and teased, "It's okay, Jack. I'll forgive you this one time, but only this one time. Now get your butt moving over to the Pavilion and then get it back over here for lunch."

Jack stood and said, "Will do. See you shortly." He saluted her on the way out.

Chapter 8

After placing her tray on the rack, Alex headed towards her office but decided to stop in hospital administration on the way.

Latetia, Don Montgomery's secretary, was working quietly at her desk. She looked up at Alex sadly and said, "Ms. Alex, how are Bridgett and Angie? I just heard a little while ago and it's just awful. Do you think Angie will be okay? I just know Bridgett must be terribly upset. Is there anything that I can do?" Latetia's liquid brown eyes were kind and reflected deep concern for her friends.

"Latetia, Angie's in surgery and you're right, Bridgett is beyond herself with grief. I wish there was something that we could do to help her and her family, but right now I think it's just a game of waiting and watching and praying." Alex watched Latetia's eyes overflow with tears as she moved from behind her desk to give her a hug.

"Sure, sure. I know you're right. We're planning to send food to Bridgett's mom's house for the next week or so. Check the Meals to Go in your email so you can participate. I'm sure that Bridgett and Angie's mom will be keeping the baby. I would imagine that Bridgett, her husband, and Angie's husband will want to be at the hospital."

"The food is a great idea and I'm happy to participate. Love the idea of the Meals to Go. By the way, do you think you can find me a temp while Bridgett is out? I would anticipate she will be out for several weeks."

"Sure. Want me to try for Mona again?"

Alex nodded in approval and said, "Yeah. That would be great. She was pretty good during those several weeks last month when Bridgett and her family were vacationing on the

Gulf Coast. And she knows me. That's half the battle right there."

"I'll do my best, Ms. Alex," Latetia said, reaching for her temporary staff file.

"Thanks. By the way, what's Don doing? Does he have anyone in his office?" Alex added, as she inclined her head towards the executive's office.

Latetia glanced at her phone. "He was on the phone, but now he seems to have hung up. By the way, you may want to think twice about going in there. He's in a pretty foul mood, so you might want to be careful. The July revenue projections came in and they were low, much lower than we expected." Checking out the look on Alex's face, Latetia added, "Are you sure you want to go in? I wouldn't if I didn't have to. I'm actually thinking about taking the afternoon off to get away from him," she smiled, rolling her eyes. "I know you. You're always up for making him mad," she teased.

"Yeah, I'm going in. He doesn't scare me anymore. It'll only take a minute and will make his day much worse," Alex added as she moved towards the door and knocked.

"Oh, that's just great. Thanks a bunch, Alex." Latetia groaned, as Alex knocked on the CEO's door.

"Enter." Don Montgomery was seated behind his massive, walnut desk, his head buried in computer printouts. He looked surprised and irritated at Alex's interruption.

"Alex, do we have a meeting?" He quickly scanned his Outlook calendar on his computer. "Nope, we don't. I didn't think so." He looked smugly at his legal counsel, always happy to be right and one up on the lovely attorney. "What do you want? I'm busy." Don glanced at Alex briefly and returned to his papers, a blatant act of dismissal. When Alex didn't reply, he looked at his watch and said angrily, "Really, Ms. Destephano! I'm very busy, and don't have time for you to stand there and gawk at me."

Anger creeped up Alex's spine and she said, "No, Don. We don't have a formal meeting scheduled, but we do have a situation we must discuss."

"Let it wait. I'm preparing for the next trustees' meeting."

Alex's impatience could be heard in her voice. "That meeting is two weeks away. There's lots of time to work on that. I want to talk to you about Angela Richelieu, *now.*"

Don looked up, irritated. "What? Who?"

"Angela Richelieu, the nurse who was attacked, beaten, and raped last night between the Psychiatric Pavilion and the parking deck."

Don was clearly annoyed. "Oh yeah, her. What a pain. Bette Farve told me about it. Too bad. Tawdry affair. Deal with it; you're the hospital's lawyer." Don shook his head, dismissed the incident quickly, and returned to his printouts.

Alex was furious at the nonchalance in Don's voice. She glared at him, her anger reflected in her face. Montgomery was a pompous man, a real horse's ass, a weak, self-serving leader and completely useless in times of stress. Alex had hoped he would leave Crescent City Medical Center after a conspiracy against the hospital earlier in the year had nearly put the medical center out of business. Unfortunately, Don had siphoned bits and pieces of the catastrophe and used them to his advantage. He'd given several interviews to the press and had emerged in the news as a media hero – a man intent on saving his hospital, preserving quality, and keeping it private and solvent in the changing health care environment. Don was a proverbial cat, always landing on his feet.

Alex's voice was calm, but forceful, as she addressed him. "Don, this situation is precarious. Angela Richelieu has been an employee at CCMC for years and is an excellent nurse. She's in the O.R. right now, fighting for her life. The hospital could be at fault here for not providing her safe access to her car — "

The CEO interrupted her rudely, "That's bullshit, Alex. Farve told me that all the nurses had been instructed to call for a security escort after hours. She did not. It's her fault if she was raped. It certainly is not the fault of the hospital."

Alex wanted to jump over his desk and rip out his carotid arteries. "You're wrong, Don. Totally wrong. How appalling you are." Alex's voice was clipped. "Her fault? How could it possibly be her fault? That's ludicrous."

Montgomery dismissed her, "Really, Alex, I am pretty busy. Can you make an appointment with Latetia?" He picked up his phone to make a call.

Alex's fury mounted. "Really, Don. Are you this dumb? How do you think a jury would view this? We've got a nurse who stayed overtime for three hours and didn't get paid for it because the hospital no longer pays nurses, or anyone, overtime. She stayed late because of patient violence on the unit. Then she's raped and beaten on the way to her car ... really, Don. For God's sake, what is wrong with you? Think about it. It's not a pretty picture."

Don was quiet for a moment, obviously thinking.

Alex continued, "We've had numerous meetings about the safety of staff, patients, and visitors traveling between the Psych Pavilion and the main hospital. We've had tons of complaints from physicians, nurses, and visitors that are on record. We've got to make some changes. I'd like a meeting this afternoon with Dr. Desmonde and the administrator that manages behavioral health under the contract agreement. Elizabeth needs to be there as well, as does Dr. Ashley. We have to handle this appropriately with the media."

Don interrupted her, "No way, Alex. Not going to happen today. I'm too busy. What is it that you don't understand? I am busy! I am running this hospital and I don't have time to stop for a stupid, 'called' meeting. Forget it."

"No, I'm not. It's a huge image concern and we all know how you worry about..." Alex said, her voice trailing off momentarily, "... the hospital's image." With these words, Alex hit her boss where it hurt him the most. Don lived and breathed, breathed and lived, CCMC's image. It was his lifeblood because, after all, it was his hospital and no one else had anything to do with the place.

Don straightened up and looked alert. "Huh, an image thing. How's that?" Don was thinking. Nothing got his attention more quickly than an incident that could affect the world-class image of CCMC.

Alex seized the opportunity. "Heavens yes, yes, definitely an image concern. And, mull this over, Don; there is a distinct possibility that the attacker could be either a patient or, even worse, *a hospital employee.*"

"What, what kind of bullshit is that, Alex? All of our staff has criminal checks done on them. It couldn't be an employee," Don retorted angrily, a self-righteous smirk on his face. "Sometimes I cannot understand why we pay you the big bucks. You'll get your meeting at 3:00. Here in my office. Now get out of here," Don said disparagingly, pointing towards the door.

Alex knew she had been dismissed, but continued to stare at the CEO, noting his impeccably coiffed hair and custom-tailored suit. She reminded herself again that the man didn't give a flip about anything except how much money the place made. He'd told her earlier that he considered patients and staff "widgets" and his job was to make the widgets work as cheaply as possible and, at all costs, make the widgets productive. Alex closed the door tightly as she left.

Latetia shook her head as Alex reemerged from the Lion's Den. "That went well, right? From what I could hear, it was pretty loud in there."

"Yep. I ruined his day," she proudly told Latetia.

Latetia smiled, gave her a thumbs up and told her that Mona would be in after lunch.

Alex thanked her and walked slowly to her office, deep in thought about the difficulties surrounding the hospital and medical center.

Chapter 9

Alex relaxed in the inner sanctum of her office. She laid her head on her desk for a few moments to fight off the headache she always seemed to notice after meeting with Montgomery. She had just called the O.R. to check on Angie and ordered lunch from dietary when Jack Françoise entered her office, accompanied by a trim, dark-haired woman. Alex judged the woman to be about thirty-five-years old. She stood behind her desk, smiled, and extended her hand in greeting to the woman as she said, "Hi, I'm Alex. Please sit down."

Françoise made the introductions. "Alex, this is Nadine Wells. She's an investigator and the NOPD expert on rape and sexual crimes. She's a forensic nurse analyst. Nadine, this is Alex. She is the legal counsel for CCMC. She's okay ... for a lawyer, I guess." Françoise grinned and winked at Alex.

Alex waved her hand to quiet Jack. "Hi, Nadine. I am a lawyer, but most of all, I'm a nurse. I don't know why Jack never says that when he introduces me," Alex said, giving Jack a reproving look.

"Whoops, sorry, Alex." Jack apologized for the second time that day.

"It's nice to meet you, Ms. Destephano. The commander has spoken highly of you." Nadine Wells accepted Alex's hand.

Alex was a bit confused and wondered who the "commander" was. Oh, yes, Jack's new job. But Jack wasn't doing anything differently as the commander than he had done as a captain. "Please, Nadine, call me Alex. It took me a moment to remember who the commander was." She gave Jack a teasing glance. "I'm not much on formality. Do you have any information on the possible rapist?" She looked

56

hopefully at Nadine, admiring her petite looks, her fresh appearance, and the fact that she was a nurse and a forensic expert.

Nadine hesitated for a moment, looking at the commander.

Françoise spoke up, "Alex, this meeting needs to be off the record. All we have is preliminary information. The guys downtown would freak if they knew we were talking to the hospital lawyer."

"Wow, Commander, I thought you were the guy downtown," Alex said laughing. "Of course, it will be off the record. I'm here as Angie's friend. Not to worry. This is completely between us. Let's sit at the conference table."

Nadine looked relieved. "Sorry, Alex. We just had to ask. Protocol and all."

"I know, Nadine. No worries. Please share."

"Well, this case is more complex than some. It presents a little differently. We usually classify rapists into three categories. The first category is the anger rapist who uses physical brutality to express rage, contempt, and hatred for his victim. The attack is usually unplanned and the rapist is seldom sexually aroused when he initiates the attack. Anger rape is usually quick, this wasn't. The medical information suggests that Angie was raped more than once. Usually with an anger rapist, the assault is one of physical violence to the whole body."

Alex was listening attentively and making notes on her legal pad. "Yeah. What about the other categories? Do they better fit with what's happened to Angie?"

Nadine continued, "Well, a power rapist initiates the attack to overcome feelings of inadequacy and insecurity. For them, to accomplish sexual intercourse is evidence of personal conquest. These attacks are planned and premeditated. There is usually no injury beyond the attack itself, although it may occur over an extended duration of time. Power rapists outnumber anger rapists two to one. Victims of power rapists have relatively minor injuries." Nadine stopped for a moment as Alex held up her hand.

"This doesn't work. Angie has extensive injuries. It seems like her attacker has attributes in both categories." Alex put her hands to her face. "You know, this stuff is sickening."

Nadine Wells nodded in agreement.

Jack Françoise suggested that Nadine describe the third category of rapists.

Nadine sighed deeply as she continued. "In contrast to anger and power rapists, the third category is the sadistic rapist. These rapists eroticize physical force. The rape may be long and involve torture, mutilation, or murder. Often times, this is the only way the rapist can achieve sexual satisfaction. Fortunately, this is the most uncommon type of rapist."

"Not for Angie Richlieu! Would you categorize her rape as one of a sadistic rapist?" Alex's blue eyes, crackling with intensity, penetrated Nadine's soft brown ones.

Nadine shook her head. "No, probably not. At least, he's not a pure sadistic rapist. Angie's rapist, at this point at least, seems to embody some of the characteristics of both the anger and the sadistic rapist. Certainly, the perp is sadistic. He bit her, beat her, crushed her skull, and sliced up her face. But, he was angry. I think our rapist is a cross between an anger rapist and a sadistic rapist."

Alex's heart was pounding in her chest. "Jack, what do you think? Do you agree with Nadine?"

"Nadine is the expert. I do agree with her. I think the son of a bitch is angry. I think he was enraged, crazy, psychotic, even."

Alex nodded, "Yeah, for sure. Nadine do you think he meant to murder her?"

58

"No. At least, I don't think so. If he had planned to murder her, he would have. He had the opportunity. He simply wasn't motivated to kill her. He wanted to disfigure her, to scare her beyond belief!"

Jack grunted. "That doesn't mean he won't come back and try to murder her, especially if it's someone she could identify or recognize. Bastard!"

Alex was anxious, "Oh my goodness, Jack, you don't think he will try to hurt her while she is in CCMC recovering, do you?"

Jack shrugged his shoulders. "Don't know for sure. Possibly. Nadine, do you have an opinion?"

Nadine's voice was uncertain. "I don't know, I just don't know. This case is a bit different. He could. Perhaps he thought she was dead or, at least, would be by the time she was found. It's hard to say. There are so many unknowns in Angie's case. We need to be prepared in case he does, Commander."

Jack nodded, "I'll take care of it."

"My Lord, what kind of profile do these rapists have? Is there a profile for this type of crime?" Alex's face paled as she considered the perp coming back and attacking Angie while she was at CCMC.

Nadine and Jack looked at each other sadly. Jack nodded while Nadine answered Alex's questions.

"Yes, these profiles usually reveal that the rapist is mentally ill. Violently, mentally ill. They are often psychotic."

"Great Day! It's looking more and more like it could be a patient from the Pavilion. Do we have any inpatients that have such a profile?" Alex's headache was getting worse.

"Don't know yet. There are several patients in the Pavilion now that are violent and have diagnoses that could suggest such a profile. However, rape is not noted in their medical histories. Dr. Desmonde and the psych team are analyzing the records that we pulled. We should know something by this afternoon. I'm sure she will talk to us then," Nadine assured them.

The conversation was interrupted by a dietary aide delivering the lunch trays. Alex, Nadine, and Jack stared at the food as the aide departed. The food looked good, but no one was particularly hungry.

Finally, Jack spoke. "Alex, there's one more thing. You ain't going to like it. Do you want to hear it?"

"Yes, of course, Commander." Alex's formal tone was indicative of her distress.

"This kind of rapist likes to revisit his victim. He likes to come back to terrorize them over and over. It could be here at CCMC or after she's recuperated and gone home. It could be in five years, who the hell knows. But, they do often return and stalk their victims."

"Oh, no. We can't let this happen! No! What do we do?" Alex's voice was approaching a hysterical level and her head was beating outside of her skull.

"When he comes back, he'll try to kill Angie. I am sure of it." Jack was feeling again for his gun. "Don't worry, Alex. In the meantime, we'll place police protection outside her room. When he comes back, we'll get him. Count on it. It's a given." Jack's face was red with anger.

Alex stared at her plate of uneaten food. She felt nauseated and was startled when Jack's cell phone rang.

He looked at the number. "I've got to go." He turned to Nadine and said, "We caught the double homicide this morning in the Quarter. A young couple. I got to get down to the coroner's office."

"Commander, you're handling that? I hear that's a bad case." Nadine's face was grim.

"Yeah, Nadine, it is. It's looking real bad. But then, this case is bad as well. Today has been nothing but bad." He looked at the lunch he had been so eagerly anticipating and said, "Sorry, ladies. I just lost my appetite."

After Jack left, Alex and Nadine talked quietly and picked at their food.

Nadine told Alex that she would be sure police protection for Angie had been arranged, "just in case". She also reminded Alex that she and Jack were operating only on a theory and that they had no hard evidence. Nadine promised to keep in touch and the two women parted, leaving Alex tearfully depressed in her office.

Shortly after she left, Alex remembered that she'd forgotten to ask Nadine about the puncture wounds on Angela's neck. She'd call and ask her later. But, right now, Alex needed a little time alone.

Chapter 10

Jack's brain was bursting as he started his drive back down to Rampart to see Maddy Jeanfreau. He was doubly concerned about Angie's safety and felt there was a risk the perp would try to finish her off, if she made it through surgery. Why did bad things happen to his friends? He'd made a ton of friends over at CCMC in the spring and the group had gotten together several times over the previous months to keep their connection alive. Several of the CCMC folks had been piqued that he hadn't invited them to his commander celebration. As it was, Jack had barely tolerated the evening. He'd only invited the few folks necessary to be politically correct. Alex, Robert, and Monique Desmond had all attended, the latter two having been his friends since childhood. He figured that if he had to suffer, his closest friends should suffer with him.

As Jack slowed his Caddy to stop for a red light, he allowed himself to think of what reason Dr. Jeanfreau could have to call him downtown for the second time in one day. He prayed it wasn't about what he feared it was. He had been ignoring the possibility since he had left earlier this morning, but the phone call from Maddy had almost confirmed his fears. If what he thought was true was correct, he wanted to bleep himself into oblivion for a few months or at least visit an obscure planet he'd never heard of.

As he wheeled his Caddy into a legal parking space, his spirits lifted. Two legal spots in one day. That must be a record for him. *Things couldn't be too bad, right,* he convinced himself. *After all, I am parking legally for the first time in months. That has to be a good omen.* But there again, it was probably his old Catholic upbringing coming back to trick him.

Chapter 11

Maddy was washing up in the autopsy room. She looked like she had aged five years since this morning. It must be a very bad day in the morgue. She saw him, brightened a bit, smiled, and pointed with a soapy hand back towards her office.

"I'll be back there in a few minutes. Got to finish getting cleaned up. Enjoy the Hershey Kisses in my candy bowl ... as if you needed an invitation," she admonished.

Jack gave her a half smile and said, "I might just do that," remembering that he had turned down lunch and a second jelly donut. Besides, he deserved it. It was a shitty day.

He made himself at home and sat at the little round table in Maddy's office near the candy bowl. He looked around. Maddy had pictures of her husband, who was a noted urologist in town, and her twin daughters, who looked just like ten-year-old Maddy miniatures. He picked up a picture of them taken at their weekend home in Pass Christian over on the Gulf Coast of Mississippi. The four looked just great, tanned, fishing poles sticking out of the sand, sitting under an umbrella on the beach, with the Mississippi Sound in the background. Maddy looked fantastic and carefree. Something she certainly didn't look like today. Jack was reading her numerous diplomas, degrees, and commendations when the petite M.E. joined him in her office. She saw Jack holding her family picture.

She shook her head. "I'd love to be over in the Pass now. Anywhere but here in this depressing morgue cutting open dead people all day."

Jack nodded, "Yeah, I bet. Me, too. I still want to take you up on that fishing trip offer when it cools off."

"You bet. Right after the lunch you offered this morning." Maddy grinned at him and asked, "What's up at CCMC?"

Jack shook his head. "Not good. An attack last night on one of the nurses who works in the Pavilion. She was raped and beaten up pretty bad. Laid in the bushes for hours until someone noticed her early this morning."

Maddy shook her head. "Oh my, I'm not surprised. The Pavilion is a festering, snake-pit, time-bomb. I've autopsied two patients who have gotten killed over there in the last couple of years. We're lucky it hasn't been worse. Monique Desmonde deserves multiple gold medals for staying in that hell hole."

"Oh, do you know Monique? I didn't know that."

"Of course, I know Monique. I love her. We female docs have to stick together, particularly in this godforsaken, good old boy network town. I don't see her as much as I'd like, but we do get together fairly often."

"Good to know. I'm afraid the perp could be one of her patients."

"Boy, Commander, I feel real sorry for you. Monique will protect her patients like they are her children. She's a marvelous physician and psychiatrist. If you ever need an advocate, she is there for you."

Jack shrugged his shoulders and rolled his eyes. "Yeah, I know. There could be a struggle. I've already figured that out. Now, why did you call me down here again on this hot as hell day when I could be eating chocolates in my air conditioned office?" Jack smiled, but his dark eyes were serious.

The two locked eyes for several moments and then Jack knew without Maddy telling him. He shook his head and said, "Oh no!"

Maddy just stared at him and said simply, "He's back. St. Germaine is back."

Jack looked miserable. "Yeah, I thought so. I was afraid of that. What the hell, here we go again." He could feel his gut tighten up and cramp. He was instantly depressed and despondent.

Maddy nodded and said, "Yeah, you're right. Here we go again. And we got zip from the bodies. We still need to identify them."

"So, I guess you're telling me that their throats were torn out just like the lady in 2009?"

"Yeah, and their wrists were slit, as well. We could get no fingerprints off the bodies so, hopefully, your team got some. You were right. The bodies had some pretty scary tattoos on them. They were definitely into the occult. They had less than 200 mls of blood that we could drain out."

Jack looked glum. "This sounds identical to 2009 and 1933, at least as far as we can tell from the police report from 1933. And God knows how many more that we never found. Anything else?"

Maddy gestured negatively and said, "Oh, there may be one thing. I don't think they were killed in the Quarter. There were scrapes to both victims' legs that were post mortem. It looks like they had been dragged. There was grass and pebbles embedded in their clothes that I am sure didn't come from the Quarter. The female's shoulder was broken, possibly from being shoved into a small space or, perhaps, she was dropped from a balcony. I can't be sure."

"I'll have the guys check around. Can you maybe pinpoint the grass or rocks?"

Maddy nodded, "Will do my best. We're running them through the database. We're also data-mining everything we know. Jack, have there been any sightings of St. Germaine lately that you've heard about?"

Jack shook his head. "Only the ones from tourists who have been on cemetery tours or have over-indulged. We are always getting St. G. sightings from drunks, at least a couple a week. We investigate, but there is nothing. We've found nothing substantive since just before the 2009 murder," Jack reported and sighed with fatigue. "Damn, I feel about 200 years old now. We don't need this Maddy. Keep it to yourself. We don't need any media hype of this stuff. You know the mayor will have a fit and we'll get the BS about hurting tourism."

"Got'cha. Okay. I'll ask the tech to keep quiet, but you know I can't promise anything. Word, no matter what you do, travels in cases like this. Just be prepared for a media onslaught."

Jack nodded, "Just do your best and keep in touch."

"You, too." Maddy hugged Jack for the second time that day. "We've got to stop meeting like this," she quipped.

"Yeah, for sure. Thanks, Maddy," Jack said as he left her office.

Chapter 12

Jack couldn't wait to get into the solitude of his luxury automobile, cut on the air, and be alone for the second time that day. He unlocked his car, laid his head back on the Cadillac's thick cushions, and closed his eyes, grateful for the darkly tinted windows. After a few moments, Jack once again forced himself to review the legend of St. Germaine. He really didn't want to, but he knew he had to. His thoughts drifted as he reviewed St. Germaine.

If there was one thing Jack knew a lot about, it was New Orleans's dark and murky underworld. Witches and black magic, voodoo and the occult, they were all part of New Orleans's dark, sensual, shadowy underbelly that Jack had learned to navigate as a rookie cop. While most cases were readily solved, it was true that the St. Germaine cases remained an enigma to even the most senior members of the NOPD, including Commander Jack Françoise and his dad, retired NOPD.

St. Germaine sightings were reported either by sober, imaginative, and/or terrified locals or by drunken tourists walking the dark streets of the Quarter at night. Legend had it that Comte St. Germaine, a Frenchman of royal lineage, had lived in Europe for many years before immigrating to New Orleans shortly after the city was settled. St. Germaine was known to be an extraordinarily wealthy man with amazing abilities, who had left France shortly before the French Revolution, fearing for his life. It was rumored that St. Germaine was a musician and could play any instrument, but favored the piano and the violin. The comte was also well versed in linguistics and was fluent in many languages. In addition, he was charming, eloquent, and an excellent conversationalist. St. Germaine had a reputation for liking the ladies, although he never married. It was also said that he liked men as well.

As Jack continued to review his knowledge of the comte, he remembered his grandfather talking about St. Germaine when he was in his eighties, expressing how unfair it was that his good friend never showed his age. In fact, no one ever knew St. Germaine's age because he never seemed to change physically. He was and always purported to be about forty years old, although he remained that age for at least a half of a century according to octogenarians who had known St. Germaine in their youth. Many of New Orleans's finest citizens had partied with St. Germaine in their youth and swore his face never aged.

In addition to being ageless and rich, St. Germaine was known to have wonderful dinner parties where his friends would dine for hours on the very best cuisine that New Orleans had to offer. Germaine was never seen to take a bite. He never ate. He only sipped red wine, pleading a sour stomach and a taste for only "white" food. The comte loved the ladies, but never had a steady girlfriend or mistress. Many New Orleanians reported he visited the brothels almost every night. In fact, Germaine was on the A list for years, much loved and revered in his adopted city. A dinner invitation from the comte was to die for, until one night when things seemed to go amiss.

St. Germaine had hosted an amazing dinner party that included guests from Europe, as well as the locals. After everyone had left, he asked a very lovely lady to have a nightcap with him on his balcony. All seemed well until the lady murmured that she must leave to prevent gossip about them. Suddenly, St. Germaine lunged for the beautiful lady, grabbed her tightly around her shoulders, and tried to bite her neck while pressing her slender body against the ornate wrought iron balcony. Fortunately, for the lady, the balcony was rusty and gave way. She plunged to the ground and landed in azalea bushes, apparently unhurt, and ran through the Quarter for safety.

The incident was reported to the police the next morning, but when the police invaded St. Germaine's home, the comte had disappeared. The police searched his home and only found tablecloths with large red splotches that appeared to be wine, although it was later determined to be part wine and part human blood. In his wine cellar, St. Germaine had stored hundreds of bottles of red wine with French and Italian wine labels, but a random testing of the cache proved them to be a mixture of wine and blood. Several cases of this wine had remained in the NOPD evidence room until it washed away in the Katrina waters a few years back, along with almost all of the evidence from the St. Germaine case. But, the evidence was clear that the bottles contained wine and blood.

As the air conditioner continued to purr softly, Jack felt himself falling asleep and gave into the feeling. It had been a pretty rough day, and it wasn't getting any better. He deserved a few minutes of shut-eye. He continued to drift off until he was rudely awakened by a blaring horn of a presumably irate driver. After flipping the driver off, Jack shook his head to wake up and shake out the cobwebs remaining in his brain from his short nap. Jack also managed to convince himself that St. Germaine was a legend and only a legend, just another good old NOLA ghost story. But, then reason and logic set in and he was forced to confront the number of unsolved murder cases and deaths where the bodies were discovered upon autopsy to have no blood or just a minimal amount of blood. The most recent case had occurred in 2009, but three other cases had occurred in the 1980s, shortly after Jack had joined the NOPD. Police records also had similar crime reports that dated back to the early

1900s. Unfortunately, a lot of those files had been lost in the floodwaters of the storm.

The unsolved cases perplexed Jack beyond belief, and it pissed him off that he had been unable to solve the crimes. He also wondered about the hundreds of people who had disappeared in NOLA over the years, never to be heard of again. Of course, many of them were prostitutes and druggies, but they didn't deserve to disappear without a trace. There were also hundreds of bodies that had washed up on the shores of the mighty, muddy Mississippi, too decomposed to identify. Fortunately, now they could often identify the corpses via DNA evidence, but even that evidence had been lost in the storm. He was no closer to solving the St. Germaine legend than he had been in the 1980s and he didn't like that feeling. It irritated him beyond belief. Then he returned to his theory that St. Germaine was a serial killer who preyed on the vulnerable and downtrodden. He continued with that thought until his cell phone rang. *Damn,* he thought as he listened, *here we go again.*

Chapter 13

After lunch, Alex made several attempts to analyze pending malpractice claims. She was totally not into it and her attention kept returning to Angie and the night before. She called the O.R. and learned that Angela was in the recovery room. A little after 2:00 p.m., her temporary secretary, Mona, checked in and Alex asked her to transcribe the depositions that were left over from yesterday. Unable to work, Alex decided to go off-campus to the psychiatric units to learn if the team had uncovered any possible suspects.

The heat was unbearable as she walked the distance between the main hospital and the Pavilion. Alex noticed the cordoned-off crime scene. The yellow-taped area showed her exactly where Angela had been assaulted, raped, and beaten. Several detectives were still trying to uncover any bits of evidence that could possibly exist. Alex wasn't surprised to see Commander François directing them. Jack waved as Alex passed. She looked at the shaded areas and shuddered when she thought of how dark it must have been last night and how scared Angie must have been. The crop of trees where Angela's body had been found was dense and the overhanging moss gave the area an eerie feeling, even during the day. It must have been awful for Angie. Alex said a quick prayer for Angela and her family.

The Pavilion loomed in front of Alex and she couldn't believe how ominous the building appeared, even in the daylight. The psychiatric hospital was a two-story converted storage building, painted grey in color, with most of the windows barred or shuttered, either to protect against the summer heat or to keep patients from looking out – or, more likely, jumping out. Alex wasn't sure which. Probably more to keep patients from jumping out of the windows, she finally decided. Some of the bars in the windows shone brightly in the Louisiana sun. They were a gunmetal color. Everything was grey. How depressing. *It was all absolutely, totally depressing,* Alex thought to herself as she entered the building.

The foyer of the Pavilion presented as much as the outside, grey and dreary. A pair of metal benches with grey, fake leather cushions was on either side of the door and a bank of elevators stood to the right. The walls were painted grey. Alex wondered what had happened to hospital green. That used to be the color in hospitals. The doors to the stairway and several other areas were locked. *Good,* Alex thought to herself, as she tried to open them.

The silence in the foyer was deafening. Alex could hear herself breathe. As she looked around, she thought about all of the sick, deranged, and criminally insane patients who had crossed through this space. Deathly quiet. It was as if the walls were waiting for her to say something.

She pushed the elevator button and it slowly crept down towards her, making a slow rattling noise. *Geez, the elevator sounds like someone rattling chains,* she thought to herself. *There was nothing normal or comforting about this place,* she thought, as the metal albatross rolled to a banging stop and the door crept open. The elevator was unmanned. There was no operator onboard. Usually, the elevator would be manned by a psych tech or mental health worker to usher people up and down the floors of the old storage building – for safety reasons, of course. As she began the slow ascent to the inpatient units, she wondered if the lack of an elevator operator was also part of the budget cuts. She sighed sadly to herself.

Alex rang the bell for admission into the closed unit. She was easily admitted and was escorted by a large man, presumably a psych tech. As they walked down the hall towards the day room, Alex was surprised by the silence. It was as silent as a tomb on the unit. Deathly quiet and dark, the sun shuttered out by long drapes.

She spoke to two psych techs, one from the day shift and one from the evening shift counting sharps. Sharps were globally defined as anything that patients could use to harm themselves. Hopefully, most sharps, along with cell phones, were confiscated on admission, but psychiatric patients who wanted to die were ingenious at finding things to kill themselves with. Razors, scissors, glass perfume bottles, aerosol cans, and any other instrument the patient could use were kept in the nurses' station. Patients were allowed to use their razors during admission but only under the supervision of a staff member.

A quick conversation with one of the psych techs alerted Alex that all sharps were accounted for, except for one razor. The tech had laughingly informed her that one sharp was always missing – nothing to worry about. "We're always missing at least one," he'd joked.

Alex didn't share his macabre sense of humor over the missing razor. In fact, she was concerned at the tech's nonchalance and casual dismissal of a dangerous instrument. Alex asked him where the staff and patients were. He directed her towards the community room on the North Hall, where the patients and staff were holding a group meeting.

Alex walked down the hall trying to remember what a therapeutic community was when her cell phone rang. Mona was calling her to tell her that the 3 o'clock executive meeting was canceled. Alex felt a tinge of impatience as she continued down the hall. She knew Don had not wanted to meet and figured that Farve had probably talked him out of it. She shook her head in disgust.

Finally, she remembered the definition of a therapeutic community. It was a model of behavioral health care that allowed psychiatry, nursing, social work, and patients to work together to establish a trusting environment at the hospital. In an effort to establish a psychiatric milieu, each group had an equal voice in the operation of the unit. The therapeutic community addressed issues and concerns that affected patients and staff. Alex paused outside the door and listened for a few moments.

Today's discussion was centered around the attack on Angie. The group leader was attempting to get patients to verbalize their feelings about the attack and share any knowledge of how it happened. About twenty faces stared at her as she entered the community room. Alex scrutinized the group, looking for a friendly face, but there were none. Only suspicious faces stared back at her.

She was surprised at the mixture of patients. Both genders and all ages were represented. Some patients looked acutely ill, psychotic in fact. A few had tardive dyskinesia, usually caused by the effects of long-term phenothiazine or anti-psychotic therapy. These patients were easily identifiable by their pill rolling mouths and shuffling gaits. One little, old, white-haired lady looked like Mrs. Santa Claus. She sat attentively in the circle, her hands clasped around her 1950s vintage pearl pocketbook. She smiled sweetly at Alex and nodded. Finally, a friendly face. She spotted Monique in the group and gave her a faltering wave.

Dr. Desmonde, once again her unflappable self, signaled her in.

Alex entered the community room and Monique introduced her.

"Group, this is Alex. She's a nurse and the attorney for the medical center. Alex is a friend of Angie's and she wants to help us understand what happened." Dr. Desmonde looked carefully at the group, gauging their reaction to Alex. She was unsure what their response would be to a stranger and an attorney in their presence. She waited calmly for their response.

After a short silence a male patient angrily retorted, "I ain't saying nothing else. Why does she need to be here? She ain't part of this here. I ain't never seen her before!"

Dr. Desmonde looked nonplussed and replied, "Anthony, Alex is Angela's friend. She's here because she cares about her. She wants to know who hurt her. She's not here for any other reason."

Anthony continued to look angry and uncertain as he muttered, "Yeah, yeah, sure. What other BS you got for us, Doc?"

Alex, unsettled for a moment, responded. "Dr. Desmonde is right, Anthony. Angie's my friend. Her twin sister, Bridgett, works with me. I'm concerned about her and what's happened to her." Alex eyed each member of the group. The silence seemed endless, an eternity. Of course, Alex remembered, silences in psychiatry were meaningful. Right? It probably wasn't an uncomfortable silence, it was simply a long silence, but for sure uncomfortable for her. Each patient looked at her speculatively. Some of them seemed skeptical and uncertain of her presence. Others looked interested in having her there. Alex met each of their stares with a straightforward look.

Finally, a female patient spoke to her in a friendly voice. "Hi, Alex. I'm Penny. I am a schizophrenic, so they say. So, I guess I must be. Anyway, I'm doing good now. It's okay with me if you stay." Penny looked around the room and then addressed the group, "She looks okay to me." Penny nodded her approval of Alex. "Whaddaya say? Can Alex stay?"

A dozen heads nodded affirmatively over what Alex perceived as a long period of time.

Only Anthony seemed unsure. He snarled at her and said, "Why in the hell would she want to be with us? We're castoffs, crazies, don't nobody want to be with us." His eyes glittered angrily at her.

Alex looked directly at Anthony and replied calmly, "Anthony, I admire your courage and your ability to voice your objections. I want to stay because I want to hear your thoughts on what happened to Angie. You know people around here. You may have information that could be useful in helping us solve this terrible crime. Angie didn't deserve what happened to her. She worked here because she cared about you." Each group member seemed content with what Alex had said. Only Anthony continued to stare at her suspiciously.

"Yeah, so you say." Anthony's voice was mocking her. "Angie got a paycheck for comin' here. She may have cared some, but the money was why she came. She's okay, I guess. But, don't hand me no bullshit. She didn't care that much. Besides, she was scared. Angie was scared of us. I know that. All of us do." Anthony looked around at the group, grinning as he spoke. His look was sinister. Several of them nodded their heads in agreement with him. He glared at Alex and growled, "I'm sure that whoever hurt her knows, too. Anyway, we know we cooperate with you or we stay here longer. I'm in for now." Anthony, still mistrustful, gave Alex a shifty look, glared at her, and then looked at the floor.

Alex said simply, even though her heart was beating full force, "Thanks, Anthony. I'll take what I can get. Don't let me interrupt. Just continue as if I wasn't here." Alex felt frenzied, uncertain. She turned to Monique, her eyes pleading with her to take up the reins of the group therapy meeting. Monique nodded at the group leader to continue. Alex was definitely out of her comfort zone and she knew the patients on the unit knew it.

The group leader continued the meeting. "Now, group, before we were interrupted, we were sharing our feelings about what happened to Angie. Rose, I believe you were talking."

Alex turned her head towards the patient identified as Rose. She looked to be in her thirties, was waif thin, and had long, stringy brown hair. Alex thought Rose looked afraid of her own shadow. She wondered if she'd been abused at some point in her life. Rose literally seemed to shrink and almost became invisible as the group stared at her.

"I … I … feel so awful for Miss Angie." Rose's voice was soft and hesitant. "She was nice to me. We talked last night, just before Jim started that fight in the day room." Rose looked around at the group and saw them staring intently at her. Her voice faltered and she began to cry. Then, she said, "Angie and I could have talked longer, but Jim ruined our conversation." She gulped, her thin shoulders heaving in despair as she burst into sobs.

Anthony's voice was hoarse with anger and resentment. "Why are you crying, Rose? You're such a little crybaby bitch. Ain't nobody hurt you yet. You're such a cowardly little piece of crap. You're a slut, just like all the women. You remind me of my…" Anthony's voice had become louder and louder as he screamed at Rose, his face livid with rage. Suddenly, he stood up and lunged towards the frail, pale woman, who seemed to shrink away from him. He was going for her neck.

"Oh, no! No! No," Alex could only exclaim. She was unable to move, paralyzed in her chair.

In a flash, Donna Meade, the nursing manager of the general psychiatry unit, a behavioral health tech, and Dr. Desmonde wrestled six-foot Anthony to the floor, pinning his arms behind him. Donna Meade left for an instant to ring the "all staff alarm" red button located by the door. The ASA was to psychiatry what a code blue was on general hospital units. It announced a psychiatric emergency and requested that all available staff report immediately to the location. Within seconds, two additional male psych techs and a second RN appeared with the syringe of Haldol, which, after a nod from Dr. Desmonde, was administered into Anthony's upper arm. The two psych techs led Anthony away to the seclusion room while the rest of the patients stared.

It was then that an acute realization hit Alex. These people, these patients, had their own culture, their own pecking order. They had their own leaders and power structure. Anthony was the power structure. Now that he was down, no one was going to say much or offer any significant help.

Alex felt safe for a brief moment. Then she realized, with a sinking feeling, that she was in a very dangerous situation. Suppose the other patients acted out? Didn't that happen often? She tried to remember from her nursing school days. Didn't one patient incident spark other patients to act out? Like an avalanche? Of course they did. She felt her heart rate pick up quickly and the hair on her arms stood up. She felt chilled. Yes. That is what happens. That's exactly what happened last night in this very place! Alex looked around furtively.

Several patients were agitated, rocking back and forth in their chairs in perfect rhythm. Another patient was plucking invisible particles from the air. Alex felt her heart fill with panic. Just to her left was another large man. He suddenly began screaming and pulling at his hair. Then he stood up and started pitching empty chairs against the window, hollering that he had to get out and save his baby.

Donna Meade looked at the patient, calmly touched his arm, and said in a soft, steady voice, "Jim, stop throwing the chairs. You're okay now. You're in the hospital and nobody's going to hurt you. Please, you're upsetting the other patients." Donna's voice was calm and quiet. She slipped her hand into the crook of Jim's arm just as he was about to toss another chair at the barred windows. He immediately replaced the chair on the floor.

Jim gave Donna a confused look. Then recognition seemed to appear on his face. "Oh, oh, oh! I gotta get outta here. I gotta go. I'm sorry, Donna. I didn't mean to cause no trouble." Jim's eyes were terrified and were full of tears. He looked ashamed of his behavior. The huge man was literally cowering before the staff and the patients.

"I know, Jim. You just couldn't help it. Let's go to the quiet room and rest awhile." Donna continued to hold his arm gently.

Then, to Alex's amazement, the large man allowed the petite Donna Meade to walk him to the secure quiet room.

Donna motioned to Monique that she needed some medication and then said to Jim in a quiet voice, "I want you to rest for a little while. We'll talk about this later."

Alex shifted her eyes from Jim and glued them on Monique. If Monique left her in the community room, there'd be no staff member at all to subdue any patient outbursts. In fact, they had been lucky that Donna had been able to quiet Jim. It would have been impossible for Alex, Donna, and Monique to wrestle the enormous man to the floor.

Several minutes ticked by. It was finally quiet. The only noise in the room was the click, click, click sound of someone clicking their tongue against the roof of their mouth and the squeaking of the two rocking chairs as the patients continued rocking back and forth.

Monique made a decision. She spoke to the patients in a cool, calm voice, glancing at her watch. "Our time is about up. Why don't you all take a break and then report to where you should be at 4 o'clock. Rose, you can go to my office because we have individual therapy at 4:15. The rest of you know your schedules."

The patients left the community room quietly. Only the two rocking patients remained. Alex breathed a sigh of relief. She was impressed with how Monique had handled the situation. Dr. Desmonde's firm tone of voice had waylaid any further patient outbursts. The psychiatrist had taken control of a potentially dangerous scenario by neither acknowledging nor discussing the situation and by redirecting energies of the patient group in a positive manner. Her behavior and poise were highly professional.

Alex glanced around, still uncertain of her surroundings. "Monique, we've gotta talk —" Alex began.

Monique lifted her index finger to silence her. "Yes, but first I've got to make sure Donna got Jim to the quiet room. Wait for me. I'll send some medicine and a psych tech back here to deal with these two." She gestured at the two remaining patients.

Alex left the community room and walked into the central nursing station, behind a door and glass windows, where she felt much safer. She was relieved to see the patients playing board games and watching the soaps on TV. She wondered to herself just how therapeutic watching soap operas could be, but figured it was better than beating up on each other and the staff. She decided to keep her mouth shut about what she thought was therapeutic. She turned and saw Dr. Desmonde in the medication room and followed her. She watched Monique select a 3 ml syringe from the locked cabinet, snap the top off an ampule of Haldol, and deftly fill the syringe. Monique continued to draw up Ativan for anti-anxiety and Cogentin to combat the side effects of the Haldol.

"Alex?" Monique intoned as she nodded towards the hall.

Alex and Monique walked deliberately down the hall to the quiet room, where they found Donna and Jim talking quietly. Jim had been crying. As they entered the quiet room, he spoke.

"Donna, I don't know what gets into me. These tempers just come. I don't know what to do. I need help. I'm scared. I never know what I'll do next." Jim was so upset, he began to sob, his voice coming out in great gulps.

Donna patted his shoulder reassuringly. "Jim, we're gonna try to help you. We care about you here in the Pavilion, don't we, Dr. Desmonde?" Donna's acknowledgment of the physician's presence drew Jim's attention to Monique.

He looked at Dr. Desmonde sadly and said, "Sorry, Doc. I just need more help. I don't know what's happened to me. Is there something else you can do to help me? A new pill or something?" Jim's voice was desperate.

"I know, Jim. I know you don't understand your outbursts and, yes, we will continue to help you." Dr. Desmonde looked sad as well. "We'll keep working on it. We've made some headway. I've made you a shot that'll help you rest. Where do you want it?"

"Can I have it in my left arm? Last time it was in my right." Jim pointed towards his left deltoid muscle.

"Well," Monique hesitated, "this needle's a little long. How much muscle do you have in that arm?"

"Doc, I got muscle. I just don't have no brains!" Jim smiled for the first time.

Alex was surprised at how handsome he was. He had a beautiful smile, dark hair, and perfect, brilliant white teeth. She guessed he was in his mid-thirties. He looked to be of Irish descent. *The Black Irish*, Alex wondered to herself, acknowledging her knowledge of Jim's bad temper. How very sad if he is really one of them.

Dr. Desmonde returned his smile as she injected the needle and said, "You've got plenty of brains, Jim. They're just a little scrambled right now. We'll get them fixed!"

"Thanks, Doc, Donna, and Alex. I'm pretty tired now. I guess I'll sleep awhile. See you soon." Jim turned over in the bed of the quiet room.

Alex was impressed that Jim had remembered her name and said so to Monique and Donna on the way down the hall.

Donna said, "Jim's very bright. I'm not surprised at all. I like him. He wants to get better and I want to help him." Donna's voice was concerned, her interest in helping the patient obvious.

Dr. Desmonde looked narrowly at Donna. "Don't let personal feelings get in the way of professional judgment, Donna. Jim's very ill, psychotic. Don't set Jim and yourself up for disappointment. Don't get too involved in this case." Monique's voice was sharp and a little accusatory.

Donna's face turned red and she replied hotly, "I hope you're not suggesting I have feelings for Jim that are other than professional! There are no boundary issues here for you to be concerned with." Her voice was cold and defensive. "It's just that most of our patients are chronic and we never really help them. Besides, most of 'em don't want help. Many are so manipulative that they can't be trusted. I doubt many of them even want to get well. Jim does. That is the impetus driving my 'involvement' in this case." Donna was enraged and felt attacked.

Monique was quiet for a moment and then spoke. Her voice was repentant and reassuring. She'd accepted Donna's rebuke with grace. She shook her head and said, "I'm sorry, I apologize. I know how you feel, Donna. I have a special place for Jim myself. But, we have to keep it all in perspective. I am sorry if you think I suggested that your involvement is anything other than professional," Dr. Desmonde's voice was pensive and apologetic. She hugged Donna around the shoulders and added, "Nice job in there, gal."

Donna hugged her back. "Thanks, Monique. But, you and I both know we've gotta do something about this place and the staffing. That situation could have gotten completely out of hand – the one last night did! My nurses are scared. Several are terrified and are planning to leave the Pavilion." Donna stopped for a minute and then admitted, "I'm scared too, and that's not even factoring in what happened to Angie. The patients are getting sicker and sicker and more and more violent, especially since we started taking the ones from the state hospital that Lester Whitset contracted for. We're not staffed for those types of admissions."

Dr. Desmonde sighed. "Yes, yes. I know, Donna. I'm trying to get more positions allocated, even if they are only muscle positions. I'd be thankful to have strong bodies to help us in emergencies like this one today. Since we've been under this contract management, it's next to impossible. We need more behavioral health techs to help us out when we have these outbursts of violence."

Alex nodded in agreement with Monique and said to Donna, "I'm concerned about your staffing, too. You don't have enough staff to handle such severely ill patients and control these kinds of situations. What's your typical census?"

Donna responded quickly. "We've got twenty-two general psychiatry beds and average about eighteen or nineteen patients. Usually, eight or so of them are overtly psychotic and have histories of violence or acting out behavior. The rest are acutely depressed or have organic brain syndrome and/or Alzheimer's disease."

Alex nodded in understanding. "How long have we been mixing the elderly and the adolescents with the others? I thought they used to be separated." Alex asked, looking questioningly at Monique and Donna.

Donna shook her head and answered, "We started mixing them at the time the contract manager started.

Whitset cut our staff twenty percent, making it impossible to run an age differentiated behavioral health unit. He maintains that a therapeutic milieu can occur with all ages together, so everyone can 'learn from each other'! Isn't that some crap? We've even had to eliminate geriatric and adolescent tract therapies. We couldn't staff them!" Donna's voice reflected her dismay.

"How's it working?" Alex asked.

"Not well, not well at all I'm afraid," Donna said. "The patients just don't identify with each other because of their ages. Mrs. Smithson, the elderly patient with the apple cheeks, is appalled when the adolescent female patients talk about their sex lives and how they have to have 'it' every day. The way they talk about sex is disgusting to Mrs. Smithson and I know it horrifies her. In fact, her son told Angie last night that he thought she was worse. He said he was gonna transfer her to Ochsner's private geriatric program. I don't blame him. She could get better care there, at least more care directed towards her age group. I'd move my mother over there, as opposed to here, so she could get better care. No question about it." Donna shrugged her shoulders.

"Is Mrs. Smithson the little lady who looks like Mrs. Santa Claus?"

Monique and Donna nodded.

"Why's she here?"

"She's in for a reactive depression. Her husband died in April and her only daughter, her caregiver, has rheumatoid arthritis and breast cancer. It's very sad, but also very typical for people in her age group. Her son is correct when he says we haven't helped her. Older patients need a different kind of care that is more structured to their place in life and their late life losses. Do you think we have been effective with her, Monique?" Donna looked carefully at Dr. Desmonde.

84

"Perhaps the meds have helped some, but basically we haven't helped her much. You're right, Donna. What we are doing isn't helping. I'm philosophically opposed to mixing these patients, but in view of managed care and reimbursement, we have no choice. I guess some concentrated care is better than none at all. At least we can watch her for suicide attempts – at least, most of the time." Monique looked sheepishly at Alex and Donna.

"What do you mean, most of the time?" Alex asked, her voice anxious.

"Face it, Alex. I usually have two RNs and two psych techs on the day shift. There is even less staff on evenings and nights. We have no security and not a lot of muscle to wrestle these people down if they have outbursts. My RNs have to assess each patient, do paperwork, run groups, give meds, handle emergencies, and participate in community meetings. The psych techs supervise the daily care of the male patients and, together with the RNs, monitor the five-step patient responsibility level. Maybe it will get better when the new health reform act goes into effect. I heard that it may."

"Five step what?" Alex asked.

Donna explained, "Well, it's really not five steps anymore, not since the length of stay decreased to three or four days, sometimes even less. It's a system of patient responsibility level used as a gauge to grant individual patient privileges. As patients improve, they're given more responsibility and freedom. On level I, patients are restricted to the floor. On level V, they may leave the floor unescorted and take unaccompanied trips off hospital grounds."

Alex's legal mind was racing. Her thoughts scared her. She interrupted Donna. "Are you suggesting that we could have possibly sanctioned an activity where one of the psychotic patients could have left the hospital last night and attacked Angie, with CCMC's blessing?" Her eyes were wide with worry.

Dr. Desmonde intervened. "No, we haven't had a patient on level V for several years, mainly because insurance won't pay. They figure if the patient can be off hospital grounds, he can be out of the hospital. Most of our patients reach level III, meaning that they can leave the unit in a group, escorted by a staff member. They go to the coffee shop for meals, the gift shop, and so on. Right, Donna?"

Donna looked pleased. "Good, Monique. Very good. You are the first attending shrink that ever understood the system! I'm proud of you." Donna grinned at Dr. Desmonde.

Alex smiled as the nurse and physician high-fived each other.

"I don't know if admissions will ever return to the pre-HMO days when a psychiatric admission actually changed behavior. According to news reports, mental health services are supposed to get better under the new health care system. Supposedly, thirty-two million additional mentally ill people will receive psych benefits and the benefits of the thirty million Americans who already have them will improve. I just don't see how that is going to happen, but it surely sounds good," Monique added. "Of course, I am totally clueless on how we are going to care for them. We have no space for more admissions now and I'm pretty sure we have more than our fair share in Louisiana," she added.

"Yes," Alex agreed. "It sounds good in theory, but it's all determined on how states interpret the "rules" set forth by the president. Some states could make as many as 500 drugs available for the mentally ill, while other states may only allow access to 250 drugs. Benefits will occur on a state-by-state basis. The same will be true for inpatient care for the acutely mentally ill and for substance abuse treatment. Some states may allow longer acute care stays or better rehab programs than others. It remains to be seen how all of that will settle out, particularly in Louisiana."

Monique looked at Alex and repeated, "Yes, particularly in Louisiana. I think we already know and shouldn't look for much to improve. There will be no silver linings for us," she added regretfully. "We'll just have many, many more patients with no place to put them. I'm not looking for any great fixes to occur in the next few years."

"Anyway," Donna continued, "getting back to your question about patients leaving the unit, each staff member is allowed to take five patients off the unit at one time. And, believe me, the patients raise hell if they've earned level III and they don't get to go. It goes back to basic trust in the building of the therapeutic environment. If our psych techs are out with patients, it's hard for the few who are left caring for the others to monitor everything. There are just not enough of us. We do usually monitor the seclusion, suicide, and quiet rooms, though. We're pretty good at that, unless there's a patient or staff emergency on the floor!" Donna looked a little sheepish.

"I'm happy to hear that," Alex said wryly to Donna. "I'll do my best to get you some more help."

Donna smiled, looked grateful, and said, "Alex, I don't mean to kick a gift horse in the mouth or anything, but Sarah Chassion, the nurse manager who heads the prison unit, is in worse shape than I am. Her patient population is much worse and more violent. Many of them also have medical needs. Lots are HIV-positive and/ or recovering dopers. That's not even mentioning the serial killers, rapists, and murderers they care for over there. As a matter of fact, Sarah swears there is a dope line coming into the prison unit. She has the same staffing ratios I do, and although my job is hard, hers is even worse." Donna looked at her watch. "I gotta go. It's almost 5 o'clock and the daycare gets ugly when you're late picking up your kids. Thanks for your time." Donna waved at them on her way out.

Monique turned to Alex. "I've got to go also. Rose is waiting for me in my office. Do you have time to catch a bite to eat with me in the cafeteria around 6 o'clock? I'd like to talk about things."

Alex nodded. "Sure. By the way, Don refused to meet with us today. Big surprise, huh! He says he has little authority on psych because of the contract management."

"Yeah, gee, what a surprise," Monique agreed sarcastically.

"Sure, I'll meet you. Is it okay with you if I review some of the charts up here? I'd like to know a little about the patients."

Monique smiled at her and laughed, "Alex, you know darned well you don't need my authority to review charts. Help yourself. But, thanks for asking! See you at 6 o'clock!" Monique flashed her a smile as she dashed off.

"Pick me up in the nurses' station," Alex said, watching the elegant Monique Desmonde rush off. She again found herself admiring the psychiatrist and her commitment to the deranged and mentally ill. *It's a heck of a job,* Alex thought to herself. *I'd never do it.*

Chapter 14

There was no one that Alex recognized on the evening shift. She introduced herself to the RN in charge who was supervising level II patients in the day room. The nurse identified herself as Joanne Waters, an agency nurse, who was helping out. Joanne laughingly asked Alex to fill her in on the patients after her review of the patient charts. She admitted she hadn't had a chance to look at any of them. Joanne also reported that one psych tech had taken five patients to dinner in the hospital cafeteria and that the other tech was making rounds. Further questioning by Alex confirmed that Joanne had never worked psych at CCMC. Joanne also admitted she knew little about psychiatric nursing and was pretty scared to be up there after what had happened "last night."

Alex shook her head as she entered the nurses' station, taking several records with her into the staff lounge. She hated temporary agency help. Why not pay their own nurses more and not spend $150 an hour for temporary nurses? *This type of care is unsafe,* she thought to herself. *This place is a catastrophe waiting to happen.* At least Farve could hire agency nurses with a background in psychiatric nursing! Of course, as Alex remembered, Farve was a believer in the warm body theory. As Farve saw it, if you had a warm body and a nursing license, you could practice anywhere in the hospital. Alex continued to reflect on the unsafe, risky environment in the Pavilion, imagining how catastrophic things could become. Her imagination in no way prepared her for the reality that was to set in a few short hours later. Psychiatric services at Crescent City were explosive, to say the very least.

Alex had reviewed about three charts and was looking at Jim McMurdie's chart when a voice behind her asked coldly, "Who, may I ask, are you?"

Alex turned around in her seat and saw a tall, cold-faced man, who was obviously furious. His face had the appearance of cold granite, his dark eyes looked like chipped, black ice. She stood up to meet his stare. She felt a bit unnerved, but her voice was strong. "My name is Alexandra Destephano. I'm the lawyer for the hospital. Who are you?" Alex's voice was equally cold and formal.

The man had soft features. His black hair was thick and curly, with abundant grey at the temples. His nose was sharp, and his lips were thick and pouty. He had a high forehead. All in all, his appearance was effeminate and Alex didn't like him. She didn't like him at all.

Alex squirmed under the man's scrutiny. His cold black eyes canvassed her tall, graceful body. Alex suppressed a shudder as his eyes stopped and surveyed her breasts, and then continued down to stare at her hips and long legs. The man was positively undressing her before her very eyes. She was totally humiliated and furious at the same time.

The man extended his hand. "Oh, I should have known. I've heard about the beautiful, auburn-haired CCMC lawyer ever since I arrived. I am Lester Whitset, the onsite contract manager over the psych, oops, I mean behavioral health department here at CCMC. I'm surprised we haven't met before."

Alex accepted his hand. It was cold, so cold Alex likened it to a corpse. It had a clammy feeling and gave her the creeps. Lester Whitset was so white he looked positively dead. *Ugh*, she thought to herself, as she shivered slightly in disgust. There was something malevolent about him. He totally grossed her out.

"I believe I was out of town when your group took over the operation of the CCMC psychiatric services. That was in March, wasn't it?" Alex knew she was right. That was when she, Jack, and Robert Bonnet had spent three weeks in Virginia, resting up from Mardi Gras in New Orleans.

"Yes, it was. I've heard a lot about you, Ms. Destephano. The grapevine has it that you're a pretty good sleuth. Are you looking through the patient records so you can find our rapist?" Whitset eyed her carefully, a thin smile on his lips, his eyes cold and unwavering.

Alex was stunned by his question. "Actually, no. I witnessed a potential disaster here today, a fight between the patients, Mr. Whitset. I'm glad we've met each other. We have some work to do up here."

"Please, call me Lester. We're colleagues, are we not? I'd be pleased to call you Alex."

Alex was uncomfortable at the thought of Whitset being a colleague. "Yes, I guess we are. In a sense." She stammered her reply, caught off guard for a moment. The man repulsed her and she wasn't sure why. He gave her the chills. She began again. "Mr. Whitset, I'm concerned about the staffing levels here on the behavioral health units. I understand you cut staff twenty percent when you took over?"

Whitset glared at her and said nothing.

"I'm convinced that staff numbers aren't appropriate to provide safe care to patients or protect the staff. As a matter of fact, I'm not sure we're meeting a minimum standard of care." Alex continued to belabor her point, uncomfortable under his stare.

Whitset's look froze Alex in her tracks.

His voice was equally as cold. "I assure you, Alex, that safety and standards are being met here in psychiatry. My company was hired to reorganize the psych department and to make it fiscally sound. I've been successful in doing just that. We are experts in Behavioral Health and behavioral health care. Behavior Health at CCMC was a money loser before we took over. I've managed to put it back in the black in six short months – an accomplishment greatly appreciated by your CEO, Donald Montgomery."

Alex was not to be bested. She gave Whitset a hard look. "Perhaps you have, but at what cost? I'm not so sure. I plan to assess the conditions here, do a risk assessment, and determine just what the care is like, from a risk management perspective, of course. I may hire a team of risk appraisers from outside of Louisiana to review our practices." Alex watched his face darken, suffused with anger, and then continued, "Furthermore, I'd like a copy of your management policies and documents to review as part of the investigation."

"Anything you want, Alex." Whitset's voice was controlled, and only the pulsing of his right carotid artery gave any indication of his rage. He continued, "My office is your office, any time." His eyes wandered over her body. "Anything else you need?" The man was positively leering at her and his intent was clear. His voice remained cold. He gave her a sly smile as he touched her hand.

Alex was startled by his touch and pulled her hand away. The man was positively vile. There was something about him that was malignant. "No, nothing. Please send your internal documents to my office ASAP." Alex turned away from him to continue her chart review.

Whitset persisted, "Alex, "I'll be happy to. Can I interest you in a cup of coffee in my office? It's a gourmet blend, one of Louisiana's finest."

"No, thank you. I'm leaving shortly." Alex didn't look at him. Her reply was short, to the point.

"Don't work your pretty little head too hard now. All work and no play makes Alex a very dull girl." Whitset's voice was hushed and Alex could feel the chill of his body behind her. Finally, he left the room, his heels clicking in a military-like fashion.

What a weird dude, Alex thought to herself. It took her several moments to relax after he left. Her heart was hammering so hard her chest wall was hurting. There was something about him that was repulsive, but she couldn't articulate it. She continued to think about him for a few minutes then returned to Jim McMurdie's chart.

She was surprised to learn that Jim was a former New Orleans police detective. He was presently on disability from the department due to mental illness. The chart indicated that he had snapped when his wife of twelve years left him several months ago, taking along their six-year-old daughter. His wife had been pregnant with their second child at the time she left. An interview with Mrs. McMurdie revealed that Jim had become more and more aggressive in his behavior towards her. In fact, he had suddenly begun accusing her of having extramarital affairs when she was three months pregnant. It was documented that Mrs. McMurdie had become increasingly frightened of Jim and had gotten a restraining order against him. Jim had become so angry at this that he had tried to beat her, which is what had precipitated her filing for divorce. Jim's medical record indicated the treatment team was hopeful that he could control his rage, anger, and jealousy through psychotherapy and with psychotropic drugs. Alex was about to read the physician progress notes in the chart when Monique Desmonde tapped her on the shoulder.

Alex jumped at the touch.

"Good Lord, Alex. I did not mean to scare you! Are the charts making you nervous?" Monique laughed at her.

"No, Monique. I guess I was just so engrossed in Jim McMurdie's chart that you startled me. Let's go. I'm famished."

As Alex and Monique left the attending chart room, Alex was surprised to see Lester Whitset sitting in the day room talking with the patients. He was joking with Jim and Anthony, who were both still pretty doped up, but out of seclusion. Both patients were laughing uproariously with the administrator. Alex moved a little closer to the entrance of the day room and saw that the three were playing cards. Rose was looking at them disdainfully, in obvious disapproval. Mrs. Smithson was knitting a sweater and smiling benevolently at them.

Alex nudged Monique's shoulder. "Is it usual for Whitset to converse with the patients? I think that's inappropriate."

Monique's eyes traveled to the day room. She shrugged her shoulders and shook her head in disapproval. "Yep, he comes in most every evening. The nurses hate it. They say he usually stays until after bedtime. Sometimes he's here all night. He's available in the late afternoons and evenings mostly. Angie told me several weeks ago that he seemed to upset the patients from time to time. I've asked him not to be so friendly, but he maintains it's part of his system of quality assurance."

"That's total BS. Can't you keep him out? It seems unprofessional to me that he should visit with them."

Monique shook her head. "I couldn't agree more, but the answer is no. I can't keep him out. I've asked him not to be so familiar with the patients, but he just smiles at me. He knows it makes me mad, so now I don't say much about it. Actually, most of the male psychiatrists disagree with me. They've heard positive things about him from their male patients. The female patients don't seem to like him. I can't garner enough support from my male colleagues to complain to Don. The whole thing actually disgusts me. Some of the male psych attendings are such pissers," Monique said, obviously piqued by her male colleagues' behavior.

Out of the blue, Alex retorted, "I don't like the man. He gives me the creeps. I just get an uneasy feeling from him. He's so cold. Yuck."

Monique looked at her curiously. "What do you mean cold? Why does he give you the creeps?"

Alex shrugged her shoulders. "I don't know for sure. I guess it's the way he looked at me. He pretty much undressed me with his eyes."

"Yeah, I know that feeling," Monica intoned. "You, me, and all the female staff. I agree. He's inappropriate as hell, but how can you reprimand someone for looking at you, not that he comes under my review? All he ever does is look. He never says anything lewd or vulgar. I wish he would because I'd love to get him out of here on a sexual harassment charge," Monique replied. "That would make my day."

"I'd love to help you, but the guy is way too smart for that. My guess is that he plays it to the hilt without ever doing anything wrong. I just don't like him. And he is so cold." Alex shivered when she remembered her conversation with him.

"What do you mean 'cold'? You've said that twice now," Monique asked.

"Well," Alex thought a moment, "When he extended his hand in greeting and I accepted it, his hand felt cold, dead, like there was no blood running through it. You know, like somebody who's had a stroke or something. It was just gross, like touching a dead person." Alex shivered at the memory.

Monique nodded. "Not sure I noticed that. I try my best not to touch him. Thank goodness, I don't see him much. He's mostly around when I'm not. By the way, Jack's going to eat with us. I didn't think you'd mind."

"Of course not. How did that happen? Does he have any info about Angie or the rapist?"

Much to her surprise, Alex saw a faint blush crawl over Monique's pale face. Her friend looked a bit guilty, as if she had been found out.

"Well," she said with some hesitation, "Jack and I are pretty good friends."

"Yes, well Jack and I are pretty good friends, too, but I don't blush when I talk about him," Alex retorted, confused by Monique's response.

"Well, we sort of decided ... well, we're special ...." Monique rambled, stumbling for the best way to describe the change in her feelings for Jack.

Alex was losing patience. Then she slowly began to understand. "What? Great day, you and Jack!" She could hardly believe it. Commander Françoise and Dr. Desmonde! Jack and Monique! Two of her favorite people. They were an item! She hugged Monique in her excitement.

Monique couldn't stop smiling. She was ecstatic.

"I just can hardly believe this. What a surprise!" Alex smiled brightly at her friend, and the oppression of the Pavilion lifted for the moment. She continued, "Monique, tell, tell, tell. Are you and Jack seeing each other?" Monique didn't respond, so Alex continued to prod her. "Your non-verbals are telling on you, Dr. Desmond. Now, spit it out!"

Monique smiled and turned bright red. "It's not what you think, Alex. We're just good friends. We've had several dates. Well, I guess you would call them dates. Do people date at my age or is it called something else?"

"Of course you date. You can date when you are ninety years old. How did it happen? Oooh! This is the best thing I've heard in days. Tell me!" Alex retorted, unrestrained in her excitement.

"Shhhhh. I'll tell you downstairs. Way too many ears up here. Let's get the elevator." Monique hushed her as she eyed one of the psych techs staring at them.

As the unwieldy elevator labored up to the second floor and then down towards the lobby, the two women chatted excitedly. Taking a seat on a drab, grey bench located in the lobby of the Pavilion, Monique reached for her purse as her iPhone beeped a text message signal. She checked the text message and said, "It's him. He's gonna be late. I'm going to call him back and see when he thinks he can get here. I'm just going to step over here so I can hear a bit better." Monique walked away from the bench and stood near a large potted plant in the corner of the lobby.

As she examined Monique from the bench, Alex was mesmerized by her changing body language. Monique's erect posture relaxed, her speech became less calm and controlled, and she looked ten years younger. Alex could have sworn she heard her giggle. Even her dark hair, pulled up into its everyday chignon, seemed to gleam brighter in the small stream of sunlight that broke through into the otherwise drab, grey lobby.

Alex was overjoyed. *Wow, this is unbelievable. I'm loving it. She loves him. I am so happy for her.* But, for just an instant, Alex felt a pang of jealousy. She reprimanded herself, bristling with self-anger at her jealously. She wished she had someone she could fall in love with, someone she could care for. She hadn't had a date since ... well, since February, when her love life had once again ended tragically. She and Robert saw each other frequently for dinner, but that relationship was questionable and uncertain at best. It seemed unlikely that Alex and Dr. Robert Bonnet could rebuild their relationship. After all, they had been married for almost five years. She worked hard at keeping her depression at bay, refusing to let it overtake and engulf her.

Her thoughts returned to Robert. He had been a brilliant surgeon. Robert lived to heal, to put people back together after major trauma. A rising star at CCMC and in the medical community at large, Robert was a luminary to the local citizens of NOLA. But in Robert's mind, he was a crippled surgeon and was totally useless. He suffered bouts of depression over his arm injury and potentially lost surgical career. When Alex had reminded him that all physicians were healers and that he could heal people medically, as well as surgically, Robert had become angry with her and shut her out. As a result, he was often depressed and moribund. She didn't know it, but Robert was seeing Monique professionally in an effort to rebuild his personal and professional life.

Robert had been the one who wanted the divorce, not her. She doubted she would ever recover from that rejection. It had destroyed her for a long time. Besides, it had been years since they had been together. They could be good friends now, but lovers? Well, who knows, but she certainly doubted the possibility. Anyway, after the spring, Alex had decided to shut herself away from romance for a while.

She was jerked back into reality from her musings when Monique rejoined her on the bench. Monique was positively effervescent after her call to Jack, her cheeks flushed, her eyes bright, and her spirit lifted.

"Jack wants us to meet him at the Palace Café. He wants to celebrate that someone knows about us. He's naturally pleased that it's you. We were gonna tell you and Robert this weekend, but now that you know about us, can we go celebrate? Can you go? Should we call Robert and invite him for dinner?"

Alex hugged Monique again. "It's your call, Monique. It's your party. I'm up for anything, as long as it involves fun. We deserve some after today!"

"Yes," Monique agreed. "For sure. Today was a bomb. I think I will. Do you know Robert's number off-hand? Never mind, it's in my cell. Where's my brain?"

Monique saw Alex's hesitation and asked, "It is okay with you if Robert comes, isn't it?" Monique returned to her doctor mode and tried to detect Alex's emotions.

"Of course it is, you crazy fool! Call him." Alex watched happily while Monique fished her smart phone out of her purse and walked towards the window to call Robert. She could tell that Monique was leaving a message on his cell. Monique was breathless when she returned.

"I left a message. Can't get to his phone, I guess. I didn't tell him anything. I just asked him to join us. When we get to the Palace, we'll call and text him again. I'm so excited about sharing our secret. We're in the open! No more clandestine relationship. It feels so good. Come on."

Alex giggled to herself about Monique's being in the open remark. "Really, Monique, it's not like you and Jack have come out of the closet!" Monique laughed as they walked towards the parking garage. Alex noticed how dark it was already though it was only 7:00 in the evening. The trees, together with the moss that hung from them, blocked out any remaining daylight. Angie must have been so scared when she walked alone in the early hours last night. As the two women approached the crime scene, Monique squeezed her hand.

After they passed, Monique continued to chatter gaily. "You know, Alex, Jack and I have known each other for years. In fact, we lived in the same neighborhood. Of course, he's older, but we even dated a few times in college, when he was at Tulane and I was in pre-med at LSU. We were never really serious, but we really liked each other."

"Really! No, I didn't know that. What happened?"

"Nothing, really." Monique looked pensive. "I think we just eventually drifted apart. There was no precipitating event, no argument, or anything. I was in medical school. Jack went into the service, came home from the wars, and became a rookie with the NOPD. Later, of course, you know that I married – a disastrous affair." Monique noted Alex's raised eyebrows at this piece of information.

"I never knew you'd been married, Monique. What happened? How long did it last?" Alex was curious.

"Oh, seven years. Seven very long years. I, for one, am a big believer in the theoretical seven-year itch. My husband was a stockbroker. He left me high and dry about ten years ago for a very voluptuous blonde and a career on Wall Street. I call it the chick du jour experience, better known to my close friends and family as Tartlett. So much for forever after." Monique looked disgusted when she described her ex-husband and his affair.

"Great day! That was pretty awful. How tacky! Did it take you a long time to get over it? I'm being snoopy, I know. You don't have to answer if it makes you feel uncomfortable."

Monique looked thoughtful. "To be honest, I'm not sure I'll ever get over it! It felt like I'd been stabbed with a knife. It took a long time for the intense pain of betrayal to go away, but it finally did. The thing that remains is the sense of a loss of trust. I really trusted Jeff. I never would've expected him to do that. I thought we had the perfect, professional yuppie marriage – minus the kids, of course." Monique was quiet for a moment. "I guess it sort of makes me afraid to love someone else, to make that kind of commitment. But, I do love having someone in my life to share things with."

Alex was nodding her head continually as Monique was speaking. "Yes, I certainly understand that ... perfectly. I felt the same way with Robert. I knew we were growing apart, but I never thought he'd want to divorce me. I was devastated."

"I'm sure you were. I think Robert knows now he made a terrible mistake." Monique gave Alex a knowing look out of the corner of her eye.

"Yes, I think he does. Well, tough for him. Now it's water under the bridge. Actually, I know he does. He told me that recently, but it's just not a relationship that I can jump back into – besides, we have lots of other things to work on. We each carry enormous baggage from that marriage and the breakup, not to mention me losing Mitch and Robert possibly losing his surgical career. I think we're both fighting demons we need to work through. Anyway, what else about you and Jack? How did all this happen?" Alex waved her hands and Monique laughed.

Monique began her story. "You know we saw each other earlier this year, during the disaster at the hospital. Well, anyway, we had coffee a few times during that…"

"Coffee and jelly donuts?" Alex couldn't suppress a smile.

"Yes, yes, oh my God, those damned jelly donuts. Anyway, I didn't see him for several months after Mardi Gras. In May, I was green grocery shopping at the French market and had stopped for café au lait at the Café Du Monde, mainly to tourist watch. I love to watch tourists in New Orleans. Jack was there, too. It was a beautiful day, not too hot. We spent the afternoon together and even had dinner. Ever since then, we've been seeing each other. It feels so good to share this with someone. I'm so glad it's you, Alex. I know how highly Jack prizes your friendship. He loves you, you know." Monique changed the subject as they reached the parking deck. "Did you drive in today, Alex?"

"No, I walked today. I have no wheels, except for Martin. Should I call him?"

"Oh, no. I have my car. It's on Level 4. Let's take the stairs, work our legs and butt muscles."

Alex groaned, but agreed.

Monique and Alex continued to talk as they climbed the stairs. Alex could feel the four flights of stairs, but Monique wasn't even winded. She continued talking as she skillfully steered her grey Volvo out of the CCMC garage and onto Canal Street, heading for the Palace Café. The two friends chatted incessantly during the short ride to the restaurant. Life was good for this hour.

Chapter 15

Monique maneuvered her vehicle right to the carpeted entrance of the Palace Café, one of Alex's favorite places to dine. The Palace was a local favorite and was owned by the famous Brennen restaurant family. Food at the Palace was to die for and the award-winning restaurant had been serving Creole cuisine in the old Werlein Music building on Canal for years. Monique generously tipped the valet at the door. She and Alex entered the beautiful eatery and spied Jack at a coveted corner table. The maître d' greeted Monique by name and accompanied them to the police commander's table.

Jack rose and kissed Monique on the cheek. He hugged Alex tightly and said, "Yo, Alex, now you know my deep, dark secret! I've had a hard time hiding this from you because I'm so happy I can hardly stand it."

Alex had tears in her eyes as she hugged Jack. "This really is a huge surprise, a gigantic one in fact!" She gazed into the happy, flushed faces of her dearest friends. "This is just perfect. My favorite peeps. I'm so happy for you all and, to be honest, a bit jealous."

Jack nodded, his face beaming. "I know, Alex, and I understand your feelings. Your day is coming, Miss Lawyer Lady," Jack teased. "Just have patience. I never thought this would've happened to an old, fat, nasty bastard like me, but, well, I'm living proof. If I can snag someone, you surely can." Jack smiled lovingly at Monique, who once again blushed at his look.

"You've got that right, Commander. I am amazed that anyone would want anyone who is as big a pain in the butt as you. You're one lucky man," Alex taunted as she high-fived Monique.

"Jack, we want to call Robert and have him join us. Will you do that?" Monique insisted, pulling at his jacket.

"Of course, honey. If it's okay with Alex. Is it, Alex?"

"Absolutely, okay." Alex nodded her head, still shell-shocked at the big, burly, fearless policeman calling her eminent, elegant, psychiatrist friend "honey". Alex had many descriptors for Monique, but honey was certainly not among them. She laughed. "You guys are flipping me out. I really need a drink. This is just great!" Alex's face glowed with happiness for Monique and Jack.

"Champagne, ladies? I've been ordered to make a phone call." Jack pulled his cell from his pocket as he signaled for the waiter.

As the commander left the table to call Robert, he appreciated the lovely decor of the strictly old-line New Orleans restaurant. He ordered a bottle of Cristal on his way to the quiet bar area, and in less than two minutes, Alex and Monique were toasting each other with beautiful leaded glass champagne goblets.

Robert responded to Jack's call. After a brief chat, Jack returned to the dining room and was happy to see Alex and Monique having such a wonderful time. Françoise was wise in the ways of life, and he knew that bad times far outnumbered the good times. He also knew that the heartache of Angela's attack and rape would surface again in the morning. He had a suspect with a psychological profile that was promising and it was one of Monique's patients. To preserve the good feelings and the festivities of the evening, he'd made a pact with himself not to allow the dinner conversation to turn to the case. After all, this was a celebration honoring him and Monique.

Jack continued to observe the two lovely women from a distance. He felt his hard policeman's heart fill with love for both of them. Of course, the love was a different kind of love for each woman. Jack had known Alex for less than a year and was very fond of her. He smiled as he remembered how the beautiful, tall, auburn-haired lawyer had stood her ground against his macho police captain's ego earlier in the year. The then 'Captain' Françoise had treated her rudely, undermined her presence, denigrated her position as the hospital attorney, and had generally been a bastard. Of course, this was the barometer the hard-nosed cop used to check people out. Alex had responded to him in a courteous and professional manner, but would not allow herself to be bullied. She immediately earned his respect, not an easy thing to do in Jack Françoise's world.

As events continued to unravel during Mardi Gras at CCMC, Françoise finally admitted to himself that Alex was some young woman. His grudging respect for her had increased. He admired her courage and cursed her fearless and stubborn spirit. Jack's fear for Alex's life had culminated in life-saving heroics for both of them, which had created a bond between them for life. Commander Jack Françoise loved Alex like a sister and best friend.

Jack continued to look at Monique. How could a gnarly, overweight, arrogant cop earn or deserve the love and attention that Monique offered him? What could she possibly see in him? Jack couldn't believe his good fortune. Sometimes, he still pinched himself when they were together. Monique was just stunning. Jack was a bit older than Monique, but she looked twenty years younger. Her long hair was still dark and her face unblemished by sun and age. She was tall, maybe even a little taller than he was, and she was positively the most exquisite woman Jack had ever met. She was sensitive and completely without pretense.

Monique already knew exactly what he was thinking and even knew how to respond to and handle his dark moods. He was so lucky. He had decided he'd take Robert's advice to lose weight and get himself back in shape, because who knew where this relationship could lead? He wanted to spend a lot of years with the lovely Monique Desmonde and he wanted to look and feel his best every moment they were together. When he returned to the table, both women were laughing heartily. Jack kissed them both on their cheeks.

"Ladies, I've good news! Robert can join us. He's leaving shortly – should be here in about thirty minutes. He can't stay long because he has to make late rounds, but at least he'll be with us for a short time."

Alex felt her heart flutter for a second and then was angry for feeling excited. *What the hell*, she thought. She admonished herself and then convinced herself how neat it would be for Robert to learn about Jack and Monique. Robert had known them since childhood. He and Monique had grown up in the Garden District. Jack had lived close by in the Uptown area of NOLA.

Monique smiled at Jack. "Good work, Commander. I knew you could get him. Did you tell him that Alex was with us?"

"I sure did. No offense, Alex, but I think he'd have come anyway," Jack teased her.

"Robert's going to be thrilled for you all. Did you tell him?" Alex asked as she looked at Jack.

Jack answered, looking pleased. "Nope, played it down. I wanted to surprise him. I've been dreaming of this night for weeks." Monique smiled and patted Jack's hand.

Alex's heart warmed at the gesture.

Jack squeezed her hand and turned his attention to the menu. "I suggest an appetizer for now then wait for Robert to order. I'm sure he'll be able to stay later than he thinks. He's not operating, so he can't have too many patients to see, now can he, Alex?" Jack looked inquiringly at her.

"I wouldn't think so. But, you know, it could be an excuse. He could have other plans," Alex speculated, changing the subject. "What should we have for appetizers?"

"I doubt that," Jack speculated, as he consulted the menu. "The Creole Shrimp is good. So is their baked spinach dip. Let's start with those," Jack suggested, as he sought approval from the ladies.

The three friends were enjoying their second glass of champagne and appetizers, unaware that they were being watched from the lobby by Dr. Robert Bonnet. Robert stood behind a column at the restaurant entrance. He was curious and intrigued by what he saw. Alex looked lovely. She always did, even on the worst of days. Seeing Alex always made his heart race, but he couldn't get over the change in Monique Desmonde. She seemed to have undergone a veritable metamorphosis. Her eyes were twinkling, her normally pale cheeks were flushed, and her entire body was relaxed. He'd never seen Monique look so beautiful, not even at their senior prom at Sacred Heart high school where she had been his date. And, to think, he'd thought Monique had been reasonably pretty at seventeen. But now, words couldn't capture how captivating she was this evening! Then, his glance shifted to Jack. Jack was laughing, smiling without reservation – very different from the day-to-day, stressed-out police commander.

What in the world was happening here, Robert wondered. Jack looked happier and more relaxed than Robert had ever seen him. His worn face, the deeply furrowed forehead, and dark eyes had lost their anxiety and fatigue. His silver hair was shining as he nodded towards the two women. Robert continued to watch his friends as an awakening thought invaded his consciousness. At the same moment, he saw Jack cover Monique's petite hand with his big, calloused one. Then he knew! Jack Françoise and

Monique Desmonde were in love. Two of his old childhood friends. This was inconceivable, but it was wonderful.

Robert felt tears jump into his eyes, but hastily wiped them away. He'd found himself much more emotional since his injury and he was overcome with delight. Monique and Jack were as different as day and night. Why, Monique was the exact antithesis of the commander. She was quiet, reserved, dignified, and cool as a cucumber. Jack, on the other hand, was loud, boisterous, volatile, and earthy. Wow, this was incredible! Robert felt his pulse quicken in delight for his two old friends. He quickly strolled towards them.

Jack saw Robert first, his policeman's intuition kicking in. He stood up, heartily shook Robert's hand, and hugged him.

Robert, charming as always, clasped Jack's hand tightly and bent to kiss Alex and Monique on the cheek.

Alex could not help but notice how handsome Robert looked. His sandy blond hair gleamed in the light of the chandeliers. His light tan suit and pale yellow shirt and tie were perfect for the sultry New Orleans evening. His sensitive, warm brown eyes quickly alerted Alex that he had discovered Monique and Jack's secret. They exchanged knowing nods. Alex felt it amazing that they still communicated so well emotionally even though their marriage had been over for years. They were often on the same emotional plane. For some reason, that pleased her. Plus, she had to admit to herself that her former husband was a hunk and very, very sexy. Her heart quickened with memories of their times together.

Robert smiled at Monique and Jack and said in his cultured Creole accent, "I've been spying on you all. I think I've been invited to a celebration. It seems there is love in the air!" Again, Robert smiled broadly at the threesome, showing his perfect white teeth. Monique blushed again and Robert couldn't stand it. He laughed at her and put his arm around her.

Alex felt her heart quicken again at the sight of her former husband. He was so charming, so handsome, and they *had been* so perfect.

"Good Lord, Monique. You look like a sixteen-year-old girl on her first date! What in heaven's name is happening! Fill me in, Commander," Robert demanded, "You've never been at a loss for words!"

The huge commander looked a bit sheepish, as well as a bit embarrassed. "Yo, Robert. What can I say? Dr. Desmonde told me she has a crush on me. Me! Can you believe it? Big, ugly, uncouth, gnarly me?"

Robert looked at Monique, his eyes twinkling. "Nope, Jack. Actually, I can't. Tell me, Monique. This just couldn't be true. You could like this big, old, ill-bred, uncouth ox?"

Monique was laughing so hard she had tears in her eyes. "Yes, yes, yes. I totally love the uncouth man. Every bit of him! Perhaps I need a shrink," she joked.

Robert and Jack both nodded in agreement.

Alex's heart warmed and she felt tears springing into her eyes as the commander bent down and kissed Monique. She didn't know if she'd ever seen such a beautiful declaration of love.

Robert was enjoying every minute. "Well, I'm glad I'm here to see this. It's pretty special and, boy, what a surprise it is! This is a reason for celebration! I vote for another bottle of wine." Robert motioned the hovering waiter.

Robert sat down next to Alex and touched her hand. "What do you make of this turn of events?"

"I'm astonished, to be truthful. But, I think it's wonderful. I'm happy for them both," Alex replied, enjoying the touch of Robert's hand and then wishing she didn't. *What is wrong with me?* she asked herself. *He is a hunk and he wants me...*

Robert proposed a toast to the happy couple and the four friends talked animatedly throughout dinner. Over coffee and dessert, Monique asked, "Robert, do you know how Angela Richlieu is doing? Did you oversee her surgery?"

Jack took Monique's hand in his. "Are you sure we want to talk about this tonight? This is our night. Let's wait until tomorrow," Jack pleaded.

Monique was quick to reply. "I do, if you don't mind. It won't put a pall on my happiness. What about the two of you?" Monique looked across the table, eyeing Alex and Robert. No one objected so she continued, "Well, let's just talk for several minutes, get an update from Robert. After all, we have the best and brightest minds at CCMC, right here, right?" Monique asked, rolling her eyes.

Jack smiled at Robert. "Dr. Bonnet, you know we don't have a chance against Dr. Desmonde and the lawyer, two of the most perceptive ladies in New Orleans, if not in the world. I guess I'll have to tell you what I know, although it's just a theory at this point." Jack noted the attentiveness of the group. "Alex, are you okay about discussing this?"

"It's okay with me. I'd like an update," Alex said, turning towards Robert.

Robert cleared his throat, but didn't look particularly happy. "Post surgery, she's okay, stable, but she's been through a lot. Dr. Goshette sutured up multiple lacerations, mostly stab wounds and most of those were superficial. We called in Neurosurgery and they had to do a craniotomy with bur holes for her head injury. She had elevated intracranial pressure and her coma had deepened. We put in a temporary VJ shunt hoping to keep the pressure out of her head. She did have a great deal of internal bleeding simply from trauma."

Jack looked impatient, "VJ what?"

Alex ignored his question. "Do you think she will wake up?" Alex asked.

"I hope so. Our main fear is that she was so hypovolemic from blood loss that we had to transfuse her repeatedly with blood. Hopefully, she doesn't have brain damage from the extensive loss of blood."

"I would imagine she lost a lot of blood at the scene. Maybe she bled out," Alex surmised. "I knew she was anemic in the E.D. Sandy thought she was bleeding internally."

"So did we. And, she was. Her blood values are stabilizing somewhat."

"Okay, dammit, okay. Enough medical talk. What is a VJ shunt and what is the H thing?" Jack was piqued and impatient. He always was when he didn't understand.

Alex smiled at the memory.

Monique laughed at Jack. "So sorry, Jack. We do talk doctorease don't we? A ventricular jugular shunt will pump the blood and fluids from her brain through a tube into her heart and then to the rest of her body, which will keep fluids from filling up in her head compressing her brain and causing brain damage. The H & H is the hemoglobin and hematocrit, blood tests that screen out such things as anemia and how your blood clots or doesn't, among other things."

Robert smiled at Monique. "Hey, that's pretty good for a shrink. I thought you all forgot everything about real medicine," he teased.

"Listen, Dr. Bonnet. I could save your life anytime. Don't you forget it," Monique smirked at him. "Remember, I'm double board certified in medicine and psychiatry!" She then turned her attention to Alex and Robert. "We have to get her through the attack trauma and rape. That is going to be hard work."

"Do you think so, Monique? She's pretty levelheaded and feisty. I hope she will be okay," Jack opined.

Alex shrugged her shoulders. "Monique, how do you think Angie will deal with this? What's been your experience in cases like this?" Alex questioned.

Monique shook her head. She looked incredibly tired and dispirited. The warm glow of the evening had burned off. "I don't know. A lot depends on her physical condition and the support her husband will give her. It's hard to predict how a woman will recover from rape and this is supposing that she does wake up."

Alex and Robert mulled this over, but didn't respond.

"Robert, what about the slice wound around her face? Did you call in plastics?"

"Yep, Alex. They sutured it. They think there will only be minimal scarring. And she's got the kind of skin that heals well. This whole thing is horrible. Malicious. It looked as though the rapist was trying to deliberately disfigure her or wipe out her face. The guy is clearly a wacko, a real sicko. Those bite marks were harrowing!" Robert's outrage at the crime was clear in his voice.

Alex could see the flush of anger under his tanned skin. *I bet he's been on his sailboat over at Gulf Shores. He looks really good.*

Alex refocused and felt herself shudder as she remembered Angie's injuries. The psychotic activity she'd seen in the Pavilion freaked her out and gave her chills. As she glanced at Monique, she could tell she was fighting with herself about revealing any possible suspects among her patients.

"Let's just hope she doesn't remember everything." Robert interrupted. "Let's be sure she wakes up first. That is still an *if.*"

"Yeah, really. Do you think she will, Robert? What's the prognosis?"

"It's guarded, Alex. There are clear concerns based on the blood loss and head trauma. We are hopeful, though," Robert added, remembering that he had just said this earlier.

Alex felt depressed. "Let's hope she wakes up soon. The sooner, the better."

Robert and Monique nodded in agreement.

Jack looked annoyed. He obviously felt left out of the conversation. "Does anyone want to hear about my theory?"

"Absolutely. We all do," Alex answered for all of them.

"Okay, it's about time. I am pretty done with the medical talk. I guess I'll have to tell you what I know, although it's just a theory at this point." Jack noted and appreciated the attentiveness of the group. He continued, "Monique, two of your patients in the Pavilion are possible suspects...." He was immediately silenced by the look on Monique's face. She was enraged.

"Jack, how could you suspect two of my patients when you haven't even talked to me? That's outlandish speculation on your part!" Monique's voice was cutting and derisive.

Alex had never heard Monique speak in that tone of voice.

"Now, Monique," Jack chided her, "I told you. This is purely speculation on my part. You asked and I'm only telling you what I think. Besides, do you think I need you to develop a theory on what happened during a crime?"

Monique looked contrite, but Alex knew she was still seething. In fact, Monique was irked.

Jack nodded and continued, "Nothing's official. Do you want to hear, or do you want to change the subject?" Jack looked at her darkly, his voice impatient.

Monique looked apologetic. "I'm sorry. You're right. I guess I spend so much time defending my patients and fighting for them that my response was purely instinct. Go ahead...." Her face was flushed with either anger or embarrassment.

Alex couldn't tell for sure.

"Okay. Remember, *it's a theory, not a reality*. I talked to one of the psych techs who told me it'd been reported on the 7:00 a.m. shift that the side stairwell door had been left open during the night. Consequently, it's plausible to think that —"

"What? The door was open! That's impossible! The whole building is secured at 11 o'clock at night by CCMC security. Besides, that door is attached to a fire alarm so if anyone had exited through it, the alarm would've gone off. It's inconceivable that—" Monique was even more angry now.

Robert and Alex caught each other's eye. Robert was looking strained, his deep-set brown eyes displaying his anxiety.

Commander Françoise threw up his hands. "Okay, that's it! No more," he said to Monique in a loud voice. "Change the subject."

There was a heavy silence. Finally, a waiter came over to offer after-dinner drinks. They all ordered Irish coffee. They needed something to fortify themselves against the uncomfortable silence. Monique excused herself to go to the ladies room, and Alex immediately began to explain Monique's position to Jack, who waved her justification aside.

His voice was impatient. "Stop it, Alex. I don't need to hear this. Monique and I have to talk about this sooner or later – either officially or unofficially. She has to open herself up to reason, for God's sake! Angie was brutally raped. The SOB may as well have killed her. She'll carry scars, inside and out, for the rest of her life ... if she lives or wakes up ... and, dammit, I'm gonna catch the pervert that did it! I don't give a flying shit if it is one of her patients or the president!" Jack stopped for a moment, as if to contemplate his next thoughts.

114

He shook his head and continued in a calm voice, "Besides, we've got to learn to communicate about unpleasant things, don't we?" Françoise was so disgusted that he pushed away from the table and went outside to smoke.

Robert and Alex looked at each other across the table. He said gently, "You know, he is right, Al. They've got to talk sooner or later. It's all part of building a relationship."

Alex knew Robert was projecting their own trouble in communicating with the difficulty Jack and Monique were having. She sighed and said, "I know, Robert. I just wished we had gotten through dinner and we hadn't started in with this stuff. The day's been emotional enough."

Robert touched her hand and said, "Monique will be okay. You can bet she's pulling herself together right this minute, and she'll be back to continue this. She's not one to let feelings of any sort hang around. Tricks of her trade, I guess. Do you think we should stay or leave?"

Monique interrupted him from behind.

She was cool and collected, but Alex could detect the fake gaiety.

"You'll stay, of course! You're right, Robert. I'm gonna get this thing sorted out now, once and for all. Where's Jack?" Monique looked around.

"Outside smoking, I guess," Robert said as he gestured with his finger out the window.

Monique looked impatient. "He's trying hard to quit. He has taken your advice to heart and cut down."

"Good, he'd better. He has ten times more reasons to live now that he has you. Now, go get the big guy and tell him to get his tail back in here so we can get this over with. I'm paying the bill," Robert said as he motioned for the waiter.

Monique started to protest, but Robert waved her protests away and demanded again that she get the commander.

115

Alex smiled. Robert really was good with people. *Maybe I will learn to love him again,* she thought. *I guess anything's possible. Maybe once I work through the hurt of losing Mitch, I'll be able to love Robert like I loved him once.* The idea seemed settling to her. She continued to think positively as she said, "Good job, Bonnet. I've never seen you push both a shrink and a policeman around in less than five minutes. I'm proud of you!"

Robert looked at her with a smile on his face and said, "Not just a policeman, Alex. A police *commander.*" He grinned. "Seriously, these people are like family to me. Even though I have a big family here in town, Monique, you, and Jack are my best friends."

"How are your parents, Robert?" Alex was fond of the elder Bonnets, one of the first families of New Orleans. The Bonnets were of Creole extraction and had lived in the Crescent City since it was settled. His mother was a gracious lady who had kept in contact with Alex even after the couple had divorced. In fact, Elisha Bonnet was one of the main reasons Alex had decided to accept the legal counsel position at CCMC. In many respects, the two women were soul mates. Alex had done exactly what Elisha had always wanted to do. She had moved away from the traditional bounds of matrimony into a profession. Elisha had never been brave enough to do so and had lived a very traditional life.

Robert's family lived in the family mansion on St. Charles Street in the garden district, where they led an active social life. The older Bonnets were young for their sixty plus years and were very wealthy. They had extensive property holdings in the French Quarter and on the riverfront. They also owned several of the finest hotels in New Orleans.

Alex had lunch with Elisha often and knew the elder Mrs. Bonnet hoped, although she would never say it, that Alex and Robert would reunite. It was ironic. Her grandmother, Kathryn Rosseau Lee of Virginia, had also encouraged Alex to reconsider reconciliation with Robert. Alex had great respect and love for her maternal grandmother and Robert's mother, but she knew the choice was hers and hers alone. Alex had been raised by her grandparents, Congressman Adam Patrick Lee and Kathryn Rosseau Lee, on their farm in Virginia. For all intents and purposes, Kathryn was Alex's mother.

Robert responded to her question. "My folks are fine. Dad said he hadn't seen you lately. They want us to come for dinner on Sunday. What do you think?"

"Sure, Robert. I love your parents. I'd love to come," she said, as she looked across the dining room and saw Jack and Monique. "Uh oh, here they come. Let's hope all goes well."

Jack and Monique were laughing and holding hands as they returned to the table. Patrons at nearby tables eyed the couple curiously.

Alex figured that several of the diners recognized either Jack or Monique.

After profuse apologies from the two lovers, all of which Alex and Robert waved aside impatiently, Monique said, "I've assured Jack ... actually, I've given him my ironclad word, that I won't interrupt him or misbehave in any way until he is finished with his theory."

The commander looked at Monique sideways. "Does that mean you're gonna misbehave when I'm done? If so —"

"No, no. I promise!" Monique was so emphatic that the entire group laughed.

"This, this, I've got to see," Robert said. "Monique could never stay quiet, you know that Jack! She was always in trouble when we were little. I'm holding her to her word!" Robert was serious, but his eyes were laughing. "Go on, Jack. Do your thing."

Françoise took a deep breath and continued, "Supposing the door was left unlocked. It's highly possible that a patient could have easily escaped from the Pavilion and committed the crime. Nadine and I reviewed three medical records and two of them stuck out conspicuously. The records of Jim McMurdie and Anthony Gavette are the most suggestive. Their medical histories both report psychoses and dangerous behavior. Anthony even has a rap sheet with a number of arrests for A & B. He's been arrested several times for malicious assaults on strangers. The shrinks think he was psychotic when he committed the acts."

"Yes," Monique agreed. "Anthony is schizophrenic. He has delusions and paranoia. He's even talked in group about having sexual fantasies involving several of the staff. I believe, I'm not absolutely sure, but I think he was arrested in Alabama for attempted rape. Was that in the chart, Jack?"

"Nope, but we will run a check with Alabama and Florida. Is Anthony prone to violence on the unit?"

Monique laughed. "Why don't you ask Alex? Anthony put on quite a show for her today! Tell them, Alex."

Alex didn't think Anthony's behavior was quite as humorous as Monique did, but she smiled to be agreeable and replied, "I'd say he got pretty violent this afternoon with another patient named Rose. She was just talking. Then she started crying, and he went after her in a rage."

"Why? What precipitated the attack?" Robert asked.

Alex looked to Monique for guidance, but she didn't offer any. "I don't know for sure. I had interrupted the community meeting. The group was trying to decide if I could stay and finally agreed that I could, except for Anthony. He wasn't too keen on it. Then, Monique was having them express their feelings about what happened to Angela. Rose was talking about her feelings when Anthony got mad, called her a slut, and went after her. Fortunately, the staff acted quickly and no one was hurt." Alex finished breathlessly, her heart racing a little at the memory.

Françoise was intrigued and asked, "What else did Anthony say? Anything specific to Angie?"

Alex was trying to remember. "He did say that Angie came to work for a paycheck and that she was afraid of the patients. That's about it. Do you remember anything else pertinent, Monique?"

Monique shook her head, while Robert remained silent.

Jack was rethinking the scenario. "Well," he finally said, "Anthony knew that she was afraid of him. It also sounds like he dislikes women in general from what he said to Rose, especially the bit about her being a slut. What do you all think?"

Monique responded quickly. "Short of giving you a long dissertation in psychobabble, it's possible that Anthony was transferring his feelings about Angie to Rose. It's hard to say, Jack. Anthony's paranoid. None of this is conclusive." Monique's voice was skeptical.

Jack looked irritated. "Of course, it's inconclusive. *It's a theory.* These are just possibilities, what ifs and wherefores, so to speak. What is conclusive is a DNA match on the hair follicles and other evidence pulled from the crime scene. I'll check on our boy with Alabama tomorrow. You never know." Jack was trying hard to be neutral.

Alex broached the next question. "What about Jim, Jack? Do you know he's former NOPD? I think he's on disability of some type now."

Jack heaved a heavy sigh. "I know Jim McMurdie well. Good cop, good guy. I rode with him when he was a rookie. He was a good man, an outstanding police officer. I'll never understand why he flipped. What about him, Monique? Do you think he could fit into this?"

Monique was clearly annoyed at Jack. She responded in an irritated voice, "Jim McMurdie is a good man. He's *still* a good guy. He's just sick. I haven't finished working him up yet. He's been on the unit for about three days and I've made a tentative diagnosis."

"Why was he admitted?" Robert asked.

Monique continued, "Mrs. McMurdie, Lynette, called me several years ago and told me that she thought Jim was having some psychotic episodes. Since Lynette's a registered nurse who worked at CCMC before their first child was born, I gave her telephone call credibility."

"I remember Lynette McMurdie. Didn't she teach critical care nursing over at LSU?" Robert asked as he searched his memory. "From what I can remember, she was a real knockout! A beautiful girl."

Monique said, "I don't know. She may have taught over there. I only remember her from the E.D. She and Jim met in the CCMC emergency department. But, you're right, Robert. She's gorgeous. Tall, fair skinned, with long, curly dark hair that she usually wears down. Anyway..."

Robert nodded his head. "Yeah. That's her!"

Monique continued, "Lynette and I had lunch shortly after her phone call and she told me that Jim, out of the blue, started accusing her of having extramarital affairs. She said she was becoming a little frightened of him because he had become so irrational. She told me that the week before she called me, Jim had run outside their house and threatened a stranger who was out walking his dog. He apparently swore at the stranger, accused him of having an affair with his wife, and threatened to kill him if he ever saw him within eyesight of his house again!"

Alex was wide-eyed. "Humph. Wow, that's pretty intimidating. Bet that man never walked his dog that way again," she quipped, trying to lighten the mood. It didn't

120

work. She paused for a moment, and then asked, "What did Lynette do?"

"Well, she tried to reason with him later. Her four-year-old had witnessed the scene and had been frightened by it. Lynette said that when she mentioned it to Jim later, he denied it ever happened. She believed he had no recollection of the event."

"Damn. How long ago was this?" Jack asked.

"It was several years ago. Anyway, I asked Lynette if Jim had been under any unusual stress or pressure and she —"

Jack jumped up from the table and exclaimed. "Damn, that's just about the time Jim was assaulted and beaten in the Quarter. From what I can remember, he was on foot patrol when he and his partner were jumped from behind by a gang of druggies, cop haters so they said. Anyway, Jim and his partner were badly beaten. They were hospitalized for quite a spell."

Monique looked at Jack and marveled at his ability to remember things, from the biggest things in his life to the tiniest details of a crime committed twenty years earlier. "You're exactly right, Jack. Jim was hospitalized for about two weeks with a head injury. He recovered nicely in the hospital. However, about three months after the beating, he experienced a sudden onset of dizziness, headaches, vomiting, ataxia, and left-sided weakness. He came to the CCMC emergency department for a workup."

Robert was absorbed, his medical mind working. "It sounds like he was having a stroke secondary to the beating. This is sounding like a very sad story," Robert said, lamenting over the Jim McMurdie story.

"Yes," Monique said, "It is a very sad case. On neurological exam, there was evidence of left dysmetria and decreased sensation to touch on the left side. Jim had no history of hypertension or any other risk factors for stroke.

His head CT scan revealed a left cerebella hemorrhage with massive effect. He had edema present near the fourth ventricle. He also had some mild atrophy of — "

Jack interrupted in an irate voice. "Yo. Wait a damned minute! Don't forget I'm here. Talk my language!" Françoise was once again furious because he couldn't understand the medical jargon. "Talk to me, not above me!"

Alex intervened, "Basically, Jack, Jim had a stroke. It also sounds like parts of his brain weren't working based on the atrophy of — "

"What in the devil is atrophy?" the commander barked at them. "Dammit, talk to me, too. I'm sitting here. You medical people are a pain in the..." Jack stared darkly into his Irish coffee, irritated that his friends were talking above him. He hated that worse than anything.

Monique smiled and patted his hand. "Sorry, Jack. Atrophy just means parts of his brain hadn't been used lately. You know the old saying that if you don't use it, you lose it? Anyway, the jealous accusations of extramarital affairs started after his injury."

Robert was intrigued. "This is fascinating, Monique. Do you think that his head injury caused his psychosis?" Robert leaned forward eagerly in anticipation of Monique's answer.

"I think it's possible. There is research to support the premise and — "

Françoise interrupted rudely. "I don't think it's fascinating. I think it's generally shitty. A policeman gets injured in the line of duty, has a stroke, and goes wacko. What the hell is fascinating about that? I don't admire the science of it. I just see the loss of a good, honest cop. Sorry." Françoise's voice was bitter as he continued to stare darkly into his Irish coffee.

Robert looked apologetic. "Sorry, Jack, I just — "

Françoise interrupted, "Save it for the medical books, Bonnet, I'm not interested."

There was an uncomfortable silence. Alex surveyed her nails and made a mental note to call for a manicure tomorrow.

Robert took a long swig from his Irish coffee and wished he'd ordered another one.

Monique and Jack stared at each other.

Finally, Monique began again. "Jack, the entire Jim McMurdie story is pure speculation. May I finish?" Her voice was calm, cool.

"Yes, of course, Monique. I just feel differently. McMurdie's a good man, was a fine cop. Now it sounds as if he could be implicated in this crime. It's unfair, it sucks, to say the very least. Of course, finish." Jack's voice was diffident as he raised his shoulders.

"Okay. Anyway, after I talked to Lynette the first time, she called again and reported that Jim was becoming increasingly depressed and irritable. His mood swings were frequent, and he'd begun drinking more than usual. She said she was becoming more frightened of him. She told Jim he had to go for help or she would leave."

"How did that go? Did he come to see you?" Alex asked.

"Yes. He came three times. He was quiet, withdrawn, and cooperative. He seemed to know he had irrational behavior, but didn't know why. He did better for a while and he and Lynette got some marriage counseling. Things were better. I put him on a course of psychotropic drugs that seemed to help, when he took them..."

"Only a short period ... what happened?" Robert remained absorbed in Monique's story.

"Typically, he stopped taking his medicine. I guess there was some sort of incident at work and the internal affairs division of the New Orleans Police Department put him on involuntary leave. Then Jim experienced extreme melancholia. He was acutely depressed."

"Why was he admitted to the pavilion last week? What was the reason?" Jack asked.

Monique shook her head sadly and answered. "Lynette and Jim were shopping for baby furniture at the mall when Jim saw a man he believed Lynette was having another affair with. He went berserk and attacked the man. His attack was vicious. Jim was psychotic and delusional at the time. Finally, the security guards at the mall subdued him and he was TDO to us. It's extremely sad."

The group digested this information slowly. Finally, Alex asked, "How badly was the man hurt?"

"Pretty bad. He'll recover, though." Monique threw her hands up in frustration. "The worst part is that Lynette, who is seven months pregnant, took their daughter to her parents' home in Baton Rouge. At this point, she's refused to be a part of Jim's therapy."

Alex thought about this for a moment and said, "Can't say I blame her. She's probably frightened to death of him. I would be. Has he ever attacked her?"

"No, he's verbally abused her, consistently verbally abused her, but he hasn't attacked physically – at least not yet, but it is within the realm of possibility." Monique's voice was low.

Jack was once again annoyed. "What kind of bullshit response is that? It's within the realm of possibility that I will attack each one of you at this table. Now tell us what you really think, Monique. I'm sick of this psychobabble."

Monique bristled and her face flushed as the blood poured to it. She managed to hold her temper. "Yes, I think it's highly probable. I think Jim has Othello Syndrome. If he'd attacked Lynette, my diagnosis would be final."

Robert was the first to respond. "Othello Syndrome ... like Othello as in Shakespeare's Othello?"

Monique nodded her head. She turned to Jack and explained. "Yes, Othello Syndrome is named for the tragic character in Shakespeare's play in which jealousy played a major role in the character's commission of spousal homicide. While the Othello story occurred in the context of a marital relationship in the play, Othello Syndrome can be applied to any generic situation involving sexual or other intimate partners. As you can imagine, there is no clear demarcation as to what comprises 'normal' jealousy versus 'morbid' jealousy."

Robert was clearly intrigued, although he was smart enough not to say so and incur Jack's wrath again.

Alex could tell. She could still read his face and anticipate what he would say. She wasn't disappointed.

"How does Othello Syndrome first appear? Is it rare? I've never heard of it. How do they diagnose it? How does the patient present?" Robert fired a barrage of questions at Monique.

"Othellos appears much like Jim's psychiatric illness has evolved. The forensic literature suggests that Othello Syndrome has appeared as delusional jealousy, sexual jealousy, erotic jealousy, and delusions of infidelity."

"How is it diagnosed? Are there criteria?" Robert asked again, his medical mind working.

"Well, sort of. Othello is often subsumed in the DSM diagnostic criteria described under delusional, paranoid disorder. There can be non-bizarre delusions of unfaithfulness, as well as auditory or visual hallucinations. Sometimes it's hard to pick up the hallucinations, if they're not clearly evident." Monique stopped for a minute to think. She continued, "Also, if bipolar syndrome is present, the mood swings may be brief or inconsequential to the relative length of the delusional disturbance. I think that's what's going on with Jim. It's hard to group human behavior into tight little boxes. Frustrates me to death, especially when people try to do it." Monique was beginning to look tired, the wear and tear of the day etched on her face.

"I think you're right," Robert surmised. "The diagnostic criteria sounds very much like Jim to me. What do you think?" Robert asked Monique.

"Yeah. It's very possible. There are two things that prevent me from confirming a diagnosis of Othello. Only one has any scientific or medical merit."

The group looked at her expectantly.

Françoise was trying hard to be patient. "Well, Doc, spit it out," Jack said carefully.

"First of all, the spouse is usually the threat in Othello. Jim hasn't physically harmed Lynette yet – although there are many cases reported where Othello patients attacked neighbors, children, and other unknown persons. Certainly, Jim fits into this mold." Monique stopped, as if examining Jim mentally.

"What's the second reason you haven't made a final diagnosis?" Alex asked Monique, gently.

Monique gave Alex a forlorn look. "It's because I don't want to. The syndrome doesn't respond very well to traditional psychotherapy or medication. It has a very poor prognosis. It's a devastating illness."

There was a long silence at the table as the four friends contemplated Jim's dilemma.

"Yeah, this really sucks, big time," Jack concurred, obviously distraught.

"Is there scientific evidence connecting Jim's head injury with the Othello?" Robert asked.

Monique nodded affirmatively. "Yeah. The best evidence suggests that Othello symptoms follow an injury of some type. As a matter of fact, there's currently a NIH research team working on identifying typical Othello lesions in the brain."

Commander Françoise, who had been thinking, looked hard at Monique. His face appeared to be carved of stone. "Monique, how dangerous are these people?" His look was ominous.

Monique's eyes met Jack's head on. "Incredibly dangerous. Jack, these patients are very, very dangerous. Othello patients harbor hostility towards others secondary to their delusional jealousy. This hostility can result in serious physical violence, including homicide. Some Othello patients murder out of morbid jealousy. These patients can be extremely violent to themselves and others."

"Are these patients dangerous only to themselves and people they know or are they dangerous to anyone?" Jack was pressing Monique for information she didn't want to give.

After a short silence, Monique acquiesced with a faraway look in her eyes. She looked out the floor-to-ceiling restaurant window as she said, "Individuals suffering from Othello Syndrome pose a significant risk to society in terms of potential violence, both in domestic and generic circumstances. Jealousy in its most severe form, the Othello delusion, plays a major role in completed homicides and spousal murders. In this situation, we know he was delusional. He attacked several men prior to admission."

Robert looked carefully at Monique and asked her gently, "Do you think Jim could have attacked Angie?"

Monique replied slowly, "I don't know. I don't believe rape is part of the syndrome. At least, I've never seen it reported anywhere in the evidence. I think that's a significant factor when we look at Jim. Otherwise, he could easily fit the picture of the attacker. He's known to be delusional, morbidly jealous." Monique stopped for a moment to think and then continued, "And he presents as classically evolving Othello Syndrome. Who knows?" She shrugged her shoulders, looking very tired. She added, "I'm wasted. Can we continue this tomorrow?"

Jack felt his phone vibrate in his pocket. As he struggled to get it out and read the text he said, "You guys timed this just right. Gotta go folks, sorry to leave such great company, but I've got another murder in the Quarter. Third one today." He shook his head. "Damn, this is getting old."

Monique glanced up and said, "Does the police commander always have to show up at every crime scene?"

Jack glared at her. "We've had this conversation. We're all tired, and, yes, *this* police commander will always show up at crime scenes and that isn't changing."

Monique looked tired and rejected. It was a good thing she had her car. She'd be damned if she was getting in Jack's car. Of course, she was instantly ashamed for having these thoughts. It was because of Jack's sense of commitment that she loved him so.

"Let's continue this tomorrow. Of course," Alex said, "we're all beat. Monique, don't be too upset. It may not even be a Pavilion patient. It could be anyone, right, Jack?"

Jack grinned at Alex. "Yep. You bet, Al. Proof is in the pudding and the pudding in this case is hair follicles, semen samples, and bite marks. "Yo, gotta go. Later," he said as he kissed Monique goodnight.

As Alex, Robert, and Monique walked towards the door of the Palace, Monique said, "I just don't get it. Why in the hell do police rush to a murder scene? They certainly can't help the victim. It's ridiculous."

"Well," Robert opined, "I think it has to do with testosterone and conditioning. And, in this case, a certain police commander who, trust me, will never change."

Alex nodded in agreement.

Monique sighed in resignation. "Yeah, that's why I love him," Monique admitted.

After hugging each other good night, Alex and Robert congratulated Monique again, who waved them away, suggesting that the romance was "old hat" now.

Robert offered Alex a ride and she accepted gratefully. During the ride home, the couple enjoyed a companionable chat. They talked about their happiness for Jack and Monique, as well as how difficult it was going to be for Monique to adjust to being a police commander's wife, if the romance got that far.

After reaching her house, Alex invited Robert in for coffee, but he looked at his watch and told her he had to get back to CCMC. He wanted to check on Angie and several other patients whose surgery he had supervised in the O.R.

Robert walked Alex to the door of her beautifully restored home, remarked how well manicured the lawn was, kissed her briefly on the cheek, returned to his silver Mercedes, and drove off.

Alex felt very alone after Robert left and wished for a few minutes that he had joined her for some decaf. But, when she realized how exhausted she was, she was glad that he hadn't. The day had been two days long. She was worn out from thinking about Angie, the crime, and the patients in the Pavilion. Besides, the celebration dinner had been wonderful, but a bit stressful at times. Too bad this had to happen to the couple now. Her thoughts kept returning to Jim McMurdie, but for some reason, her intuition told her he didn't do it. After assuring herself that there was no concrete evidence to implicate him, she went into her kitchen, poured herself a glass of milk, found some chocolate cookies, and took them into her bedroom.

Milk and cookies in the bed were Alex's treat after a long, hard day. She supposed it was the child in her, and tonight she needed to nurture that child because her day had been so terrible. She changed into her nightgown, climbed into her antique, Victorian, walnut bed, and flipped on the TV with the remote. She watched the late news, pleased there was no mention of Angie's rape and beating. The press had virtually persecuted CCMC earlier in the year when patients had been attacked inside the hospital. Alex clicked the TV off and began to rethink the day. She was too tired to be analytical, so she focused her thoughts on Monique and Jack. When her eyes began to feel heavy, she snapped off her light and went to sleep.

At 3:30 in the morning, she was awakened out of a dead sleep by the constant, shrill ringing of the phone on her bedside table. She picked up the handset drowsily.

"Hello," Alex said sleepily.

Someone was trying to talk to her. It was a woman, but she was hysterical. Alex couldn't understand her words or recognize her voice. The woman was babbling.

Alex sat up in her bed, interrupted the caller, and said clearly, "Please slow down. I can't understand what you're saying." By this time, she was wide awake, adrenaline pulsing through her veins.

"Alex, Alex, it's me! Monique. Get here as soon as you can. The Pavilion. It's horrible, just horrible!" Monique started sobbing again and hung up the phone.

Chapter 16

Depression weighed Jack down like a ton of bricks as he made his way back down Canal to the Quarter. He was upset over his potential disagreement with Monique about her patients, as well as a nagging feeling that their careers would always present a challenge to their relationship. He guessed he'd just have to figure out a way to maneuver around it. He certainly knew he would try. He still couldn't believe the beautiful Dr. Monique Desmonde wanted him. Damn he was a lucky SOB. He jumped as his police scanner blared in his ear. He was surprised to hear the voice of his PR man, Jason Aldridge. *Oh shit,* he thought to himself. *This couldn't be good. What is Jason doing out this late at a crime scene? This must be bad.* He picked up his receiver, a sick feeling in the pit of his stomach.

"Yo, Jason! What's up? Are you at the scene?"

"Commander, are you close?" Jason's voice sounded tense.

"Yeah, I am turning into the Quarter now. What's up?"

"We'll talk when you get here. Hurry up."

"Gotcha! I'm turning in now." Jack signed off, secure in the knowledge that whoever was dead was important. His sense of dread only increased as he searched for parking on the narrow streets of the Quarter. Bourbon Street was party central with all the sex shops and no one seemed to have any idea that there was a corpse down the street. Jack doubted they would have cared even if they had known it. While the Quarter was the center of tourism in New Orleans, as well as a beacon of history and architecture, it was also home to some of the most heinous crime scenes in the world. And, it was Jack's beat. It had always been Jack's beat. He loved the

French Quarter, but he feared its steamy streets and deviant personalities.

What a bitch, Jack thought to himself. *There is no parking to be found anywhere. Not even illegal parking.* Jack circled a few times and finally pulled his silver caddy into a private driveway. He put his light on the hood in case the owners should come out and complain.

As he started walking towards the scene, Jack tripped over a body on the ground. The body groaned and rolled over, so Jack kept on walking briskly through the oppressive August night. He saw the blue bubble lights of at least six NOPD police cars, dizzying as they competed with the red lights of the emergency vehicles. As he hurried down the rough, aged, and bumpy sidewalk, it struck him that the crime scene location was close to the scene from last night – or, rather, early this morning, to be more specific. As he got a little closer, he realized that the crime scene was in the *exact* location as the one less than twenty-four hours earlier. *Damn,* he thought to himself. *What The Fuck! Here we go again. What the hell is this all about? This is definitely gonna suck. Why the same place? I wonder if it's the same perp. It has to be.*

Jason spotted the commander and walked towards him, a frown on his face. Jason could see the finely etched lines of worry and stress in Jack's face, highlighted by the circling beams of the police cars.

Then, Jack noticed that there were two bodies, two victims, in the same exact spot where the two kids had been found earlier. The meat wagon was pulled to the side in another alley.

"What the hell, Jason, there are *two* bodies? *Again?* What do you know?" Jack demanded.

"Yeah, and they're not the typical guys we usually find down this far in the Quarter."

"Yeah, I see. They're wearing some pretty expensive threads," Jack observed, as he noted the custom-tailored suit on one of the victims. The other man was dressed casually in khakis and a polo shirt. His face was literally blue. Really blue. Jack had never seen anyone so blue from death. He hoped it was the blue police lights making the guy look worse than he really was. But he wasn't sure. Jack shined his flashlight on the guy. Yep, the guy's nails were so blue that they could have passed for black. For a moment, Jack wondered if the vic had on black nail polish. The guy in the suit had on a wedding band and the other man had on a Rolex watch.

"Is the Rolex real or a knock off and do we have any ID?"

"Commander, yes and yes. The Rolex appears to be genuine and IDs have tentatively been established. Both men had their wallets in their pockets, so robbery doesn't seem to be a motive, unfortunately. Between the two of them, they were carrying several thousand dollars." Jack continued to stare at the bodies, saying nothing as Jason continued, "Bad news, Commander. Here comes the mayor. I can spot him and his entourage a block away."

Jack gave Jason a dark look. The Mayor of New Orleans was Jack's boss and his sworn enemy. He really didn't need this after the day he'd had. "What the hell, who invited them to this party and who the hell else is coming?"

"I hope no one, sir," Jason replied. "Trust me, the only person I invited was you."

"Then why the hell are the mayor and his buddies here?" Jack demanded, sensing the beginning of a huge cluster. "And why is the man in the suit blue? Did he choke or something?"

Jason shrugged his shoulders and replied, "Clueless. The M.E. should be here any minute. I hear there's another murder over in the third district."

Jason continued to check out the body. "Maybe he was strangled or puked," Jason offered, looking closer at the dead man.

"Damn, he's as blue as any dead person I've ever seen. Who the hell are they?"

"Not good, Commander. The blue guy is Senator Beau LaMont, our infamous Senator from Louisiana."

Jack's face was incredulous. "No way. No way that's Beau LaMont! Couldn't be! It looks nothing like him. This guy is skinny. LaMont is a pretty heavy dude from what I remember. Couldn't be."

Detective Vern Bridges hailed Jack, walked over, and joined in on the conversation. "Commander, you been home yet?" Bridges teased.

"What the hell, Bridges, I just saw you here a few hours ago. Are you bringing these bodies in from Kenner?" Jack grunted as he slapped his detective on the back.

"Heck no. We don't have anything like this out in the burbs. That's why I gotta come to town for some action. Kenner police just sit around and eat donuts. You know that, Commander."

Jack gave Vern a wide grin. "Yep, best donuts in the world are on Airline Highway. Who the hell are these stiffs, Bridges?"

"Jason's right, sir. Yeah, Commander, that's LaMont. He had one of those fat surgeries done a year or so ago and lost over a hundred pounds. He does look entirely different, but for sure, that's him. I mean he looks different because of his weight. Not because he's blue, although that's different as well," Vern stammered and couldn't help but laugh.

Jack clapped Vern on the back. "Geez, Bridges, you're a funny man. You get all the good ones. How'd you get so lucky to catch both double homicides? Nobody I know has ever been this lucky."

"Guess it's just because I'm your best detective, Jack," Vern quipped.

Jack nodded. "Who's the other dude? The one with the slit throat?"

Detective Bridges shook his head and gave Jack a solemn look. "Commander, this guy looks just like those kids from last night. Do you see any blood?"

"Shit, no I don't." Jack looked around. "Was he killed here or just moved here after the kill?"

"Don't know, too early. But guess who he is, Commander."

Jack gave Bridges an irritated look, "I don't know, Santa Claus? Just spit it out, Detective, it's too late for games. Who the hell is he?"

"It's, at least according to his wallet, Hayes Hunter."

"Hayes Hunter? Hayes Hunter? That name's familiar, but who is he?" Jack scratched his head trying to remember.

"He's the head of the Democratic National Party. *The* Democratic National Party, not just Louisiana. He and LaMont were in NOLA finalizing the plans for the Democratic National meeting this fall. They were last seen —"

"Oh my God. Oh shit," Jack said just as he heard the mayor holler his name. Jack cursed under his breath and stared at his team. "We just have all the luck don't we, guys. Two fricking politicians dead in my backyard."

Jack turned around slowly to face the angry, pig-eyed, newly elected mayor of New Orleans. "Mr. Mayor, you're out late tonight," Jack said in a condescending voice. He saw Jason Aldridge flinch at his sarcasm. Jack guessed he didn't make Jason's life any easier.

Mayor Anthony Devries ignored Jack's comment and said, "Commander Françoise, let's put our differences away for a few moments. What has happened here in our beloved

French Quarter? Is it true that Senator LaMont and Mr. Hunter have been killed?" The mayor's little pig-like eyes were wide and he looked frightened.

Jack's eyes narrowed as he gazed at his nemesis, Mayor Anthony Devries. "Yeah. That's right. Mr. Mayor, that's precisely correct, and a better question is – how in the hell did you know?"

Devries bristled at the deprecating tone of the commander, "Really, Françoise, tone it down a bit. I am your boss, and I am happy to answer your questions. I am invested in bringing this to closure immediately. We have a lot riding on this."

"Yeah, I bet you do ... like questions about whether New Orleans is a safe enough place to host the Democratic Party right, Mr. Mayor?

Devries ignored the commander's sarcasm. He personally hated the commander and had tried to block his promotion, but was unsuccessful because Jack had too many friends. "And to answer your question, my office received an anonymous tip less than an hour ago that two VIPs were dead in the Quarter. We came right down here immediately. Now, what do you know?"

"We know we got two stiffs, one of them is blue, and the other looks like someone tried to cut his head off. The M.E. hasn't gotten here yet. You can take a look for yourself," Jack offered, gesturing expansively with his arm.

Jason Aldridge interrupted, "Mr. Mayor, did you trace the call and does anyone know where the two gentlemen were earlier this evening?"

The vice-mayor offered up some information. He caught Jack's attention, as Jack actually liked the vice-mayor. "We tried to get the State Police to trace the call, but the conversation was too short, even though it was transferred through the city network. Our security people got nothing."

Jack introduced Detective Vern Bridges to the mayor's entourage and announced he was the lead detective on the case.

Bridges gave an update on the murders, as best he could, and informed the mayor that the M.E. should be along shortly.

The mayor looked around impatiently and said, "Detective Bridges, is that all you know? That's really nothing. All we really know is that they are dead."

Bridges was getting pissed, "Mr. Mayor, you are correct. We don't know much, but the bodies are hardly cold and the M.E. hasn't arrived yet. We'll know a great deal more when he or she does arrive. One thing we do know is that both men were last seen together at one of the Vampire Bars downtown. And, that was about two hours ago."

For a moment, there was total silence in the air at the crime scene. Even the police sirens seemed to cease.

Shit, Jack thought to himself. *It just keeps getting better.*

Chapter 17

Alex's heart was pounding as she leapt out of bed. She hastily combed her long auburn hair and pulled it up into a chignon. She considered wearing jeans and a cotton sweater to the hospital, but decided against it. She had no idea what she was up against and didn't know if she'd be able to return home to redress later. Besides, her grandmother always told her to dress her best when things looked the worst or when she was facing the unknown, good advice Alex always heeded. Sometimes, just knowing you look good makes things seem easier.

She quickly selected and stepped into a pale blue linen dress with a matching jacket. She added a hand-painted blue floral scarf, a long string of pearls, and low-heeled shoes that completed the look. As she checked her appearance in her full-length mirror, her mind was racing with possibilities. The knot in her stomach and the pain in her chest were reminiscent of the terrible tragedies that occurred only a few months ago at Crescent City Medical Center – a myriad of tragedies resulting in utter chaos and damage from which the hospital was just now beginning to recover.

Alex was debating whether she should drive to the hospital or call for Martin, her faithful cabdriver, when the phone rang again. She answered it with apprehension. It was Jack.

"Yo, Alex, I'm sending a patrol car around to get you. Are you ready?" Françoise's voice was low and gruff.

"Yes, Jack. What's going on? What happened?" Alex asked, feeling frantic.

"You'll see when you get here. Trust me, that's soon enough." Jack's voice was hushed but ominous.

Alex, fully dressed, paced in her elegant living room waiting for the uniformed policeman to pick her up. She was so anxious she forced herself to take deep breaths to calm down and think more clearly. She snapped on several lights and seated herself in the blue, silk, Queen Anne chair flanking the marble fireplace so that she would be able to see the lights of the police car through the French doors.

Each minute seemed like an eternity. The ticking of the grandfather clock slowed time to a crawl and thundered in her ears. If she only knew what had happened, she could be spending this time deciding on the best way to handle the crisis. For a moment, Alex was irritated at Jack for not filling her in. Obviously, Monique couldn't have. Monique could hardly speak. Alex forced herself to calm down. She looked around the room, admiring the soft pastel colors. She had designed the room herself and had used many of the Virginia antiques she had found at Wyndley, her grandparents' Virginia estate. She'd found other antiques in New Orleans on Royal and Magazine streets, the city's antique haven.

Her thoughts turned to Mitch. He'd loved this room and had often said the room captured the "essence of Alex" and personified her spirit, personality, taste, and love of beauty. Alex felt her eyes well up with tears at the thought of Mitchell Landry, the man she had loved and had lost so violently. She could still conjure up Mitch's face. His dark wavy hair and startling dark eyes were crystal-clear in her mind's eye. Alex loved him and missed him greatly. She was just about to let herself slip into one of her "Grand Funks," as she referred to them, when there was a soft knock on her door.

Her heartbeat accelerated again. She hadn't seen any lights. Was she daydreaming? She peered out the window and looked for a police car. She didn't see one. She wondered if she could have been so obsessed with her thoughts that she had imagined the knock. No, there it was again. A very soft knock. Alex walked over to her door and peered through the peephole. She knew she couldn't be too careful these days. Just last week, the *Times Picayune* had published an article stating that Louisiana was the most dangerous state to live in with the murder rate ten times the national average. Anyway, it was pretty clear that violence against the elderly, preschoolers, and women was escalating and Alex was always careful when answering her door.

She looked through her peephole. She still couldn't see anything. It was dark. She stepped back, rubbed her eyes, and looked again. It was still black. She couldn't even see the light from the porch lanterns. Alex felt her heart racing. She knew she'd heard a knock on her door – hadn't she? She was feeling a little dizzy from her rapid heartbeat, fatigue most likely, and fear.

For a second, she was beginning to think she was crazy. Then she heard voices on her loggia. She looked through the peephole again. Looking back at her with an innocent, enigmatic smile on his face was Lester Whitset the administrator from the Pavilion. Behind him was a uniformed New Orleans policeman.

Alex opened the door and stared at the two men.

Lester Whitset's eyes roamed over her, from top to bottom. He spoke first. "Evening or, should I say, morning, Ms. Destephano. Sorry to awaken you so early, but – "

"What are you doing here, Mr. Whitset?" Her voice was harsh and uncertain. "Commander Françoise told me he was sending a police officer to pick me up and take me to the Pavilion." Alex knew her tone was aloof and rushed. She felt short of breath just looking at the man. He gave her the creeps. He was vile. Besides, she wasn't pleased that Lester Whitset knew where she lived. In fact, it frightened and made her uneasy.

Whitset gave Alex another long, appraising look and said in a soft, sensual voice, "I was at the Pavilion when the tragedy occurred. Dr. Desmonde was extremely upset, so I decided who to call in." He shrugged his shoulders and said innocently, "In the interest of expediency, I decided to personally pick you up, particularly since we most likely have a legal situation on our hands."

Alex decided she wouldn't be ruffled or perturbed by the administrator. She said clearly, with no room for argument, "Thank you, Mr. Whitset. I'll travel with Officer Bennett." She was straining to see the police officer's badge in the darkness. "The commander was kind enough to send me a ride, so I'll honor his kindness by accepting it. I'll see you later." Alex's voice was formal and remote. She locked the door and brushed by Whitset to walk with the uniformed policeman to his car. Usually, Alex was friendlier and not so curt, but Lester Whitset made her blood run cold.

"Are you all right, ma'am?" The policeman asked officiously. "That man didn't bother you, did he?"

"No, Officer Bennett. I just didn't expect him to come to my house at 3 o'clock in the morning. I didn't like seeing him here…." Her voice trailed off.

"It does seem a bit unusual that he took it upon himself to pick you up. I'm glad I pulled up behind him. The commander would skin me alive if I returned without you," the officer admitted.

Me, too, Alex thought. She smiled at the young policeman and inquired, "Do you know what's happened over at CCMC? The commander just called me and told me to come at once and that he was sending you to pick me up. Other than that, I'm clueless."

Officer Bennett stared at Alex's huge blue eyes, wide with anxiety. "I don't know, ma'am. I was the closest unit to your house and I haven't been over to CCMC yet. I guess there's been some kind of accident. They're sending for the crime team again. I heard it on the radio."

Alex's heart sank. Her intuition told her it was patient related violence. She hoped in her heart that none of the staff or patients were injured badly. She had to do something about the staffing and security in the Pavilion. Don Montgomery, idiot that he was, would just have to listen to her.

As the bright lights of CCMC became visible in the darkness of the night, Alex quickly noted that the area around the Pavilion was blazing with activity. The blue and red sirens made her dizzy. When Officer Bennett dropped Alex off at the door, there were at least six NOPD cars and a dozen or so other cars parked in the circular drive in front of the main entrance. Alex saw Monique's Volvo in the group. She also noticed Don Montgomery's shiny, gold Porsche. Just seeing the CEO's car convinced Alex that it was going to be a night, or morning, from hell.

The heavy Pavilion doors were guarded by members of the NOPD. Alex had to show her hospital ID to enter the building. On the drab grey bench, where Monique and Alex had talked just a few hours earlier, sat a handsome, well-dressed, middle-aged couple. The wife was trying to comfort her husband, a distinguished white-haired gentleman. The man was red-eyed, obviously upset. The couple looked at Alex curiously.

Alex wondered who they were and how they'd gotten past the police. She smiled at them as she waited for the elevator. They didn't give her a response. She guessed she'd know their identity soon enough. As she stood in the lobby, she was keenly aware that the couple was staring at her. She wanted to speak and offer some comfort, but decided against it. Instead, she smiled at them and nodded.

A police officer was operating the elevator. He also asked for her ID and then pushed the button for the second floor. The Unit was locked, but Alex was quickly admitted by a pale-faced psych tech.

Whitset came in within seconds of Alex. He touched her shoulder as he passed by her on the way to his office and said, "Have a pleasant ride, Alex? Sorry if I frightened you earlier." He gave her a smirking smile and disappeared.

Alex ignored him and looked around for Françoise and Monique.

The psych unit was electric with activity. There were three staff members talking with police in the nurses' station and Alex noticed several patients sitting in the day room. Two were catatonic and sat rigidly staring, without blinking, at the television set mounted high on the wall. One patient's body posture was grotesque. He was wearing only a T-shirt and boxer shorts. His legs looked like spaghetti noodles, wrapped around each other in a grotesquely contorted fashion. His arms were bent at the elbows and perpendicular to each other. His hands were fixed in a position that suggested he had just finished strangling somebody. His fingers were spaced apart and curved, just as though they would fit around someone's neck. His nails were long and untrimmed. Alex cringed at the contorted patient. His tongue was hanging out of his mouth and his eyes were bulging. He looked as though he had just finished killing his victim. He was even drooling. Her total body shuddered in disgust.

This place is horrible, she thought, as she continued to look around. Another patient was pacing frantically around the room, never slowing his pace. His face was so devoid of expression that it looked like a mask. His continual motion made Alex dizzy.

143

The third patient was restrained in a chair, clearly hallucinating. He was speaking directly to President Obama and God, asking them to have Michelle fix things. Alex watched him briefly as President Obama apparently answered him. She shook her head at the disorganized, incoherent thinking of the man. Suddenly, he burst into loud, silly laughter that had a surrealistic tone to it. *How could Monique do this every day?*

Alex again scanned the day room. Over in a corner, looking most uncomfortable, was a young New Orleans policeman named Josh Martin, whom she recognized as a protégé of Jack Françoise. Alex motioned and caught his eye. He finally saw her and waved.

Josh Martin was an attractive young man. He wore his uniform to perfection and approached Alex with crinkly eyes and a wide smile that stretched over a generous mouth.

"Ms. Destephano. I'm glad to see you. This place is incredible!" Josh scratched his head and looked around wildly. "Look at these people! I'm supposed to be guarding them!" He rolled his eyes and continued, "To tell the truth, I'd rather be in a shootout or chasing a burglar than sitting in here. In fact, I'd rather be losing the shootout!" Josh gave a short laugh, looking around nervously.

Alex smiled at the young man. "Yeah, they're pretty unique, aren't they?" Then Alex changed the subject and anxiously asked, "Josh, what's going on? Where's the commander and Dr. Desmonde?"

Josh gestured towards the North Hall and said, "They're down there. The bigwigs are meeting in the community room. Go on down. It's pretty safe. Most of the patients are either asleep, doped up, or in seclusion."

"Thanks, Josh. You okay here?"

Josh looked uncertain. "Yeah, I guess so … but what do I do if they go off? The commander told me I couldn't shoot them! Heck, he even threatened to take my gun away from me, just in case I was tempted."

Alex laughed. "They look pretty controlled at this point. Keep your eye on the pacer, though. He could be a problem."

Josh grimaced, wavered, and returned to his chair, continuing to watch the eerie threesome he was supposed to be guarding.

"Josh," Alex hissed at him, "Move your chair closer to the door. You never put yourself in a corner with a psychotic patient close by. You'll want to get out if the going gets rough. Don't let them block you in, ever."

"Yeah. Good idea. Thanks, Ms. Destephano." Josh couldn't move his chair quickly enough to get himself closer to the double doors of the day room.

Alex walked down the hall towards the community room, her heart again thudding in her chest. She knocked on the door and a grim-faced Don Montgomery admitted her.

Don's greeting was tinged with scorn. "It's about time. Where in the hell have you been? I can never find you when I need you. When I don't need or want to see you, you're hanging around my office!" Montgomery's normally grating voice had a caustic edge to it.

Alex ignored him. Sweeping feelings of déjà vu encompassed her. *This is just like before,* she thought. Just like February, right before Mardi Gras. *Even the players are the same,* she thought to herself as she looked at the group assembled around the table. Monique was sitting next to Jack, her face tear-streaked and pale.

Jack was fighting strong emotions not to overly comfort Monique, while working hard not to beat the hell out of the pompous CEO as he railed out at Alex.

Jack looked like hell. It was clear he hadn't been home at all. He must have come here straight from the murder in the Quarter. A nurse was also present. Alex assumed it was the night shift charge nurse. Missing were Dr. John Ashley, the chief of medicine who was out of town, and Bette Farve. The other person in the room was Whitset, who waved and smiled benignly at Alex, greeting her as if she was his best friend. Monique hardly seemed to notice Alex's entrance.

"What's happened?" Alex's voice was cool, but she was seething with anger at Don Montgomery's disrespect.

Montgomery's voice was loud and testy. "We have a dead patient – a dead, whacko patient – *that's what happened*!" He looked around impatiently and continued, "A dead crazy, right here at CCMC. I just love it." Montgomery's voice dripped sarcasm as he peevishly added, "Where's Elizabeth? We've got to cover our asses on this one with the media. Where is she, Alex?" Don demanded, his face red with anger.

Alex shrugged her shoulders and said, "I don't know where Elizabeth is. I would imagine home in bed unless someone has called her. Did anyone call?" Alex looked around the room.

Everyone gestured in the negative. No one spoke.

Don's harsh voice broke in again. "Desmonde, you're the medical person here. Call Tippett and get her in here. *Now!* I can't expect anything from you physicians." Don glared at the psychiatrist.

Alex could feel Monique's fury and she saw the telltale blush of anger climbing her bruised and battered body.

After several moments, Monique stood, stared at Don, recovered herself, and said clearly, "Mr. Montgomery, I'll be happy to call Elizabeth Tippet. Generally, the unit administrator, who in this case would be Mr. Whitset, calls. But I gather that hasn't happened, so—"

Whitset jumped to his feet, his eyes flashing, and harshly interrupting Monique, said, "How dare you single me out in front of a group for a responsibility I never knew I had. I will get you for this —"

Monique didn't let him finish, "Don't threaten me, Mr. Whitset. We'll talk about this later." Then she turned to face Don, leaned over so she was inches from his face, and said, "As I was saying before Mr. Whitset interrupted me, I will call Elizabeth, but I won't respond to any more of your callous behavior or profanity. Is that clear to you?" Monique's voice was calm and cool and her intent was clear. She had regained her professional demeanor.

Alex telepathically cheered her on. *That's my girl,* she thought. *Go Monique.*

Alex noticed the ruthless look Whitset gave Monique and it sent shivers up her spine. The look was downright evil and Whitset had even bared his teeth. He was furious at her and Alex was afraid he would physically hurt her or sabotage her. She had to remind Monique to be careful and watch out. She turned to Jack and immediately knew that Jack had seen the look as well. His face revealed his anger and he looked like he wanted to strangle the administrator.

"Just get Tippet in here," Don roared. He glowered at Dr. Desmonde again and said, "I run this damned place, such as it is. I'll say whatever I want to, when I want to!" Montgomery pointed his finger in Monique's face and said, "Don't try to bully me, Desmonde, with your calculated, psychiatric bullshit. If you knew how to run a psychiatric service, we wouldn't have patients murdering each other."

Alex's heart was racing frantically, skipping beats. She felt hot all over. Murder! So that's what happened. It wasn't just a dead patient, but one that had been murdered. On the psych unit at CCMC? Murder involving patients? Oh My God! Oh, no! This was worse than she'd expected. Her legal mind was boggled with the thoughts of it, not to mention the repercussions. A million thoughts were racing through her head all at once.

Monique continued standing, undeterred by Don's anger, ranting, and rudeness. She stated again, her voice firm, "Mr. Montgomery, I'll call Elizabeth, but I want you to guarantee that you will conduct yourself in an acceptable manner and cut the vulgarity and innuendos."

Don nodded his head and threw up his hands. "Just do it, Dr. Desmonde!" His voice was scathing and his emphasis on the word *doctor* was derogatory.

Monique left the room to call Elizabeth Tippet, the young woman in charge of media relations at CCMC.

Alex looked frantically at Jack Françoise. "What happened, Jack? Who was killed?"

Françoise was positively grey with fatigue. He looked at Alex and spoke softly. "An elderly patient, Mrs. Smithson, was found dead in her room about an hour and a half ago. She had been stabbed repeatedly. She'd only been dead for a short period of time. Her body was still warm."

Alex's stomach lurched forward and she thought she would be sick on the large walnut conference table. She immediately remembered Mrs. Smithson from the day before. She was the little, white-haired lady who had been admitted with depression. Just yesterday, Alex had questioned Monique and Donna about the clinical judgment of placing an elderly, depressed woman on a unit with so many violent patients.

Her voice was hushed. She could hardly form her words. "Oh God, not Mrs. Smithson. That little, white-haired lady who was knitting yesterday in the community room? The one who looks like Mrs. Santa Claus? The little lady with the apple-red cheeks?"

Whitset was clearly loving Alex's reaction. His smile was inappropriate. He couldn't wait to respond. His voice was remarkably clear and sounded gleeful, "Yes, Alex dear, that's her. But she doesn't have apple cheeks anymore and the knitting needle is now stuck in her mouth.

Alex was stunned, her jaw dropped in shock.

Even Don looked surprised at the sound of Whitset's voice, but his surprise was short lived. To deflect attention from his administrator, Don moved closer to Alex, his face leering into hers. "Looked like Mrs. Santa Claus. You've got it, Alex," he said sarcastically. "Mrs. Santa Claus has been murdered at Crescent City Medical Center by her next-door neighbor, Mr. McMurdie, our inpatient member of the New Orleans Police Department on the wacko unit. Right, Commander Françoise?" Don Montgomery turned his sarcasm on Jack and glared at him.

Alex could see Jack struggle for control. Jack despised Montgomery, who he had disliked before the mayoral election. Now he had two sworn enemies.

The CEO continued, "One of your protégés wasn't he, Captain Françoise? NOPD's finest. Great work!" Montgomery spit his words at the police commander.

"It's Commander Françoise now," Monique said automatically. "He is the highest ranking officer in this police district."

"Well, whoop-de-do! Everyone knows the New Orleans police are all crooked, incompetent, or on the take," Don snarled, staring at Jack.

Alex placed her hand on Jack's arm as if to restrain him from knocking Montgomery senseless, a dream the commander had coveted for months. The blood was bad between the CEO and the police commander – very bad, in fact. Alex knew that the meeting could easily erupt into a free-for-all between the two men and that the commander would lose, not physically, but most assuredly politically. She also knew Don would be a bloody mess. There was nothing Don would like more than to get Françoise fired, or at least, reprimanded. Jack's judgment returned with a touch of Alex's hand. He sat down. Alex noted with some relief that Monique had returned to the room, her composure intact.

Françoise settled down and looked at Alex. His tone was grave. "It looks, at least from the preliminaries, that McMurdie is guilty. He was covered with Mrs. Smithson's blood."

Alex fought another visceral response and thought about how she could possibly keep herself from throwing up. It had been hours since she had eaten. "Who found Mrs. Smithson?" Alex questioned.

"I did," responded the nurse at the conference table.

Alex turned to look again at the nurse. She looked familiar, but Alex couldn't quite place her. She thought for several moments and then remembered her from the evening before. She was a nurse from an agency, who had been working evenings ... the nurse who had admitted to Alex that she had no psychiatric nursing experience. *This is just great,* Alex thought to herself. *A jury will love this. We're fish bait on this one. This really sucks.*

Alex spoke to the nurse. "Didn't we talk earlier? Weren't you on the evening shift? Sorry, I can't remember your name."

"I'm JoAnne Waters. Yes, we did talk and I was on evenings. The agency couldn't find anyone else to send for nights, so I volunteered. I guess the word's out around town about the nurse that was attacked and raped. Anyway, I agreed to stay over, you know, do a double. I didn't know I'd signed up for murder."

Alex noticed that Joanne was super pale and had tears in her eyes. "You were the one who found Mrs. Smithson?" Alex asked.

"Yes, I found her when I was making rounds at 2:00 a.m. She was dead. I immediately called security and they called the other people who are here. Mr. Whitset was already here, in his office, and came out when I was making the phone calls."

Whitset was here. What the hell was Whitset doing here on the night shift? "Did something happen on your shift that could've caused something like this to happen?" Alex looked speculatively at the tearful, frightened RN.

Joanne answered in a quavering voice, "No. Nothing. The evening was quiet. The patients were doing well. There was no trouble at all." At that point JoAnne turned to look at Lester and said, "Wouldn't you agree, Mr. Whitset? You were here until after midnight."

Whitset gave the nurse a sly smile. "Yes, it was quiet. I agree. I left shortly after midnight to grab a coffee and returned to my office to do some work." He looked around the group as if to be sure that everyone heard him.

"Anyway," Joanne continued, "On the night shift, shortly after Mr. Whitset left, there was a big ruckus on the prison unit next door. They called a stat page for help and I sent my two psych techs over. Apparently, several inmates were trying to attack a third man and my techs were tied up for some time. I was alone on this unit. There was a lot of noise and screaming that I could hear from the prison unit. The noise woke up several of our patients who became alarmed and frightened. One was a new admission. I medicated him, along with two others, and told them all to go back to sleep. I guess that was what I was doing when the murder occurred … I didn't hear anything. I promise you, if I had known this had happened or heard Mrs. Smithson's bell, I would have gone there immediately. She went to bed around 9:00 and was sleeping soundly at midnight. I had no idea ...." Joanne started crying softly into a tissue, deftly handed to her by Whitset.

Alex pondered Joanne's remarks for a few seconds. She looked at the commander who nodded his head. Jack also believed Joanne's story. Alex turned her gaze to Whitset and asked him coldly, "Why were you here so late, Mr. Whitset?"

Lester gave Alex a placating smile. "I frequently work late, Alex. I make it a point to be on the unit at different times during the day and night so I can evaluate the quality of care the patients are receiving. It's my own system of quality management, you see. I'm a clinical and administrative manager. Besides, I love being here at night. It's quiet and I can get so much more work done than during the daylight hours." His voice was soft and smooth, even sensuous.

Alex found herself once again mesmerized by the man's voice.

He continued to smile at Alex the entire time he was talking. Then Whitset added, "Besides, I don't like imposters working at my hospital. I oversee all operations, clinical and administrative."

Alex was confused. "Imposters? What do you mean, imposters?" Alex questioned.

Whitset hesitated for a second and said, "Imposters, people that pretend to care for patients, but who don't know how. People who aren't in tune with patient needs and don't understand them are imposters. Many psychiatric staff are actually imposters – they pretend to be someone they aren't."

Alex nodded her head slowly. "Did you happen to hear or see anything that made you suspicious before you left?" Alex guessed that Jack had asked the same questions earlier. She glanced at the commander out of the corner of her eye and saw he was listening intently, his notebook open in front of him.

Whitset glared at Alex steadily, with a lewd look in his eyes. His eyes dropped to Alex's breasts and stayed there for several moments before looking back up into her face.

Alex could swear he was leering at her.

"No, not a thing, Ms. Destephano. I checked the situation on the prison unit, headed for my car, and went out for coffee." He continued to stare moodily at Alex, his eyes wandering over her body suggestively.

Alex stared back at Whitset. Her gaze wandered over his rumpled shirt and pants. It was pretty clear to her that he hadn't been to bed. Perhaps he had napped in his office because he was a mess.

Lester continued to gawk at her, his eyes wandering over her body as if trying to catch her off guard, daring her to say something that questioned his story.

Alex said softly, "Sorry you were awakened from your slumber, Lester. You must have been napping on your sofa in your office. That must be why your clothes are so wrinkled." She gave the administrator a sweet smile. "I guess we were all awakened abruptly."

"No problem, Alex. I'm a light sleeper. I'm used to rising for any occasion. Any occasion. You remember that." Whitset gave Alex an indecent look. His eyes were half closed and his mouth was open as he looked at her. A little bit of spittle had gathered at one corner of his mouth.

Alex flashed a look at Jack, who nodded his head, a nod that was imperceptible to anyone else in the room.

Montgomery was glowering at her. He said, "Alex, have you finished your inquisition? If you have, I'd like to hear more from Françoise about his buddy that murdered dear Mrs. Santa Claus." Montgomery's eyes glittered rudely at Alex and Jack.

Dr. Desmonde interrupted Don. "Mr. Montgomery, her name was Mrs. Smithson and her son and his wife are waiting for you downstairs. I suggest you learn her name before you meet with them." Monique's voice was sharp and she was clearly annoyed and irritated with him.

"I'll be damned if I'm seeing them. That's your job, Desmonde. You're the shrink and this travesty is your fault." Montgomery gave the psychiatrist an ugly look. "Are you out of your mind? I have no intention of ever seeing them or associating myself with anything that has happened or will happen over here in this insane asylum. You should have given them more pills to knock them out. Damn situations such as these. I just don't have time for this," Don added, as he slammed his fist on the conference table.

Monique was livid, but held her tongue and remained aloof.

Alex, clearly incensed, resisted an impulse to rail out at Don Montgomery. She could feel Françoise's body tense up beside her. He was so angry his body was radiating heat. She touched Jack's leg and said in a steady voice, "Really, Don, as CEO you and I both need to see the Smithsons. This is a terrible crime and we need to —"

Don interrupted her, his voice piercing her brain. "You just don't get it, do you? You don't know just how gruesome this crime is, Alex. Tell her, Captain Mighty Mouse," Montgomery said as he glanced at the New Orleans Police Commander, refusing to acknowledge his new title.

Jack overlooked Montgomery's slur and looked contemplatively at Alex. "The scene's bad, Alex. Grizzly crime – one of the worst I've seen in my time and…"

Alex remembered the violent crimes earlier in the year. Nothing, nothing could be worse than those crime scenes. Nor could anything be worse than what had happened to Angela the night before … could it? Alex was uncertain and asked herself these questions as she turned to Jack.

"Jack," she interrupted, "Nothing could be worse than what happened in February. Those crimes were horrible." Alex still had nightmares about them, even six months later.

Judith Lucci

Jack sighed audibly. "This is a little different. It's different in another way." He paused for a moment as he saw Elizabeth Tippett enter the room.

The lovely, dark-haired Elizabeth looked strained. Dressed casually in jeans and a white shirt, Liz had opted to get to CCMC quickly. She looked stunning for 4:30 a.m., prepared to take command of the media fracas certain to erupt shortly. Apparently, she'd heard there had been a murder. She sat down opposite Don and Monique.

"Thanks for coming Elizabeth." Alex smiled hesitantly at her friend. Elizabeth's job as the director of media relations for the hospital was difficult, especially for a young woman who had only two years before received her Master's degree in Communications. Elizabeth had earned her stripes via a baptism by fire earlier in the year, when the press had swooped down on CCMC like vultures, making mincemeat of the place and broadcasting the medical center's dirty laundry to the entire world. Elizabeth had stood her ground and represented the hospital well during those difficult times. As a result, she'd forged an excellent media network, which now worked to the hospital's advantage. She'd earned respect and admiration among her colleagues. She was incredibly well respected.

Alex continued, "We've had some trouble here, Liz. Apparently, one of the patients attacked and murdered another patient and Jack was —"

Liz gestured to Alex to stop. "I know, Alex. The policeman outside told me. Do you have any details?" Elizabeth looked around the group and immediately extended her hand and introduced herself to Whitset and Joanne Waters, the two people she didn't know at the table. Joanne murmured a greeting to the media director.

Whitset spoke, "Miss Tippett, I assume it's 'Miss'?"

155

Whitset drew out the 's' in 'Miss' until Alex wanted to throttle him.

Elizabeth nodded, but said nothing.

Whitset continued, "I am so delighted to meet you. I'm in charge of the Pavilion and very happy to be meeting all of you from the 'other side' of the medical center, particularly those of you who are beautiful." Once again, Alex felt mesmerized by the sound of his voice. It was melodious and comforting to her ears. His voice was directly opposed to his appearance, which Alex found repulsive.

If Elizabeth was surprised or appalled, she didn't show it. She gave a half smile and turned to Alex. She was all business and Alex loved it.

Whitset looked annoyed that she hadn't responded to his compliment. His eyebrows were arched in disapproval.

"Commander Françoise was just about to fill us in when you arrived. Would you continue, Commander?" Alex asked.

Commander Françoise gave Elizabeth a quick smile. He'd become friends with her earlier in the year. The commander was well acquainted with the administrative players at CCMC. He knew their strengths and weaknesses. Most of them he didn't respect at all. As a matter of fact, he detested them.

"Hi, Liz. It looks like one of the patients attacked and murdered an elderly woman, Mrs. Smithson, sometime after midnight. The crime scene's a bloody mess."

Elizabeth nodded. "I understand the patient was stabbed. Is that correct?" She looked around the table and was surprised to find Whitset smiling as Jack described the situation.

"Yeah, you're right. But this ain't no ordinary stabbing. Mrs. Smithson was stabbed repeatedly with a long, thin, instrument. Probably at least seventeen times, as best we can determine."

Don interrupted rudely. "It was her knitting needle, you idiot. Couldn't you tell?"

The commander gave the CEO a dark, murderous look, said nothing, and then continued, "The murder weapon has not been confirmed yet, at least not officially."

Jack glanced at Elizabeth and Alex staring at him. Both women were speechless. Joanne looked at her hands, and Monique was staring at an imaginary spot on the wall. All seemed to be trying to disassociate themselves from what the commander was about to say.

Alex looked out of the corner of her eye.

Whitset was gazing intently at Françoise. Whitset's countenance was reverent, almost holy. He looked excited, practically orgasmic, as Jack uttered the next few words.

"Mrs. Smithson was stabbed at least seventeen times with what appears to be her blue knitting needle. She was stabbed repeatedly in the eyes, ears, and the nose and mouth areas. I'm sure the medical examiner will tell us that she died as a result of the murder weapon piercing her brain. It's as if the murderer wanted to totally disfigure her – to wipe out her face." After a pause lasting a few seconds, Jack added, "He did."

Alex felt the bile rising into her mouth. She was hot, so hot … and flushed all over. She felt ill again. She was afraid this time she'd be sick on the conference table for sure.

Jack reached towards her, thinking she would faint.

Elizabeth left the room, apparently to compose herself.

They could hear retching in the restroom down the hall.

Monique looked unwell, her pale face covered with a sheen of perspiration.

The room was so silent you could hear a pin drop, each person caught up in their own thoughts about the brutal murder.

Alex prayed for composure and felt it gradually returning. *Thank God*, she thought.

Whitset looked pleased. Everyone else seemed in shock.

After several moments, Alex managed to ask, "Did Mrs. Smithson try to fight back? Did she cry for help?" She felt tears in her eyes rise as she imagined the horrible death the little, apple-cheeked lady had endured.

Jack looked steadily at Alex. "We don't know if she called for help. Most likely, she did at first. The M.E. will have to determine precisely what happened. Remember, only Joanne was on the unit. The psych techs were next door."

Alex thought Jack was being evasive. She asked again, "Did she fight back?" For some reason, this was important to Alex. She didn't know why, but she needed to know if Mrs. Smithson had an opportunity to fight for her life.

Françoise held Alex's eyes to his and said, "No, Alex. She didn't appear to fight back. She couldn't. Her hands were tied to the bed. She had on wrist restraints. As a matter of fact, she had on four-point restraints. Her hands and her feet were tied down." Jack's voice sounded dead and weary as he told her.

"But why? Why?" Alex demanded loudly. Her voice was shrill, almost a screech. "She didn't look like a patient who needed to be restrained. Side rails, a Posey vest, maybe … but four-point restraints!" She looked wildly at Monique. "Why, Monique, would you order four-point restraints for a harmless, little, old lady."

Dr. Desmonde said softly, "We didn't tie her down, Alex. Her killer did."

Alex was so devastated by the insanity of the crime she could scarcely think. Her body felt weak, exhausted, and immovable. She felt faint. A look of dread crossed her face as her mind clicked through questions to ask. She was afraid to ask the question. She looked at the people around her.

Monique and Jack were gazing steadily at her. Montgomery and Joanne were preoccupied with their own thoughts. Whitset was staring at her as well, his eyes unreadable. His cold eyes bore into her face. His mouth was curled upward in an eager, expectant smile. Her stomach again turned as she looked at him.

Alex continued to gather the strength to ask the next question. Her hands were pressed on the top of the conference table, the tips of her fingers bloodless due to the pressure she exerted against the table. She looked directly at Dr. Desmonde and Commander Françoise.

Her voice was low, breathless. It came in small, short gasps. "Was she ... Mrs. Smithson ...?" Alex couldn't say the words.

Monique looked in Alex's startled blue eyes with her clear gaze. She knew what Alex was trying to say and she replied, "Yes, Alex. We believe Mrs. Smithson was sexually assaulted, that she was raped and beaten. It's horrible, atrocious, and horrendous." Monique's voice broke and her eyes filled with tears.

The room was still, very still. Everyone was gaping at Alex. She finally looked around and said to Commander Françoise, "Jack, could you leave the crime scene undisturbed? I'd like to take a look at it in a little while. First, I need to do a little thinking."

"Sure, Alex. Sure. The CSI team is in there now. We've got some time. Ain't nobody going to touch nothing in there. Forensics arrived and will be in there for hours. Biggest problem we got, as I see it, is dealing with Mr. and Mrs. Smithson and figuring out who did this. He insists on seeing his mother's body. Nothing good is gonna come out of that." Françoise shook his head in anticipation of the event.

"I certainly wouldn't recommend that, would you?" This statement came from Whitset. The group stared at him. His

159

voice was high and he was laughing. "You can't even see her face – it's gone! He probably wouldn't even know that it is his mother. But, on second thought, perhaps it will help him deal with his loss." He looked around the group, gauging their response.

Monique and Alex glanced at each other, sharing a look that communicated their disgust with the man, as well as their questions about his inappropriate behavior.

Monique looked at him curiously. "No, Mr. Whitset. We'll discourage the Smithsons from seeing their mother. As a matter of fact, Ms. Destephano and I, hope Mr. Montgomery will see them shortly."

Whitset interrupted Monique and said, "I'll be glad to see the family. After all, I am the administrator for psychiatric services here at Crescent City. Besides, Don, you don't need to be involved with this, particularly since you aren't comfortable. Right?" Whitset gave Don an old boy, placating look and patted him on the back.

Montgomery gave a broad smile. "Hell, no. You go, Lester. I hate this kind of stuff. Makes me look bad. This one's going to hurt, too. Where the hell is Elizabeth? Hasn't she had enough time to puke her guts out?" Don glared angrily towards the door.

Alex spoke, "I'll bring Elizabeth up to date. We'll figure out a media strategy and pass it by you." Her voice was cold, and she stared at Don, disgusted again at his inability to deal with unpleasant situations. Of course, he was always available to claim the praise for everyone else's achievements and awards. What a bastard. She was finding it harder and harder to tolerate him.

"Okay." Don looked relieved. He looked at his watch. "I'm going home. It's only 5:00 a.m. I still have time for some shuteye. Don't bother me until noon. I'll be in sometime around then."

160

Alex and Monique eyed each other with amazement as Donald Montgomery left the room. Joanne asked to be excused as well.

Jack was incensed by the chickenshit administrator's lack of interest and leadership. He uttered a string of profanities under his breath at the CEO's behavior.

Monique stepped on his foot to shut him up.

Whitset had been watching them closely, enjoying their disillusionment with Don. He smiled at them and said in a cold, but smooth voice, "Mr. Montgomery doesn't need to be involved in this. I can handle it myself. No problem. When shall we meet with the family?" His eyes were clear and he was completely composed. He seemed eager to see the Smithson family and he was getting off on splitting staff between Don and his administration team. He rubbed his hands together in anticipation.

Alex reached across the table and offered the administrator her hand. "Later. Let's see them after lunch. Thank you, Whitset. We'll keep you posted." Alex's voice was low and throaty.

Monique and Jack met each other's eyes, questioning Alex's strategy as they rose to leave.

Whitset held on to Alex's hand just a little too long and then returned it to her, his eyes again raking her body. "I'll be waiting to hear from you, Alex," he said softly. He nodded to the others and left the room.

Alex shivered at his arctic cold touch and watched him leave.

Françoise spoke first and roared, "Let's get outta here. What the hell was that, Alex? That little pervert incites my killer instinct."

Monique nodded in agreement.

Alex didn't respond.

On their way down the hall, they ran into a pale and wan Elizabeth, who immediately started to apologize even though the three tried to wave her apologies away.

Alex said roughly, "Save it, Liz. I want to get outta here. Let's go to my office."

On the way out of the Pavilion, Françoise caught up with Josh Martin and told him to keep an eye on Ms. Tippett.

The police officer agreed and gave Elizabeth a concerned smile. He asked her, "Are you all right, Ms. Tippett?"

"Yes, thank you, Josh. It's been a little rough this morning." Elizabeth smiled brightly at the police officer.

"It's going to be a long day, Ms. Tippett. It's just a little after 5:00 a.m.," Josh said, gesturing to his watch. "Let me know if there is anything you need."

"Yes, I know. I'll make it. I've done it before." Elizabeth waved bye to Josh Martin and caught up with the others at the elevator.

Alex wondered if there was a new romance in the making. She turned to comment on this to Jack and Monique, but they were obviously tied up with each other. Once again, Alex felt loneliness engulf her.

"A little romance in the making? He's good-looking!" Alex joked and poked Liz in the ribs.

"Sure, Al," Elizabeth quipped. "I'm sure Officer Bennett thinks I'm really attractive, especially after he heard me throwing my guts up in the ladies room." Elizabeth laughed and shook her head and added, "The irony of it all. He is really cute. I could go for him!"

"Don't get too excited, Liz. It probably raised the protective instinct in him. I understand policeman have a bad case of it," Monique joked as she looked sideways at Françoise.

Françoise nodded his head. "Yep, we do. We like to protect all of the good-looking ladies. I am training Josh right," he reminded the three ladies, and then said, "I'll meet you all on the first floor. I still don't ride in elevators if there's another way down." He looked sheepishly at Alex and Monique, a little ashamed of his continual elevator phobia.

They laughed at him, and after a couple of seconds, he joined in. "Laugh all you like – but remember, if the power goes out, I won't be the one stuck in a tin can or, in this case, an iron albatross!" With that, he turned and headed towards the stairway. Fortunately, the Smithsons had left the foyer of the Pavilion, relieving the stress of the group on the ground floor.

Chapter 18

Françoise drove the three women to the main hospital in his prized silver Cadillac. Jack loved the luxury of his wheels. Jack defended the expense by saying he spent days at a time in his car. Besides, when he needed to move, he needed to move, and the car was fast. Fortunately, since he was now the commander, he got less grief from the higher-ups.

Alex pressed against the cushions in the backseat and directed the air-conditioning vent towards her. She loved the tinted windows and the comfort of Jack's car. It was already hot and it wasn't even 6 o'clock in the morning. *Damn New Orleans in August,* she thought to herself. "Do you think the crime scene in the Pavilion will provoke any further violence?" she asked Monique, who was sitting in the front seat next to Jack.

Monique looked at Alex through the rearview mirror and replied, "I'm not sure. I hope not. But anything can set them off. After the last two days, we could have a riot!" Her tone was light, but her face was dead serious. "We've got to step up security on the unit, at least for the next few days. I guess I'll have to check with Whitset." Monique looked aggravated at the thought. "He is such a slime ball," she added.

Françoise minced no words when he spoke to the women. "I'm going to tell you gals straight up. He raised red flags for me! I think that bastard's as nuts as most of the patients. Strikes me as a real psycho." He looked at Monique sitting next to him in the car and tried to catch Alex and Elizabeth's eyes in the rearview mirror.

Alex was quick to respond. "I agree, Jack. The man gives me the creeps. I despise the way he looks at me. Besides, I

164

think he knows something. He is so sneaky. He looked as though he couldn't wait to talk with the Smithsons. It was almost as if he was looking forward to it. I don't trust him at all."

Monique turned around and looked at Alex. "Is that the reason you are playing patsy with him, Al? It's pretty dangerous, even if he is sane. I think the guy's a leech at the very least." She studied Alex's face in the backseat. "What's up with that?"

"I don't know for sure. I agree with Jack and I think he knows something, too. I'd like to psych him out. There's no way he went to bed last night. His clothes were rumpled and…"

"He could've put the same clothes back on, Alex. Besides, he never said he went to bed. You just inferred that. There's no proof." Françoise looked again at her through the rearview mirror.

"It's proof to me that he's a liar! That's a good beginning. So far, he's a leech and a liar. Why is he always at the hospital at night? It just doesn't add up!" Alex stopped for a minute, thinking. She asked suddenly, "When did he see Mrs. Smithson's body?"

Françoise shrugged his shoulders and looked at her in the rearview mirror. "I don't know. He could have gone in there at some point. I'll check with my men. They were stationed in the room. Why?"

"Because he came to my house to pick me up this morning a little after 4; he beat the police. He said he knew her face was gone," Alex said with a chill. "There is something about him that just wigs me out."

Monique cautioned her. "Alex, you seem to hang on to every word he says and you are playing mind games with him. It's very serious and you shouldn't do it. I frankly don't like the way you're interacting with him. It could be dangerous."

Alex was silent for several seconds trying to find a way to express her feelings. She was a little piqued with Monique's critique of her behavior. "You know, Monique, you are right. There is something about him that I find powerful and I am at some level fascinated with him. I know it sounds crazy, but I find something about him mesmerizing."

Monique turned around and glared at her. "Alex, you need to get over that. The man is at least sociopathic based on his behavior today. He relished, actually loved, the crime scene and was excited by it. Please, please be careful around him. He may mistake your attention and assume you are 'coming on' to him."

Alex felt defensive, "Really, Monique. I wasn't born yesterday. I can see through him and am sure I can handle myself around him. Don't worry."

Elizabeth took all of this in and added, "I agree with Alex, there is something about him that is charming, even if it is in a sick sort of way. But, trust me," she patted Monique's shoulder, "Alex and I can handle ourselves. Not to worry."

Monique still looked uncertain and said, "Okay, just be careful and don't play any games with him."

Françoise was thoughtful and said, "You girls listen to Monique. He's a slimy little bastard and I'd like to kill him. I'll check him out today. That being said, I imagine he saw Mrs. Smithson when the nurse, Joanne, found Mrs. Smithson's body.

Alex was thoughtful and pensive. "You know, you're probably right, but the timing is important, Jack. We know he didn't see her after I arrived. There wasn't time."

"I know. I realize that. I'll check into it, Alex. Don't worry. The man is messed up at best. He even gives me the creeps." Jack turned to Elizabeth. "What do you think, Liz?"

"Commander, I can't honestly say. I'd never seen the man before this morning and then only briefly, but he is weird. He does seem to like Alex, though." She looked at Alex and laughed. "You lucky girl," she teased.

"Wow, thanks, Liz," Alex responded ruefully.

Françoise pulled his big, silver Caddy up directly in front of the hospital. "Alex, you think I'll get a ticket if I park my wheels here?"

"If you do, Jack, I'll fix it for you. But you'll have to repay me when I get my next one in the French Quarter!" The group laughed at the idea of a lawyer fixing a ticket for a cop.

"Thanks. I'm gonna go by the cafeteria and pick up some donuts and cinnamon buns. You make the coffee, Alex. You gals want anything special?"

"I'll eat whatever you bring, Jack," Monique said, as she smiled at him brightly.

"Ditto for me," Alex said, deciding she deserved some junk food and carbs to get through her day."

"I'm in, Commander, I'll take whatever," Elizabeth added.

Thirty minutes later, seated at the conference table in Alex's office, they all felt better. After several cups of coffee and a little sugar buzz, Alex and Elizabeth were talking nonstop and Monique was less wan. Eventually, the conversation returned to the crime.

"Where's Jim McMurdie in this, Jack? Do you think he's responsible for the murder?" Alex glanced at the commander, who was slowly munching his third jelly donut.

Jack was noncommittal, savoring his jelly donut. "I wish they'd learn to make low-fat, low-calorie donuts. Sure would help my weight and cholesterol. To answer your question,

Alex, McMurdie's in chains in his room at the Pavilion. I don't know if he's guilty or not, but it looks bad for him. What do you think Monique?"

"I don't know. He was covered with blood when we found him sleeping in his room. That was after we discovered Mrs. Smithson's body. At least, there was blood on his hands. We searched his room, but we didn't find anything. He became upset when he saw the blood and he started crying. He'd been heavily medicated both around dinnertime and at bedtime. He had enough Thorazine to quiet an elephant. It's the heaviest dose he's had since admission. I don't know ... he could have, but I'm not convinced. Most people would have slept for forty-eight hours after receiving that much Thorazine. Jim's not that big of a guy."

"Does he have a history of violent outbursts?" Elizabeth asked Dr. Desmonde.

"Yep," said Monique. "He has delusional jealousy concerning his wife. I think he has Othello Syndrome – a syndrome named after Shakespeare's character who killed his wife in a jealous rage. I haven't made a final diagnosis yet. Jim's had some violent outbreaks during his admission and assaulted several men prior to coming in. He thought they were having affairs with his wife. He's very sick, psychotic, and delusional."

"Why haven't you confirmed your diagnosis, Dr. Desmonde? What's holding you back," Elizabeth asked with growing curiosity. It wasn't like Monique to procrastinate about anything.

Monique was quiet for a moment reflecting on how she had been asked the question the night before. "It's probably because I don't want to and I need more time to study his case. The syndrome has a poor prognosis. Another reason is that the violence is usually directed towards the spouse in Othello's – not other people. Of course, Jim is delusional.

Other than that, Liz, Jim McMurdie is a classic example of Othello." Monique's voice was sad and pensive.

"So, Monique, do you think McMurdie could have been delusional and thought Mrs. Smithson was his wife? Would that be a possible motive for the crime?"

Alex marveled at what a good thinker Liz was. It was a good question.

Monique shrugged her shoulders helplessly. "Of course, that's possible, Elizabeth. I've thought about it myself."

Françoise leaned forward expectantly. "Dr. Desmonde, do you think Jim McMurdie could be responsible for the rape and beating of Angie, as well as the attack and murder of Mrs. Smithson?"

"Commander," Monique's tone was cool, aloof, "I told you yesterday and I'm telling you again today, I don't know! I just don't know! Do you understand that? If I knew, I'd tell you!" Her face was flushed with resentment.

Alex gave Elizabeth a quick look and intervened to diffuse the situation. "Jack, there are twenty-five patients in the Pavilion who could be responsible for the rapes and deaths. Plenty of them are overtly psychotic. Besides, you said the forensic evidence would tell. And, it's possible it isn't a patient." Alex's voice was calm, but her teeth were gritted and Jack understood the "back off" look she gave him.

In a way, Jack Françoise was a little ashamed. "I accept your reprimand, Alex. You're right. Sorry, Monique. I'm having the department run a check on our local felons in the area. If the door of the unit was open Monday night, it could have been opened last night, too." He saw that Monique's face was livid with anger now. "Let me out of here before you're all mad at me. I can tell this isn't going well for me," Jack said plaintively as he rose to leave.

Jack's departure was interrupted by the surprising appearance of Lester Whitset in Alex's office, unannounced and unwelcome. His shadow in the doorframe seemed to dim the beauty of Alex's well-appointed inner sanctum.

Alex loathed the sight of him, but remained fascinated with him – a fact that totally disgusted her.

"Oh, sorry if I interrupted anything. I didn't think of calling first." Whitset had the same angelic smile on his face as he looked around at the group, knowing they were shocked to see him. "I'm especially glad to see you, Commander. I found something you might be interested in. I was going to give it to Alex, but since you're here ..." Whitset turned his head, gave Alex a sweet smile, and withdrew a shirt from a plastic bag – it was covered with brown stains.

The room was deathly silent. All eyes were focused on Whitset. He looked directly at Monique, his eyes cold and glaring. "I just found this shirt in the bottom of Jim McMurdie's locker on the unit. It looks like dried blood – certainly older than today's massacre." Whitset turned towards Monique and said in a sneering voice, "Really, Dr. Desmonde, I expected more professional behavior from you."

Monique felt a flush come over her. Whitset's words stung her like the bite of a thousand fire ants. She didn't know if she was embarrassed or just enraged. She tried to will away the crimson in her cheeks. She muttered in a small voice, "I beg your pardon?"

Whitset continued, sneering at Monique, who looked like a deer cornered in the headlights. "I thought you had the unit searched by the staff yesterday. And, Commander Françoise, I thought your men searched as well?"

Jack stared at Whitset, his face impassive.

Alex could see and feel the invisible steam of anger that poured from his ears.

Jack's eyes cut into Whitset's face and he looked like he could kill him at any moment.

Whitset stared back at him with his cold fish look, nonplussed, carefully surveying the reactions of the commander and the CCMC group. "I'll leave this 'evidence' with you, Commander. I trust you'll handle *it* appropriately. By the way, you may want to test it for the nurse's blood." Whitset's voice and manner were condescending as he handed the bloodied shirt to Commander Françoise. He turned to leave, but on his way out, said to Alex in his soft, sensual voice, "See you later, Alex, my pretty lass." He smiled his pure, beautiful smile at her and abruptly left the office.

Alex shuddered in disgust. Françoise erupted. "That bastard boils my blood and gives me the creeps at the same time. There is something wrong with him. He's not human. He slithers around everywhere, just like a little worm. I think I'll rush that background check on him!"

Monique was quiet. Finally, she said, "Dammit! We did search the unit. Twice! We gave everything over to you all, Jack. Where on earth did he get that shirt?"

"I don't know, Monique, but my men searched as well." Jack's voice was irate. "I'm not sure the evidence wasn't planted."

Alex intuitively knew there was more to Whitset than met the eye. She asked Monique if she knew anything about his background.

Monique thought for a moment, and then shook her head negatively. "Nope, I know nothing. Montgomery made the connection and hired him early in March. I wasn't even allowed to interview him." Monique tossed her head in anger. "If I'd interviewed him, we'd never have hired him!"

Elizabeth changed the subject and asked, "Dr. Desmonde, since I'm not a clinical person, can you tell me what motivates a person to work in psychiatry?" Elizabeth's question was straightforward and Alex thought it was a darned good one. Jack looked at Elizabeth with renewed respect. Obviously, after her experience on the unit today, Elizabeth was skeptical about why anyone would want to work with such patients.

"That's a hard one, Liz," Monique said in a bemused voice. "I have my own theory. It's not scientific, but I think it's pretty accurate."

"Shoot," Françoise ordered, as he sat back down and sipped his cold coffee.

"I think most people go into psychiatry because they want to know more about themselves. I certainly did. I grew up in a house full of hidden agendas that needed tending one way or another. My childhood was full of secrets. My mother was a socialite and a closet alcoholic. My father was a control freak. He thought he could control my mother by controlling her booze. He was wrong. Alcohol merely cloaked my mother's real illness. She was chronically depressed and suffered from major depressive disorder. When my father realized he couldn't control her, he concentrated on controlling his business. He spent seventy hours a week away from home. The three of us – my sister, my brother, and me – grew up with no parents to speak of, no emotional support, no strong relationships with anyone, and no one to listen to us. We took care of each other. There was no one to help us grow up strong and sound." Monique's voice faltered, she was becoming upset.

Jack put both hands on his coffee mug. He was dying to hug Monique, but he didn't dare.

"You certainly did well, Dr. Desmonde," Elizabeth said, trying hard to preserve the physician's waning self-esteem.

"Yeah, at the time I thought I did okay. I was the oldest and I remember some of the good times when my family wasn't so dysfunctional. My brother and sister weren't so lucky." Monique stopped for a few moments, thinking about her past. Then she continued, "You see, I had my grandmother. She was strong, wise, and loving. She was a positive influence in my life when I was very young. She helped me a lot in my early years. Unfortunately, she died when I was eleven. My brother and sister didn't have her as a role model. They never knew families were supposed to love you, care for you, and nurture you. It was hard for them."

"What about your brother and sister? How are they now?" Alex was associating Monique's past with her own. Her own mother was mentally unstable and reclusive. Alex had never known her father, Louis, very well. He had deserted them when Alex was three years old, apparently unable to put up with her mother's behavior. Alex had felt deserted with no father. It was painful to think her father had left her and hadn't loved her enough to keep in touch. This was the same pain she'd felt after Robert's rejection of her. Two men had deserted her.

Monique looked sad. She said with tears welling in her eyes, "My brother died fifteen years ago in a drunk driving accident. He inherited my mother's booze genes, I guess. My sister lives somewhere in California. She's pretty whacked out. She still acts like it's the 1960s. I rarely hear from her."

Françoise put his hand over Monique's. He'd known about her brother and sister, but didn't know how sad and lonely her childhood had been. It made his heart heavy and made him want to protect her even more.

Monique dabbed her eyes with her sleeve and continued, "Anyway, when I took psychology in college, a light started going off for me. It was like, 'yeah, I recognize this … yeah, that sounds familiar.' That's when I knew I'd try to spend my life helping other people build confidence, self-esteem, and positive coping skills. I guess I just want to help people find their way in life. So, getting back to your question, Liz, I think people choose psychiatry because they are also looking for help. In fact, some of them may be a little bit sick." All three of her friends were listening intently, nodding their heads in understanding.

Monique continued, "I'm not just talking about physicians and nurses. I also mean social workers, music therapists, and other caregivers. I think in some ways we're looking for validation that we're not alone, that some of the things we do are okay and are done by other people, too." Monique gave a bright, false smile. "Anyway, that's my theory, such as it is."

Alex asked cryptically, "Is this in any way akin to Whitset's imposter theory?"

"Hell, no! It's not even close! That got my attention though," Monique said, shaking her head in reference to the imposter theory. "He is very strange and possibly pathological."

Alex's thoughts returned to Lester Whitset. She thought about him for a few seconds. "I'm not sure Whitset's all he's cracked up to be. I think he's one of those 'little bit sick' people you mentioned who choose psych as a great place to hang out, possibly to hide."

Françoise roared, "A little bit? Hell! That SOB is totally crazy!"

Monique contemplated Alex's statement and arched her finely etched eyebrows. "Could be, Alex, could be. You never know. But, I hardly think he's responsible for these crimes and murders. Granted, he is a weird one. Probably has a personality disorder of some type. Forget him." She waved her arm in dismissal of Whitset. "Anyway, lots of bright and creative people suffer from various forms of mental illness."

"Oh yeah, like who?" Jack roared in a deprecating voice. Jack's world was clearly defined in black and white. He couldn't imagine any nut bunnies being bright or creative.

Monique glanced at him in disbelief. "Jack, really. Open your eyes. There are millions. Look at Winston Churchill and Edgar Allen Poe for starters. Also, Abraham Lincoln who, as history reports, was prone to melancholia. Lincoln was most likely bipolar, as was Churchill."

"Weren't there lots of artists who had diagnosed mental illnesses?" Elizabeth asked, fascinated.

"Yes, many of them were also bipolar. Vincent van Gogh and Paul Gauguin, to name a couple. Certainly they were creative."

Jack was not buying a word of it. "Is that why that dumb SOB cut off his ears?" Jack inquired as he shook his head.

Monique gave Jack a dirty look and continued, "I believe it was only a piece of one ear that he cut off. There are many famous writers who also had a diagnosed mental illness – Walt Whitman, Mark Twain, Cole Porter, Ernest Hemingway, and our own Tennessee Williams suffered from major depressive syndrome, as did Virginia Woolf and Sylvia Plath. Who knows? If we'd had Lithium, Lamictal, and Prozac years ago, no telling what these artists' contributions to music, art, and literature would have been! Lots of severely ill patients are extremely talented," Monique added, finishing her diatribe on a high note.

"This is very enlightening, but somehow, I don't think it's going to make Bridgett or the Smithsons feel better about their dead and/or maimed family members." Françoise's voice was sarcastic, as he looked at his watch. "But, thanks for the review, Monique. I didn't know so many famous people were bipolar." Jack felt a bit guilty for demeaning Monique's profession. He would have to work through his opinions of and bias against psychiatric patients. After all, it was Monique's life work. He glanced over at Elizabeth and Alex. "Sorry to break up the party, but I need to get downtown and get some work done," Jack said.

Monique stood and said, "I've got to go as well. I'll see you all later. I've got patients starting in a few minutes. Anyone free for lunch?"

"Sure. Hospital cafeteria at 12:30 okay?" Alex asked, as she glanced at Jack and Monique. They both nodded and walked out of the hospital. Elizabeth declined, but walked outside with them. Alex, Monique, and Jack continued to the car and Alex watched as Jack gave Monique a quick peck on the cheek as he opened the door for her. He looked around quickly to see if anyone could have seen. No one was anywhere close to the silver Caddy.

"Give it up, Commander. The windows are tinted. You're safe," Alex teased him. Monique smiled up at him from the seat. Jack looked smug, embarrassed, and a little like the tomcat who stole the cream.

Elizabeth smiled, looked at Alex, and said, "Well, this is news. It looks like the two of them are an item. That's pretty cool."

Alex returned the smile. "Yes, it's very cool, but let's keep it quiet until these crimes are solved."

"Gotcha, mum's the word," Elizabeth promised on her way out.

Chapter 19

Alex felt her armpits begin to sweat as she and Commander Françoise walked down the hallway to Pavilion II. She didn't want to do this, but she knew she had to. She knew there'd be a huge lawsuit against CCMC and she needed all the information she could get. This was absolutely a case of wrongful death. CCMC would pay; the question was how much would it cost them? She would certainly sue if Mrs. Smithson was her relative and, as hospital attorney, she felt compelled to review the crime scene. They were about to enter the room when they ran smack into Nadine Wells in the hall. She looked disturbed, but crisply professional.

"Have you been in, Nadine?" Jack asked.

She shook her head.

"Are you ready to go?" Jack looked carefully at the police expert.

Nadine nodded her head, still not speaking.

Jack was getting irritated and you could hear the impatience in his voice. "What the hell – cat got your tongue, Nadine? This ain't going to be pretty, Alex, Nadine. It's pretty awful. One of the worst crime scenes I've ever seen. Just expect to see the worst."

Neither woman replied, so Jack continued, "You can't even imagine it, so don't try." Françoise looked hard at the young, beautiful attorney and the grim-faced forensic expert. Alex seemed to be wavering.

Françoise scrutinized her and said, "You sure you want to go, Alex? You don't have to. We've got plenty of pictures."

"Nope, I'm going," Alex said in a firm voice. "Got to. Remember, Jack, I've seen some pretty horrible things already this year."

"Yeah, but this is worse, and no puking – either one of you. I can't take any more of that today," Jack said, as he thought back to February. "You ready?"

Alex nodded.

Nadine opened the door and stepped into the alcove of the room. Both of them gasped at the smell that greeted them.

Alex was assaulted by the stench of death. It enveloped her and caught her unaware. The metallic smell of old blood and decay entered her nostrils. She was overcome with wooziness. She felt cold and clammy. Even with the air-conditioning set at fifty degrees to delay decomposition, the smell was overwhelming. She looked at Nadine, who seemed to be struggling as well. After several moments, Alex plunged forward and peered around the curtain of the room.

Alex could barely stifle the scream that came from her mouth as she viewed the remains of Mrs. Smithson. Her knees were weak. She felt dizzy and lightheaded. The room was covered in blood. It was all over the bed and the pale yellow walls. And the smell, it was even worse than the smell in the alcove. The smell, salty and fetid, turned Alex's stomach. It was like a scene from a horror movie. The room was a red print of destruction, the aftermath of a massacre. Alex couldn't look closely at Mrs. Smithson. She took some deep breaths and regrouped slowly. Finally, she turned to look down at the body. It was a hideous sight.

Alex, incapacitated and paralyzed at the sight of the elderly lady, clutched futilely at the air for support. Emotions were clouding her objectivity. These emotions turned into distress and shock as she continued to look around the room.

Mrs. Smithson no longer had a face. Her eyes had been completely gouged out by the knitting needle. Alex couldn't even tell if they were open or closed. Her nose was a torn piece of flesh that was barely connected to her face. There were numerous stab and puncture wounds all over her head.

Her ears had been desecrated in the attack. Most of her beautiful silver hair was matted with blood. The knitting needle protruded ominously from her mouth. Alex felt her knees buckle and Jack caught her. With effortless ease, he held her up until she felt strong enough to support herself. Alex barely noticed when Nadine left the room.

Alex gasped. "I can't believe this. This is terrible – horrible. What kind of a despicable, loathsome animal could mutilate a little old lady like this? My Lord, Jack! This is ... there are no words to describe this."

Jack stood silently next to Alex and nodded in agreement, his arm around her shoulders for support, and led her to a chair. He nodded his head silently, tears in his eyes.

Nadine returned to the room and continued to view the body objectively. She had said nothing since reentering the room.

Alex was impressed by her dispassionate inspection of the body or, at least, she thought she was.

Jack said quietly, "I don't know, Alex. It's bad. The perp is ... an animal. No human could create such brutal devastation."

Alex rose from the chair and walked back to the bed. She studied the body of Mrs. Smithson and noticed that the elderly lady's hospital gown was pulled up to her chest. Her small, frail hips were completely exposed. With tears in her eyes, she asked the Commander, "Can we cover her up, Jack?"

Jack hesitated for a moment, unwilling to disturb the crime scene, and then wavered. "Yes, I'll cover her up. She deserves that much dignity. Okay with you, Nadine?"

"Yeah, Jack. Trust me, I've seen enough. We've got pictures, right?" Nadine's voice was terse and despondent.

"Yeah, got plenty of them."

As Alex and Jack moved towards the bed, Alex saw that the patient's call bell on Mrs. Smithson's right side was covered in blood. It was clear to Alex that Mrs. Smithson had rung the call bell repeatedly for help. Her trained eyes immediately traveled the length of the electric cord to the wall outlet, where the bell was connected to electrical power. The bell cord had been pulled out of the wall. The alarm had long ceased ringing – perhaps even hours before the patient had died. Whoever did this was smart enough to disconnect the bell from the wall. But who? A patient? A staff member? Someone with knowledge of hospital equipment had killed Mrs. Santa Claus. Alex just knew it.

"Jack," Alex said breathlessly at the upsetting discovery. "Did you notice that the call bell had been disconnected from the wall? This call system is antique and it won't ring if it has been disconnected from the wall. So, even if someone had been close to the nursing station, the bell would not have rung in there. It has been disconnected from the operating call system in the patient's room!"

Jack shook his head. "No, I hadn't noticed. There were so many folks in here earlier I didn't notice. I am sure the CSI team picked it up. Shit! Unbelievable. This murdering SOB knew what he was doing!" Jack's face had taken on a fierce look. His normally cautious eyes were dark, brooding, and as hard as black coal. He trembled with anger and outrage at the pain and fear Mrs. Smithson must have endured.

Alex and Nadine watched quietly as Jack put the scene together.

"This bastard knows hospitals. This maniac restrained the poor lady in four-point leather restraints and disconnected her call bell. He knew his way around this unit!" Jack's face was flushed with anger. His eyes had turned into burning sockets in his head. He thought his head was about to explode.

Nadine continued quietly examining the body. "Look here, Commander. Check this out." Nadine was pointing to an area on Mrs. Smithson's fragile right shoulder.

Jack crossed over to Nadine's side of the bed. He looked at the mark. Their eyes met with recognition. "Nadine, these look like puncture wounds on her neck. What do you think?"

"What is it? What is it?" Alex implored as she tried to see around the two police officers.

Nadine looked at Alex coldly. "It's a bite mark, Alex. Our killer here is the same man who attacked, raped, and beat Angela. He's probably already selected his next victim."

This was more than Alex could handle. Her face immediately crumpled. She left the room and the locked unit and walked briskly back to her office on the main hospital campus not even noticing the heat of the day. She was still cold with fright. Sticky from the New Orleans heat, but cold on the inside. Alex shuddered as she passed the yellow-tagged crime scene where Angela was assaulted.

She nodded briefly to Mona on the way in and then closed and locked her door. Then Alex cried and cried. She cried for the violent acts committed against two completely vulnerable and undeserving women. She sobbed until no more tears would flow. She vowed to herself that she would make every effort and use every opportunity within her power to make Crescent City Medical Center a safer place for patients and staff. She also decided that she would no longer compromise her own personal value system for the good of the hospital, no matter what or who got in her way. She would work based on her own values and ethical beliefs. The hell with Don! For a short while, Alex sat at her desk, oblivious to the world around her. She began to wonder if she was losing her own mind.

Chapter 20

Shortly before noon, Mona knocked softly on Alex's office door. Mona knew that Alex was upset and hated to disturb her, but she felt she needed to check on her. So far, she had been successful in holding off the hordes of people searching for the hospital attorney this morning and she had managed to successfully stall and reschedule most of her meetings. Still – Mona hated to bother her. Alex had been so distressed when she returned from the Pavilion a little while ago. Mona had heard her crying in her office.

There was no answer to her knock. Mona hesitated, thinking before she knocked again. If she hadn't received the phone call from Donald Montgomery, she wouldn't bother Alex. But, as usual, Montgomery had acted like such an ass on the phone she knew she had to notify Alex. Hesitantly, she knocked again on Alex's door.

"Come in. Door's open," Alex said, her voice faint and hard to hear.

Mona opened the door slowly and stood in the doorway. "Sorry to interrupt you, Alex, but Montgomery has called an emergency meeting of the hospital executive committee about the attacks. Latetia called about an hour ago." Mona sounded apologetic for interrupting.

Alex picked up on Mona's hesitation. "Thanks, Mona. It's okay. Thanks for letting me know. I'm okay now, but I did lose it this morning. When's the meeting?"

Alex spoke in a flat voice and she looked whipped. She didn't sound or look better to Mona. Mona examined her critically. "It's at 2 o'clock this afternoon in the executive conference room. Latetiaa said something about a press release and some other matters that will be discussed. You sure you're okay, Alex? You're looking mighty beat up!"

182

Alex smiled at Mona's typically Mississippi description of her. "I'll be okay. I just look terrible because most of my makeup has worn off. I cried it off. I'll put it back on before the meeting. Thanks, Mona." Alex hesitated for a moment and added, "I appreciate your concern. Thanks for letting me cry and giving me the time to do it. I know you rescheduled all of my meetings."

Mona nodded and left the office. As Mona returned to her desk, she thought about Alex. Alex had been up practically all night, had been through hell, and was going back for more this afternoon. Mona silently agreed with Bridgett, who adored Alex. They had discussed how amazing Alex was and how great a role model she was for women. Bridgett had confided to Mona that she thought Alex was insecure with men and had also whispered that she didn't think Alex had ever gotten over her marriage to Dr. Bonnet. Besides, it had only been six months since her relationship with Mitch Landry had ended so tragically. *Poor Alex*, thought Mona. *She has so much, but she also has so little.* As she returned to her computer, Mona was infinitely grateful for her husband, her two small children, and her little house in Kenner. She was thankful for being able to work part-time and was totally glad she wasn't the high-powered Alexandra Destephano. Regardless of how beautiful she was, how much money she made, or how much respect she garnered, Alex's life was hell.

Chapter 21

Alex checked her watch. It was half past noon and time to meet Monique and Jack for lunch in the cafeteria. She sighed. She was exhausted and felt as if she was a hundred years old. Every iota of energy had been drained from her. She walked into her private bathroom to redo her makeup and was shocked at her appearance in the mirror. Mona had been right – she looked bad, really awful. She looked like hell. No question. For the first time, she noticed small dry lines and wrinkles in the corners of her eyes and around her mouth. Her flawless fair skin was pasty white and her normally lustrous auburn hair looked dull and lifeless.

I'm really a mess! I look terrible and feel like hell! As she repaired the damage to the best of her ability, she made a pact with herself to take some extra vitamins and get more exercise. She needed to get more rest as well. That would help. Finally, reasonably pleased with her appearance, she headed towards the cafeteria when her thoughts were interrupted with what she was sure was a telepathic message from her grandmother, Grand. Kathryn Lee had always told her to look her best when she was on her way to slay her dragons and Montgomery and Whitset were certainly the dragons du jour. Bastard dragons, actually.

Alex smiled when she thought about Grand. She made a mental note to call her tonight. She missed her grandparents and she missed Virginia. She was beginning to hate New Orleans. Her mind flickered to the job offer on her desk. Maybe, just maybe, she ought to consider it. It would take her home to Virginia. Besides, her grandparents were getting older and, even though the congressman hadn't slowed down a bit, Alex had noticed some fatigue and weariness in her grandmother that she had never seen before and it bothered her. Just thinking about her home in Virginia and her grandparents lifted her spirits and gave her the energy she needed to move forward. *God bless them,* she thought.

Alex steeled herself for the rest of her day and admitted that it totally sucked, as she walked towards the hospital cafeteria. As she contemplated her afternoon, she frowned. She wasn't looking forward to meeting with the Smithsons, especially with Whitset present, and she knew the executive meeting she was headed to was going to be a battle or, more likely, a sham.

She waved at Monique waiting for her outside the hospital cafeteria.

Monique grabbed Alex by her arm. "Let's get out of here, Alex," Monique hissed. "Whitset is waiting for you in there. I told him you'd left the hospital for lunch and that you would meet him at about 1:30 on the unit to talk with the Smithsons. I figured you didn't want to eat with him."

Alex's blue eyes were sharp and her voice was brittle. "You figured right. Only, I want to meet him somewhere else. I'll call Mona and tell her to have Whitset and the Smithsons meet me in my office conference room at 1:30. I don't want them witnessing anything unpleasant in the Pavilion and thinking again that their mother should not have been admitted there."

"Good idea, Alex. The fire is going to be hot enough anyway. No sense adding more fuel."

Alex nodded in agreement. "Let's run over to the Cajun Café. I'll call Mona from there. Is Jack coming?"

"Nope. He's downtown running checks on Anthony and our boy Whitset." Monique smiled grimly at Alex. "Jack also says he has to meet with the medical examiner this afternoon."

"Why? Anything special happen?" Alex looked speculatively at the psychiatrist.

"No, not that I know of. I think he just wants to drop off some pictures of Angie so the medical examiner can compare them with Mrs. Smithson. You know Jack. He's pretty involved in this. Actually, he's so emotionally involved it bothers me."

Alex looked critically at Monique. She took a risk and said plainly, "Yeah, I know. Let it go, Monique. We're all involved and Jack's M.O. for years has been to become personally involved in his cases. That's the type of cop he is and that's why he's where he is. Police officers like Jack François are few and far between."

A faint blush was perceptible on Monique's pale cheeks. Alex knew she was trying to control her anger. She spoke again, her voice matter of fact. "Monique, I'm not trying to offer advice or cause trouble, but Jack is Jack, and that's how he operates. It's just part of him that you'll have to get used to or not—"

Monique interrupted her, her voice cool. "All right, Alex. I've got it. Let's table this for now. I'm too tired for another emotional shakedown and so are you. I know you're right and I know I can't change him. It would've been easier if his first case with us as a couple hadn't occurred on my medical unit."

Alex laughed at her friend. "Yep, for sure, it certainly would've been – but sometimes life's a shit sandwich and we all have to take a few bites!"

Monique laughed at Alex's description, which she knew came straight from the mouth of Congressman Adam Patrick Lee. Alex seldom used profanity and, when she did, it was for emphasis. By this time, they were in front of the restaurant. "My, my, my, where are your genteel Virginia manners and where did you learn to speak like that?"

"You know exactly where that came from because you've been there!" Alex eyed the door thankfully. "Good, no wait.

We can go straight in. And, the manners, I left them at home – better watch me at the table. Order me the special and I'll call Mona."

The Cajun Café was a small coffee shop inside the CCMC complex. It was usually filled with patients, staff, and family members for lunch, but for some reason the lunch traffic was light today. The food was authentic Cajun cuisine and the chef took great pride in his menu. The café was gaily decorated with a Cajun bayou motif and watercolors of New Orleans street scenes painted by a local artist. Monique slid into the back booth at the rear of the restaurant, while Alex fished in her purse for her phone. By the time Alex finished her call, Monique had ordered iced tea and crawfish étouffée for both of them. Pierre, the owner and chef of the Cajun Café, was arguing good-naturedly with Dr. Desmonde over the proper Cajun spices for étouffée.

When Chef Pierre saw Alex, he bowed gallantly from the waist and said with a big smile on his face, "Miss Alex. I'm honored. Please enjoy your meal. I'll send a special chocolate dessert your way. You know, I know your favorite."

Alex smiled her thanks and she, Monique, and Pierre chatted for a few minutes before the chef left the women alone to enjoy their lunch.

The service was quick and within several minutes, they were eating the rich, delicious étouffée. Alex asked how things were going at the Pavilion.

Monique looked at her sideways. "Well, pretty well, I guess. That should be obvious since I was able to get over here for lunch. Most of the patients are still heavily medicated. Several others are depressed ... that is, more depressed than usual. Overall, there's still a feeling of shock up there. Things could break bad tonight or tomorrow when the patients rally and start to talk about things – you know, when the meds wear off. The community meeting should be interesting today and tomorrow, especially since we canceled all privileges!" Monique rolled her eyes as she imagined the backlash she would get from Anthony.

Alex sighed. "Yes, I suspect you're right. We've got to get Don and Whitset to agree to hire more security at the Pavilion for the next few weeks."

"Good luck with that, Alex," Monique said in a sarcastic voice as she arched her eyebrows. "Whitset told me this morning he wasn't authorizing any increased help – either professional or security. He maintains the unit is safe –"

Alex interrupted her, her face flushed with anger and her voice defensive. "That's insane! That man's crazy! If it was safe and we had enough staff, Mrs. Smithson would more than likely still be alive today."

Monique held up her hand. "Save it for the executive meeting, Alex. We will need all the support we can muster to fight the boys. From what I can tell, Whitset has Montgomery in his pocket. It's pretty disgusting." Monique pulled vigorously at her chignon and several large masses of her dark hair came loose.

Alex was astounded at how "human" Monique had become in the past few days. Before, the distinguished psychiatrist, while always supportive of Alex and friendly, had been aloof, cool, and unapproachable – or, at least, unapproachable in a proverbial human sort of way. Now, she seemed to be real – a real person like Alex, who struggled endlessly with the trials and tribulations of working in a male-dominated organization. It wasn't that Alex had a problem working with men in general; it was just that she had a problem working with incompetent people … and most of the incompetent leadership at CCMC was male.

Thank goodness, she was meeting this side of Monique Desmonde. It was going to be great to have a colleague to hang out with who was part of the same dysfunctional organization. Of course, she had Elizabeth, but Elizabeth was much younger and Alex was both her boss and her mentor. It wasn't quite the same. Dr. Desmonde was a power broker in the organization.

Alex touched her shoulder and said, "Monique, in some respects these events, terrible though they are, have created a bond between us. We'll work through this together."

Monique squeezed her hand in return and said, "I agree. Two heads are better than one and I need all the help I can get."

Alex nodded and continued, "Let's figure out a strategy for this afternoon's meeting with Don Montgomery." She thought for a moment and said, "How about you approach the need for more security from a patient and staff safety point of view and I'll approach it from a legal and image position. We ought to be able to get what we want. Don's hot button is the CCMC image and he wants no airing of our dirty laundry."

Monique looked uncertain. "I'm not so sure, but I hope you're right. We have to go," she said as she ate quickly. She checked her watch. "We're meeting with Whitset. I invited myself, hope you don't mind?"

"Not at all. It's going to be hard. I'm glad you're coming! The poor Smithsons. I'm dreading it. It's still so horrible." Alex had a tragic faraway look in her eyes as she remembered the scene.

"Yes, it's horrible and Whitset's horrible, but we've got to meet with them. I'm still angry that chickenshit Montgomery isn't coming. It makes me furious when he dodges these nasty issues!" Monique was mad.

She only cursed when she was really mad, kind of like Alex. They saved the profanity for when it really mattered. Another lesson from Alex's grandmother.

Alex shook her head and said sarcastically, "Now, Monique, where are *your* genteel manners? Surely, you know by now that our esteemed CEO only pays attention to the positive things that happen here. Don thinks he's a deity and the only person who does any work!"

Monique smiled ruefully at Alex. "Hell yes, I know." To quote an observant police commander, 'Donald Montgomery is an incompetent SOB.'" Monique and Alex both laughed as Alex's phone sounded, signaling a text. It was Mona texting her, "Get in your office quick!" Monique excused herself and quickly headed to the ladies' room. As Alex was gathering her things, an enraged Donald Montgomery grabbed her shoulder roughly.

"Where the hell is Desmonde? I want to talk with both of you. Where the hell is she?" Don's voice was loud and people at nearby tables looked at him sharply.

Alex was shocked by Don's behavior. "Monique's gone to the ladies' room. Please lower your voice."

Don continued to hurl angry and profane epithets at her, while a number of patrons eating lunch in the café turned to stare at the well-dressed man whose speech would make a sailor blush. One gentleman stood up as if to intervene on Alex's behalf. Even Chef Pierre had emerged from the kitchen, wielding a large chopping knife. He was looking questioningly at Alex. She smiled, but with a small movement of her finger, she motioned for him to go back into the kitchen.

Alex's voice was soft. "Don, what's the matter? Come on over and sit down." She gently grasped the CEOs arm and led him to the table where she and Monique had just finished their lunch. Alex saw that people were still watching them and she smiled courteously at the people around them. Alex hated scenes. She also hated to see people make fools of themselves because it embarrassed her. Don did it frequently and she still hated it. By this time, Monique had returned and sat down.

Don sat down. Alex and Monique looked at him expectantly, waiting to hear the cause of his most recent outburst.

The CEO looked around the restaurant and saw for the first time that people were staring at him curiously. He lowered his voice and quietly blasted his words at the two women, his voice hissing a torrent of swearwords like the air escaping from a dying sailor.

"Why in the hell didn't the two of you take care of the Smithsons? The man literally stormed into my office a few minutes ago demanding to see his mother. Damn you all! Both of you are useless, incompetents. Why didn't you talk with him?" Don's face was so red that Alex thought he might have a stroke. Monique hoped he would.

Monique glared at him and answered his questions. She was as angry as Montgomery, but much more in control. "Mr. Montgomery, did you really want Mr. Smithson to see his mother with a knitting needle hanging out of her mouth? Did you want him to see her blood and brains on the walls? Did you want him to see that his mother no longer had a face? Do you think that would've settled him down?" Monique's voice was strong and quiet. Her intent was clear, and her argument was strong. Monique glanced over at Alex, who seemed to be silently cheering her on.

Donald Montgomery turned his eyes away from the straightforward glance of his chief of psychiatry. He was quiet for several moments and then said heatedly, "Hell no! That would not have been good ... but ... it's still your fault. If ... if ...." Don was groping for words. "I don't see why you all didn't see them hours ago and calm them down. He's in my office threatening to call the press. Says he's going to sue Crescent City for all it's worth. Said his mother was brutally murdered in my hospital by one of my patients. The man's insane!" Don's red face had turned grey and he was shaking, obviously anticipating an onslaught of press reporters and TV cameras. "Where do people get these lies?"

Alex and Monique stared at each other in disbelief. What was going on with Montgomery? Didn't he remember the murder?

Alex spoke to him. "Don, his mother was murdered in the Pavilion. She was murdered in our hospital and Dr. Desmonde talked with the family this morning. We asked you to see them as well. You refused. You told Lester Whitset and me to see them. We're seeing them in a few minutes. Do you remember any of this?" Alex watched Don closely as his anger and rage returned.

Montgomery glared at Alex as if she were a moron. He raised his voice and said impatiently, "Of course I remember the murder in the Pavilion. As far as I'm concerned, the Pavilion isn't CCMC. We're a world-class hospital. Those wackos don't count when we look at the good things that are done here. Psychiatry isn't an important part of the hospital! It never has been. The Pavilion is a dump. It's a loser. As a matter of fact, I don't even consider psychiatry a part of this hospital at all." Don was thinking.

Alex could see the wheels turning in his mind. He was completely oblivious to the look of contempt Dr. Desmonde was giving him.

He continued, "Hell, I'm not even sure that psychiatry is part of the practice of medicine! Those sons of bitches never get well. They never even get better. They are just leeches on society. It's a losing battle all the way around. Even the psychiatrists are half crazy!" Don looked smugly at Alex and Monique and folded his hands on the table, as if patiently waiting for their anger.

Alex thought she could see smoke pouring from Monique's ears. She was speechless at Don's diatribe and accusations. She could feel energy, negative energy, radiating from Dr. Desmonde. Monique could hardly contain herself. Alex tried to settle the physician down by placing her hand on her arm, but it was useless.

Desmonde was not to be quieted. She rose and stood over the CEO, her face faintly flushed and her dark hair and eyes glistening in the artificial light of the restaurant. "Montgomery! You know something. Your behavior is infantile, it's inexcusable. You are an idiot. You treat this hospital like a toyshop, lining up your favorite toys and beating up and discarding the ones you don't like. That's what you did to the psychiatric service. You sold us out to contract management. Psychiatric services have been going downhill ever since." Monique paused for a moment and began again, her voice seething with anger, "Frankly, Montgomery, I think you need a bed in the Pavilion. Not only are you an idiot, you have a behavioral disorder!" Monique stared down at the CEO, clearly repulsed by what she saw. With a quick glance at Alex, she stalked out of the café.

Donald Montgomery was silent for a moment and then he turned to Alex and laughed. "Our famous shrink looks pretty good when she's mad. She is much easier on the eyes when she's irate. Maybe I should make her angry more often. Then I can almost stand to look at her!"

Alex was enraged at Don, but refused to play into his sexist remarks. She said quietly, "Don, psych is a part of CCMC and the situation over there will affect the hospital and our image. You may as well prepare for a lengthy wrongful death action and a lot of negative publicity." Alex watched Don as reality set in. She chastised herself for feeling a bit victorious. She had humbled the CEO. "How did you leave Mr. Smithson?"

"Not well. I sent him to your office. He's probably there now. Take care of him, Alex. Handle it, and do it right. I don't need this stuff so soon after February!" Don was actually pleading with her. His voice was quiet.

Alex used the situation to her advantage and said, "I'll do my best, Don. At the executive meeting this afternoon, I expect you to approve additional permanent staff positions for the Pavilion, as well as a temporary increase in security – at least until this stuff clears up. Deal? We need strong young bodies up there for security, as well as professional caregivers permanently." She looked carefully at Don, contemplating her next move.

Don shrugged his shoulders. "You give me a good argument, you'll get the money. Farve maintains that psychiatry is well staffed. So does Whitset. Just keep these people out of my office – the crazies and their crazy relatives. I'm busy and I don't have time for this kind of stuff. Understood?" Don was recovering from his momentary lapse into fear and uncertainty.

Alex shook her head negatively, signed her lunch check, and headed for her office.

Don, since he was already there, decided to have lunch. What was left on Alex and Monique's plates looked pretty good. He waved for the waiter. Things were quiet for him. He had over an hour until the executive committee meeting, so he settled in for a tasty lunch. Besides, he deserved it. It'd been an awful day, and he did run the place. He was entitled to a reward.

Don was a lucky man. He had no idea how close Chef Pierre had come to putting crushed glass into his lunch.

Chapter 22

As Alex made her way back to her office, she became more and more infuriated at Don Montgomery. The man was an absolute egomaniacal idiot. Monique was right. The CEO probably did have some sort of a personality disorder. She wondered if asshole was a legitimate diagnosis in psychiatry and asked herself how much longer she could stand working for him. Again, the letter from her colleague in San Francisco surfaced in her mind. Maybe she would consider it. It was only a year and she could return to New Orleans if she chose. Dealing with Montgomery was getting pretty old and very tiring.

Alex paused outside her office door for a few moments, contemplating the best way to handle the Smithsons and the sad tale of their mother's death. When Jack had spoken with them earlier, it had been difficult enough, but he had kept with the police procedure and said nothing about how the crime had occurred. She shook her head, as if to clear it, hoping for some clarity on the best way to manage the conversation. When she entered her outer office, Lester Whitset was sitting on her sofa reading a magazine. Mona was not at her desk. Alex's heart began to beat frantically – just seeing him made her uncomfortable. He was repulsive. She felt her stomach flip-flop.

Whitset rose when he saw Alex, his eyes raking her face and body. "Alex, you're looking amazingly well for such a long day. Marvelous in fact!" His voice was soft and seductive.

Alex pulled back reflexively as his hand touched her wrist. The coldness of his fingers sent a shiver through her. "Are Mr. and Mrs. Smithson here? Where's Mona?"

"Your secretary just took them into the conference room. She's getting them coffee. She seems to be obedient enough – she a good worker?" Whitset smiled balefully at Alex.

"Obedient? What do you mean by obedient?" Alex looked suspiciously at the administrator. Obedience was becoming a theme in Lester's conversations.

"You know what obedient means, Alex dear." Whitset's voice was soft, almost hedonistic. "It means that she did what I asked her to do as soon as I asked her to do it. She scurried right out of here. I like that!" Lester had a half smile on his face and his dark glittering eyes were locked with Alex's blue ones. He moved closer to her. She could feel his breath on her cheek, and for some reason, she was powerless to move back. It was if he had a strange hold over her. Whitset continued to talk with her in the same soft voice. "Another pretty girl. Mona is her name, isn't it? She looks like a darker version of your regular secretary, Bridgett. They're the same size ... just the hair is different. Isn't that correct?" He continued to stare at Alex, his dark eyes raking her face as his look commanded her attention.

Alex could barely suppress the shudder she felt crawling up her spine. And yet, there was something about him that fascinated her and made her feel powerless. It was almost as if there was an electric energy between them. She was startled. A dozen thoughts were dancing through her head. How did Lester Whitset know Bridgett? Did he know she was Angie's twin sister? Did all of these things mean something? She was frantically trying to sort the information through her tired brain as Whitset continued to leer at her.

Just at that moment, the door opened and Bridgett walked in. She looked terrible. Her face was streaked with tears. She had a gold cross in her hand.

"Oh, Alex. It's so horrible. This is all been so dreadful." Bridgett was crying pitifully. Her voice coming out in gasps.

"The nurse in the ICU just gave me Angie's cross. She's not doing well at all. She still won't talk to me – they say she can't! I don't think she is conscious, but her eyes are open and she stares at the wall. Alex, will she get well?" Bridgett burst into fresh tears.

Alex walked over to hug Bridgett. "Sure she will, Bridge. She'll be okay in a few days. It'll take some time." Alex continued to hug Bridgett, conscious of the gaping, sly smile Whitset was giving them. It was almost pornographic, she thought. Whitset was relishing Bridgett's pain. Bridgett seemed unaware of him. Alex doubted that Bridgett had noticed him in her grief.

She held Bridgett close for a few more moments, becoming more and more uncomfortable with the effect Whitset was having on her. He was openly smiling at both of them. He looked pleased with himself and Alex didn't understand why. He seemed to enjoy the secretary's grief. He was enjoying it – feeding on it! It was as if he were a voyeur, basking in Bridgett's abject misery. His smile turned benignly gleeful, and once again, spittle formed in the side of his mouth. He continued to leer at them, as the two women comforted each other.

Finally, Alex broke the embrace. "Bridgett, this is Lester Whitset. He's the contract administrator for psychiatry."

Whitset stepped forward and took Bridgett's hand.

Bridgett visibly flinched when he touched her.

An involuntary reaction, Alex guessed.

She said, "Oh yes, Mr. Whitset. My sister mentioned you to me. I'm pleased to meet you." Instantly, Bridgett dropped Whitset hand, as if touching him was unpleasant to her.

Whitset seemed to pick up on Bridgett's feelings toward him. "Sorry if my hands are cold, my dear Bridgett. Poor circulation, I suppose. But you know what they say about that

...." His eyes gleamed at her as he continued, "Cold hands, very warm, warm heart."

Bridgett just stared at him, speechless.

Whitset was nonplussed and continued, "I liked your sister. She seemed to be a competent nurse, although she was not as obedient as I would've liked. I do hope she improves soon."

Obedient, obedient. There was that word again, Alex thought. The word continued to frighten and grab at her, but Alex remained silent. Alex was also troubled by Whitset's use of the past tense, "liked your sister" and "seemed to be competent" – it gave her a sick feeling in her stomach.

Bridgett said nothing, but nodded her head. She turned to Alex, "Do you know where I could get another chain for this necklace? I have a feeling that if I could fix it and get it back on Angie, she will get better. She got this cross and a St. Christopher's medal when we were confirmed at St. Anthony's as children. She always felt it protected her. See, I have one just like it." Bridgett opened the neck of her blouse to show Alex.

Alex heard an unusual noise. She turned sharply towards Whitset. She thought she heard a giggle come from his mouth. He was leering at both of them, his mouth open and his eyes bright with a strange light in the fervor of his enjoyment of the scene. He looked insane, crazed.

Alex turned to Bridgett. "Yes, I'll get it fixed this afternoon and bring it back this evening. Trust me, I promise," she reassured Bridgett. "I'm going to get Mona so she can be with you for a while. Mr. Whitset and I have a meeting to go to. Wait for me here."

Bridgett looked around frantically. She saw Whitset staring at her. His cold black eyes were raking her body with a sense of familiarity.

Alex saw his eyes rest on Bridgett's right shoulder. *Oh My God,* Alex thought. *What is wrong with this man?* Whitset was licking his lips. Then, Alex chided herself. She had to be imagining these things, but she was alarmed at the attention and reaction Bridgett was getting from Lester Whitset.

Bridgett noticed his gawking as well. She clung to Alex and said quickly, "No. No, Alex. I'll come with you. I want to catch Mona up on a few things in your office."

Alex picked up on Bridgett's discomfort. She took her arm and ushered her into the private office. She examined Bridgett carefully. Bridgett's eyes were wide with fright. *She feels it, too,* Alex thought.

Mona entered Alex's office from the conference room on the right. She stared at both of them with surprise. "What's with you two? You look like you've seen a ghost." Mona eyed them cautiously.

Neither woman was able to speak. Both were tied up in their own thoughts.

Bridgett, her fear subsiding, began to cry again, her shoulders shaking as her blue eyes welled over with tears.

Alex took charge, sending Mona numerous messages with her eyes. "Mona, show Mr. Whitset into the conference room. I presume the Smithsons are already in there?"

Mona nodded affirmatively.

"Then, take Bridgett out through the back door for coffee. Put the phones on forward. Still better, Bridgett, go on over to the coffee shop. Mona will meet you in five minutes – okay? Can you do that?"

Bridgett seemed to be in a trance, but she nodded her head. She said quietly to Alex, "Angie didn't like him. She said he was trouble in the Pavilion and that he stirred up the patients. He gives me the creeps. I think he's bad."

Alex held up her hand to stop her. "I know, Bridgett. We'll talk later. Now go! Mona will be there soon."

Bridgett left the office via the back conference room's door, as Mona went to get Whitset.

Alex attempted to compose herself and went into the conference room.

Mr. and Mrs. Smithson were seated at the far end of the table in Alex's conference room. They were dressed in the same clothes they'd been in at 5 a.m. and both looked worn and sad. Mrs. Smithson was drinking black coffee and Mr. Smithson had a can of diet Sprite. He stood deferentially as Alex entered the room.

Alex smiled once again, thinking how handsome Mr. Smithson was. She walked towards the distinguished gentleman. "Mr. Smithson, I am Alexandra Destephano. I am the legal counsel for the hospital and I want you to know that—"

"Legal counsel? So you're the hospital lawyer? I thought we were meeting with administration. Does anyone know anything that is happening around here?" Mr. Smithson's voice was deep and his face was flushed. He was impatient and angry.

Alex tried to ease his concerns. She said softly, "I'm representing administration. Mr. Whitset will be joining us and I believe Dr. Desmonde will be coming, as well."

Alex turned as Whitset entered the room. She watched him stand to the side of the table, glaring at the weary, older couple. There was no concern or compassion in his face for the Smithson family. His face was set in an ominous scowl and he looked prepared for battle.

Alex introduced Whitset to the Smithsons and was appalled when Whitset ignored Mr. Smithson's outstretched hand. He waved it aside and sat down. He turned his glittering cold eyes towards Mrs. Smithson and stared at her. The gentle-faced woman seemed nervous at his look and her hands fell to her lap, where she began to play with the catch on her pocketbook.

Alex began, "Mr. and Mrs. Smithson, on behalf of the hospital, I'd like to tell you how very, very distressed and sad we are over your mother's death. We're very sorry about the circumstances and hope that—"

Mr. Smithson, still smarting from the rebuke by Lester Whitset, interrupted her. "Thank you, Ms. Destephano. I understand that. My wife and I want some answers."

Alex nodded, urging him to continue.

"We want to know precisely how my mother died, and we want to know exactly why my mother died. We've had no information at all. When Dr. Desmonde talked with us this morning, she only told us that my mother had died – that she had been murdered!"

Alex felt her heart sink. She hadn't wanted to do this. She began, "I understand that Dr. Desmonde told you this morning that your mother had been attacked and murdered by someone, possibly another patient and —"

"Yes, yes, we know that." Mr. Smithson was clearly impatient. "How did she die? By what manner did she die? Did someone shoot her? I don't mean to sound short, but you've jerked us around since 4 o'clock this morning. I tried to see your CEO, Mr. Montgomery, and he literally threw me out of his office. I don't mind telling you, Ms. Destephano, that didn't sit well with me." Mr. Smithson sat back in his chair tiredly. He looked exhausted.

Alex took a deep breath and said clearly, "Mr. Smithson, your mother was stabbed – with a knitting needle."

There was a silence that seemed to last for hours.

After an audible gasp, Mrs. Smithson ventured a few words. "A knitting needle? *Her* knitting needle?" Her voice sounded incredulous. "Could being stabbed with a knitting needle kill you? It seems impossible. Are you sure?"

"She was stabbed more than once," Alex said, wishing she had someone there she could count on for support. She looked over at Whitset who was staring at the wall, smiling to himself. The wheels seemed to be turning in his brain. Alex prayed he kept quiet and behaved.

"How many times?" Mr. Smithson looked directly at Alex.

Alex didn't respond. She was thinking.

"Ms. Destephano, I asked you, how many times?" Smithson's voice was loud and demanding.

Alex's composure was dwindling. She fought for control and said, "She was stabbed many times. I don't know for sure. We'll know more when the police and coroner's reports come in. I can assure you that—"

Alex was interrupted when Dr. Desmonde entered the conference room and sat down quietly next to Mr. Smithson. Alex had to admire the man, his control, his fortitude, and his determination. Of course, he was pissed – she would be, too!

Mr. Smithson turned to Monique. "Dr. Desmonde, you told me in the wee hours of dawn this morning that my mother had died in a hospital accident. You didn't tell me she had been stabbed with a knitting needle! Now, everyone claims they don't know how many times she was stabbed!" Mr. Smithson put his elbow on the conference table and placed his chin on his hand so that he was looking directly into the pale, wan face of the lovely, but very stressed, psychiatrist. "You need not repeat what Commander Françoise told me. I want to know about the hospital's role in the death of my mother."

Monique gave Mr. Smithson her full attention. Their eyes were locked together.

"Now," he continued, "I want to know everything you know about my mother's death. Do you understand?" His voice was quiet, but demanding.

Monique nodded at Mr. Smithson. "Yes, I understand. I know you must be very upset over your mother's death and I understand that. We all are. But, we are not sure what exactly happened. Conjecture about her death will only be more upsetting. As soon as we know everything, the police will update you again. As soon as the investigation is complete, I'll speak with you again if you would like. Please let me know if I am repeating what the commander told you."

Mrs. Smithson interjected, "Dr. Desmonde, we only want to know if our mother suffered. Did she?"

It was so quiet in the room you could hear the clicking of Mona's computer two rooms away. You could also hear the distant linen carts and x-ray machines rolling down the halls. Far off, someone was laughing. Alex wished she were with them and not here in this room with these poor, sad, grief-stricken people discussing the elderly Mrs. Smithson's horrific death.

Monique remained silent and looked at her hands for several moments, then looked back at the Smithsons. Finally, slowly, she said, "Yes, it is possible your mother may have suffered. We'll know for sure when we get the autopsy report." Secretly, Monique hoped that the gentle, elderly lady had suffered a stroke or a heart attack and had died instantly. This thought was helping her manage her own fragile emotional survival. Although it was unlikely, she was taking some comfort in the possibility.

Mrs. Smithson was crying softly into a tissue.

Mr. Smithson's eyes were red-rimmed as he looked at Alex and Monique and said quietly, "I admitted my mother because she was depressed over my father's death and my sister's illness. She was not chronically mentally ill, do you understand, she was *not mentally ill*. She'd never been depressed. You, Dr. Desmonde, assured me that this was the best hospital for her —"

A sob escaped Mrs. Smithson's mouth and she said to her husband, "Please, honey, let's not talk about this now. There is nothing Dr. Desmonde can do. Let's just go home, I am so tired."

Mr. Smithson turned to comfort his wife and said tearfully, "Two weeks later, she's stabbed to death in what is supposed to be the best hospital in New Orleans. I repeat, *how did this happen?* I expected this hospital to take care of her – to help her. Why didn't you? I trusted you to make her better!"

There was silence. No one spoke. What was there to say? Everyone just continued to sit uncomfortably in the conference room.

Mr. Smithson tried to speak again, but his voice broke. He stopped for several seconds to catch his breath, composed himself, and then said, "My mother was a gentle soul. She never hurt anyone. She didn't deserve to die like this."

Alex looked over at Whitset. He was watching Mrs. Smithson cry softly. He had a pleased look on his face. His mouth was turned up in a sly, half smile and he looked as if he was worshipping her grief. He was enjoying himself and was enjoying being a part of this heartbreaking meeting! *What the hell was going on?* Alex just couldn't understand Whitset. It was like he got off on grief, enjoyed it, and even relished it. A glance over at Monique confirmed to Alex that she wasn't noticing Whitset's behavior. Her attention was focused on Mr. Smithson who continued to vent his feelings.

"You know," he said, "it seems to me that something's wrong here. If my mother suffered, that must be your fault. If she was so brutally killed ...." He looked towards his wife, as she was seized with a fresh torrent of tears. He took her hand, pressed it for comfort, and continued, "If she was stabbed over and over, then why didn't somebody come to help her? I'm sure she cried for help." Mr. Smithson looked back and forth between Monique and Alex. *"Why didn't somebody come help her? Answer me! I demand an answer!"* His voice was loud and harsh.

Suddenly, without warning, Lester Whitset jumped from his seat. His tone was harsh, cruel even, his face only inches from Mr. Smithson's, "Listen, Smithson, we told you we were sorry. Isn't that enough? We don't make promises when we admit people to the hospital. Particularly old people —" He stopped as Alex kicked him hard in the leg.

Smithson stood, faced the younger man, and raised his voice, "What did you say? *What in the hell did you say about old people?"* Mr. Smithson's voice was getting louder. "Say it again, dammit! What's this about promises and old people?" Mr. Smithson was taller and heavier than Lester Whitset and Alex watched as a brief flicker of uncertainty crossed Whitset's face.

Whitset momentarily gained control of himself. Then he lost it completely. His appearance changed and he looked like a pouty little boy. His slicked-back, G.Q. hair fell forward and he looked at his hands and smiled. Then he began to speak, his lips pouting as he began a singsong litany. His head moved back and forth, keeping time with his voice, *"We're so sorry, Mr. and Mrs. Smithson. We're so very sorry your mother was murdered in – our hospital. Please, please forgive us."* Whitset's voice ended on a high note.

Alex was dumbfounded, paralyzed with shock at his behavior. Monique was speechless. What the hell was happening? It seemed like Whitset was making fun of the incident. His words were rhymed and spoken in iambic pentameter. His voice was the voice of a child in kindergarten. Alex couldn't figure out whether he was being rude and condescending or was just crazy.

The Smithsons were flabbergasted by Whitset's behavior.

Dr. Desmonde stared at him strangely. She slipped Alex a note telling her to call the hospital chaplain. Alex rose to leave the room as Monique again turned to the Smithsons, who were still shell-shocked by Whitset's words. She sighed with fatigue. She and Alex would now have to deal with Whitset.

Monique took Mrs. Smithson's hand and said to the older couple in a reassuring voice, "We will tell you everything as soon as we get the information. Is there anything else you need? Can I arrange for a cab to take you home?"

"Is there anything else we need to know now?" Mr. Smithson's voice was morose. He was grey with fatigue and grief. Mrs. Smithson looked like a shocked, broken puppet.

"Yeah," said Whitset, his voice loud and commanding. "Yeah, you may want to know that your mother was also raped."

Mrs. Smithson responded with a bloodcurdling sound. Mr. Smithson made the low guttural sounds of a wild animal in intense pain.

Whitset smiled his gleeful, enigmatic smile at the grieving couple, turned to Dr. Desmonde, and simply said, "Well, they needed to know, didn't they? They did ask if there was anything else."

Monique didn't reply. She continued to stare at Whitset. A realization about the man was sending tingles up her spine. He belonged on the Pavilion but not as the administrator.

Whitset flinched under her intense stare and looked at his watch. When he looked back at her, it began to happen. Dr. Desmonde's face was turning to plastic. *My God, the bitch is one of them*, he thought! Whitset could tell from the way the fluorescent light highlighted the sheen of her pale face. He felt a terrible noise in his head and struggled for control. He wanted to reach out and rip her head off. *The bitch*, he thought to himself. *How had she kept her secret so long? Was he losing his ability to identify them?* He stood abruptly and said, "See you shortly in Montgomery's office."

Alex was hanging up the phone when Whitset came into her office.

He grabbed her shoulder and said gleefully, "I told them everything, it's all done. See you in a few minutes."

Alex stared at him as he raced from her office. She couldn't decide whether he was happy, sad, or just crazy. She just couldn't figure him out.

Alex returned to the conference room and found both of the Smithsons in tears, devastated over their mother's death. Monique was doing her best, but she too was having difficulty keeping her composure. Her eyes were full of tears. Alex supposed they were tears of frustration, as well as grief. Alex and Monique stayed with the Smithsons, offering as much comfort as they could until a priest took the heartbroken couple away.

Chapter 23

The room was deathly quiet after the Smithsons left. Monique and Alex sat quietly for a few minutes, each trying to figure out what had happened. Finally, Alex couldn't stand the silence any longer and spoke.

"Monique, talk to me! There's got to be something wrong with Whitset. Did you see him in here? It was as if some type of transformation occurred and a kid broke out! It's like he went to another planet or something! What's wrong with him? I think he's psycho!"

The psychiatrist didn't respond, caught up in her own thoughts. A dozen possibilities were racing through her mind. It was clear in her professional judgment that Whitset had some sort of psychiatric disorder – only she didn't know what. She'd never seen evidence of any overtly psychotic behavior. He'd always seem grounded in reality, although he was very strange. Of course, her interactions with him were limited and minimal because, truthfully, she didn't like or trust him. Monique knew that psychotic patients were often highly manipulative and could cloak their behavior well. The only clinical behavior she'd witnessed had only just happened a few minutes before and she couldn't make a judgment based on just that one incident. She needed verification and validation of what she was thinking. Somehow, she had to figure out a way to corroborate her suspicions. Of course, there was the sexual thing he seemed to have with Alex, but that wasn't conclusive either. Monique didn't know and needed more time.

"Monique. For heaven's sake, what do you think?" Alex persisted and grabbed her arm, pressing for an answer.

Dr. Desmonde shrugged her shoulders and shook her head. "I don't know, Alex. It could be any number of things.

There's definitely something wrong, but I just don't have enough information. Anyway, I need to call Jack and find out if he's checked Whitset out."

Alex was not to be mollified. "Do you think he has multiple personalities? That sure seemed like a child that came out in here!" Alex's voice was shrill, as she looked speculatively at her friend.

"I don't know, Alex. It's possible, but multiple personality disorder is pretty rare. If he has it, I guess we've seen at least two of them – the child and the sensual adult. Anyway, it's pure speculation on our part. Multiple personality disorder is extremely difficult to diagnose and treat. I think Whitset's more of a sociopath – he has a sociopathic personality or an antisocial personality disorder, as we call them now. Anyway, I've got to get out of here. I want to check in with Jack and go over to the Pavilion to check on things. Then I'll meet you over in Don's office."

"Okay, Monique. We've got about twenty minutes. Don't be late."

Monique nodded her head and waved at Alex as she left. Her mind was troubled as she walked back to the Pavilion. She was definitely suspicious of Lester Whitset. She couldn't casually blow him off anymore. She didn't think he was involved in the violence at the hospital, but she was troubled by the fact that he spent so much time with the patients, not to mention that he was her administrator. Her intuition told her something was very wrong with the man. He gave her an intense feeling of fear and free-floating anxiety, the origins of which she could not explain or articulate.

As she walked back to the Pavilion, Monique worked up an intense sweat. The August heat was stifling – it was hotter than hell. Even though she was a native of New Orleans, Monique could barely stand the heat. It weakened her. Sometimes she was convinced that it actually crippled her physically and emotionally. It almost assuredly brought out the worst in everybody – colleagues, patients, and families. As she entered the Pavilion lobby, she made a conscious decision. She was going to search Lester Whitset's office. Who would know? She'd never get caught if she planned it right! Right?

Monique used her unit keys to let herself into Pavilion I. Things seemed almost normal. She checked with the charge nurse, who reported that Jim McMurdie had remained in seclusion since he threatened suicide earlier in the day – directly after Whitset had confronted him with the bloody shirt. Monique knew Jim thought he'd killed the elder Mrs. Smithson. The police questioning had been hard for him, even though the officers had been gentle with their questions. After all, he had been one of them.

On the spur of the moment, Monique decided to check on him. She walked down the hall towards his seclusion room, where she ran smack into Anthony Gavette who blocked her path in the hallway. He looked belligerent.

"Hey, Doc. What gives? They say you ain't coming to community today. Why not? Aren't we important to you anymore or are you more concerned with the dead people?"

Dr. Desmonde looked at Anthony. His face was tight and threatening. She said quietly, "Of course you are important. More important than ever. It's just that I have a meeting to go to, to see about getting more staff here so that we can all feel safer."

"Don't give me that crap, Doc. I feel safe. Plenty safe. Besides, I ain't afraid of nobody. Ain't nobody messin' with me. I may mess with other people, but ain't nobody messin' with me!" Anthony's body language was tense and angry.

Monique looked up at Anthony, her heart pounding a little. She decided to push the envelope, asking him quietly,

"What exactly are you saying? Have you been hurting someone?"

"Hell no, Doc. I just want you at that meetin' today so I can get my privileges raised another level. I'm ready to be promoted to step three so I can get the hell out of here. The nurses say you got to sign off on it. Right?" He looked at her expectantly.

"Yes, that's right, but we're not raising anybody's privileges around here now. We've got to wait for things to settle down a little bit and —" Monique stopped for a second and looked straight at her often violent, schizophrenic patient.

He was getting mad, really mad. His face was red and his eyes were glazed over. He started moving towards her in a menacing manner. "Listen to me, bitch, you useless, cold-blooded pig. I'm going to kill you. You hear, you Dr. Pig?" Anthony's voice was low, but threatening. His eyes were gleaming with an evil intent.

Monique knew she was in trouble. She felt her normal calm demeanor slip away. She knew she couldn't let him know she was scared. She never took her eyes off Anthony's face as she felt around her for something to throw for help. She wasn't close to an ASA red button. The nearest one was at least three feet away. She let her eyes wander for one brief second before she was convinced that no one was nearby. She only hoped someone was in the nursing station watching the security monitors.

It only took Anthony that one brief second to realize that Monique was frightened. Her fear gave him the edge he needed. The moment her eyes left his face, Anthony knew he was in charge. Quick as a flash, he reached out for the psychiatrist's slender white throat and wrapped his huge hands around it. At first, he exerted only a little pressure on Monique's neck, enjoying the fear and terror he saw in her eyes. Anthony had a fleeting remembrance of how much fun killing was. He should do it more often. He liked the sense of power it gave him. He applied a little more pressure, watching her eyes dilate with fear at the certainty of her fate.

He began to talk to her in a soft, sensual voice, "You're a pretty lady, Doc. Wish I had time to get a little piece, but I guess there's not much time left in this life for us – at least for you. Maybe in another life. That's okay, though. Squeezing your neck is almost as good as...." Anthony was surprised that he was so sexually stimulated. This killing thing felt good. He would do it more often, he thought, once he got out of this hellhole. He'd steal the shrink's keys and escape. The thought gave him another pleasure thrill.

Anthony applied a little more pressure.

Monique began to feel dizzy and felt her body grow weak. Anthony moved his face in position to kiss her and Monique became furious. In a last ditch effort to free herself, she brought her knee up sharply between his legs. He gave a yelp like a wounded dog when she kicked him. He grabbed his crotch, hurling profanities and vulgar epitaphs at her as he lay writhing in pain on the floor. Monique ran for the red button, pushed it, and then threw a stainless steel bedpan down the hall to attract attention as Anthony struggled to his feet.

Within several seconds, a powerful, young psych tech grabbed Anthony from behind and wrestled him back down to the floor. Anthony fell down on his stomach, moaning and holding his testicles.

In a matter of seconds, Donna Meade appeared with a syringe full of Haldol. As she squatted on her knees beside Anthony to inject his arm, the patient gave a huge yell, let go of his testicles, and grabbed Donna's crotch. In an instant, he had ripped through her uniform pants and pantyhose, while Donna lay writhing in pain on the cold linoleum floor.

Monique immediately retrieved the syringe and jammed it into Anthony's outstretched arm, sighing with relief when several additional psychiatric aides showed up and carted the angry patient off to the seclusion room on the far hall.

Dr. Desmonde immediately ducked into the utility room and returned with a blanket, which she placed over the moaning Donna Meade. Monique tried to talk with her, but the nurse manager was in too much pain. She also appeared to be shocky. Monique checked her pulse, finding it weak and thready and her blood pressure low. She ordered a stretcher and waited until two attendants had taken Donna over to the main CCMC emergency room. *My God, what a day!* she thought. *And it's only 2:15 in the afternoon.*

Sensing that the staff was now in control of the unit, Dr. Desmonde escaped to her office and locked the door. After forcing herself to calm down, she called Don Montgomery's office to tell them she was running late and would be over shortly. She breathed a sigh of relief when Latetiaa told her they were starting at 3 o'clock. The meeting was delayed for an hour because Bette Farve had a prior commitment – *probably at the hairdresser*, Monique thought ruefully. *What a bitch!* Thinking about Farve raised Monique's blood pressure and she actually felt better. She could handle Farve, no problem. It was some of the others that were scary. Farve was passive aggressive and a pain in the ass, but nothing like some of the other major players of the day.

After a few minutes, Monique's thoughts returned to Lester Whitset. She was still tempted to search his office, but her eagerness had been waylaid by Anthony's attempt on her life. Besides, as Monique reviewed the scenario with Anthony, she considered the possibility that Anthony was a more likely suspect in Angela's rape and Mrs. Smithson's murder than either Whitset or Jim. Anthony was totally psychotic now. God knows what he could do.

Monique continued to think about Anthony. Anthony Gavette did have a history of malicious assault. But, was it sexual assault? Monique couldn't remember. Her heart fluttered once again when she allowed herself to realize how close she'd come to death. Another minute, and well....

Monique shook off those thoughts and returned to Anthony. He was a diagnosed schizophrenic and did have delusional behavior. Besides, this was the second time in two days he had gone after a woman. Yesterday he'd tried to attack Rose in the community meeting. Monique had considered the behavior a manifestation of Anthony's jealous rage, but then, an attack was an attack.

Gosh, Monique continued to think to herself, w*as it only yesterday? It seemed like ages ago. Then, today, he had attacked her.* That was certainly a notable escalation of psychotic behavior. Both assaults had been accompanied by profane sexual language. She dared herself to look at her hands – they were still trembling. She put her face into her hands to make them stop. She was still frightened, and frustrated, for tons of reasons, and she was scared. She'd never been scared on her own psychiatric unit before. These feelings were new and she didn't like them. She needed to talk to Jack, but she couldn't reach him. She felt defenseless and very vulnerable. Monique didn't like vulnerability, not at all.

Chapter 24

Alex was uneasy. She'd been put off when the meeting had been delayed. She, too, had decided that was another manifestation of Farve's uncooperative, passive aggressive behavior. Farve remained useless. Unfortunately, she knew that Farve's management style was similar to that of many nursing leaders. Farve neither supported nor appreciated the efforts of the great nursing staff at CCMC and rarely advocated for them in tough situations. Her style was more one of nepotism and fear. Hence, her nickname was Bigfoot in polite company, but she had more ribald nicknames that were used in the back of the cafeteria. With the initials B.F., it didn't take much imagination.

It was well known that Bette had pet nurses. One of the male nurses in critical care served as her on-call gardener, weeding her garden and mowing her lawn. Another nurse baked cookies for her every week and catered her dinner parties at no charge. Of course, they were rewarded – with favors, promotions, and extra time off. It was so unfair and so unethical. Alex just shook her head. This favoritism had to end.

Alex's thoughts turned from Farve to Whitset. She was convinced he was playing a large part in the current events at Crescent City Medical Center. She wondered if Jack had been able to find out anything on either Whitset or Anthony Gavette. She'd ask Monique after the executive meeting. Alex was so deep in thought that she jumped when her private phone rang.

"Alex here," she spoke into the phone.

"Alex, it's Sandy Pilschner. We've got Donna Meade over here in emergency..." Sandy paused, waiting for a response from Alex. When none came, she continued, "Did you know there was another incident over the Pavilion?"

Finally, Alex squeaked out a "no."

Sandy continued, "Apparently one of the patients whacked out and tried to strangle Dr. Desmonde ... Alex, are you there?"

"Oh, no, no. What happened?" Alex's voice was a whisper.

"I don't know much, Alex. The techs had to hurry back. They said the place was wild and they couldn't stay."

"Is Monique all right? Is she all right?" Alex repeated to herself in her anxiety.

"What?" Sandy seemed confused for a moment. "Oh, Alex, I'm sorry. I wasn't clear. Yeah, I guess she's okay. Dr. Desmonde isn't here. Donna Meade is. She's the one who's hurt. The tech said Dr. Desmonde seemed okay."

"How's Donna doing?" asked Alex.

"Well, I guess she's doing as well as any woman can – who's just had most of her lady parts ripped at. She's in a lot of pain ... and in shock, too."

"My God! I can't imagine." Alex cringed at the thought. "That's horrible, just hideous. Who did it?"

"Yeah, it is. Awful. No question. I don't know who did it. You know, Alex," Sandy paused briefly, "I would never work in the Pavilion. It's dangerous, and it's a hellhole. I think Angie hated it."

"I expect she did, I sure do. It is *a hell pit*. I understand perfectly, Sandy. Perfectly." Alex silently agreed with her. She would never work there, either.

"Gotta go, Alex." Sandy's voice was brisk. "We've got red blankets on the way in. Just thought I'd keep you up-to-date."

"Thanks, Sandy. I appreciate it," Alex said as she hung up the phone. She was in a state of bewilderment. She rubbed the chill bumps that had formed on her arms, as she thought about what happened to Donna and Monique. Something had to give up there or the whole place would spontaneously combust. *I've got to call Monique,* she thought to herself, *and make sure she's okay.*

Monique answered Alex's call on the first ring. She hoped her disappointment wasn't reflected in her voice. She had hoped it was Jack returning her call. Monique assured Alex she was not injured and promised she could see for herself shortly. Then, Monique decided to take the plunge. "Alex, do me a favor? Go over to Don's office and make sure Whitset's there. If he is, call me right back. I want to take a quick look in his office and I sure as hell don't want him to catch me."

Alex felt a quickening in her gut. "Monique, are you sure? Suppose someone sees you?"

"I'll be very careful, don't worry. Just call me back as soon as you get over there." Monique's voice sounded strong and steady.

"Okay, I'm with you. Give me about five minutes. Just be careful – promise me." Alex's voice was pleading and Monique detected a tinge of fear.

"Promise. You got it. Just call," Monique said as she hung up the phone.

Alex called Monique back a few minutes later and reported that the coast was clear. Latetia had confirmed that Whitset was in Don's private office and Alex had even interrupted them to be absolutely sure. She tolerated the ridicule in Don's voice with a small degree of triumph. At least Monique wouldn't be apprehended by Whitset as she quickly searched his office.

Dr. Desmonde walked quickly down the hall towards Lester Whitset's office, nodding briefly to staff, patients, and family members. She waved aside the questions of several staff, assuring them that she was okay and would return to the unit later.

She failed to notice the curious glances that several patients in the day room gave her. It was completely out of character for Dr. Desmonde to rush. She was the coolest, calmest, most collected cucumber that most of the patients had ever seen.

Rose was relatively indifferent to the physician's movements, but was concerned. She'd been worried about Dr. Desmonde for the past few days and had heard through the patient grapevine that Anthony had just attacked her. Rose, in her confused and flustered state, really liked Dr. Monique. She decided the physician might need some help, so she decided to follow her.

As Monique entered the hall between Pavilion I and Pavilion II, she looked around furtively. The last thing she needed was someone reporting to Whitset that she'd been hovering and snooping around his office. Her heart froze when she thought of the possible repercussions, but she shook off the fear. Monique looked around again, just to be safe. The coast was clear.

She didn't see the waiflike profile of Rose peering at her from around the corner.

Dr. Desmonde tentatively turned the knob on Whitset's door. It was locked. *Just my luck*, she thought to herself. She thought for a second and then pulled the master key to the psychiatric unit from her pocket. She inserted the key into the lock, her heart pounding in her chest. She'd never broken into anything before. *Please Lord, please Lord, let it open*, she prayed to herself. She was in luck. The lock clicked with a slight turn of her wrist and she pushed the door open. She entered Whitset's office, closing the door softly behind her.

The first thing that struck the psychiatrist when she opened the door was the darkness of the office. The heavy curtains had been drawn over the double windows opposite the door. As her eyes adjusted to the darkness, she noted that the office was immaculate. Nothing was out of place. Whitset's highly polished walnut desk was completely clear of any notes, files, or correspondence. The leather desk set and inkstand were easily visible. The round, leather container held four different colored ballpoint pens. Several pencils with sharp points were also in the container. A bookcase held several psychiatric reference books and several recent journals were on an end table, next to a pair of leather side chairs. All in all, the office looked like a magazine advertisement for office furniture. It was as if no one really worked in the place. It didn't even have a scent. It smelled like nothing. Monique sniffed again. Well, maybe it did smell like something. She could smell something metallic. It had a salty, metallic scent, kind of like old blood.

After looking around a second time, Monique decided the most impressive thing about the office was that it was unimpressive – except for its neatness, which was pretty typical of an obsessive personality. She continued to look around carefully, convinced that if she searched closely enough, she'd find something. She walked around to the side of Whitset's desk and switched on his brass desk lamp. A warm glow from the light bathed the office in a comfortably colored hue. The polished wood of the desk gleamed brightly in the lamplight. Monique's eyes searched the desk and nearby bookcases for any possible clues.

Once again, her senses were heightened to the metallic smell. What was that smell? As she tried to open the desk drawers, her eyes noted something glistening in the lamplight. It was hanging out of the bottom left desk drawer. Monique reached to pick it up and found it was a slender gold chain that was caught in the drawer. She tried to pull it out, but couldn't because it was stuck between the drawer and the desk frame. Monique reached down to examine the chain more closely. She saw that the chain was broken and missing several links. The clasp was in place. The chain looked like one a woman would wear. It was much too fragile to be male jewelry.

Monique tried for several moments to detangle the chain from the desk drawer. Convinced that she couldn't remove the chain, Monique looked around the office again. Her eyes fell on Whitset's diplomas, which were hanging neatly on the wall over his bookcase. He had an undergraduate degree from some university in Europe. His graduate degree was a Master's in business administration from the University of Pennsylvania. Monique looked closely at the date on the MBA. The degree was conferred in 1966. Immediately, her heart started beating hard. It seemed impossible. Whitset certainly didn't appear old enough to have received a Master's degree in 1966! She didn't think he was over forty-five. If he had received a Master's degree in 1966, he must be a lot older than she thought he was – how then could he look so youthful? Monique intuitively knew that it wasn't Whitset's degree. She quickly looked back at his undergraduate degree. It was awarded in 1963. Damn, that was impossible!

As she stood contemplating this information, there was a soft knock on the office door. Her heart sank. She immediately killed the light and ducked behind the desk, holding her breath for what seemed like an eternity. Her pulse beat rapidly. Wow, the smell was overwhelming. What was that smell? At that point, Monique noted a green bottle, the shape that red wine came in, on the bottom bookcase near the back. She picked it up a sniffed. *Oh My God,* the smell of old wine and metal about knocked her out. She had to take several deep breaths to recover. *Whew,* she thought to herself. *If I drank that stuff, I'd be loco, crazy too.*

After several minutes of silence, Monique rose from her hiding place and slipped surreptitiously out of the office. When she reached her own office, she pulled out her personnel file on Whitset. Her eyes scanned his resume. His date of birth was recorded as January 27, 1951. Monique smiled a half smile. She knew Whitset was smart, but she doubted he was smart enough to have been awarded a Master's degree when he was only fifteen years old! Her watch beeped. It was almost 3:15. She rushed over to the main campus to the executive meeting, her face highly colored because of her discovery.

Chapter 25

Alex was getting antsy at the meeting. She found herself fidgeting in her chair. Where was Monique? Where was Commander Françoise? She'd expected that he would attend the meeting to report on the progress of the investigation. Don was obviously getting cross about being held up by his "employees." Farve was droning on and on about how safe the psych units were and how other hospitals didn't have the sophisticated monitoring systems that CCMC had installed several years ago. Farve maintained the staffing numbers in the Pavilion were better than the staffing numbers of several hospitals considered competitors to Crescent City Medical.

Alex wanted to hug Robert Bonnet, present at the meeting because he was acting chief of surgery, when he interrupted Bette Farve's drone.

Robert directly addressed the nurse executive in a reasonable tone, "Ms. Farve, how can you suggest that the Pavilion is safe? Only last night an elderly patient was murdered and no one heard her screams because the only staff member was on the far hall, a long distance from where the incident occurred."

Bette raised her eyebrows and gave the handsome surgeon a dirty look. "Dr. Bonnet, last night was an extreme and unusual situation. There'd been an emergency over on the prison unit. All other staff had been sent over there to handle it. This is an isolated incident!" Farve gave Robert a tight little smile.

Elizabeth spoke up, "It may be an isolated incident, but it still has a heavy impact. There should be enough staff to cover the unit, even when there's a problem. When the media gets a hold of this, as I believe they already have – based on

222

the stack of messages on my desk – we're going to be in for some nasty, negative publicity." Elizabeth Tippett used her advantage well and looked straight at Don Montgomery.

Montgomery didn't respond, but Whitset did. "I believe we are blowing the repercussions of this incident out of proportion in relationship to the actual threat. Accidents happen in hospitals. They happen every single day—"

Elizabeth interrupted the psychiatric administrator, "Really, Mr. Whitset, accidents and incidents do occur in hospitals regularly, but it's a bit extreme to have a patient murdered by another patient on the psychiatric unit. I believe you're the one underestimating the potential disaster here."

Alex wanted to give Liz a standing ovation. She was proud of Elizabeth for the way she was standing up to Whitset. She had emerged from a shrinking violet just a few months ago to a strong member of the executive team. She was a master at dealing with the press and sorting out difficult, press related issues. Elizabeth had a well-connected press network, which complimented her ability to perform her job well.

Whitset stared at Liz and gave her a chilling look.

Even Alex could feel the coldness his manner exuded.

He said in an icy voice, his black glittering eyes raking the media director's face and upper torso, "My dear, I do believe you're wrong."

Elizabeth maintained her composure and said simply, "No, Mr. Whitset, I'm right." She turned to Bette Farve and said, "Besides, it's clear to me that our sophisticated equipment you mentioned, Ms. Farve, was useless last night – particularly since there were no staff members available to monitor it!" She glared at the nurse executive, her eyes displaying her displeasure.

Bette just stared at the table. There was nothing she could say.

Alex and Robert both eyed each other after they saw the look of intense hatred Lester Whitset gave Elizabeth Tippett. Elizabeth seemed not to notice. Alex was glad. It was bad enough that she and Robert were worried.

Montgomery checked his watch and eyed the group. "Where in the hell is Dr. Desmonde? And, where is that useless police commander? I was sure he would be here to entertain us with his consistent incompetence." Don looked around at the group to see which of the members appreciated his humor. Bette Farve and Lester Whitset both smiled broadly.

Alex, per usual, was disgusted with Don. She said, "Don, I believe Dr. Desmonde is on her way. There was another incident up on the unit and —"

Whitset about fell out of his chair, "What incident, what happened?"

Alex looked around the room and said, "I don't know the details. Monique will tell us when she arrives."

Don was livid and his faced flushed bright red. "Shut up, Alex. I know what happened and I don't care about that." Don paused as the door to the conference room opened, "Well, well, well, look who finally made it," Don sneered as Monique entered the conference room.

Robert was angry as well, but his voice was calm. "Don, please watch what you say and keep this meeting professional. Dr. Desmonde and Ms. Destephano don't deserve your sarcasm and disrespect."

Alex flashed Robert a smile. She could hardly believe the CEO had told her to shut up.

Don ignored Robert and said, "Dr. Desmonde, I don't recall you telling me I was going to need double staff to take care of these wackos. Did you tell me that, Dr. Desmonde?" Don's voice was demanding and so sarcastic that Alex could feel Robert get ready to say something else to him. She placed her hand on Robert's arm and whispered to him to let Monique handle Montgomery.

"No, I didn't tell you that precisely, Don. What I did tell you was that there was a distinct possibility our workload would increase significantly and that we may need more staff later. That, I believe, is when you, as our esteemed leader, hired Mr. Whitset's company to manage the psychiatry service!" Monique's voice was disdainful and patronizing.

Whitset had been watching the exchange with a great deal of interest. He interjected, "Yes, Mr. Montgomery did hire us around the time he signed the state contract. He was obviously worried about the costs of caring for such a diverse population of psychiatric patients. My company assured him that we had helped many other hospitals do the same type of thing we have done here at Crescent City – successfully managing a changing population of psychiatric patients without increasing costs. We're successful here. It's a good model." Whitset smiled broadly, his thin lips curling over his small rodent like teeth.

Monique could hardly abide Whitset's tiresome ponderosity. *What a pile of bullshit*, she thought to herself. When she couldn't stand it any longer, she addressed the pompous Whitset.

"Mr. Whitset, your model may be a good financial model for the hospital, but it is a poor clinical model. I'm sure the only reason it's saved the hospital money is because you cut staffing positions."

If looks could kill, Whitset would have eradicated Monique. But, he remained silent.

Elizabeth Tippet pushed her long, dark hair back and looked at Whitset as though he were a moron. "I'm a bit confused by your comments. I wouldn't call these recent events successful, Mr. Whitset. I'd call them tragic. I agree with Dr. Desmonde. I vote we increase the staff to the levels she's suggested. It's pretty clear to me that we're understaffed over there. I, for one, don't want any more of these patient or staff incidents to occur."

"I second Elizabeth's suggestion. I trust Dr. Desmonde's judgment implicitly in these matters." Dr. Bonnet smiled warmly at Monique and continued talking. "She is a nationally known expert in her field and she knows the internal needs of her department."

Don Montgomery gave Robert Bonnet a deprecating look.

He'd always hated and distrusted the surgeon. In some respects, Alex believed Don was jealous of Robert.

"Thanks, Bonnet. What a surprise! You physicians never disagree with each other." His voice was laced with sarcasm and disdain as he sneered at Robert.

Montgomery turned to Whitset. "What do you want to do, Whitset? It's really your call, you know. You're in charge of the Pavilion. If you think we need the staff, we'll work it out."

Alex intervened. "Don, I object to giving him this authority. He's hired contract help. This system is an administrative disaster. I would certainly like him on our team, but I wouldn't give him the authority to make the decision. In fact, I don't think he has that authority based on hospital by-laws and policy."

Whitset's eyes shot daggers at Alex, his black eyes penetrated her face.

Alex could feel the coldness he exuded. She could feel the chill as it washed over her.

Don shrugged his shoulders and looked at Whitset. "Don't know, Whitset. What do you think?"

Whitset managed a complete turnabout. He looked at the group, nodding at Donald Montgomery. His smile was pleasant and his voice congenial. "Thanks, Don. Thank you all for your input. I'm not in favor of hiring additional staff. We don't need them. According to my numbers, CCMC is well staffed. The staff we have are competent and are used to caring for the type of patients we admit. Secondly, our productivity would drop if we hired ten new positions. It would take us over six months to hire and train them. Hiring these people makes no business sense at all – particularly because we don't need them. I figure these positions would cost us better than $1 million the first year. I'm against it."

Bette Farve nodded her head in agreement with Lester Whitset. "I quite agree with Mr. Whitset. If we have money for positions, Don, I'd much rather put the FTEs in critical care or on the medicine units. Psych is doing okay. Besides, it's hard to fill psych nursing positions. We have to pay them more because of the perceived notion that working with these patients can be more dangerous. I'm against increasing the staff over there." Bette rolled her eyes at the "perceived notion" that caring for psych patients could be dangerous.

Monique interrupted, "Perceived notions, really Bette, you are intolerable. Two nurses have been attacked in the Pavilion!"

Alex gave Bette Farve a disgusted look and shook her head. One thing about Bette was that she never disappointed. For some reason, she always expected that the nursing leader would emerge as supportive of nursing and their needs. Farve never did. *I ought to be used to her by now,* Alex thought. *At least I know what to expect,* she mused. *I guess it's better than people shooting from the hip. Expect nothing, get less. That's going to be the way I approach her.*

Alex spoke, "I recommend, from a legal standpoint, that we fill the slots. We have a file full of complaints from patients, staff, and visitors about how unsafe the Pavilion is. We're required by law to provide for the reasonable safety of those who visit our premises. If we don't, we could be liable for all types of actions."

"Now, now, now, Alex. Perhaps you're being a little overzealous. Aren't you flaunting your lawyer credentials?" Lester Whitset looked at her, a mollifying smile on his face. His voice was so low she could hardly hear him.

"Absolutely not, Mr. Whitset. I'm only being reasonable and prudent, doing my job as the hospital attorney. Dr. Desmonde has offered a convincing argument, substantiated by statistics, that we are severely understaffed here in psychiatry. Her numbers aren't even adjusted for the severity of our patient index or patient population. Our overall patient acuity is higher than that of any other hospital in New Orleans. Therefore —"

Alex was interrupted by Whitset as he jumped up from his seat and leaned across, practically lying on the conference table across from her, his face white again with fury. He looked like a little boy who was pouting. "We will not hire any additional staff! It's my decision, and it's final! It's no longer open for discussion." Whitset stared around the room.

Alex was incredulous. How dare that creepy SOB undermine her? She looked at Don and said, "Don, really, we must have some type of closure here."

Montgomery looked at the hospital lawyer and shrugged his shoulders. "It's Whitset's decision, Alex. He has the last say. It's in his contract."

Alex was incredulous. "No, no, Don. You're wrong. *It's our contract.* Whitset is contracting with us. We are in charge here. We are driving the bus."

Robert looked scornfully at Whitset. "What's in this for you, Whitset? A bigger bonus based on dollars saved at the end of the year?"

Whitset said nothing and continued to look around the room.

228

Alex's sense of smell was assaulted by a strange odor. She couldn't quite place it, but it was very familiar. She looked around to see if anyone else noticed it. Whatever the smell was, it had a metallic taint.

Elizabeth said clearly, "I must go on record here as being positively opposed to this decision."

Robert and Alex nodded their heads in agreement with Liz.

Monique Desmonde, still standing at the wall-mounted board with her statistics clearly in sight, looked at the group and quietly, but assuredly, said, "I disagree completely with Mr. Whitset. The Pavilion is a powder keg. Anything could happen up there at any time. In fact, it already has."

The silence was deafening and no one spoke.

Montgomery looked at Whitset for help and support, but Whitset didn't seem to be paying attention.

Monique continued as she locked eyes with Don Montgomery and said to him, "Don, don't take this as a threat. Take this as a fact. If those new positions are not approved by noon tomorrow, I will personally call a press conference. I'll tell them, as the former chief of psychiatry at Crescent City Medical Center, just how unsafe patient care is here. I'll tell the press in great detail about the attack and rape of Angela Richelieu, mentioning her commitment to her work, her unpaid overtime, and the unavailability of a security guard to walk her to her car. I'll also talk about the death of Mrs. Smithson in great, gory detail. I'll describe her injuries – the way in which the knitting needle protruded from her mouth and the fact that her face had virtually been eradicated by her murderer. I'll also mention her patient call light – about how it was covered with her blood and how it was disconnected from the wall. I'll tell the press how Mrs. Smithson, as an elderly, loving grandmother and great-grandmother, frantically called and called for help while she was being brutally raped and *murdered because there were no available staff to come help her.* I'll tell them where the staff was, both of them. I'll tell the *Times Picayune* and the *Associated Press* how *both* of our staff members were on the prison unit trying to prevent the inmates from raping the new admission."

Monique stopped for a few moments and looked at the group, as if surveying the effects of her words. Then she continued, pulling down the neck of her blouse. "Finally, I'll show them my neck, my bruises. By tomorrow, this redness will clearly delineate the hands that tried to strangle me an hour or so ago on the nursing unit. Then, I'll describe the patient attack on the nurse manager. Good story, don't you think?" Monique's pale face was red with fury, anger, and wrath as she continued, "It should keep the tabloids busy for several weeks. Trust me, if you think our Mardi Gras press was bad this year, wait until this hits TV, radio, Facebook and burns up Twitter and the local news all over the country. It will go viral in a matter of several hours. I may even uplink a YouTube video of my injuries!"

Montgomery looked as though he were going to cry, "Monique, no! You wouldn't do that! You couldn't!" He was pleading with her.

"Don, I can and I will. Count on it. I want an answer by noon tomorrow. I want the positions at mid-to-upper salary scales and I want to hire them myself." Monique gave Lester Whitset a sideways glance as she left the room. His look chilled her to the bone, but she didn't care. She was on a roll. "I don't need Mr. Whitset's assistance with any of the human resource issues. As a matter of fact, I would prefer Mr. Whitset not interact with the patients at all," Monique concluded, as she shut the door behind her.

Alex glared at Whitset. She was shocked, but pleased at Monique's ultimatum, although she was afraid for her. The look on Whitset's face was one of unmitigated hatred and rage. Alex was scared for her friend and her heart raced at the potential danger Monique could be in.

As Whitset watched Dr. Desmonde leave the conference room, he saw her turn into one of them. When she had given him that glance, he had seen it. She was one of them. An imposter. Whitset felt his heart speed up. A hot flush came over him. He was sweating. Could he be wrong? There were so many lately. No. He'd seen right. Right in front of him, Monique Desmonde's face turned into plastic – just as he thought it had earlier in the day. Then, he hadn't been sure, but, now, he was positive. Whitset found himself becoming nervous and agitated. He felt like he was being suffocated. He had to get out of the room. He looked around at the others. They looked okay. Their faces had real skin. Suddenly, he got up from his chair and left the room. The noise and screaming in his head was all he could stand. There was no way he could stay for idle conversation.

Don watched him leave and said sarcastically, "Great, he's a lot of help. What a piss poor manager." He turned to Alex.

"Do you think Monique will go to the press? Will you help me?" His voice was pleading, even begging.

Alex hated Don's pleading, whiny voice. She was silent for a few moments. "I don't know, Don. Dr. Desmonde is a woman of principle. She feels strongly about things in the Pavilion. She's felt strongly for a long time. In addition to the security issues, she's convinced that the treatment milieu is inappropriate for optimal clinical outcomes. She maintains that mixing ages and placing depressed patients on the same unit with acute psychotics is inappropriate and substandard." She paused for a few seconds. "Yes, Don. She may indeed go to the press. Robert, what do you think?"

Robert Bonnet looked at Alex and Don. He nodded affirmatively. "No question about it – I'm sure she'll go. I've known Monique most of my life. What Alex says is absolutely right. Besides, she has nothing to lose, and a great deal to gain—"

Don interrupted, reverting to his little boy destructive act. "Nothing to lose! Hell, I'll fire her ass! I'll jerk her privileges! I'll black list her from every hospital in town!" His eyes gleamed in anticipation of destroying Monique.

Robert laughed at him. "Montgomery, Monique Desmonde is one of the leading psychiatrists in the United States, with an impressive international reputation to boot! Besides, she said she would quit. She's known globally for her work with adolescents and more recently, she's built quite a reputation for herself as a forensic psychiatrist. For God's sake, Montgomery, she's a consultant to the CDC and NIH on mental health issues. She can get a job anywhere. She could write her ticket to Hopkins or Harvard tonight and be there next week."

"I'll be damned if she'll get one in New Orleans. I'll see to that," Don ranted and threatened.

Robert snorted at the CEO. "You are powerless on this one, Don. Monique's currently an attending professor in psychiatry at Tulane, has staff privileges there, and an open invitation to head the service at Oschner. The only reason she has stayed here is because you got the state contract and she was interested in building her forensic practice. You'd better give her what she wants."

Don looked dismal. "I can't. I really can't. It's Whitset's decision – it's in the contract."

"That's BS, Don. You are in charge of CCMC. Where's the contract? I've never seen it!" Alex was furious. "You shouldn't be entering into agreements with other groups without my advice. That is what you pay me for!" Alex looked at him disdainfully. Don was such an idiot and an appalling leader.

232

"I'll have Latetia copy it. See if you can work around it." Don looked scared. "Alex, please talk to Dr. Desmonde. Make her change her mind. She'll destroy us!"

"I'll talk with her, Don. But you best talk with Whitset. He's the problem."

"I will. Let's get out of here. You all think about this and let me know what we should do." Don dismissed the rest of the executive team with a wave of his hand. He disappeared into his private office and shut the door tightly.

Alex and Robert walked slowly towards her office, talking quietly to each other.

Robert said to Alex, his voice low and serious, "You know, Al, Whitset really bothers me. He looks crazy himself. Did you see the way he looked at Monique? At Liz? I swear, I think he'd like to kill them both."

"Yeah, I know, and probably me as well. The man absolutely chills me to the bone. I think there's something wrong with him, too. Monique thinks he probably has some type of personality disorder. I know Jack was going to run a check on him today. By the way, Robert," Alex said, lowering her voice to a whisper, "Monique was going to search his office this afternoon. That's why she was late getting to the meeting. Intuitively, I think she believes he's involved in some of the stuff in the Pavilion."

"Do you mean Angela or Mrs. Smithson?" Robert looked shocked.

"Oh, no, I don't think so. She's just concerned that he spends so much time with the patients. She thinks he agitates them or something. Causes patient outbursts. Anyway, I'm going to go over there and try to see her."

Chapter 26

Whitset felt confused on his way back to the Pavilion. He had taken several wrong turns in the main hospital. The voices were screaming in his head. He was so hot, so terribly hot. He stopped to sit on a bench in the shade to rest for a few minutes, but it was still stifling. It'd been a hard day for him. He'd been up a long time, almost twenty-four hours. He always felt bad when he didn't sleep well and the voices seemed to wear him down more. He placed his face between his hands, pleading with the voices to leave him alone. He was too tired to listen to them. Besides, he was worried about all the imposters that were showing up. They were ganging up against him. There were so many, three in just the last few days. Before that, it'd been years since he had seen one of them.

Lester began to think back. He'd never forget the first one he'd met. It was at school, a teacher of his in Alabama. He had been twelve years old then. She'd been mean to him and ridiculed him in front of the class. He'd wet his pants and everybody had laughed at him. He could still see their faces – all of his friends. Their mouths were huge and their lips painted red like the red of a clown's mouth. They were leering at him. They were making fun of him and taunting him repeatedly. They'd even made up a rhyme. He could hear it now. They had sung it to him on the bus over and over again:

"Whitset, Whitset, can stand no stress
Whitset, Whitset is a real big mess
Whitset, Whitset is such a mess
Whitset, Whitset just peed his pants!"

234

Lester couldn't stand it. After that, the kids never left him alone. He'd become the class whipping boy. He began to hate school and retreated into himself. Then, one day, his teacher had kept him after school and made him write on the blackboard 300 times, "I will pay attention in class." He remembered being mad and feeling completely powerless. He had completed his punishment and turned around to face his teacher ... and then it happened. He saw her turn to plastic! He watched her face become hard and immovable. He saw her eyes turn into two inflexible pieces of blue plastic. He watched in horror and fascination as her lips became fixed in a red, stiff, hard smile. Her hands, below the cuffs of her blouse, had also turned to plastic. Her nails turned a shiny pink plastic, like seashells. Then, they told him to do it ... the voices ... and he had. He felt triumphant! After all, she was an imposter. It was his responsibility to "do away" with imposters. His voices said so.

Then there was a huge blank in his life. Whitset didn't remember the next few years. He thought he'd been in school trying to learn to behave better. Anyway, he hadn't seen any imposters for a long time. He could only remember one other one and he pushed her out of his mind. He had loved her and she had laughed at him. Finally, he saw her turn to plastic, too. And then, well, he had had to do it. Even if it was his brother's wife. He felt tingly at the memory. He liked the feeling he got when hurting other people.

He got excited now just remembering the feeling of squeezing her neck. God, that was such a long time ago. It was too painful to remember, but the pain felt good and energized him – at least, for a while. Suddenly Whitset felt tired. He closed his eyes for a brief moment and awoke with a start! Had someone spoken to him? They must have because he had heard a voice. It was five o'clock in the afternoon. People were walking from the Pavilion towards their cars. He looked over at the yellow tape and wondered what it was doing there in the trees. Then he remembered. Oh yeah, the nurse. He remembered that night and pleasure riveted through him. He got chill bumps all over his arms. He could feel the hair stand up on the back of his neck. Lester shook his head furiously. He didn't want to think about that now. He had to get control back. He was much too tired and his head was beginning to ache.

Whitset rested a few minutes longer and then finished walking to the Pavilion. The air-conditioning in the lobby felt so cool. The blast seemed to revive him. So very cool. He sat on the grey vinyl bench for a few minutes. He began to feel better, much better. His strength came back and his head cleared. He pushed the elevator button, unlocked the door to Pavilion II, and headed towards his office. It was pretty quiet. Everybody was in the day room eating dinner. Rose, the waif, waved at him from her room when he walked by. Whitset didn't respond. He continued the walk down the hall towards his office.

He opened his office door. Immediately, he knew. *Someone had been in here. Someone had been in his office.* He could smell it – no, not it, her. It was a female smell. Just a slight, slight odor. He felt himself getting angry. Who had been in his office? He began to hyperventilate as he looked around carefully. Nothing seemed to be disturbed. His desk drawers were still locked. He took out his keys and opened his bottom right drawer to check his stash. It was there. He breathed a sigh of relief and began to calm down.

His relief was momentary. He was furious about the invasion of his private space. He stalked out of his door and locked it securely. He walked into Rose's room. Why not? Her room was the closest to his office. Maybe Rose saw something. She was lying on her bed and gave Whitset a shy smile in greeting.

His voice was charming, honey coated. "Rose, it's your good friend, Lester. How are you doing?" Whitset gave Rose his best smile. He sat next to her on the bed, holding her hands. "I like your blouse. Is it new?" His voice was soft and sensual. His eyes rolled up and down her slight body.

Rose nodded her head. Her eyes transfixed on Whitset's face.

"Give Lester a big smile and then Lester will give Rose a big kiss," Whitset said in a childish voice as he moved closer to her.

Rose smiled at him. She didn't really like Lester, but she was so lonely. Besides, once he had made her feel really good. Just a couple of nights ago. They had done the dirty thing or, at least, they had almost done the dirty thing. Somehow, Anthony had found out and that was why he had been so mad at her yesterday. Somehow, Anthony knew she had been with Lester. Rose continued to smile and think. Men usually just ignored her, except for Anthony. He said he really loved her. She didn't really know. Men had said that to her before and, besides, Lester was being nice. She kissed him back.

"That's good, very good," Lester's voice was soft, almost a whisper, as he continued to kiss Rose over and over. His hands undid the buttons on her blouse. Rose gave a little sigh as Lester's soft hand reached for her tiny breasts. As he continued to kiss and fondle her, he asked her softly, talking baby talk to her, "Did little Rose see anybody go into Lessie's office today? You know, when I was at the meeting?"

Rose didn't say anything, but Whitset picked up on the almost imperceptible stiffening of her body. He continued to kiss her, kneading her breasts and fondling her body. He said sensually, "Lester knows that Rose knows who was in his office. Rose had better tell Lester if she wants him to stay and play with her."

Rose was silent. Whitset immediately withdrew his mouth and hands from her body.

Rose moaned in disappointment. It was cold where his lips had been and she shivered. She opened her eyes wide and looked at him. "Please, Lester, please. It feels so good. Please play with me," she begged.

"Only if you tell Lessie who was in his office this afternoon. That's only fair. Then, I'll play with you all night. That's only fair." Whitset's voice was indignant, self-righteous.

That was all Rose needed to hear. She asked in her little girl voice, "Promise, Lester? Do you really promise?"

"Scouts honor. I promise. Tell Lester and we will play with each other all night." Whitset gave Rose another long, lingering kiss.

Rose, her eyes closed, said softly. "It was Dr. Desmonde. She was only in there a couple of minutes."

Rose opened her eyes as she felt Whitset's hands turn cold. His face was white and his eyes were dilated. She was frightened. She wished he would get up, but he just laid there, his body was so cold that she was freezing where she had been so warm a few minutes before.

Whitset was beside himself with anger. God, he hated that shrink bitch. She'd been a pain since his first day. Always wanting to do things right. Always wanting more staff and more supplies. Always wanting to disorder Lester's perfectly ordered life. Today she had gone too far. She would pay now.

He continued to think, becoming angrier by the minute. First, she'd threatened to close down the hospital and now she'd broken into his office. Then, she turned into an imposter. She was one of them. In his anger and fury, Lester ripped off Rose's polyester slacks and thrust himself into her. He needed a release. Please, somebody, anybody, give me a release, he cried to himself. Let me make it this time. Let me get off! It was such a big deal for him sometimes. Then, other times, it wasn't a big deal at all. The uncertainty made him mad and unsure of his sexuality. He lusted for power and obedience at all times. That also included the obedience of his body.

He continued to go at it. Please, he deserved it today. He needed the release. It had been a horrible day. He thrust and thrust and thrust.

Rose lay beneath him, whimpering silently. "Please stop, Lester. You're hurting me. I want you to play nicely with me." Rose smiled tearfully at him.

Whitset glared at her. "Shut up, you little bitch." He grabbed her face in his hands and hissed at her, "If you tell anybody we did this, I'll kill you!"

He jumped from the bed and disappeared silently from Rose's room, leaving her crying silently into her pillow.

Chapter 27

It was late afternoon and Alex was frantic. She could not find Monique anywhere. She had called the Pavilion before she left the hospital, and the staff had assured her that Dr. Desmonde wasn't there. Alex, feeling increasingly apprehensive and useless at work, called Martin's cab, dropped Angie's cross at her jewelry store over on Magazine Street, and went home. Even Martin's humor and jokes had not been able to cheer her up on her way home. She was worried and had a bad feeling in the pit of her stomach that made her fearful.

She glanced at her kitchen clock for the tenth time since getting home. It was almost seven o'clock in the evening. She phoned Monique again and left a voicemail. The charge nurse at the Pavilion told her that Dr. Desmonde had turned over her calls to the senior psychiatric resident at six o'clock that evening. Alex, her frustration mounting, tried to reach Jack. When he didn't answer his cell or text, she called police headquarters and was told that Commander Françoise was unavailable. Alex pressed the watch officer for more information and declared an emergency. The officer finally admitted that the commander was out of New Orleans for the evening, working on a case somewhere either in Mississippi or Alabama. He wasn't sure. The man offered to put Alex in contact with someone else, but she refused.

After the phone call, she chided herself, thinking that Monique and Jack were spending a quiet evening alone – out of New Orleans, probably in an isolated hideaway on the Gulf Coast. That kept her satisfied for a few minutes. If they were together and she was this worried, she would probably murder them herself for not answering her frantic messages and texts.

Time wore on. Alex didn't like what she was feeling. She was so unsettled; she poured herself a second glass of wine and sat on the sofa in her living room. As her mind clicked through the events of the day, she kept refocusing on the look that Whitset had given Monique in the executive committee meeting. His behavior towards the psychiatrist had chilled her to the bone. It terrified her. It was evident that he was enraged with her. Essentially, Monique had the power to put Whitset out of work and, more than likely, Whitset knew that as well. This concerned Alex because she didn't think Whitset was normal or rational. His behavior with the Smithsons had been unnerving, particularly that singsong routine she had witnessed. Oh, if only she could reach either Jack or Monique, she would feel so much better. Besides, she knew Monique had found something in Whitset's office and her curiosity was killing her.

She jumped up when she heard a knock at her door. She ran from the living room to the foyer and felt a twinge of disappointment when she saw Robert on her porch. Well, not disappointment, but she had hoped it was Monique. She opened the door, smiling. Robert looked great. He was impeccably dressed, clean-shaven, and his eyes sparkled at the sight of her. *He truly was a hot guy*, she thought to herself.

"Hey, what a surprise! What's up? Have you heard from Monique or Jack?" Her voice sounded strained and she looked stressed.

Robert looked surprised at her greeting. "No, Alex, why? What's happened? Has something else happened?"

"Nothing. Nothing really. At least, nothing I know of. I've been trying to reach Monique since right after the meeting this afternoon and I can't find her. The hospital said she turned over her calls. She doesn't answer her home phone or her cell and ..." Alex paused for a moment and continued in a concerned voice, "Oh, Robert, I guess I'm frightened for her. I'm afraid Whitset might go after her. He was so angry!"

Robert nodded in agreement, his face also showing concern. "Yeah, that he was. Have you been able to locate Jack?"

"No, I've tried. I pressed the watch officer at NOPD. He said Jack was out of the state, that he was investigating over in Alabama or Mississippi. I would think his cell phone would work over there, wouldn't you?" Alex paused for a moment, thinking. "I bet he found something out on Whitset. He said he was going to run a check on him in Alabama!" Alex was breathless for a moment then her face fell.

"What's the matter, Alex? If he found something out on Whitset, that's good, isn't it?" Robert looked at her intently.

"Yes, of course it is! I had convinced myself that he and Monique were off on some romantic interlude or something. I guess I'm a hopeless romantic. Heaven knows, they certainly deserve it after today."

Robert attempted to look cheerful. "Well, maybe they are investigating together. Anyway, I'm sure they're fine. Have you had any dinner?"

Alex shook her head. "No ... would you like for me to make something for us? I could whip us up something simple. Salad or something."

"I'd be glad to take you out, if you'd like."

"No, Robert, thanks. I prefer to stay in. I feel better here, particularly if the phone rings and it's either Jack or Monique. How about a fresh chicken salad and a glass of pinot noir?"

"Well, you know they can reach you on your cell, Alex. But, that being said, chicken salad and wine sounds great. Are you sure I'm not imposing? We could order out," Robert ventured.

"No, no. It will get my mind off things to be busy in the kitchen. I appreciate the company. I hate to be anxious alone. Come on back to the kitchen."

Robert and Alex retreated to Alex's newly renovated gourmet kitchen. Robert looked around, once again pleased at how beautifully Alex had renovated her New Orleans home. He reminded himself that he had never really appreciated her talent and abilities when they were married. He guessed he would be sorry for that for the rest of his natural life. He eyed the oak kitchen furniture appreciably and said, "I still love this furniture."

Alex smiled at him. "Yes, it's beautiful. One of our best purchases ...." They both remembered the beautiful fall afternoon when they had purchased the lovely antique oak furniture during a sojourn to the Virginia countryside. They had absolutely no money at that point in time. Robert had been a resident at the University of Virginia and she was a staff nurse in the ICU at the University hospital. They had fallen in love with the honey-colored oak furniture and had purchased it on impulse. Robert had worked three straight weekends in the emergency department at Martha Jefferson Hospital and Alex had worked many overtime shifts to pay for that extravagance. It'd been worth it. They'd dined on it during their marriage and spent many evenings sitting around it talking with good friends. Additionally, the couple used the table as a desk and spent many evenings studying around it together when they were students. The table, chairs, and sideboard were so large they had practically taken up the entire student housing apartment.

Alex was again remembering their first meal together at the table, how it was followed by a night of splendid and unparalleled passion in their marriage – the night she became pregnant with the child she later lost. That seemed to start the downward spiral of what she thought was a perfect marriage. She guessed Robert was remembering the same evening. Suddenly, they were interrupted by the shrill ringing of her telephone.

Alex quickly picked up the receiver. It was Donald Montgomery. She winced at the sound of his whiny voice.

"Destephano, have you gotten Monique Desmonde straightened out? This shit is bothering me. We can't have her blabbing to the press. Not good for us. Not good at all." Montgomery was whimpering into the phone.

Alex gritted her teeth and mouthed to Robert that it was Don. "No, Don, I haven't talked with Monique. I've been calling her since right after our meeting. I don't know where she is."

"Shit, she's probably at home writing her press release. Fix this, Alex. I mean it! Your butt's on the line!"

Alex could hear the irrational anger beginning to surface in the CEO's voice. "I'll do my best, Don. Did you look at Whitset's contract?" Alex skillfully returned the ball to Montgomery's court.

"No. I had a cocktail party to go to. I'll have it on your desk in the morning." Don was whining again.

"Good. Make sure you do. Whitset's the major player here. Make sure you can control him. I'm not your problem and neither is Monique." Alex knew her voice was condescending, but she didn't care.

"Dammit, Alex! Desmonde is the problem, not Whitset!"

"Don, you and I both know that there are a dozen Whitset's for every Monique Desmonde. You need to stand tall on this. If you lose Dr. Desmonde, you will lose psychiatry at CCMC."

"I don't give a damn about psychiatry! Let the wackos go! I just don't want any bad press!"

"You'll destroy our reputation as a world-class hospital. You must have a psychiatric service to keep the world-class

244

designation. You're going to get bad press if you don't get Whitset in line. After all, you are the CEO." Alex knew she was venturing on the fringe, but she didn't care. Don had already tried to fire her once this year – back in February. Her appointment by the hospital board of trustees made it impossible for Don to fire her without their approval. And, so far, they really liked her.

"All right, all right. Just fix Monique." He was backing down and his voice was contrite.

Alex rode her advantage home. "Look, Don. Think about it. Your win-win position is to keep Dr. Desmonde and psychiatry – even if Whitset and his management company have to go. Think about that."

"Okay, okay. Just keep Desmonde away from the press, promise?" Don's voice was placating now, sugarcoated.

Alex was disgusted. "I won't have to keep Monique from the press if you give her what she needs to provide safe, reasonable, standard care. Get the picture, Don?" Alex's voice was defiant.

"Yeah, yeah. I'll do what I can. You do your part." He clicked off the phone without saying goodbye.

"Bye to you too, you idiot!" Alex slammed down the phone. "I hate that Motherfucker," she grumbled to Robert.

Robert laughed. "Whoa! That's rough talk for you, Alex. Can I assume your boss hung up on you?"

"You bet he did. Slimeball!" Alex was quiet for a moment. Then she said, "Robert, I'm going to tell you the truth. I don't know how much longer I can stand working with him. He's an absolute idiot, a model of incompetence. He's the Peter Principle personified. I have a very interesting opportunity on my desk at the hospital. A large, managed care group is looking for a corporate attorney. Of course, I would have to leave New Orleans ..." Alex demurred a bit. "I'll never understand why the board keeps him here."

Robert gave her a matter-of-fact look and said, "Sure you do, Alex. For all of his faults, we all know why they keep Don around. Montgomery is a financial wizard. Crescent City is one of the few hospitals in New Orleans that is financially solvent. No one cares that he's rude, inappropriate, and non-appreciative of nurses, physicians, and other providers. No one cares that he's insensitive to needs of patients, staff, and families. They only care about money. *We* are making money and that is ultimately what it's all about – the bottom line, like it or not. CCMC has held together when other hospitals have gone out of business or have been bought up by conglomerates. Don will skillfully maneuver CCMC through health care reform. He understands the health care portability act better than the politicians that wrote it. That, my dear, is very simply Mr. Montgomery's strength."

Alex sighed. "Yeah, I know, Robert. But Don truthfully doesn't give a rip about the care that patients receive. He doesn't even know about clinical care. It seems unlikely that his success will continue."

Robert shrugged his shoulders. "Rest assured, it will continue as long as he keeps giving the physicians the technology they crave and the raises they deserve. I hate to give the man any accolades, but he's doing a fairly good job, all things considered. Even the nursing salaries are competitive, I hear."

"Yeah, but the quality of care is dropping and the working conditions suck. The nurses have absolutely no support. Bette Farve treats them like street workers, not like professionals. Money is important to nurses, but so is professionalism, research, and continuing education – important aspects of a nurse's role that Farve refuses to recognize. Motivation and morale is almost zilch at CCMC among nursing staff." Alex shook her head, "It's actually very sad because CCMC has some of the best nurses I've ever seen."

"Yes, a fact which the physician group is profoundly concerned about. None of them like Farve." Robert paused for a moment and winked at her, "Don't say anything to anyone, but I think Farve may take a fall in a few months."

"Robert," Alex's voice was gleeful, "That's the best news I've heard." She ran over and hugged him.

"Shish. Don't say anything. It is definitely in the making. I've just come from a medical staff meeting and Ms. Farve's leadership, or lack of it, was the topic of discussion. I'm sure it will happen. Just be patient. Besides, I don't want you anywhere other than New Orleans!"

Alex smiled to herself. She was enjoying the feel of being in his arms again. When she broke off the embrace, Alex literally danced around the kitchen making a gourmet salad of lettuce, cherry tomatoes, cucumbers, and fresh chicken breast. She even pulled out her food processor and made Robert's favorite salad dressing, a creamy vinaigrette, for old time's sake.

Robert knew what she was doing and was secretly pleased. Once again, he could kick his own ass for divorcing her.

"Robert, let's set the table in the dining room! It's been a long, lousy day. It deserves a good ending. No shoptalk at all. The china is in the linen press. I have a bottle of barrel-fermented Virginia chardonnay that should go well with the salad. It's great! Estate bottled at Windy River Winery, a new winery close to my grandparents' home in Hanover County. Grand shipped me four bottles last week. She's impressed with the quality – what do you say?"

"Why in heaven's name would I argue with such a beautiful lady? I'm on my way to set the table." Robert was feeling happy and lighthearted as he moved into Alex's formal dining room. He switched on the brilliant crystal chandelier. It glowed magnificently against the pale blue moiré of the wallpaper. He adjusted the dimmer switch to a low light level until Alex's antique silver service glistened in the light. The silver candlesticks and fresh flowers were beautifully set against the antique mahogany and cherry of the dining room furniture. Robert sighed in appreciation as he looked around the room. The Sheraton banquet table gleamed in the light of the chandelier. Again, he was awed by Alex's taste. He wondered briefly if Mitch Landry had been a part of the house's renovation. A flicker of jealousy flowed through him. Then he realized that Mitch couldn't have been. He remembered they had started seeing each other three months after Alex had moved in to the renovated townhouse. The flat was obviously Alex's creation alone. For some reason, that pleased him.

He continued to think about the relationship between Mitch and Alex, as he removed the heavy silver from the drawer of the sideboard. He'd known Mitch for years and had been a little perturbed when he had learned that Mitch and Alex were dating. Of course, Mitch had been charming. He was sincerely sorry at the way things had ended. But, to be honest, it did allow him an opportunity to win Alex back. Oh, and how Robert wanted her again. He had been such a fool – young and foolish, a real macho idiot. He could admit that to himself now. Monique had helped him see that.

He had wanted Alex to be a typical haus frau, a stay at home wife and mother. That was what his mother had been. Of course, his mother had always done civic and charity work. She was a proverbial do-gooder. Back then, that was what he thought all men wanted, a wife that stayed at home and cared for the home and children. He never thought a man wanted a professional wife, one who shared his world. Looking back, he guessed it was a culture thing. He'd just recently realized that marriage in the world he lived in was very different than the world his parents shared.

Thank goodness for Monique Desmonde! Now, due to her influence, he saw things differently. He wanted Alex, just as she was. Actually, since he had gotten older, Robert had learned that his mother had given up her professional career for his father. She had been a well-known classical violinist. Of course, it hadn't been all bad. She was the first lady of Louisiana when his dad was governor, and now she was a ranking senator's wife. Still, Robert realized, his mother had made considerable sacrifices throughout the years, missed opportunities she could never regain.

As Robert opened the antique linen press, he felt a little maudlin. The china was the same. Alex was still using their wedding china. It was English Aynsley, the pattern, Capistrano. He hadn't liked the china when they were married. He had considered it too busy, garish in fact. Now he thought the colors were beautiful and the birds magnificent. What a purist he had been in those days! He'd wanted china that was white, with a platinum ring around the edge. He had possessed no imagination at all back then, only a preconceived notion of what a wife, a woman, should be.

Alex had fought him on the china decision, telling him continually that if the Queen of England dined on Aynsley, so could they. He had acquiesced, but had never liked the china with its colorful birds and flowers. Now he touched the plates fondly, as if trying to atone for his former dislike. He loved the china. It was beautiful. It was so very Alex, beautifully designed, etched, and colored. He had just finished setting the table when Alex appeared in the doorway with the salad in a large cut glass bowl and a silver basket full of French bread.

"Robert, you did great! When did you learn to set the table? Good job ... I'm impressed." Alex really was pleased.

Before and during their marriage, Robert would never have helped her in the kitchen, much less have set the table. She looked around. The silver, china, wine and water goblets were perfectly placed on the table. She continued, "If you light the candles, I'll get the wine. It's chilling in the silver ice bucket in the kitchen."

Alex was thinking about how much Robert had changed, as she returned to the kitchen. He was a wonderful man. Kind, good, even tempered. A healer. Would she ever recover from the distrust and feelings of abandonment he had left her with? Maybe, just maybe, she could. She felt her heart beat pick up. Maybe they could get back together. She knew Robert was interested. She believed Robert loved her and always had – but he did have a lot of baggage. He had been an excellent surgeon prior to his injury earlier in the year, and while he seemed to be coping well with his limitations, Alex knew he was prone to depression. Of course, what man wouldn't be? He had been at the precipice of national fame prior to his injury and had pioneered several surgical techniques that were now written in the medical books. After all, it was quite possible that a brilliant surgical career had ended in a gun battle at the Endymion extravaganza during Mardi Gras.

Alex also remembered that Robert was a wonderful lover. She briefly allowed herself to think back to their married years and, as her heart quickened, she felt her legs weaken. Even when they weren't getting along, they had always had a consuming passion for each other. They had been great lovers. She felt a little nervous about the dinner. What was going to happen? What would she do if one thing led to another? Well, she made up her mind. She would just savor the day. Wasn't that the avant-garde thing to do? Besides, it'd been so long. There had only been one other man in her life since Robert, a physician in Texas. She and Mitch had never been intimate sexually. Why, it'd been over two years. No wonder! Alex's heart began to flutter.

Robert reappeared in the kitchen. She heard the sounds of Vladimir Horowitz, her favorite pianist and Robert's favorite as well. He had remembered and played the CD for her. She was beginning to feel wonderful. She felt the tension drop from her body like a discarded garment.

Robert smiled at her – a deep, caring, and sensual smile. She looked into his eyes. She knew the look, the sensitive eyes that smoldered and bespoke of countless pleasures to come. He said in his deep voice, "May I escort the lovely lady into dinner?" He was so gallant, so cultured, so ... French. So sexy. She loved this.

Alex laughed a little nervously and accepted his arm. "Of course ... I'd be honored," she said, remembering her Virginia upbringing.

He seated her to his right, and he sat at the head of the table. He deftly poured the wine and served her salad.

For a moment, Alex had a flashback. This evening was so typical of the evenings she and Mitch had spent at her house. Only Mitch had been seated at her table. No other man had ever graced her dining room. She pushed the thought from her mind, not wanting to think about Mitch tonight. Mitch wasn't an option any longer.

She had a fleeting thought of what her grandmother, Kathryn Rosseau Lee, would do in a similar situation. It was easy. Grand would tell her to go for it. Grand was such a pragmatist, a wise lady and so fair with people, their flaws, and relationships. Besides, hadn't Grand encouraged her in March to try and rekindle her love for Robert? Hadn't she urged her to consider reconciliation when they'd been in Virginia in the spring? Grand had suggested this and Alex had brushed it off, way too raw from the death of Mitch.

Actually, Alex couldn't be hard on her grandmother, her mentor. Grand had suggested to her in her exacting, precise, and practical way, "Alex, my dear, real love comes only once. Robert was your first love, just as Adam was mine. People fall in and out of love with each other many times throughout a marriage. My generation, we put up with each other, but you younger folks run for divorce – an easy out which prevents people from trying to work things out—"

Alex had interrupted her grandmother, angry and defensive at the conversation. She'd accused her grandmother of blaming her for ending her marriage. Boy, she had some raw nerves back then.

Kathryn had denied this, saying only that she was sure Robert still loved and wanted her. Because the conversation had been painful for Alex and the loss of Mitch so recent, Alex had abruptly ended the conversation. Her grandmother had assured her that she understood and asked only that Alex keep an open mind with regard to Robert's intentions. She asked that Alex be honest with herself. Grand also mentioned she knew Alex had secrets locked in her heart, as Grand did herself. Alex had found this remark particularly perplexing. One day when she wasn't so emotional, she would ask Grand about her secrets.

Robert interrupted her thoughts. "Alex, what are you thinking?" His dark eyes bored into hers.

"I was just thinking about Grand. Something she said to me when we were home. It's nothing really. How's your salad, Robert?"

"It's wonderful! Just as you are, Alex. I'm going to savor this evening – it's perfect!"

Robert reached for Alex's hand and rubbed it gently, tracing the veins in her hands softly. Alex again remembered the passion of their marriage. She decided to let herself be romanced and lured. It felt so good.

Robert continued, "You know, Alex. You're so fortunate to have had your grandparents. They are fine people. The very best actually. I admire them both."

She laughed. "Even Granddad? You always said you never had a handle on how Adam felt about you. Has that changed?"

Robert contemplated her remarks. "No, I guess not. But, I still admire Adam Patrick Lee. He's one of the most noble and ethical men I have ever met." He looked a little sheepish. "I don't think Adam Lee thinks any man is good enough for his Alex."

Alex smiled at him.

"And you know what," Robert continued, "He may be right."

Alex smiled at Robert. Their eyes locked. He continued to stroke her hand. She looked at him, conscious that she was going to have to make a decision very soon – a decision that could possibly affect the relationship for a long time, maybe even forever.

Alex said to Robert gently, "Robert, I don't have any dessert. Sorry." Alex pretended to ponder this impropriety.

He finally said, "Well, I guess I'll accept a dance instead. Isn't that Richard Clayderman?"

Alex nodded. Clayderman, a popular pianist, was playing a romantic medley of songs. They moved into the living room to dance. Alex was pleased that Robert had cut off the lamps and had lit the electric wall sconces. The room was romantic, the sconces casting a warm, mellow glow over the pastel furniture.

Robert and Alex began dancing, each caught up in their own thoughts about the rest of the evening. It was a wonderful feeling for Alex. She felt like a teenager. It seemed so right. After all, Robert had been her husband. That made it feel especially right. Besides, it felt perfect in his arms. It was so familiar.

Robert was thinking the same thing. He felt sure he was interpreting Alex correctly. He wanted her to want the same things as he did. He wasn't looking for a one-night stand. He was looking for the opportunity to reclaim his wife. He said to her softly, "Alex, I love you. I've always loved you. I want to be with you, but only if you really want me."

She moved her head from his shoulder and looked at him directly. His eyes were smoldering with passion and love. She knew the delights they held.

She said simply, "I want you, too, Robert. I can't promise anything forever, but I want you."

He pulled her closer and kissed her. A long, lingering, passionate kiss.

Alex felt her heart beat faster and her legs and arms become weak with anticipation. She was aware of the degree of Robert's passion, as he held her in his arms. She took his hand and led him into her bedroom. "Give me a moment, Robert, so I can brush my teeth."

He laughed at her, remembering that this was Alex's prelude to love. He said, "I'll do the same."

Alex went into her bathroom, stripped off her clothes, and changed into a satin gown. She reemerged and found Robert waiting for her in her bed. No, it was their antique walnut bed with the deeply carved rosewood ten-foot headboard.

For a moment, Alex was infinitely glad she had Helene, her cleaning lady, continue to put satin sheets on her bed. Over the past couple of years, she'd laughed at herself for using them, but now, it was worth it.

She smiled shyly at Robert and he pulled her into bed. She fell into his arms. Robert was naked and she felt his muscled, lean body press against her as they embraced. She breathed a sigh of contentment as he kissed her. It was beautiful. It was poignantly familiar, it seemed so right. It was right, Alex convinced herself. She loved the way he smelled, so fresh and masculine. She was giving herself up to a night of ecstasy, when the phone rang. Robert gave a little, sad moan. Alex giggled and picked it up. It was Monique. Alex felt guilty. She had forgotten all about Monique and Jack.

"Alex, can you meet me? I have got to talk to you! I can't find Jack!" Monique's voice was strangely hollow and frightened.

Alex looked at her alarm clock. It was almost 11:00 p.m. She said, "Of course, Monique. Are you okay? You sound frightened. Where are you?"

"I am frightened and I'm at home. Would you like to come here?" Monique picked up on Alex's hesitation. "I could come there, but I'm not sure that someone ..."

"No, you stay there. I'll come over. I'll be there in about twenty minutes."

"Thanks, Alex. I appreciate it." Monique sounded relieved.

Alex looked at Robert, who smiled at her sheepishly. "Could I have a rain check," she asked demurely.

He laughed. "You bet! You can have any kind of check you want. Monique okay?"

"I think so. She said she was frightened and wanted to talk." Alex became apologetic. "If it was anything or anyone else, I would've said no, but ..."

"Alex. It's okay. Believe me, I understand. Want me to go?"

"No. But if I need you, I'll call. Deal?"

"You bet. I'll drop you off."

Robert and Alex looked at each other shyly. Robert finally said, "I won't look, if you won't look."

"Okay ... another deal. Shut your eyes!"

"Okay." Robert pretended to shut his eyes as his beautiful former wife bounded naked from the bed, clutching only a sheet. She had the elegance of a gazelle. She turned around and smiled at him as she ran into the master bath.

God, she's beautiful, he thought to himself. *She looks like a goddess with her alabaster skin and perfect body. She hasn't changed at all. In fact, she looks better now than she did ten years ago.* He was right. Alex's long legs and buttocks were perfectly formed. Her tiny waist was the same. If anything, she had improved. He sighed as he retreated into the guest bath to dress. *Well,* he thought to himself, *it was almost a perfect night.* It was certainly more perfect than he had ever dreamed of on his way over. Robert smiled to himself. *I love her,* he thought. *I really love her. Please God, please make her want me back,* he prayed to himself.

Chapter 28

Lester Whitset was having a rough evening. He was furious about Dr. Desmonde breaking into his office. He also knew that Anthony Gavette had seen him come out of Rose's room. That had pissed him off, especially when Anthony started screaming rape while hurling obscenities and threats at him. Lester decided he really didn't give a damn about Anthony. Anthony was the least of his problems.

The voices had been screaming at him all night, since he left the hospital and went home. He had tried to stop them, but couldn't. His head was hurting so badly, that Whitset decided on a chemical fix, something he rarely did. Sometimes it helped calm the voices down and send them away. The booze and pills made him feel mellow and he deserved it. It'd been a bad day. Then, when he was calm and could think better, he could decide what to do about that imposter shrink bitch.

Lester went to his bar and poured himself a tumbler full of scotch whiskey. After gulping the golden liquid, he went into his tiny bathroom to look for his Xanax. Damn, the bottle was empty. He'd have to steal some tomorrow off the medication cart. He refilled his tumbler again and drank it all.

Finally, the whiskey was helping. The voices were fading. He thought again about Rose. He knew she would be loyal to him. She had shared in his little game. He continued to think about her as he drank heavily. He suspected Rose had told Anthony about the little game they'd been playing. Whitset considered Anthony his closest equal on the unit. He also knew that Anthony coveted the little waiflike patient.

Anthony had told Lester one night, over a week ago, that he had wanted Rose for his own. Whitset had laughed at

Anthony, reminding him that he was, after all, only a patient and not the administrator, like Les, who had the pick of the female patient litter. Anthony had gotten mad, but Lester calmed him down, assuring him that he liked his women tall and lush, like Angela Richelieu – not like the skinny little waif, Rose. Eventually, Anthony had cooled off, feeling confident that Lester was telling the truth.

Whitset had put on a real show for Anthony and had spent most of the evening watching the beautiful nurse as she worked on the unit. Anthony had watched his every move. Whitset had even followed Angie into the glassed medication room, making obscene gestures behind her back in an effort to prove his point to Anthony and the other patients watching from the day room. Anthony had seemed pretty convinced. Whitset had thought what a dumbass Gavette was. Just a stupid, ignoramus crazy.

Whitset smiled as he remembered how he foiled Anthony. Yes, Anthony was close to his equal, but of course, Lester was the superior being. The two men had a lot in common, but Whitset was the leader. After all, he was the administrator and Anthony was a lowly patient without any power. Lester had all the power, except some that the shrink bitch thought she had. He mustn't think about that, he told himself. Tut, tut, for Anthony Gavette. He smiled as he relived the evening. As soon as Anthony had been medicated and hauled off to bed by the psych tech, Whitset had reentered Rose's room.

As the evening wore on and Whitset continued to drink, he daydreamed about the night with Rose. It had been good, so good. Rose was exactly what he had needed. The two had played like children, naughty children of course, for over two hours. Lester had been able to be himself with her. He was so happy when he had learned that Rose likes the simple little games of house that he had made up. He became more excited when he learned that Rose hadn't minded when the big burglar came in, killed her husband, and then raped her in the special way that only Lester knew how to do. He had ignored Rose when she had cried for help. He knew she loved it.

Whitset shook himself when he realized he had drooled all down the front of his shirt. He got up to get a towel and shuddered when he thought of Angela Richelieu. She was a big, gross, woman pig. He had hated her. Still did. She was trouble. She wasn't obedient. She never had been – like Rose. He felt grossed out at the thought of Angela. He knew he'd have to take care of her if she woke up. *It kind of made him happy ... it would be a pleasant "chore"*, he thought to himself.

Whitset began to feel agitated again and poured himself another glass of whiskey, drinking it quickly. It was good. Booze really did help him. He felt better. He was calm. Whitset looked down at his pants. He had a huge hard on. He thought about Rose again and smiled to himself as he checked his watch. It was a little past nine. He knew that pretty soon it would be lights out at the Pavilion. He had just enough time to finish his drink and go to the Pavilion to sample a few more of Rose's favors. Maybe he'd get off this time! And, afterwards, maybe he'd go into Anthony's room and lord it over him. Tell him about the little game he and Rose played, about how she preferred him to the big, powerful Anthony. Lester smiled and clapped his hands in anticipation of his plans for the evening. He felt like such a naughty boy.

His phone rang. It shrilled endlessly in the still apartment. At first, Whitset was disoriented. He had only gotten one or two phone calls in the six months he had lived in New Orleans. They had been from long distance telephone services trying to sell him cheaper long-distance rates. He picked it up. It was Don Montgomery.

"Whitset, is that you?" Don Montgomery, demanded. "Say something to me, dammit!"

Whitset recovered swiftly. "Don, what's up? Where are you?"

"I'm in my car on the way home. Have you decided to hire the staff we talked about?" Don's voice was laced with static. The cell reception was terrible.

Whitset was annoyed. He hated cell phones. He said clearly, "No, I'm not hiring anyone. I told you my decision today. We don't need all that staff. It costs too much and it's stupid."

"Whitset," Don's voice was placating, "We have got to do something, or else Desmonde will go to the press. You heard her today. Whitset, just hire them temporarily. We can get rid of them when all this quiets down. Nobody will listen to her story in two weeks or a month. I think we should give her what she wants – at least for now." Don's voice ended in a whine.

Whitset, hardly sober, reviewed his options. "Don't worry, Don. I'll take care of Desmonde. I'll talk to her again."

"She's not going to back down. I know the woman. You have got to give her what she wants now. Do it, Whitset, it's worth it. I promise it will be a temporary fix."

Lester felt himself losing control. The voices were back, telling him to get the shrink bitch. He could barely talk coherently. "I said I would take care of it, Don. Don't worry. See you tomorrow." Whitset hung up the phone.

"Whitset, you sound funny. You sure you're okay?" Don repeated his question again before he realized the administrator had hung up. The CEO said out loud in his car, "You had better take care of it, you damned asshole! If you don't, I'm canceling your contract and I'll make sure you never get another job anywhere." Don floored his gold

Porsche and drove recklessly down Canal Street towards his house.

Whitset sat on the sofa. The voices had completely taken over his head. In his mind, he again saw Dr. Desmonde turn to plastic in front of him. He was going to have to do what the voices told him to do. The imposter shrink had to be stopped. After all, wasn't that his mission? He was supposed to get rid of all the imposters. They told him so. Whitset grabbed his tie and left his French Quarter apartment.

He wandered aimlessly for about an hour through the sultry New Orleans heat into the Vieux Carre, trying to decide what to do. He sat on a bench, holding his head, trying to argue with the voices. Nobody looked at him. After all, he was in the French Quarter of New Orleans with all kinds of people from all walks of life. He fit right into the crowd. He finally acquiesced to the voices and entered a phone booth to look for Monique's address. Phone booths were a bit of an anachronism in most cities, but New Orleans still had them. Phone booths were still around for the throngs of people who could not afford cell phones. He found no listing for Monique Desmonde.

He was furious. Why didn't the shrink bitch have an address? Maybe imposters didn't really live in houses. They seem to appear only now and then. Perhaps they were already dead. Whitset batted this idea around in his head for a few minutes. It certainly seemed plausible to him. Finally, an idea dawned in his drunken head.

Whitset reached for his cell phone and called CCMC information. He identified himself and the hospital operator bought his story and gave him Monique's phone number and address. He was in luck. She lived on Royal Street in the Quarter, only a few blocks away. He dialed the number and got a machine or voicemail. He was livid. He hated answering machines and voicemail. His calls were too important to be picked up by a piece of equipment. Machines represented more of the technology he hated. In frustration, he slammed the receiver down, chipping a large chunk of plastic out of his iPhone.

The voices were loud again, screaming at him. Whitset entered a bar and ordered a double whiskey, which he downed in rapid time. He had a second drink. It was now almost 10:30 p.m. He walked over to the wall phone in the bar and dialed the psychiatrist's phone number. She answered on the first ring. He could see her cold, plastic face talking to him. Her lips were just as red as his teacher's had been – taut, thin, and inflexible. He would change that. Soon. She said hello three times before he hung up. He decided to have another drink or two for the road and the work ahead.

Chapter 29

Monique was unnerved by the hang-up phone call. She pressed redial, but no one spoke or answered her repeated "hello". There was just a dead, ominous silence. Whitset listened on the other end of the phone, relishing the increasing panic in the shrink bitch's voice.

Monique tried to convince herself that she was being paranoid. It could've been anybody – even a wrong number. In desperation, she dialed Jack's home phone and cell again. No answer. Then she paged his beeper, entering her number with the 911. She waited fifteen minutes for a return call, but her phone didn't ring.

Jack, Jack, where are you, she said to herself. *I'm frightened half to death. I have to find you. I have the answers you need.* Monique, her hands shaking, looked up the non-emergency phone number of the NOPD in the New Orleans phone directory. Finally, after an endless amount of time, she was connected with the watch officer. He chuckled when she asked for Commander Françoise.

The watch officer said, "The commander sure is popular tonight, Dr. Desmonde, and you're the second person looking for him. He's out of New Orleans. He's investigating a crime over in Alabama. He's been gone and unreachable all afternoon."

Monique was panicked. "Has he called in?"

"Nope, not since six o'clock this evening. Said he would be unavailable until morning."

"Can you reach him? It's really urgent." Monique was working hard to keep the hysteria out of her voice.

"No, ma'am. If the commander could be reached, he would've left a number. If you need help, I'll send a blue and white over," the watch officer offered, trying hard to be helpful. He felt sorry for the poor lady. He knew something was very wrong.

"No, no. I'm all right. I'll call a friend." Monique managed to say, as she was fighting for control.

"Listen, Dr. Desmonde, if you're in any danger, just tell me. I'll send a car over. The commander said that if you called and needed anything, I was to give you everything you needed, plus more."

Monique smiled at the watch officer's remarks and said, "What I need is Jack Françoise. I'll call a friend to come over. Thanks. If the commander does call, please tell him to call me stat."

"Huh, stat? What do you mean?" The watch officer didn't understand and he'd picked up on the frantic sound of Monique's voice.

"ASAP. As soon as possible," Monique clarified.

"Yes, ma'am. I will. Take care now. Good night."

Monique laughed a little hysterically. "Yes, I will. Thank you."

After Monique hung up the phone, the watch officer radioed the mobile unit closest to Monique's house and asked them to drive by periodically. They assured him they would. It was a good move on the part of the watch officer, a very good move. Besides, he didn't want to piss off the commander. He'd done that once before and was, to this day, stinging from the rebuke. No one ever wanted to mess with Commander Jack Françoise – not because he was a commander, but because he was Jack Françoise.

Monique decided to call Alex and was relieved that she was coming over. Alex had a good analytical mind and would help her sort out what she needed to do. Finally, after an endless period of time, she heard a knock at her door. Alex was standing on her porch. Monique noticed the silver Mercedes with the lights on out front.

"Alex, thank goodness. I'm so glad to see you. Who's in the car?"

"It's Robert. He dropped me off. He was over for dinner and we —"

"Oh, I'm so sorry," Monique interrupted her. She looked at her friend. Alex looked lovely. Her eyes were as blue as the denim work shirt and jeans she had hastily donned for her late-night visit. Her beautiful face was flushed and her eyes were shining. Monique didn't think she had ever seen Alex look so ravishing. She continued, "I interrupted something, didn't I?" Her voice was apologetic.

"Monique, it's okay. I'll tell you about it later. What's up? You look scared, frightened to death. I've been trying to find you all evening. Where were you?"

"I was so angry after the executive committee meeting, that I decided to go to City Park and walk off my frustrations. Then, I went over to the Art Museum to see the Monet exhibit." Monique paused for a moment, capturing in her mind again the beauty and elegance of the French artist's late works at Giverny. "It was magnificent ... and sad. Alex, you really must go."

"I will, I will. Then what happened?" Alex asked impatiently.

"I went to the Pavilion. It's a good thing I did. One of my patients had been raped, Rose, remember her?"

Alex's heart sank. Another attack and rape. When would it end? "Of course I know Rose. Is she okay? Who raped her?"

"Physically she's okay. She won't tell who did it. One of the psych techs found her lying in her bed whimpering. She wasn't in the day room for supper. That's when they went to search for her and found her sobbing. I tried to get her to tell me who did it, but she just looked at me and cried."

"Was it Jim or Anthony?"

"No, impossible. Both of them were locked in seclusion. I don't know who it was. Anyway, we sent her to the emergency department. She hadn't returned to the unit when I left...." Monique's voice trailed off.

Alex pondered her comments. "I can't imagine who did it. With Jim and Anthony locked up, our saga has a new twist. I guess we'll know later." Alex looked at her friend. She had become very quiet. She was sitting on the sofa, twisting her hands.

"Monique, what else happened? What else do you know? Tell me, for goodness sake!"

"This sounds crazy, Alex. Bear with me, but it's true. Whitset is not Whitset."

"Huh, what! What the hell are you talking about? For heaven's sake, Monique, spit it out. Make sense." Alex's voice was snappish. After all, her friend had just interrupted the first potential sex she had had in years.

"Stop interrupting me, Alex. I'm doing my best." Monique paused for a moment, as if getting her facts straight. "This afternoon when I searched Whitset's office, I noticed the diplomas on the wall were dated 1963 and 1965. Whitset doesn't look old enough to have graduated that long ago. So, I went to my office and looked in the personnel file at his resume. He lists his date of birth as being 1951. It's inconceivable that he could have graduated with a Master's degree in 1965. Whitset is an imposter. I don't know who in the hell he is, but I'm convinced that he's parading around as a psychiatric administrator without the education."

Alex was quiet, taking all of this in. Finally, she said, "Who do you think he is, Monique?"

Monique shook her head. "I don't have a clue. I think he's probably a former psych patient who somehow got hold of the real Whitset's degrees and has been pretending to be him for years! Unbelievable, isn't it?"

266

Alex sighed deeply. "Yes, it is, but it does explain his outbursts this morning. He's definitely a crazy."

Monique glared at her. "Come on, Alex, cut me some slack. You know I hate that term. It's unfair to label people like that."

Alex waved Monique's objections away. "Okay, sorry. Anyway, we have an unbalanced, possibly very mentally ill man running our psychiatric service. Now, that's a real legal problem! Monique, did you find anything else in his office that could lead us to figure out who he really is?"

"Alex, I'm freezing to death. Do you mind if I open the French doors for a few minutes? Maybe we could go outside for a few minutes so I can warm up." Monique's teeth were chattering, more from fear than the air-conditioning.

"That'll warm you up. It's still in the high eighties out there. Hot and sultry. Nope, I don't mind. Let's do it."

Monique unlocked the deadbolt on her French door and walked out on the balcony.

Alex followed her. It did feel a little better. Alex was cold too.

"Do you mind if we sit out here for a few minutes? I promise I won't keep you out here long. As soon as we warm up, we'll go back in." Monique rubbed her arms, as if to rub away the uncertainty and chill bumps.

Alex smiled, "Of course not. These chairs look pretty comfortable." Alex seated herself. "Monique, this is really a lovely balcony." She admired the perfectly manicured, flowering plants in hanging baskets. "You're quite a gardener."

"As are you. Yes, I love working out here. It's a great stress reliever. Where were we?"

Alex thought back for a second. "I had just asked if you had found anything else in Whitset's – or whoever he is – office?"

"No. Place was obsessively neat and clean. It was very dark in there. Drapes were completely drawn. There was nothing else significant."

Alex pressed for more. "Tell me everything you remember about the office, Monique. Was there any correspondence on his desk, books, anything like that?"

Monique thought hard. "He had some current psychiatric journals and textbooks lying around. The most significant things were his degrees. Of course, I could've missed something. Someone knocked on the door when I was in there. I thought I was going to have a heart attack! Scared me to death! My heart was racing!"

"What did you do?" Alex could imagine Monique's fright and it bothered her immensely that someone knew she was in there. "Who do you think it was?"

"It could've been the cleaning staff. Anyway, I crouched under his desk for a few minutes."

"Did you go through his desk drawers?"

Monique raised her eyebrows at Alex and laughed, "Of course, I did. I was playing super snoop. It was the usual stuff. Oh ..." Monique's voice trailed off again.

Perceiving that Monique had remembered something, Alex urged her. "What, Monique, what else did you see?"

"It's probably nothing. His bottom right drawer was locked. There was a fine gold chain hanging out of it. It looked like a woman's gold chain. I only noticed it because I was hiding on the floor beside his desk." Monique's voice was noncommittal as she told the story to Alex.

Alex's head had started thundering. She felt the hairs on her neck stand up. Her entire body went weak all over and she felt dizzy. She said to Monique in a strained voice, "Monique, are you warm enough to go in? I'm feeling really warm!"

The psychiatrist couldn't see Alex's face in the dark, but she distinguished the change in her voice. She knew something was wrong. She said, "Sure, I've warmed up. Let's go in and have some ice coffee."

Neither woman saw the crouched body of Lester Whitset hidden behind the latticework and a massive copper planter at the end of the balcony. He'd heard every word the women had said and he was enraged. The voices were screaming in his head. Kill ... Kill ... Kill. Whitset was drenched with sweat. *Would the voices ever stop?*

Chapter 30

Alex could barely breathe as she entered Monique's living room. She was weak and trembling all over. Monique looked at her strangely. "What is it, Alex? What is it?"

For once, Alex was too frightened to speak. She was speechless.

Monique instructed her in an authoritarian tone of voice. "Alex, take some deep breaths and calm down. You've got time. What you've got to say will keep until you get control of yourself." Monique sounded stronger than she felt. She was terrified at the look in Alex's eyes. After a minute or so, Alex was able to speak.

"It's Whitset. It's Whitset," she gasped, stopping to take a breath. "Monique, Whitset's the one that raped and beat Angie!" Alex gasped out the words, her heart racing and pounding in her chest.

Monique stayed calm. She faced Alex, standing by the French doors. "Whitset? How do you know, Alex? What makes you so sure?" Monique noted the fast pounding and beating of her own heart.

"Because … because … the chain, the gold chain you saw, goes to her cross, her religious medal. Bridgett brought it to me today in the office. I took it to a jeweler this afternoon to have the chain replaced." Alex was so weak from her discovery, she wasn't sure she could stand.

Monique felt the force of the earth coming down on her shoulders. She could hardly speak. She was so frightened. She was about to ask Alex whether she thought Whitset was involved with Mrs. Smithson's murder, when, to her horror, her French door opened and Lester Whitset entered her living room carrying a long metal pipe.

Alex turned and froze in place. Monique looked like a marble statue. She was transfixed. All color had drained from her face.

Whitset stared at Monique. It happened again. She was so white. She was plastic. Once again, right in front of his eyes, she had turned to plastic. So, he had been right. The voices were screaming at him to kill the shrink. Lester watched in horror and fascination as Monique's face assumed a hard, shiny appearance. Her green eyes turned into emerald green plastic ovals. Lester could hardly stand what he was seeing.

He stared at the psychiatrist and said in a cold, measured voice, "I'm going to kill you, you shrink bitch imposter. They are telling me to!"

Monique spoke to him through her pale plastic lips. Lester was startled because she could speak. He had never heard an imposter talk and it confused him. Once they turned, they lost their voice, but, he recognized her voice. Yes, he said to himself, it's her, it's still the shrink bitch. Even though she's plastic, she is the same bad person.

Whitset made no response to Monique's question. He continued to look at her, a slow smile spreading across his face. He looked very pleased with himself. Finally, he turned towards Alex and said to her in a slow and sexy voice, "Alex, I'm so glad you're here." He shook his head a little, as if to clear it. "As soon as I take care of her, we can leave. I wasn't sure you would meet me."

Whitset raped her body with his eyes and returned to her face, his eyes boring into hers. Alex ventured a look at him out of the side of her eyes. His intent was clear. Whitset meant to rape her. A large amount of spittle had again gathered at the side of his mouth and had begun to run down his chin.

Alex stood mutely trying to decide the best thing to do. Whitset moved closer to her, reached out and gingerly touched her. She flinched at his touch.

Whitset became angry. He gawked at her, squinting as if to see her better. Was she one of them too? No, she didn't appear to be. Her face stayed the same. He reached out and touched her face. It was warm and soft. She didn't move. Lester was satisfied. Alex was real. She wasn't an imposter like the bitch standing next to her.

Alex stood there, like a dead person, while Whitset began to run his hands over her body. He put his face next to hers and started to kiss her. She was overwhelmed by the smell of whiskey.

Suddenly, he pulled back in anger. He was furious. He screamed at her. "You whore! You slut! You've been with somebody else! Who is your lover? Who have you been with, whore?" Whitset was dancing around with rage, waving his lead pipe madly.

Her voice was frozen. She tried to talk, but couldn't. Only grunts came from her throat. She looked frantically at Monique.

Monique had been contemplating the best approach to use with Whitset. She decided to try a blunt one – one that would catch him off guard and give them an opportunity to defend themselves.

Monique addressed Whitset, her voice hard. "Whitset, what are you doing here? Don't you know the police are watching this place? They're probably looking for you by now."

Lester looked at Monique and laughed, the sound of a maniac – a loud, piercing, surreal laugh. "Shut up you bitch imposter! Just shut up!" He moved towards Monique and pushed her hard against the sofa. She fell backwards on it. "I'll take care of you in a minute." He turned to Alex and said in a sad, soft voice, "How could you do this to me, Alex? How could you betray me? You know I want you. I love you. We've been special for a long time. How could you be with someone else?"

"Lester, I didn't." Alex finally found her voice and it was soft. "You look so tired. Why don't you just sit down for a few minutes and I'll get you something cold to drink. Then, we'll talk."

Whitset smiled at Alex, the same slow, seductive smile that gave her chills. He said softly, "You're a bad girl, Alex. You're very naughty. Very, very, naughty. Lester's going to make you pay for being naughty."

Then Whitset began to sing to her, once again in that childlike voice that rhymed.

"Alex is a bad, bad girl,
Bad as all girls in the world,
Lester's going to make her pay,
Lester's going to have his way, way, way, way…."

The sound of his voice and the emphasis on the word "way" froze Alex's blood. She stood paralyzed with fear as he approached her.

Whitset's stride was broken, disjointed, as he moved towards Alex with an evil and threatening look on his face. He hurled himself towards her, the lead pipe raised in fury. He swung the pipe at her head, but Alex ducked, barely missing contact with the lead. She felt the cool rush of wind whistle by her ear. The stark realization of what was happening propelled Alex into action. She moved behind the chair, ducking another swing of the pipe.

Monique came to life and attacked the administrator from behind. She jumped on his back, her arms around his throat as she shoved her knee up into his groin. With a loud yell, Whitset threw her off and she fell to the floor, striking her head on the edge of a marble table.

Whitset laughed at her as he clutched his groin. "Look at you, you plastic bitch. I see your plastic head did not split. As soon as you wake up, I'll really fix you. I'll split that plastic head!" Then, he began to laugh again – the high pitched, rumbling laugh of a maniac. The sound was the most evil cacophony that Alex had ever heard. She bent to the floor to help her friend.

Just then, the phone rang. It rang three times, as Alex, who was sitting on the floor by Monique, and Whitset each looked at it. Finally, Monique's voicemail clicked on and Alex heard Commander Françoise's voice.

He was desperate. "Monique, where are you? Answer the phone!" There was a pause, and then Jack's voice continued, "Stay inside and lock your door! I have information on Whitset. He is parading around as his brother. I think he's Weston Whitset, the brother of Lester Whitset. If it's him, and I'm sure it is, he was locked up in the hospital for the criminally insane in Alabama for years after killing two women and possibly more. I've been here in Alabama all night gathering information. I've called the precinct and they'll be checking on you." Jack's voice stopped again. Finally, in a desperate voice he said, "I love you, Monique. I'll be there soon. Please stay safe."

Whitset went into a rage after hearing the message. He took his lead pipe and beat the phone repeatedly with it. He ripped the phone plug out of the wall. The low sound caught his attention. He whirled around in his mania and saw that Alex and Monique were talking softly. Monique was attempting to sit up. He gave another furious howl and swung the lead pipe at Monique's head, striking her fiercely on the right side. Monique immediately slumped and lost consciousness.

Alex cringed at the sound of the pipe breaking Monique's skull. She knew Whitset's blow had been a deadly one. She watched helplessly as Whitset cut Monique's face with a knife he had in his belt.

Alex stood up slowly, seething with hate and rage at her attacker. Her voice was filled with fury and wrath. "You crazy bastard, you've killed her!" Alex grabbed a porcelain lamp and hurled it towards Whitset. It missed him, but landed on the wrought-iron balcony, breaking into a thousand pieces.

Whitset laughed again, the high pitch sound of a maniac, as he sprang towards Alex, knocking her to the floor. He began ripping off her clothes and hitting her in the face.

She fought against him furiously. It was a losing battle. Whitset had the superhuman power of the criminally insane.

Chapter 31

Officer Josh Martin came on duty at 11. He'd learned and reported that Ms. Destephano and Dr. Desmonde had called the precinct looking for the commander. The watch officer had described Dr. Desmonde's voice as desperate. The commander wanted the doc's house watched and Josh agreed to cover it for the shift. Josh knew the commander had special feelings for the psychiatrist, but he didn't know what they were and, really, it wasn't his business.

He smiled to himself as he drove into the Quarter. He'd spent a pleasant evening with Elizabeth Tippett. They had talked about the events at CCMC, superficially of course, and he knew that Elizabeth thought something was wrong with Whitset. Josh had experienced similar feelings earlier in the day as he watched Whitset interact with patients. Anthony, the big guy, had told him on the sly that Whitset was one of them – "one of the gang" was specifically how the wacko had put it. Josh hadn't given it much thought since and wasn't quite sure he understood what Anthony meant.

Josh, like most policemen, hated wackos. He'd only had a little experience with them, but he knew some of them were really dangerous, especially if they did drugs and drank booze. *It just seemed to make them crazier.* , he thought.

Josh drove down Royal Street. It was the second time he had cruised by Dr. Desmonde's house. The front light was still on, but the French doors leading to the balcony were open. He stopped the police car just as he heard something breaking on the balcony. He immediately radioed for help, took out his 9 mm and raced towards the house, taking the steps two at a time. There was no answer at the door, so the young officer scaled the balcony and entered the living room.

He saw the prostrate, bleeding form of Monique Desmonde on the floor and saw Whitset on top of another woman. Josh aimed his gun at Whitset's head and said "Freeze!"

Nothing happened. Apparently, Whitset didn't hear him. Josh went over and kicked the administrator in the back. It was then that he saw Alex Destephano, her clothes all in disarray. Josh was appalled at what Whitset had done to her – or may have done to her. The extent of the attack was unclear, so Josh could not be sure.

Whitset looked up in surprise at the policeman. His pupils dilated with hatred. Then, in a flash, he jumped the police officer, knocking his gun from his hand as he ran out the French doors. Josh went after Whitset, but before he could catch him, Whitset jumped from the balcony and disappeared into the Quarter.

Alex was lying on the floor. Whitset had beaten her severely in the face. Handprints were visible on her face. Her lip was bloodied and there was a considerable amount of blood pouring from one eye. Josh bent over her and said quietly, "Ms. Destephano, can you hear me?"

Alex was dazed, unable to talk, but nodded and pointed towards Monique.

Josh felt for Monique's neck pulse. It was beating faintly. He felt sick as he looked at the long slash mark circling the psychiatrist white, perfectly oval face. He reached for the phone to dial 911, but the phone was dead. He grabbed his radio and called for an ambulance.

Then he turned his attention back to Alex. She seemed more coherent and asked, "Is Monique alive?"

Josh nodded his head. "I called for help. Alex, did he hurt you?"

She gave Josh a tight smile and said, "Josh, he cut Monique's face after she was unconscious. He cracked her skull. I heard it break when he hit her with the pipe. Oh, no ..." Alex's voice began to break.

Josh tried to hug her to offer some comfort, but she pushed him back frantically. Then, she started sobbing. Finally, she said, "Josh, call Dr. Bonnet. Call the hospital and get them to connect you. Please. He has to come take care of Monique."

Josh left her for an instant and radioed the hospital. He returned to tell her that Dr. Bonnet was on his way. He also retrieved a quilt from Monique's bedroom and covered the psychiatrist with it.

Alex was attempting to rearrange her clothes when she heard the police car sirens outside the apartment. Within seconds, the house was crawling with NOPD and an ambulance was outside.

Robert appeared a few minutes later. Alex waved him towards Monique. After a cursory examination of Monique, Robert ordered an immobilizing board. He called the hospital and talked directly with neurosurgery. He returned to Alex, took her hand, and said simply, "Monique's unconscious. She's in a coma. Her pupils are barely reactive. She'll need surgery. They're waiting for her at CCMC. It doesn't look good, Alex."

Alex was so traumatized, the right questions wouldn't come – that is, not the questions that she, as a nurse, would have ordinarily asked. She let Robert hold her while she sobbed quietly. Alex was still unable to speak.

Robert sensed this and didn't ask any questions.

Josh told Alex and Robert that they had made contact with Commander Françoise and that he would be there within minutes. He also reported there was a citywide manhunt for Whitset. The police were combing the Quarter looking for him. Josh was confident he would be apprehended soon.

Robert thanked him, but waved away the questions he was trying to ask Alex. She looked up at him gratefully.

Alex continued to let Robert rock her in his arms. She felt so guilty ... and dirty. She hadn't been able to help her friend, and besides – she shuddered when she thought about it and broke out into fresh sobs as the ambulance took Monique away.

Robert eased Alex onto the sofa at the same moment Commander Françoise entered the house. His face was strained and as dark as a thundercloud.

"Where's Monique?" He bellowed. "What the hell happened here?"

Robert shook his head sadly. "She's on her way to CCMC. Whitset attacked both Monique and Alex. Monique has a head injury. They'll do surgery as soon as she arrives."

Jack sat down, a broken man. He stroked Alex's face. "Are you all right, honey?"

Alex nodded, her eyes filling again with tears. "I'm sorry, Jack. I just couldn't do anything. He came at us like a maniac. He was so strong. I tried so hard, but I just couldn't stop it."

"It's okay, Alex. You did what you could. We'll find the little bastard, whoever he is, and he'll pay for what he's done. I need to talk to Officer Martin for a few minutes. I'll be back."

Josh and Jack retreated into the kitchen. Josh reported to Jack what he had found, describing in detail the slash to Monique's face and how he had discovered Whitset and Alex. He saw Françoise's face darken again and noted the curious light that came into his eyes, the killer light. It was the famous Jack Françoise killer light that he had heard older officers describe. He was sure that it was only a matter of hours that Whitset had left on this earth.

"Martin," Françoise asked in a quiet, but demanding voice. "Did Whitset rape Alex?"

Josh looked at the floor and back up into the commander's face. He replied, "I don't know, sir. Her clothes were torn. I just can't say for sure. It certainly looked like it could've happened."

"Did you ask her?"

"I asked her if Whitset had hurt her and she turned the conversation towards Dr. Desmonde. She wouldn't answer me, Commander. I tried to ask her – twice." Josh looked despondent.

Françoise nodded his head, as he felt the anger spread throughout his body. "Robert, come in here for a moment," he barked from the kitchen.

Robert appeared immediately. The men talked in low tones for a few moments.

Finally, Commander Françoise said to Robert, "You've got to find out if Whitset raped Alex. If he did, she needs to go to the emergency room."

"But, Jack," Robert began, "She's been beaten and terrorized. Can't we give her some time?"

"No. No. Hell no. We need the evidence against him. Do you want me to ask her to go with you?" Commander Françoise's voice was firm and he gave Bonnet a hard look.

Robert wanted to accept Jack's assistance, but he knew he couldn't. He shook his head negatively and said, "I'll do it, Jack. You may want to go to CCMC and check on Monique. I'm worried about her."

"I will. I'm going now. Then I am going to find and kill Lester Whitset." Commander Françoise was reasonably calm.

Robert and Josh both knew that beneath the calm façade was a roaring lion, out for blood – blood to avenge Monique and Alex.

"Jack, Jack, come here. I've got to talk to you for a minute." Alex was calling for Jack from the living room.

Jack went to Alex, and sat by her on the sofa. "What is it, Al?" He asked gently.

"You have got to search Whitset's office. Monique went in there today, and she found a gold chain hanging out of his bottom right desk drawer. I'm sure it's Angie's chain. Bridget brought me her cross today and I had it repaired." Alex's voice trailed off, remembering the teary scene in her office. Then she continued, "Monique also discovered that the college degrees in Whitset's office couldn't be his."

The commander nodded his head. "Yeah, I know they aren't. He's a fake, an imposter. I think he's Weston Whitset, Lester's crazy brother. I've got to go. Anything else, Alex?" Jack looked at her sharply.

Alex shook her head. "Not that I can think of. I know there's more, but I can't think of anything now. I'm just so tired..." Alex looked away, uncomfortable at the commander's direct gaze.

"Alex," Jack's voice was gentle. "Did Whitset rape you?"

Alex didn't answer. She looked at the commander and began to cry again.

"You must tell me, Alex. It's important. If he did, we'll need the evidence to convict him. You'll need to go to the hospital and be checked. "

Alex pulled her hand away from Jack's. She got up and left the room.

Robert and Josh looked at her disheveled, torn clothes. Then they looked at each other.

Jack's face was suffused with anger and he shrugged his shoulders as he said to Robert, "You've got to find out for sure, Robert. Need the evidence. Need it bad!" The commander's voice was rough and emotional.

"The hell with that evidence, Jack. I need to get her to CCMC to get her face treated. Besides, you're probably gonna kill him anyway." Robert's voice was short and angry.

"No, take her over to Community Memorial in Gulfport. Alex doesn't need the ignominy and stress of being treated for rape in her own hospital. Check her in under an alias. I'll call and make the arrangements. Take her now, dammit, I mean it." Jack saw Robert hesitate and said roughly, "*NOW*, I mean it. And, check on Monique. Make sure she gets the best CCMC has. Do you understand?" Jack was glaring at his boyhood friend, his temper hanging by a thread.

Robert nodded. "Yeah. I'll do my best, Jack. Now, get out of here." His voice and his eyes were tired.

Jack whispered to Josh on the way out, "Get Nadine Wells over here to see Alex. Let her decide about the rape. And, get Alex's statement when Nadine is with her. Move dammit, move now!"

Josh disappeared from the room to call Nadine.

Robert intervened, "Please, Jack, you have got to calm down. I know you are stressed, we all are, but there's no place for temper in this—"

Commander Françoise pivoted around and stared at the physician. "Dammit, Bonnet. This lunatic practically killed Monique and probably raped Alex. He raped and beat Angie Richelieu. He probably killed Mrs. Smithson as well. Don't talk to me about my temper. My temper's the only thing giving me the energy to move right now. Understand? If my temper wasn't acting up, I'd be dysfunctional with grief." Françoise stared at Robert, his eyes full of tears.

Robert walked over to him and hugged the big, burly policeman. The two men stayed in an embrace for several moments, each crying silently for what they had lost.

Françoise broke the embrace, "The next time you see me, Robert, Whitset will be dead. To hell with court justice."

Robert nodded, powerless to stop him.

"Take care of my girls, Bonnet. I'm trusting both of them to you." Françoise slammed Monique's French door so hard that the glass shattered and fell out.

Alex reemerged from the bathroom.

"Al, you've got to tell me about Whitset and what he did. Jack said we've got to get the evidence soon – you know that." Robert's voice was gentle and he moved over on the sofa so she could sit next to him.

"I'm not going to any emergency facility. Not CCMC, not in New Orleans, and not in Mississippi. I refuse to submit to any examination." Her voice was adamant, stubborn.

He asked gently, "Why, Alex? It was a situation you couldn't control. You're not guilty of anything."

Her voice was morose, her eyes filled with tears, "I'm just not going, Robert, I'm not. Now leave me alone about it, please." She laid her head down in his lap and pretended to fall asleep. She needed to be alone with her thoughts to try to put together exactly what had happened. She needed to think through what she should've done. She was feeling so guilty – about a lot of things. She should've saved Monique. Finally, she fell asleep on Monique's sofa.

A half an hour later, Josh opened the door for Nadine Wells. They talked quietly in the kitchen for a few minutes and Josh motioned for Robert to join them.

Robert seemed uncertain about Nadine. When he learned she was NOPD's expert on sexual crimes, he retreated into himself.

Nadine perceived the change in Robert's behavior and assured him she wouldn't badger Alex. She mentioned they had met shortly after the rape of Angie Richelieu.

Robert seemed surer of the petite Nadine's concern for Alex and went to awaken her.

Nadine held up her hand, motioning for Robert to wait a moment. She asked him, "Dr. Bonnet, what is your relationship to Ms. Destephano?"

He flushed a little bit at the question. It would have been easy to answer before last night. He didn't know what to say and stammered his reply, "Well ... well, to be honest, Ms. Wells, Alex and I were married when we were students and lived in Virginia. We divorced about four years ago. Alex moved to Texas and I moved to New Orleans. I'm from here ..." Robert's voice trailed off, unsure of exactly what it was the woman wanted to know.

She continued to look at him, their eyes locked. "And now, Dr. Bonnet, what is your current relationship with Alex?"

Robert was uncomfortable. Her directness was bothering him and he didn't like it. He felt guilty and defensive for some reason. He remained silent.

Nadine turned to Josh. "Josh, could you leave Dr. Bonnet and me alone for a few minutes?" Josh nodded and hastily left the kitchen. Nadine continued to look at Robert, whose defensiveness was turning to anger. His lean, handsome face was red. She repeated her question, her voice adamant, "Dr. Bonnet, it's important that you answer my question for your sake and for ours."

"Why, why in the hell do I have to answer your question? I haven't done anything illegal or wrong." He was stubbornly defensive.

"I must know if you and Alex are sexually intimate. If you are, and have been recently, it could complicate any evidence we gather tonight. That's the reason for the question. Otherwise, I agree. It's none of my business."

Nadine saw Robert's shoulder sag. "Ms. Wells, I love Alex. I'd like to marry her again. We're presently good friends and have been since earlier this year. I assure you

284

there's no evidence from a sexual encounter that would complicate a police rape investigation. I promise you."

"Then why are you so uncomfortable?" Nadine looked at him shrewdly, still persistent.

Robert was amazed at the woman's perceptiveness. "Tonight, at least earlier tonight, Alex and I had dinner at her house." He smiled at the memory. "I believe we could have complicated the evidence if Dr. Desmonde hadn't called Alex at 11 o'clock. Actually, Alex and I were … well, the phone rang, but nothing had happened." He looked sheepish, even a little embarrassed.

Nadine smiled at him and touched his shoulder. "I'm sorry she called and spoiled it for you. Trust me, there will be other times. Thanks for being honest with me, Dr. Bonnet. Can I count on your support – emotional and physical – to get Alex through this?"

"Yes, absolutely. What do you want me to do?"

"Help me help her remember what happened. I believe, based on what Commander Françoise and Officer Martin said, it's possible Alex doesn't remember what happened. She may not know if she was raped or not."

Robert was flabbergasted. "You're kidding. I'd never have thought that."

"It's a protective reflex that many women have after a rape. It's a dissociation mechanism that's commonly associated with sexual crime and abuse. It sounds as though her clothes, while torn, were basically intact, so I'm hopeful that she wasn't raped. Let me rephrase that, I'm hopeful she wasn't actually penetrated. She was most assuredly raped in the greater sense of the word, and Alex will view it that way. It's critical for her recovery and continued mental health that she knows for sure so she can learn to deal with it. Do you understand what I'm saying, Dr. Bonnet?"

Robert nodded mutely and followed her into the living room where Alex remained on the sofa. Damn! It was a lot easier being a surgeon than a shrink or mental health worker. Being a surgeon was quick and simple and you got results right away – not so much with mental health stuff.

Nadine shook Alex gently.

She opened her eyes slowly. They were liquid blue in color, the color of bachelor's buttons in the summer. She struggled to sit up.

Robert noticed that her right shoulder was drooping. A fractured clavicle, he surmised – the same arm that had been injured in February.

Nadine spoke softly, "Alex, Jack asked me to come over and talk with you. Josh and I need a statement about what happened here tonight. Are you up to talking?"

Alex nodded, looking to Robert.

Clasping her hand tightly, Robert assured her he would stay with her.

Nadine was pleased that Bonnet was so cooperative. So many men were either useless or macho machines in times like this. He would be a good support for Alex, if she'd let him. For some reason, Nadine's intuition told her she wouldn't.

Josh began, "Ms. Destephano, do you mind if I tape your interview? The commander asked me to get your permission. If you would rather I didn't, I won't."

Alex smiled at Josh, "You can, Josh. It's okay. Call me Alex."

"Thanks, Alex." Josh cut the recorder on, giving the date, time, describing the crime scene, and naming the people present at the taped interview.

"Tell me what happened tonight, Alex. You can go as slowly as you like. I've got three tapes with me. We've got plenty of tape and plenty of time." He handed Alex the microphone.

In a clear voice, Alex talked into the machine. She began with the phone call from Monique and ended with the entrance of Josh Martin. She cried when she related how Whitset had beaten Monique with the lead pipe and how he had cut her face after she was unconscious. She made no mention of rape, but recounted in great detail how Whitset had sung his sick little rhyme to her and how he had torn her clothes. Her hand was gripped tightly by Robert throughout the interview, which took about twenty minutes.

Nadine and Josh nodded their heads as she spoke, asking questions to clarify and expand her statement.

Josh seemed satisfied and looked at Nadine for direction.

Nadine picked up on his cue and said to Alex, "You described how Whitset pushed you to the floor and ripped your clothes. You didn't tell us what he did to you."

Alex looked confused. "What do you mean I didn't tell you? I told you everything that Whitset did!" Her voice was angry, defensive.

Nadine persisted. "You've got bruises on your face, a black eye, and an injured shoulder. Did Whitset hit you when he had you on the floor?"

Alex looked thoughtful. "Why yes, I suppose he did. Who else could have possibly hit me?" The tone of Alex's voice implied she thought Nadine's question was ridiculous and stupid. Her tone was condescending, very much unlike Alex's normal voice.

"Did Whitset do anything else to you that you haven't mentioned?" Nadine continued to look thoughtfully at Alex, who shook her head negatively.

There was a silence for a few minutes while Nadine and Josh reviewed their notes.

Robert continued to stroke Alex's hand. He smiled at her gently and said, "It's almost over, Al. Soon we'll go."

She smiled back. She was so tired. All she wanted to do was take a shower and sleep.

Nadine looked up from her notes and said, "I have another question for you, Alex. Listen carefully and answer me as best you can. It's important."

"Okay, Nadine. But, hurry up. I'm tired and I want to get cleaned up so I can go to CCMC to check on Monique."

Nadine could tell that Alex was getting impatient. Nadine's dark eyes searched Alex's deep blue ones as she asked the question in a matter of fact manner, "Did Lester Whitset rape you?"

Alex was flustered, her voice angry. "Nadine, I told you everything that happened that I can think of. Don't you understand that I'm tired and I want to go home? I've been awake for over twenty-four hours."

Nadine continued to look steadily at her. She asked again, "Did Lester Whitset rape you, Alex? Did he penetrate you?"

Alex jumped angrily off the sofa, her injured shoulder drooping. She shrieked at them, her voice loud and quavering, "I told you everything I know. I want to get out of here, now." She looked around frantically for some means of escape. Her eyes rested on Robert, and she said to him, in a small and broken voice, "Robert, please make them leave me alone. I said everything I can remember. I want to go home. I want you to take me, please!"

He felt his heart constrict as he looked at her, her eyes liquid pools of grief. He felt his reserve melting. She was so dejected, so sad. He glanced over at Nadine Wells, who gave him a dark look that clearly told him to keep his mouth shut.

He looked back at Alex and said gently, "You've gotta answer Nadine's question. It's important to know whether

Whitset actually raped you. If he did, we need to get you to the emergency department for an examination."

Alex became hysterical. "No ... no ... no ... I'm not going anywhere. Don't you hear me! I'm not going anywhere! I've told you what I know and I am leaving! Don't any of you try to stop me!"

Nadine stood in her way. Her voice was crisp, chilly. "Calm down, Alex. Shut up and stop all the noise, now! None of us wants to hear it. Just answer the question."

Robert was becoming more and more uncomfortable with the line of questioning. He thought Alex was being harassed. He was about to interrupt and protect her when Josh Martin placed his hand on his shoulder in restraint and shook his head.

Nadine asked again, her voice clear, "Did Lester Whitset rape you, Alex?"

She dissolved into tears. She was sobbing so hard her shoulders were shaking. Her voice came out in large gulps. She was hyperventilating.

Robert held her in his arms, reassuring her that it made no difference to him. He told her over and over that he loved her.

Finally, Alex calmed down a little and said in a small, still voice that was almost a whisper, "I don't know. I just don't know. I can't remember!"

Nadine leaned over and put her arms around Alex. "It's all right if you don't know, Alex. A lot of women don't know. They can't remember. They repress the terror of what happened to them." Nadine continued to offer her reassurance for several more minutes until Alex calmed down.

Alex clung to Robert's hand and turned to face the police officers. "You mean there are other women who don't know if they have actually been raped or not?"

Nadine smiled and responded, "Yep, Alex. That's right. You are certainly not alone in this. What's important now is that we get you examined so that we can tell—"

Alex shrank from the thought of a rape examination. It was so humiliating and embarrassing. She remembered having to do them when she worked in the emergency department. "No, no, I won't go."

Nadine looked at her firmly and said, "You've got to go, Alex. If you don't, you will never know if you were physically raped and the uncertainty will haunt you forever. You'll never recover emotionally from the experience." Nadine turned and prevailed upon Alex's relationship with Robert. "You've gotta go get checked out now so you and Robert can work through this together."

Robert was nodding his head, aware of the implications that could result if Alex never knew whether she was forcibly raped by Whitset. "Nadine's right, Alex. We need to do all we can so we can work through this. I'll take you to Memorial Hospital in Gulfport."

"Jack has made the arrangements, Alex. We'll check you in under an assumed name. No one will know you have been there. It'll be confidential. I'll go as well if you like." Nadine squeezed her hand.

Alex looked from Robert to Nadine. She said to Robert, "Would you mind if only Nadine went with me? I'd rather you go check on Monique. Besides, someone will recognize you there."

Robert was surprised and a little hurt. "Of course, Al, whatever you want. I am anxious about Monique. I'll see you back at your house around lunch time – okay?" He raised his eyebrows questioningly at Nadine Wells.

"Yes, that will be enough time. She can even get a few hours' sleep. We'll call your cell when all is done." Nadine thought how lucky Alex was to have a man like Bonnet on her side.

It was after five o'clock in the morning when Nadine and Alex left Monique's apartment on Royal Street. Alex was about to ask Nadine if she could go home to take a shower and change clothes when she remembered that she couldn't. It would destroy any evidence they had against Whitset. It made her crazy that she didn't know whether she was raped or not. What kind of an idiot was she?

There was little conversation between the women as they drove out I-10 towards the Mississippi Gulf Coast. Alex slept most of the way, exhausted beyond belief. When they pulled up in front of Community Memorial Hospital, Alex said very simply to Nadine, "You know, Nadine, no matter what they find, I have been raped." Her voice was teary. She sounded so fatigued and depressed.

"Yes, Alex. You have been raped. You are absolutely right and how well I know."

Alex looked at Nadine curiously, as they entered the emergency room door.

Chapter 32

Weston Whitset was frantic. He was hiding, partly occluded in a doorway setback in the Quarter, a wine bottle in his hand, looking like most of the drunks at that time of the morning. He'd been running forever. He still couldn't believe that the police officer had barged into that shrink bitch's apartment and he hadn't heard him! Damn the voices! If they hadn't been talking so loudly, he wouldn't have been taken by surprise. He cursed the voices out loud. Several people walking by looked at him curiously, but he didn't care because he figured they were as drunk as he was.

Weston continued to think. It had just been getting good with Alex. He had been watching her for several months and gaining control over her had become his life's work. Sex with her was a necessity; "a driving obsession" is what that shrink of his in Alabama would have said. Weston knew she had wanted him too. He'd seen it in her eyes several times in the last couple of days. Of course, she had tried to hide it from the others. He had picked up on that. But, he knew she wanted him. Weston couldn't believe she had been playing hard to get over there at Monique's. She was acting like a tease. He hated prick-teasers! What a slut! Well, that had been part of her game. But, he had showed her, hadn't he? Just like the nurse pig. He smiled at the memory.

Weston stayed in the doorway, drinking his wine. The voices were quiet now, allowing him to think without interruption. Well, at least he had killed the imposter shrink bitch. There was comfort in that. He had heard her skull crack! It was a beautiful sound – better than any symphony Weston had ever heard. It had been wonderful! He had almost gotten off on the sound itself. Weston smiled as he remembered the terrorized look on her plastic face. The powerful, plastic shrink bitch. Her plastic, fake head had cracked under his trusty pipe. He loved it. Weston jerked his head up when he realized he was drooling again. The liquid had run down onto his shirt.

Far in the distance, he heard police sirens. He guessed he had better keep moving. He felt panicked again. Where should he go? Where could he go? The voices were screaming at him, just screaming. He tore at his face and his hair, trying desperately to quiet them down. Then, he started walking. He stayed close to groups of tourists in the Quarter, attempting to blend in.

His wine bottle was empty, and he needed a drink. He decided to duck into one of the bars, and he knew just the bar he was going to! It was on the other side of Dauphine Street. They would never look for him there! It was a male Vampire Bar and he'd been before. He just loved the place. So many people like himself. He checked his watch. It was almost 2:00 a.m. One thing about New Orleans, you could drink twenty-four hours a day and the male Vampire Bar never closed until dawn. He was good for five or more hours. He'd figure things out by then ... how to make his next move.

Weston sat in the dark pub for several hours, drinking double bourbons. He enjoyed watching the men flirt with each other and pretend to feed on each other's blood. And the costumes, wow, so Goth, devilish, fancy, and expensive. Some of the guys were pretty funny, others ... well ... he wasn't sure about them. There was a rumor that the Sire visited this vampire club. Weston didn't really know what the Sire was, but he had been told that if the Sire chose you, well, you were set for life. He didn't really know.

The men were really interesting in the way they communicated. The place was a regular tearoom, lots of action. Men just came and went. All kinds of men, pretty men, studs, bodybuilders, executive types, Voodoos, Occults, and, his favorite, daddies with little kids at home. He loved these best. They were so perverse that he was envious of their skills. What double lives they led! They made it with their wives at night, were appropriate with family members and work, had kids, coached the Little League, and then they came out at night and acted out their perversions. It was disgusting, but Weston loved disgusting and perverted. He shook his head. The more he thought about it, the more it calmed him. It was a little wicked, and Wes loved wicked.

He continued to watch the men. It was fascinating! It was entertaining to watch the men seduce each other. First, there was the eye contact, then the emotional seduction, then the preliminaries, then the fake blood sucking – at least, he thought it was fake – and then the trip to the restroom, or outside. Then, finally, came the release, Weston supposed. He guessed the alley behind the bar had seen some action. He smiled to himself. Maybe he should consider "crossing the line." Maybe he had been missing some good stuff all these years.

Weston especially liked guessing who would emerge the most powerful of the dyad. Who was who? Who was in control? Who became obedient? Wow, the more he thought about it, the more excited he felt. He continued to watch the men flirt and preen for each other. Hell, maybe he should start playing the vampire part. He'd been "into" it in his youth, but had gotten bored and left it alone for years. It looked to him like the vampire craft had grown a lot since the early years. *Very interesting*, he thought to himself.

Studying these men really calmed him down and shut up the voices. He noted that he was usually right – you could tell at the takeover who was the most powerful! Weston only wished he could have seen some of the kills. He could only fantasize. Weston had never been one for homosexual sex, but … maybe he ought to consider it sometime. After all, variety was the spice of life. He smiled to himself.

It was after 5:00 a.m. Weston was the last customer left at the bar and the bartender offered him a blowjob. Weston declined. The bartender, enraged at the refusal, told him to get the hell out. Weston complied.

The voices were remaining quiet and now he could decide what to do. He had to make some plans. It would be daylight soon. Where was he going to hide? What was he going to do? Then, the next steps came to him. He knew exactly where he was going! He would be safe there for at least three or four days.

He would be safe until this stuff died down.

Chapter 33

Jack Françoise was beat, angry, discouraged, and in so much emotional pain he could barely think. He knew he was in the worst possible situation a police officer could be. He recognized he was vulnerable and knew he should turn the case over to someone who was not emotionally involved. Of course, no one really knew that he and Monique were lovers, no one but Robert and Alex. It had been a secret. Was that only two nights ago they had celebrated at the Palace Café? Would he and Monique ever make love again? Would they ever speak again? The possibility that they wouldn't terrorized Jack and took him to an emotional place he had never been before, a place he hated.

He could feel the hot tears pouring down his cheeks. He couldn't begin to describe the pain he felt when he looked down at Monique in the intensive care unit at CCMC. Her beautiful face was pallid, her bright eyes closed. The angry, red streak around her face made by Whitset's knife was clearly visible under the fluorescent lights in intensive care. The sight made Jack want to kill the man even more.

One tube came out of her nose and was hooked to wall suction to keep her stomach emptied. The second tube was hooked to the machine that was helping her breathe. Every now and then Monique coughed, as if she was trying to cough the tube out of her mouth and nose. The nurses said that was good. When she coughed, her eyes opened up wide and they stared straight ahead. Her eyes looked terrified. Jack asked the nurse if she was blind. She assured him she wasn't, but Jack wasn't convinced.

Every time the ventilator alarm went off, it scared Jack to death. He was afraid she had stopped breathing. The nurse explained that Monique was fighting the ventilator. She also said that Monique could probably breathe on her own, but the neurosurgeon wanted her intubated for the surgery and the first few days afterwards, just in case. So, the nurses sedated Monique to keep her calm and from fighting the tubes.

Jack hadn't been able to stay in the intensive care unit long. He felt helpless, useless even. He didn't understand what was happening and he didn't like the feeling. He gratefully accepted a cup of coffee from Monique's nurse and sat down in the doctors' lounge to think – and plan his revenge.

A quick call to headquarters confirmed what the commander expected; the citywide manhunt for Whitset was so far unsuccessful. Where in the hell was that little pervert? What do the insane crazies do when they're scared? Where do the wackos go? Jack pondered these questions as he finished his coffee and left Crescent City Medical Center to begin his own personal manhunt for the bastard who had destroyed the love of his life and raped his best friend.

Chapter 34

Whitset knew the police were still searching for him. He ducked in and out of the darkened alleyways in the French Quarter. He crossed Canal Street and walked several blocks towards the lovely residential section that surrounded Crescent City Medical Center. He entered the hospital through the radiology department located in the oldest part of the main building. It was completely darkened and desolate. No one was around to see him and Whitset smiled at his luck. He rounded the hall, walked towards the service elevators, and pressed the button that would take him to the sub-basement.

As the old very tarnished elevator groaned and creaked towards him, Whitset smiled at the cleverness of his plan. He told the voices how stupid they were and admonished them for bothering him earlier. After all, he was Weston Whitset, almighty and all-powerful. He needed nothing from the voices that had assumed the identity of his dead brother, Lester, so many years ago. It had been such a clever scheme, and it had worked so well.

For years, Weston had masqueraded as his brother and held positions in psychiatric administration that permitted him to continue feeding his needs without fear. It had been a marvelous game. Weston smiled as he remembered the fun he had at other wackos' expense. God, it had been good. All that sex, all the fun, always emerging on top, being in charge of an army of crazies. Weston emerged from the elevator with a dreamy smile on his face as he remembered his escapades. Everything had been just perfect until that damned, plastic shrink bitch had begun to get in his way.

Where had all these plastic people come from? He hadn't seen one for years. Now, he wasn't certain how many there were. But, of course, Dr. Desmonde had been the only one. He had killed her. Weston became sexually aroused again as he thought about cracking her skull.

And, that damned nurse. She was a pig, but such a temptress. He had wanted her badly. He had to have her, and he had. It had been simple. It had been ecstasy. A night to remember.

He would go back for more when things quieted down, he decided. He'd enjoyed her terror so much that he savored it. That's why he didn't kill her. He wanted it again, the high he got from her fear, from her terror. Angie, the temptress. Angie, the pig. He'd get it, soon, and when he went for her again, she'll be so frightened that the experience would be the best he'd ever had. Maybe he would get her while she was still on the hospital ward. What a lark! What fun! That would be a real coup. Of course, this time he would have to kill her. Whitset smiled broadly at his ingenious plan. He wondered if she had woken up yet.

He continued his fantasy as he walked through the darkened tunnel of the medical center. Huge steam pipes hissed at him as he walked by them. The sound was comforting. The steam cleared his mind. He carefully jumped around to avoid deep pools of water. He couldn't see the pools of water, but Weston could feel they were there. Weston liked knowing what was around. Every now and then, he waved and joyfully greeted a large rat or an enormous New Orleans cockroach. They were his friends. Several rats were albinos and had pink, inquiring eyes. They neither bothered him nor required anything from him. Hapless creatures. Helpless, like he made his victims. He loved hapless and helpless.

Weston wished he had a light as he entered the stretch of tunnel between the Pavilion and the main hospital. It was pitch black. There was only a single light bulb about every fifty feet. The engineering people never entered this part of the tunnel. The heating and maintenance facilities for the Pavilion were located directly under the building itself. Weston cursed a little as he wiped the cobwebs from his face. He hated spiders. They reminded him of women who were both hateful and as dishonest as woven webs of intrigue around full-blooded men. *Such a useless exercise,* he thought to himself. *No wonder they had to be put in their place. Women – disgusting pigs.*

Finally, he reached the seldom-used elevator under the Pavilion. He smiled and congratulated himself on the ingenuity of his scheme. They would never find him, not right here in the Pavilion. The tunnel and the elevator were Weston's secret. He had used them many times to enter and leave the hospital secretly, most recently when he had "used" the nurse. He had even left the outside door to the stairwell open to confuse people. He smiled at his cleverness. He felt himself aroused again at the memory of his night with the pig nurse, Angie.

The elevator opened into an old supply room, which was now part of one of the seclusion rooms. A thin wall and heavy metal door separated the supply room from the small seclusion cell. Of course, Weston had a key to the door. He was sure no one else did. He doubted if anyone even remembered the door was there – except for the patients in seclusion, and no one listened to them.

Weston remembered late last March when he had entered the hospital through the tunnel and the elevator. He had been surprised to find the seclusion room occupied by a young, beautiful woman who had just been admitted for severe depression. Of course, she had been suicidal and hostile, which is why the shrinks had secluded her. He would never forget the look of fear in her eyes when he entered her room through the metal door. It had been an unexpected surprise for him, too. A very pleasant surprise indeed, as it turned out. Of course, she had screamed, but the seclusion rooms were soundproof. How handy. How fortunate! And, his timing had been just right. He had entered a few minutes past midnight and knew he had a full two hours for fun before the next rounds by the hospital staff.

It had been two great sex-filled and sex-crazed hours. The girl had a beautiful body and Weston had used it fully for his convenience. He couldn't remember how many times he had gotten off, but it had been good. *Ah, life was good,* he thought to himself as he remembered his fortune. After the initial sex act, which never involved penetration, the woman had been submissive and even begged him to kill her. He had accommodated her by helping her slit her wrists. He hadn't wanted to and would've liked to have visited her again, but was afraid the shrinks might believe her story. She just hadn't been insane enough. Besides, the best sex of all had been giving it to her while she bled to death. That had also been the best part with the old lady, but she had been an imposter, so it really didn't count as much. She had been a plastic, old lady bitch, and she deserved that knitting needle just where he placed it.

Ah, the power of it all, the supreme triumph. Orgasm for one at another's moment of death. Ultimate power, ultimate control. Didn't the shrinks call that something? Necrophilia or something? He liked the word. It had a pleasant ring to it. Several other times he'd enjoyed "fruits" of the room, but had never derived the same satisfaction he had the first time. The first adventure was always the best for him. It was a great setup. Crescent City Medical offered him everything he needed, even a huge bonus at the end of the year for the cost savings he had instituted. His bonus would be even more now that the plastic shrink was dead.

A sudden thought alarmed him. He broke out into a sweat. Suppose the room was occupied tonight? What would he do? Then he relaxed. It would only be a woman in the room. No problem. The seclusion room was on the women's side of the Pavilion. It was available only for female seclusion. No sweat after all. Cool. Maybe someone would be waiting for him tonight. Maybe even Rose. Weston breathed a sigh of relief. He was tired and the voices and all the whiskey had finally hit him. He was super human, but everyone had a limit. He walked off the elevator and inserted his key into the lock of the heavy metal door.

As the door creaked open and a shaft of light appeared from the overhead light, Weston felt fear for the first time in his life.

Facing him in the room was the drug crazed, raging face of Anthony Gavette.

Weston was frozen in place.

Anthony stared at him and said quietly, "I've been waiting for you, you slimy bastard. You took my Rose!" Then Anthony lunged at Whitset, knocking him to the floor.

Chapter 35

The rape treatment at Gulfport Memorial had been just as awful as Alex had expected. It was the most humiliating experience she had ever endured. Even though the physician had been kind, she thought she heard some joking outside her cubicle. Nadine's quiet reprimand had convinced her she was correct.

She breathed a sigh of relief when she was discharged. The ride back to New Orleans was quiet, both women deep in thought. Finally, Alex asked, "When will I know? When will they tell me if I've been raped?"

"The physician told me he would run the labs himself. He said he would get back to me this afternoon." Nadine glanced over at Alex, aware that she was depressed.

"That long? Why so long?" Alex's voice sounded pitiful.

"They do a lot of testing, Alex. You know that. Try to get some sleep now." Nadine's voice was chiding. She was getting pretty tired, too.

"I just want a shower and something to eat. Then, I want to go to CCMC and check on Monique. I'm really worried about her." Alex's voice faltered as her eyes filled with tears for her friend.

Nadine nodded. "Yes, I talked with Robert. He's also very concerned. Monique's still in surgery. They're doing a craniotomy. She has a depressed skull fracture."

"Did she regain consciousness before the surgery?" Alex was afraid to hear the response.

"No, she didn't. She was completely unresponsive. Robert's also in surgery. Said he was hopeful that once they relieve the pressure in her head, she might regain consciousness, maybe even come back full force." Nadine reached for Alex's hand and pressed it. "You know how these things go, Alex. It could be either way." Her voice was sympathetic. The look she gave Alex understanding.

Alex flinched as she remembered the sound of Whitset's lead pipe splitting Monique's skull. She would never forget the sound it had made, not as long as she lived. She shuddered to herself and cried silent tears for her friend.

"It's so unfair, Nadine. Monique and Jack had just found each other. They're in love. Did you know that?"

Nadine jerked her head and stared at Alex. Her eyes were closed, her head laid back against the seat. Hell no, she didn't know that. She said softly, "No, Alex, I didn't know that. Thanks for telling me."

Alex made no response until Nadine woke her in front of her house. Nadine made them both a sandwich, while Alex showered and dressed. It was afternoon. Then, they left for CCMC.

Chapter 36

Don Montgomery was pacing furiously back and forth in his office. Elizabeth Tippett and Josh Martin were sitting at a small conference table. In front of them was the morning edition of the *Times Picayune*. The lead story on the front page outlined the tragic attack on Angie Richelieu and the death of Mrs. Smithson.

Elizabeth finally spoke, "Don, for heaven sakes, sit down. Your pacing is driving me nuts. Stop it!"

Montgomery turned on her. "Tippett, what the hell is going on here? Tell me again! Are you sure Whitset is responsible for the attacks on Alex and Monique Desmonde?"

Elizabeth sighed and turned to Josh Martin and back to Don. "Yes, absolutely. Officer Martin was there! What other proof do you need? He interrupted the attack on Alex. Monique was already unconscious. Whitset is definitely responsible. Can't you get that through your head?" Elizabeth was tired, worried about Alex and Monique, and sick of Don.

Don sat down and glared at Josh Martin. "Where in the hell is Commander Françoise? That useless bastard should be here helping us clean this shit up!"

Josh bristled at Montgomery's reference to the commander. Jack was his hero and he worshiped the ground he walked on. He was short on energy, patience, and time. He mustered up some self-control and said in a derogatory voice, "Mr. Montgomery, Commander Françoise is out searching for Whitset now. There's a citywide manhunt for your administrator. I'm leaving here now to meet up with him, if I can find him."

"No need. I'm here, Josh. No need to hunt." The three of them looked towards the doorway of Montgomery's office

305

and stared at the exhausted Jack Françoise. Jack was so grey with fatigue and anxiety that he appeared to be an apparition. Jack touched Elizabeth's shoulder and sat down.

Officer Martin rose in deference to his commanding officer. "Commander, can I get you anything?"

Jack shook his head negatively and addressed Montgomery. "Is Alex here yet?"

Montgomery stared at the commander and said, "Hell, no! I heard she'd been attacked by Whitset. Is it true?"

Françoise nodded. "Yeah, Whitset attacked Alex and Dr. Desmonde. I understand she's still in surgery. Anyone check on her?" Jack looked at all of them dismally.

Elizabeth answered, "Yeah. I called up about an hour ago. She was still in surgery. They said it would be several more hours. They're doing a craniotomy, Commander. She has a severe skull fracture. Why not come with me to my office and I'll call again." Elizabeth stood alongside Josh, and the three of them left a speechless Don Montgomery in his plush executive office.

As the trio walked towards Elizabeth's office, Jack's cell rang. He looked at the number. It was Nadine's cell. He said, "I'll catch up. Let me talk to Nadine. I think she's with Alex." He stopped and sat in the lobby, while Josh and Liz waited expectantly.

Jack returned and gestured with his hand. "Let's go to Alex's office. She and Nadine are over there.

Alex and Nadine were sitting at the conference table in Alex's office. As soon as Jack entered, Alex went over and hugged him. She could feel his silent tears as they embraced. Alex said softly, "Jack, we don't know anything yet. Let's be positive. Robert's up there, so you can be sure she's getting the best." She continued to hold Jack, feeling him shudder as he grouped for composure.

Finally, he let go and smiled at her. "You're looking pretty good, Miss Lawyer Lady. You do have a few bruises and a shiner. Everything else okay?"

"Yep, I'm doing okay. Promise. Nadine has been great. Can you get her a raise?" Alex winked at Nadine.

"I'll do my best." He looked at Josh and Nadine. "Can we talk privately?" He looked sideways at Elizabeth.

"I get the message, Commander. I've got to go clean up our image with the press anyway. You guys be good while I'm gone, okay?" Liz gave them all a big smile. She hugged Alex when she left and said, "We'll talk later, Al. I'm glad you're okay. You don't look too bad for a chick who has been up all night," Elizabeth joked, as she left them alone.

Alex smiled at her friend. "Yes, Liz. Later. I'm doing pretty okay. Say some prayers for Monique."

"I've been praying for you all since about three o'clock this morning. And by the way, you two owe me. I've been sitting with Don for hours, listening to him rant and rave. Steer clear of him if you can. He's a wild man again."

"Gotcha, Liz. Thanks," Alex said.

Elizabeth gave Officer Martin a special smile as she quietly closed the door of Alex's conference room.

Jack sat down wearily in a chair and said to the group, "I got the preliminary forensics on Angie. We ain't got zip. Nothing."

Alex gasped, "What? Nothing? How can that be?"

Nadine spoke quietly, "It's probably because so much time elapsed between the rape and the collection of the evidence. What about blood and hair samples, Jack? Are they conclusive?"

Jack's face brightened. *Damn*, he thought to himself. *I really am in bad shape. I'm almost useless.* He had forgotten about the evidence, except the rape forensics. "Hell, yeah, we got the hair and skin. We even got the damned bite mark. I can't wait to catch the little pervert." Jack, clearly in a brighter mood, rubbed his hands together in anticipation.

Alex was still confused. She felt her heart fluttering with fear. She looked at Nadine and said, "Nadine, why don't we have any ABO groupings? Surely, there should be something!"

Nadine understood Alex's fear. "I guess the specimens weren't collected soon enough to build a good case. Anyway, the genetic markers could only implicate Whitset if —"

She was interrupted by Commander Françoise, who said tersely, "Nadine, suppose the man's a non-secretor? Then we'll never be able to determine..." Jack's voice trailed off as he stared at Alex, whose face had flushed a bright red. She was staring at the conference table, unable to speak.

Nadine knew what they were thinking. If Whitset was a non-secretor, then Alex might not know if she had been physically raped or not. She'd never come to closure on the subject. *Damn*, Nadine thought. *This just isn't fair.*

"Alex," Nadine began, "We don't know anything yet."

Alex stood. She was in the greatest rage she could remember. "Shut up, Nadine! Shut up all of you! None of you know that humiliation, the ignominy, I just endured at that Podunk hospital. All of you just get out of my office!" She looked wildly at Josh, Nadine, and Jack. "I said to get the hell out of here, now!"

Jack was shocked. He'd never heard Alex curse like that before. He stood to try to comfort her. As he reached for her, she pushed him away, fighting back hot tears.

Nadine remained seated and looked up at Alex's tear streaked face. "Alex, I know exactly what you've been through. I've been through it myself. We'll leave now, but I'll be back here in one hour to see you."

Alex stared at them as they left her office. Then, she put her head down on her conference table and wept, crying for herself, Monique, Jack, and Robert. Her life would never be the same. She just knew it. There was no way it could be.

Commander Françoise, Nadine Wells, and Josh Martin reconvened in the hospital dining room, all of them staring tiredly into their coffee.

Finally, Jack said, "How bad was it in Gulfport?"

"It was as bad as always, Jack. Nothing different or unusual. It's just a demeaning experience for any woman, or man for that matter." Her voice was clear, but her eyes had a faraway look in them.

Jack cleared his throat, uncomfortable with what he was about to say. Finally, it came out. "Nadine, I didn't know that you had been—"

Nadine interrupted him. "I know you didn't, Jack. It's not something I've ever revealed during a case." She looked bluntly at Jack and Josh. "Make sure this goes no further."

"Of course, Nadine. Your secret is safe with us. Right, Josh?"

Josh nodded his head affirmatively and said, "Right, Commander. Right, Ms. Wells. No one will ever know." Personally, Josh never wanted to piss off either the commander or Ms. Wells. They were both pretty scary in their own right.

Chapter 37

Robert Bonnet was deeply troubled. As he stood in the shower in the O.R. suite, the warm water seemed to remind him only that he was still alive. He was numb all over. The rest of the world seemed cold to him, cold and unkind, and out of sync.

Monique's surgery had progressed well, but Robert was depressed by the extent of her head injury. The neurosurgeon, Dr. Van Hansen, wasn't hopeful for much of a recovery. In fact, early in the surgery, after assessing the extent of her injury, the buildup of intracranial fluid, and its compression on the brain, he had recommended they close, take three EKG readings, and then make a decision. Robert had objected vehemently, even though the clinical picture looked grim.

At a later point, the neurosurgeon had pointedly questioned whether Monique should even have any plastic surgery, suggesting it was a waste of time and doubtful that Monique would ever even ask for a mirror if she ever regained consciousness.

Robert again objected angrily. A volley of harsh words had followed.

Robert really didn't like Van Hansen. He was lousy at the bedside and had the "surgeon rude, superior personality". But Robert knew he was also a great technical neurosurgeon. In the end, the plastic surgeon had come in and done a fairly good job of reconstructing Dr. Desmonde's face where Lester Whitset had tried to obliterate it. Of course, only time would really tell how good she would look, if she even lived.

Robert continued to chastise himself. Perhaps the neuro doc had been correct. Maybe he wasn't seeing Monique's injuries for what they were. Part of the time during the operation, he had found himself remembering their youth together. They had been great friends. They still were. Then, his thoughts returned to the "celebratory dinner" they had shared only two days before. Jack and Monique had been so happy that night. Oh, there had been a few tense moments, but Robert knew the two loved each other beyond belief. Now, he had to go tell Jack that things didn't look so good.

"Bonnet, wake up! Are you still in there? You're going to be a prune if you don't get out." Robert recognized the voice of one of the male O.R. techs. He opened the shower door and grabbed a towel.

"Yeah, I'm coming out. Give me a minute." Robert left the shower and was changing into clean scrubs when the tech approached him again.

"You okay, man? You look awful. You're all wrinkled." Tom Finney, the O.R. tech, looked him up and down. He smiled at Robert and gave him a look of encouragement. He studied the surgeon's face and said, "Listen, man, you know how those damned brain guys are. They thrive on pessimism. They always predict the worst ... not sure of this, not sure of that, and all that horseshit. Then, they look like Santa Claus or the tooth fairy when the patient wakes up and starts bitching about the nursing care. Brain surgeons practice more savior behavior than the rest of you. Don't let him get you down!" Tom slapped Robert on the back.

Robert smiled at the aging tech. He had known Tom for years, even before he was operating at CCMC. Tom had been a nursing assistant first and then an O.R. tech. He knew patients and he knew doctors. "Thanks, Tom. You're right. I'm really down about Dr. Desmonde."

"Listen, Doc. If anyone can pull through a skull fracture, it's Monique Desmonde. She's a fighter, and a stubborn lady. Don't write her off. She'll come back, if only to prove her jackass surgeon wrong. Wait and see!" Tom gave Robert a big hug before rushing down the Hall. "Gotta go. See you, Doc. Get some rest. You look like hell."

Robert waved at the spry tech and smiled. "Thanks, Tom." He entered the physician's waiting room and called Alex's office. No answer. That concerned him. Then he called Jack's cell. Jack answered and agreed to meet him in the recovery waiting area.

Robert finished dressing and walked slowly into the recovery area. His injured arm was killing him. It was numb and felt like someone was sticking pins in it. He brushed the sensations off. It was just fatigue. It always got like that when he was tired. He checked on Monique in recovery, and learned from the nurses that she was stable and had been transferred straight up to the neuro ICU. The room was empty except for Jack and Nadine, who were seated together on a couch, talking quietly.

Robert stood in the doorway. The pair hadn't seen him. Robert felt his eyes fill with tears as he saw the goodhearted, hard-nosed policeman. If he looked bad, then Jack looked ten times worse. The commander was suffering. He looked old and tired. His body language spoke of complete misery and severe emotional pain. His face was, well, what was it? Robert had never seen the look that Jack had on his face. He continued staring at him from a distance, as his mind searched for a word that described how the commander looked. Finally, it dawned on him. It was fear and Robert had never seen Jack truly frightened.

Jack's face was a mask of fear. The commander was desperately afraid of what Robert Bonnet, his friend the surgeon, would tell them about Monique.

Robert approached Jack, who looked deep in thought, and gently tapped his shoulder. The commander jumped at his touch. He looked at Robert anxiously. Robert sat on the coffee table opposite Jack and Nadine. Neither man spoke.

Nadine, fearing the worst, reached for Jack's hand.

If he was standing in front of a firing squad, Robert was sure Jack wouldn't be as afraid as he was now.

"Hey, man. How are you?" Robert asked tentatively. The silence was endless. Françoise seemed afraid to ask, and Robert didn't want to talk. His mind was formulating the best way to tell Jack that all estimates to this point suggested that Monique would be a vegetable.

Jack's eyes implored Robert to tell him something good. Robert knew he couldn't ethically do that.

Finally, Robert said, "Jack, the surgery went well. Monique's in recovery." He paused for a moment, groping for the best words. "To be honest, Jack, the neurosurgeon isn't optimistic about her recovery. Her injury was extensive..."

"And...?" Jack asked in a small voice. If the situation hadn't been so serious, Robert would have laughed at Jack's voice.

"We don't know. The next twelve hours are critical. He put in a shunt to drain the fluid off of her brain." Robert watched as Jack's shoulders sagged and then continued, "But, I'm hopeful that she'll regain consciousness —"

Jack interrupted and said hoarsely, "I don't care if she never practices medicine again. I just want her to be able to be with me, to love me, to stay with me. I love her, Robert. I loved her as she was, and I'll love her for what she'll be. I don't care what she's like after this. I'm going to marry her and take care of her. Do you understand?"

"Of course I do, Jack. And, I'm going to pray that you get your wish. We'll all pray for that, won't we, Nadine?"

Nadine nodded and continued to hold Jack's hand. She asked Robert, "Dr. Bonnet, have you experience with patients like Dr. Desmonde?"

"Yes, I do. I'm not offering any false hopes. I never do. I simply want to say that medicine has been proven wrong many, many times. Monique may come out of this and do fairly well, great even. But, Jack, she'll never be exactly what she was, if she's anything at all. You must understand that."

"I understand, Robert. And I love her. Just keep her alive for me so she has the chance to talk again. Will you do that for me, Robert?" The commander's eyes were filled with tears.

"Of course I will." Robert touched his friend's shoulder. "I will do everything I possibly can. You know we all love her, too."

"Can I see her?"

"She's in the Neuro ICU, the neurological intensive care unit. There are a lot of machines. But I'll take you, Jack. Nadine, would you like to go?"

Nadine checked her watch and shook her head. "I'm going to Alex's office. We've got an appointment. Will you meet me there afterwards, Jack?"

"Yeah. I will," Jack said in a small voice.

"Is Alex okay?" Robert asked and looked directly at both police officers.

Nadine hesitated for a moment.

Robert immediately picked up on the hesitation and said, "Is Alex okay?" His voice was low, demanding.

"Yes, physically she's okay. Emotionally, she's drained. You can see for yourself after you two visit Monique. I'll be in her office."

At that moment, the telepage operator stat paged Commander Jack Françoise to the Pavilion. Jack said in a sour tone, "Screw the Pavilion. I'm going with Robert!"

"Let me answer the page, Jack. Otherwise, they'll keep stat paging you over and over. We need a little time and a little silence." Robert reached for his cell, called telepage, and talked for a moment.

Nadine saw his face pale a little.

He smiled at them and said, "Another incident at the Pavilion. It'll wait, Jack. Trust me."

"I do. I don't give a damn about that place anyway. Now, let's go." Jack glanced at Nadine and said, "We'll meet you and Alex in her office. Then, I'll check in the Pavilion." Jack gave Nadine a forced smile and left with Robert.

Chapter 38

Weston Whitset wasn't used to feeling fear. He didn't like it. What the hell was Anthony Gavette doing in the female seclusion room? Fleeting thoughts raced through his mind, as Anthony wrestled him to the floor and knocked him senseless in the face.

Weston knew he had the edge. Even though Anthony was powerfully built and was heavier than Weston by at least fifty pounds, Weston was smarter. He let Anthony knock him around a few times. Then, he stuck his fingers into Anthony's eyes and gave him a fierce kick to the groin. Anthony, momentarily blinded, screamed, and fell backwards. Weston sat on top of him and said, "Anthony, you're a dumb, crazy, worthless piece of shit. Let me tell you about me and Rose."

Anthony lay docile under Weston, mesmerized by his cold, black marbled eyes.

"Yeah, Anthony, let me tell you what it was like with your woman. She's like any other piece. If you're nice to her, she'll put out. No question about it. You see, me and Rose, we got this game. We talk baby talk to each other and I play with her."

Weston was enjoying himself so much that he ignored the hiss that came from Anthony's throat. He continued, "You see, Anthony, you may be a big man and all, but what I got is packaged just right for your poor little Rose. I sing her a few baby songs, sort of like nursery songs, and then we play married. She likes to play married. She pretends she's a little housewife, the little woman of the house, taking care of the plants and cooking me meatloaf. She loves the game. Then, we start to wrestle, you know. I usually sing to her while I wrestle, and then she starts to take her clothes off for me. Sometimes she knows I'm coming, so she doesn't put any on

..." Weston caught Anthony's angry look and used it to his advantage.

"Yeah, sometimes all she has on is a little teeny nighty. Now, tonight she had on a new blouse. I made up a little song about her new blouse and it took her about two seconds to take it off, and then ... well, you know, it was pretty good. Not too great, but not bad for a crazy woman. Basically, she is much too skinny for me. Just a bag of ... no real tits, not like Angie."

Whitset felt Anthony stiffen under his body. He said in a placating, singsong voice, "Oh, did you want Angie, Anthony, the big tits nurse? Well, too bad, I got her. She was mine and she was good. Anyway, Rose ain't much, even at her best. She looks like a little beggar girl when she's naked, all bones. Of course, Anthony, that probably makes a big man like you feel better, feel good. And then when she puts her..."

Weston was enjoying himself. He loved to inflict pain on others. He was enjoying himself so much that he was unprepared for the primal scream and thrust from Anthony that sent his body flailing against the wall. Momentarily stunned, he was defenseless when Anthony grabbed him and started beating his head against the hard tile floor. Beating it over and over. Whitset's last thoughts were those of searing pain, as he remembered his classmates laughing and taunting him on the school bus.

Anthony couldn't stop beating Whitset's head against the floor. He was obsessed. He beat the administrator until blood ran from his ears and mouth. The back of his head was literally flattened from the beating. Satisfied that Whitset was dead, he threw his body into the closet, closed the metal door, and went to sleep in his bed in the seclusion room. He would tell them at group tomorrow that the administrator was dead in his closet. Anthony had sweet dreams about the congrats he would receive tomorrow from his fellow patients. He knew they hated Whitset. He had been one of them, but the balance of power had been unfair. Now the balance was fair. Whitset was dead and in Anthony Gavette's mind, that was really fair. He smiled in his sleep at the thought.

Bye, bye, Lester, you son of a bitch. Forever!

Anthony had great dreams all night.

Chapter 39

The night had been endless. Alex had not slept at all. She had been plagued with nightmares and wished she had accepted Robert's offer to spend the night at her house. Consequently, she was exhausted, mentally and physically. She had sent the talkative Mona home for the day, unable to handle any extraneous noise or conversation. She had called the Neuro ICU and been advised that Monique's condition was unchanged. She was still in a deep coma.

Alex was deeply depressed. She considered calling her grandmother in Virginia, but knew Kathryn would pick up on the despondency in her voice. Her grandmother was just smart like that and she could read Alex like a book. She didn't want to upset her grandparents and have them chartering a jet to New Orleans anytime soon.

As Alex sat at her desk, she remembered the day in February, just after Mardi Gras, when she had received Mitch's last letter. In essence, it was his declaration of love. For some reason, Alex pulled out her copy of the letter from her desk and reread it. It only made more hot tears come into her eyes and she began to cry harder and wish things were different. Alex knew her life would never be the same. She knew she had to leave New Orleans and start over. Things here were just too impossible. There had been too much heartbreak in such a short period of time. First, February, and now all of this.

She continued with her morbid thoughts. She could easily identify her losses – Jack, Monique, Mitch, and possibly Robert. And for what? New Orleans had brought her nothing but heartache and grief for the last six months. The first year and a half had been okay, but lately…

As she continued to think, her eyes strayed to a letter she had received from her colleague in San Francisco. A large managed care organization was seeking a hospital attorney to set up an in house legal counsel office. The position was only for a year. Her friend was urging her to come for an interview, assuring her the organization would meet any stipulations she required. Alex began to consider it.

San Francisco sounded like a long way to go alone and start over. Virginia, Texas, New Orleans, San Francisco.... Was this a logical progression for her career? But, was that what she wanted, a career? Or did she want something else? Hadn't she said only a short time ago that she wanted a husband and a family?

Alex laughed out loud and began to consider how screwed up she was. Her grandparents would die if she moved to California. The congressman was convinced the place was doomed and had been waiting for it to fall off the face of the earth forever.

At this point, though the opportunity was sounding more promising. Perhaps she should find a position in Virginia after New Orleans. Now, that was a thought. Her grandparents were growing older and she wanted to be closer to them. She missed them dreadfully. And, she missed Virginia, the horse farm and her horse. Still, Alex continued to think as her office door opened. *Good*, she thought, *a distraction*. Anything was better than thinking about the last forty-eight hours. Standing in front of her was Nadine.

"For heaven's sake, Nadine. Sit down. You're looking at me like I might suddenly go into orbit. I'm better. I think. No, I promise." Alex gave the forensic nurse a brave smile.

Nadine sat down across from her and said, "Robert just spoke with Jack. The picture is not good for Dr. Desmonde. If I read between the lines, Robert is trying to offer Jack some hope. But, I really don't think there is much, at least based on what Robert is saying at this point." Nadine looked sad and she barely knew Monique Desmonde.

The sharp intake of air seemed to crush her chest. Alex knew her voice was breathless when she responded. "How did Jack take it?"

"Okay, I guess. He only wants her to talk to him. Says he's planning on marrying her, no matter what."

"I guess you know they have a secret relationship. But of course, you do, I told you in the car coming back from Mississippi. I only learned several days ago. They were so happy. Robert and I had dinner with them two nights ago – to celebrate. I think they had planned to marry. They were so happy." Her voice trailed off, unable to believe that so much could happen so quickly and be so devastating.

"Yeah, I know. You told me. I hope she comes out of it. They'll be down here shortly. Robert was taking Jack to see Monique in the ICU again." Nadine's voice sounded glum.

Alex shuddered. "Oh my, I hope Jack's able to keep it together. I wish I were with him. If you know anything about hospitals, a PACU or ICU can be scary and intimidating, to say the least. "

Nadine nodded. "Dr. Bonnet will do a good job. He's a kind, sensitive man." Nadine paused for a moment and looked at Alex directly. "You know, Alex, Dr. Bonnet loves you as well. Did you know that?"

Alex looked uncertain. "I don't know, Nadine. We have a lot of issues to work on. We were married once and Robert's been troubled with his arm. I can't say for sure things will ever work for us. He's prone to sadness and depression and I don't want to live with that."

Nadine nodded and looked at her quietly, "That's part of his Creole blood. Do you want things to work out, Alex?"

Alex said in a tired voice, "I don't know, Nadine. There is too much happening now. Too many other things to work on. We'll see."

"Will you promise to allow Robert to help you work through this thing with Whitset? Your recovery from the rape will be the same no matter what the lab test determines. Do you understand that?" Nadine looked at her, her dark eyes locked with Alex's blue ones.

"I don't know. I just don't know. I'm pretty confused now. We'll see. I will promise you that I won't shut —" Alex was interrupted when Robert and Jack walked into her office. They both had a sense of urgency about them.

Robert walked over and hugged her for a moment. He could feel how stiff she felt in his arms. He sighed and looked at Jack.

Françoise said in a rough voice, "We've got to hightail it over to the Pavilion. There's another corpse over there!"

"My God, now who, Commander?" Nadine asked in a breathless voice. "Is this ever going to stop?"

"Don't know, Nadine. Josh just paged me again. He said to get over there ASAP. He and Elizabeth are up there and the forensic team is coming."

Alex looked and felt weary, as she gathered her legal pad and purse. She asked, "Did anyone call Don Montgomery?"

"I'm not calling the SOB. Let's move!" No one stopped to argue with Françoise.

Chapter 40

The Pavilion was bristling with activity. Once again, the place was crawling with police. Sandy Pilsner met them at the locked door and ushered them in. Sandy announced she was covering for Donna Meade, who was still out from the injuries inflicted on her by Anthony Gavette.

"Sandy, you just keep showing up like a good penny every time something bad has happened." Alex reached out to hug her.

Sandy hugged Alex back and said, "Thank goodness for the added security. This place is crazy! All the seclusion rooms are full and the place is finally sort of stable. Let's go back to the community room." Her voice was quiet and subdued, but her high color reflected the intensity of the situation.

"Who is dead? Tell us, Sandy." Alex's voice sounded desperate as they walked down the hall and entered the community room. She quickly looked around, relieved that only staff she knew were present.

Josh Martin met them at the community room door. He quietly ushered them into the room. His eyes were strangely bright. He looked pleased, even happy.

Sandy sat at the head of the table and addressed the group. "At the morning group meeting, Anthony announced that he had a dead body in the closet in the seclusion room. No one really paid any attention to him. He had been locked in seclusion since his attack on Donna. Anyway, he began a long story about how his seclusion room had an elevator in the closet and how someone had come in his room last night. He told us how that someone had been using the seclusion room for his fun house and love nest and how that same someone had raped and killed a female patient earlier this year. One of the nurses remembered the suicide of a young woman in that room late this spring. I began to take notice, so I called Officer Martin here and he and I went with Anthony into the seclusion room. He was right. There is an elevator and the body..."

"Who the hell is in there?" Françoise's voice was furious. "Martin, have you secured the scene?"

Josh nodded and said, "Why don't we just show you, Commander, all of you if you'd like!"

Alex felt her fear increasing as they walked down the hall, passed the nurse's station, and entered the last seclusion room. Smears of blood were on the floor and the wall.

Josh moved ahead of the group and opened the closet. There, on the floor, in a pool of blood, hair, and brain matter, was a very dead Lester – Weston – Whitset.

A pitiful cry came from Alex, as she crammed her fist into her mouth and fainted into Robert and Josh Martin's arms.

At the same moment, Donald Montgomery entered the room, screaming and cursing because he hadn't been called immediately. When he saw the dead Whitset, he turned and started upbraiding Jack Françoise for shoddy police work.

Don's voice was loud and angry. "What the hell, Françoise? Why didn't you find this man last night? What the hell is he doing dead in a closet in my hospital? You and your officers are worthless pieces of shit! How am I ever going to explain this one – to the media, to the board? My own administrator, dead in his own hospital on his own unit. What the hell am I supposed to say?"

Françoise's dark eyes gleamed hatefully at the pompous Montgomery. He said in a scathing voice, "I don't really give a shit what you say, Montgomery, but listen to this. *Your* administrator, whom *you* hired *all* by yourself, was an imposter. He wasn't even a hospital administrator. The bastard didn't even have a college degree. What kind of a moron are you?"

Montgomery looked at Jack with disbelief and said, "Listen, you stupid son of a bitch. Whitset is exactly who he is—"

Jack grabbed the hospital administrator by the shoulder and shook him as he interrupted Montgomery's tirade. "Listen, you idiot. Lester Whitset was really Weston Whitset. Lester, a bona fide hospital administrator, died years ago, and Weston, a deranged mental patient who spent most of his life confined for aberrant behavior, assumed his identity. He was a rapist and a murderer. Did you check him out, Montgomery, or did you just hire him because he promised to reduce costs?" Françoise paused for a moment, and then continued to go head to head with the red-faced CEO.

By this time, an audience had gathered outside the room. Françoise continued, completely out of control, his emotional agony unleashed. He said harshly, "By the way, Donald, how big was Whitset's percentage this quarter? What was his bonus for saving costs at the expense of patient care? Thousands of dollars? Talk about incompetent, look in the mirror, you weasel-faced son of a bitch."

Montgomery was white with anger and unable to speak.

Françoise was enjoying the scene, but was still angry. He said, "Never mind, you little ingratiating asshole, you don't have to tell me! It's a matter of record that the *Times Picayune* will be hot to know. You're a cheap, stingy, son of a bitch!" Françoise sneered at the CEO.

Montgomery was livid with fury. He lunged towards the commander. Josh Martin was about to come to his commander's defense when Françoise slammed his fist into the administrator's face, cold cocking him onto the floor. A rousing cheer went up from the group.

Alex completely missed it. When she came to, Robert took her home, where she slept for hours.

Chapter 41

Alex woke up in her bed in a cold sweat, hearing muffled, choking sounds. Where are they coming from? She looked around her darkened room. It's me, she noted. She felt like she was being suffocated. Her body was rigid and heavy. The illuminated dial of the alarm clock next to her bed said 3:00 a.m. At first, Alex's mind was numb and frozen. She felt acute pain in her shoulder as she attempted to roll over. Then, it all came back to her and an agonizing sound came from her mouth as she began to scream.

Immediately, Robert Bonnet was at her side.

She continued to cry uncontrollably. Robert attempted to take her into his arms to comfort her, but she resisted, pushing him away forcefully. She turned her body away from him and curled up into a little ball in the fetal position in her bed.

Robert was desperate. He didn't know what to do. Every effort he made to comfort Alex made him feel increasingly useless. He was tempted to call Nadine Wells for advice, but decided against it. He knew the policewoman had put in the long hours and deserved a good night's rest. After all, she had told him to expect something like this since Alex was in the initial phase of rape trauma syndrome. He tried to remember the things Nadine had told him to expect, but his tired mind refused to let him think back to their conversation. Gradually, Alex's crying slowed to a muffled sob, and Robert went into the kitchen to make her some hot tea. When he returned to her room with a tray, Alex was sound asleep.

Robert went back into the kitchen where he sat for several hours, reminiscing over his life with Alex and the tragic events of the past few days. He felt miserable, guilty. He had enough to contend with before, and now he had no idea where it would lead or whether Alex would ever recover. Finally, he returned to bed, depressed and sad.

He rested fitfully in Alex's beautifully appointed guest room. His mind kept returning to the attack on Alex and Monique. Why hadn't he insisted on going in with Alex when he dropped her off at Monique's house? Why hadn't he sensed the danger? How could he have been so stupid? Robert continued with his self-deprecation until he could think of nothing else to blame himself for. This was all his fault. It was his fault Alex and Monique had been attacked. It was his fault the marriage had ended and that knowledge was utterly painful to him.

He felt tears jump into his eyes. The dinner he and Alex shared only two nights ago had been so promising. He had begun to think that perhaps Alex would marry him again. Now, they had all of this to work through – the rape, the medical problems with Monique, and Jack's grief. Of course, he had been grappling for months with the thought that he would never be able to operate again. A surgeon without hands, an amputee, that's how he perceived himself. That in itself had caused him to be terribly depressed over the past six months. And now all of this. He could only hope and pray that he could cope.

Robert checked his watch for the third time in twenty minutes. It was almost six o'clock in the morning. He checked on Alex and she was sleeping peacefully. He then phoned the neuro intensive care unit at CCMC. The nurses reported that Dr. Desmonde was the same, stable but unresponsive. Robert could only guess how Jack was doing and figured he was feeling just as useless as he was. Thank goodness, he wasn't in Jack's position. At least Alex could think and talk, but Monique probably wouldn't ever come out of her coma. She probably wouldn't even wake up. Tomorrow, they would do the first EEG to measure her brainwave activity. He prayed that the swelling had decreased. He wasn't ready to tell Jack they needed to disconnect the ventilator and let her die. Please, Lord, he prayed to himself, don't let that happen.

Robert returned to the kitchen and made coffee. The annoying feeling in his gut told him he was hungry, but he had no desire to eat. He continued to sit at the table, silently drinking coffee and reminiscing over all the mistakes he had made in his adult life. He only wanted his childhood again, just to be young and carefree. Finally, he was aware that Alex was behind him. He could feel her presence.

She smiled tentatively at him, touched his shoulder, and asked, "Could you share your coffee with me?"

He stood immediately, "I can do better than that. I'll let you have your own cup."

Alex had huge coffee cups, just like the ones Alex's grandmother had in Virginia. Robert removed a brightly decorated porcelain cup from the cabinet, made Alex a cup of coffee in her Keurig, and set it down in front of her with a flourish. He was pleased that she looked so rested and relaxed.

Alex savored the rich flavor of the New Orleans coffee. She murmured her appreciation, "Mmm, this is good. I feel like I may be human again. Thanks, Robert. Thank you for staying with me and for always being there for me. It means a lot, especially in times like these."

Robert smiled, feeling a little brighter. Alex looked lovely this morning. Her hair was down and its curly reddish-chestnut color beautifully framed her delicately colored face. Her eyes were clear and blue. There were no signs of tears, dark circles, or fatigue. Only the black eye and the drooping shoulder told of her recent misery.

He said lightly, "You look rested this morning, Al. You must've gotten some sleep."

"Yes, I did. I remember awakening during the night and crying. It all came back to me, but I decided that today's another day and we need to move forward. Have you checked on Monique?" Her voice and her face expressed her concern about her friend.

"Yeah, I have. There's no change. It's still pretty early, Alex," Robert said, noting the crestfallen look on her face. "You know that." His voice was soft, but definitive, as he attempted to comfort her.

Alex nodded, stirring her coffee. She looked up and asked, "Did Anthony Gavette kill Whitset?"

Robert nodded. "Yes, he did. Apparently, Whitset had a secret access to the Pavilion. He used the old tunnels that connected the Pavilion to the main hospital building. Most people had totally forgotten they existed. That's how he had been coming and going secretly for months."

"Wasn't something said before I fainted about his killing a patient in there?"

"Yep, he did. He told Anthony, who reported it to the psych staff, and it checks out. I talked to Jack last night, who confirmed that a young woman admitted for depression a few months back had committed suicide in the room by slashing her wrists. The staff never knew where she'd gotten the razor. Apparently, Whitset gave it to her – at least, according to Anthony. Or, who knows, perhaps Whitset slashed her wrists and watched her bleed. He seemed to be that crazy."

"Did he rape her?" Alex asked and continued to stare into her coffee.

"I don't know. I don't think they can prove that, but Anthony said Whitset told him all about it. I would guess it's probably true. Whitset was a sick man." Robert looked carefully at Alex.

"Also, Jack seems to think Whitset probably did slash the woman's wrists because there was a bottle of wine and human blood found in his office. They were mixed together. I think forensics is going to type the blood and see if it matches the dead woman's."

Alex was appalled and her face was disbelieving. "What, you think Whitset bled the woman's wrist into the wine bottle? How disgusting!" She shuddered at the thought.

Robert nodded. "Yes, grotesque and disgusting. Somehow, he got the blood into the wine bottle. Unbelievable!"

"Un huh, you bet. Real sick. You're sure he's dead?" Alex's voice was tremulous.

"Positive. I'm absolutely sure. I saw him."

Alex looked relieved, "I'm glad. Very glad. I guess that's not the best way to feel, but I'm glad he is dead".

Robert reached for her hand. "I think it's a very honest and appropriate way to feel. I feel the same way."

"Good," Alex said brightly. "I feel vindicated, and I'm hungry. Let's eat. What should we have?"

"I'll cook, you get dressed. You know that breakfast is the only meal I can make." Robert paused for a moment and said with a smile on his face, "By the way, Alex, do you remember what Jack did to Montgomery?"

Alex looked confused. "What Jack did to Don? No, I don't think so."

Delight was written all over Robert's face as he told her, "He cold-cocked him! Knocked the hell out of him! It was great!"

Alex burst into laughter. "You're kidding! When?"

"Yesterday, just after you fainted. I wanted to take a picture with my iPhone, but didn't. Everyone standing around gave Françoise a huge cheer!"

Alex continued to laugh. "I'm sorry I missed it. Jack's been dying to do that for a long time and Montgomery finally pushed him over the edge. I just wish I'd seen it —" She was interrupted by the phone.

Robert answered and said, "Speak of the devil." It was Jack. They talked for several moments. Robert gave a delightful war whoop and hung up the phone. He was smiling a huge smile.

"Robert, what is it? What did he say?" Alex's voice was excited, inpatient.

"Jack swears that Monique just squeezed his hand. He swears she can hear him. He said she opened her eyes!" Robert was ecstatic.

"What do the nurses say? Do you think Jack could've imagined it?" Alex felt hopeful but looked uncertain.

Robert stared at her and said firmly, "No. If Jack saw Monique with her eyes open and felt her squeeze his hand, then it happened."

Alex smiled happily, "Let's hurry up and eat. I want to go see for myself."

"Me, too. Get dressed and we'll eat in a hurry. Jack also wants to give us the final information about Whitset before he closes the case."

Alex felt her happiness ebb away and felt fear engulf her. *He must have the results of my lab reports,* she thought to herself. *At least I'll know.* Then, she remembered. *Well, maybe I will know something.*

The couple ate a quick breakfast and hurried to the hospital. They found Jack in the waiting room outside the intensive care unit. He looked forlorn, exhausted, and gloomy. His face brightened when he saw Robert and Alex.

"That damned doctor who operated told me there was no way Monique squeezed my hand. He said her brain is too swollen for her to do anything like that."

Alex felt her heart sink. She looked for reassurance. She walked over and gave Jack a huge hug.

Robert said to Jack, "If you felt her squeeze your hand, then she squeezed your hand." Robert reassured him with a smile. "I'm going to go look in on her." Robert was mentally cursing the neurosurgeon. What a bastard the man was; but that being said, he was a great neurosurgeon.

"I'm going to go, too. The hell with that man. How about you, Alex? By the way, you look mighty good today." Jack leaned over, hugged her again, and gave her a kiss on the cheek.

Alex turned towards him and winced as her shoulder reminded her it was broken, smiled, and once again returned the hug offered by the thickset, kindhearted police commander. She whispered clandestinely, "I heard you knocked out my boss!"

Commander Françoise's eyes lit up and he smiled from ear to ear. "You're damned right, I did, Al. I would have kept hitting the son of a bitch if Josh Martin hadn't stopped me. Little prick has had it coming for months..."

"Probably all of his life," Alex surmised.

Chapter 42

Alex had a hard time controlling her emotions when she looked down at Monique Desmonde. She had forgotten how horrible craniotomy patients looked after surgery. Monique's eyes were both black and her face was swollen. She wasn't recognizable. Alex managed to keep herself together, but felt her heart sink as she heard Jack talking softly to her. She also began to talk to Monique. But there was no response. Monique seemed to be in a deep coma. Alex was beginning to doubt what Jack had seen. She looked over and saw Robert reviewing Monique's chart. He shook his head at Alex and came to the bedside.

Robert and Alex stood quietly looking at Monique.

Jack continued to hold her hand and talk to her. Finally, he said, "Well, she ain't talkin' now, but that doesn't mean she won't wake up a little later, right, Robert?"

"That's right, Jack. Let's go." Robert's voice was gentle.

"Nah, I'm staying a while longer. Can we meet in your office later this morning, Alex? I'll have everything by then and I'll give you both the finals. Nadine's coming at 10 o'clock." Jack looked sad.

"Sure, Jack. We'll see you then."

"I'm going to the O.R. to get a shower and change my clothes. Either of you need anything?" Robert asked.

"No," Jack and Alex said in unison.

"I'll walk out with you, Robert. See you in a little while, Jack. You want any donuts?" Alex asked in a teasing voice.

"No, I'm not hungry lately," Jack said a little dismally. He knew what his friends were thinking.

On the way out of the unit, Alex asked Robert, "What do you think, Robert? Do you think Jack just wanted to believe Monique was coming out of it?"

334

"I don't think anything. I'm just praying Jack is right." Robert's voice was tense, and Alex could feel his disappointment. "That being said, she's still in a deep coma and I certainly didn't see any response at all."

Chapter 43

Mona, Bridgett, and Latetia were drinking coffee and gossiping in Alex's office. All three stood and hugged her when she came in.

Bridgett looked rested and she was laughing. "Guess what, Al? Angie's much better today! Last night she began to come around. She began talking about the attack and said it was Whitset who attacked her. Angie was a little emotional when Jack told her that Whitset was dead. It takes her a while to understand stuff, but then she said she was glad."

Alex hugged Bridgett again, as her secretary continued to talk.

"Anyway, she seemed relieved that Whitset was dead. Nadine told her that her responses were natural, well, you know, normal. Anyway, she is so much better, and I feel so grateful to you all." Bridgett looked like her old self. Her blond hair was piled high on her head, her blue eyes were sparkling, and the rings of fatigue around her eyes were gone. Her clothes, once again, were outrageous. She wore a pink mini-skirt, an orange tank top, and a lime green blazer. She couldn't be any brighter. She even had on three-inch gold heels and the largest lime green necklace and drop earrings Alex had ever seen.

Alex shook her head when she noted Bridgett's outfit, but was so happy for her that she just said, "Bridge, I'm so glad. I know Angie's going to be fine now. She is strong and practical, just like you, and she will be able to work through it. Besides, she has her husband and Jessica to pull her through. They'll help her refocus her life."

Bridgett hugged Alex again and said, "Alex, will you help me help her? You are so good at helping people with things."

336

Alex felt her heart start to beat frantically. She understood then that Bridgett didn't know that Whitset had attacked and raped her as well. Alex didn't know if she would be able to help herself, much less Angie.

"I'll do my best, Bridge. You know that. And by the way, you're so bright that most people would need sunglasses to look at you today. What an outfit!" If Bridgett picked up on the hesitancy in Alex's voice, she didn't let on.

Bridgett looked a bit chagrined. "Yeah, but I wanted to look cheerful for Angie. Believe me, she had plenty to say to me about my outfit. She's so conservative. She doesn't dress like me at all anymore. She used to hate it when Momma dressed us alike in bright colors."

Latetia, laughing at them, commented, "Yes, Miss Bridgett, now, she does wear the bright clothes. No question."

Alex's spirits rose as she looked at Leticia. "Latetia, how's the boss this morning?"

Latetia smiled coyly at Alex and said, "Well, Miss Alex, Mr. Montgomery isn't in this morning. I doubt he'll be here for the rest of the week. Rumor has it that he has a black eye, among other injuries." I even heard he needed to see his dentist 'cause he lost a few teeth!" Latetia was smiling broadly, her white teeth shining.

Alex held up her hand to stop her and said gaily, "Say no more, Latetia. Let's just revel in rumors and the memories! And, Miss Mona, how are you today?"

"I'm alright, Alex. I'm glad to see you're looking so good. Much better than yesterday! I guess I'm a little sad, though. Looks like I'll be out of a job soon. Bridge is coming back next week." Mona looked a little forlorn.

"Get off it, Mona. You know you can only stand working a week at a time. If you need some extra work, I'm sure Alex can arrange it. Right, Alex?" Bridgett winked at Alex.

Alex smiled at both women. "Yeah. You bet. Just let me know, Mona."

Bridgett changed the subject. "How's Dr. Desmonde, Alex?

Alex shook her head. "Not good, Bridgett. She's the same. She's in a coma. Dr. Bonnet is hopeful that she'll regain consciousness soon. Her neurosurgeon is less hopeful."

Bridgett and Latetia looked sad.

Mona said expectantly, "Commander Françoise was in here earlier. He said she had squeezed his hand."

Alex nodded her head and said, "Yes, I know. He told me, too. But now, she seems to be back in a deep coma." There was silence and Alex continued, "Bridgett or Mona, could you have dietary send up some coffee and donuts for us? Jack and Robert are coming over soon and will be in my office."

Bridgett said with some authority, "The commander just needs to be patient, Angie was in a coma too, and now she's just fine."

"Why don't you remind him of that, Bridgett, when you see him today," Alex suggested. "He could use a perk."

Bridgett gave Alex a bright, dazzling smile. "I'll do just that, Alex. The commander is a good man."

Alex nodded in agreement, while Mona went to call dietary. Then, she waved goodbye to the secretaries and went into her office.

As Alex savored the silence and elegance of her office, she noted she had less than an hour before Jack, Nadine, and Robert would show up. It occurred to her that no one knew about her rape except for Jack, Robert, Josh, and Nadine. That was comforting. If Bridgett or Mona knew, she would've picked up on it. Alex felt some relief that her confidentiality was intact.

As she continued to think, she again noticed the letter
from her friend in San Francisco. Alex found herself reading
the letter and scanning the organization's annual report. Her
interest in setting up their legal department was heightened.
More than ever, she felt a pressing need to get out of New
Orleans and away from Crescent City Medical Center for a
while. Perhaps she could arrange for a year or two sabbatical.
Maybe by then, Don would have quit and she could come
back. She was infinitely sick of him and his juvenile antics.
But she might as well forget California. Her grandparents
would have a fit, particularly the congressman. She really
needed to get closer to Virginia. It occurred to her that this
was the second time she had had these thoughts in a very
short period of time. *Maybe, though, she should consider
California for a year.*

Mona buzzed her and said the others were in her
conference room. Alex went in, her heart pounding, as if she
were about to be executed. Now, she would find out if she
had been forcibly raped or not. Then, she could make plans
and get on with her life.

Jack, Robert, and Nadine were drinking coffee and
talking quietly. Only Robert was eating a donut. *A bad sign*,
Alex thought. Jack had never turned down a donut before.
She studied his face as she sat down. It was dismal as he
spoke to them. He looked like a whipped puppy.

"I don't have much to tell you," he began. "First of all,
Whitset was responsible for the rape and beating of Angie
and the murder of Mrs. Smithson. The evidence is conclusive;
the bite marks match up perfectly."

Alex and Robert sat quietly and Nadine said, "Go on,
Jack, what else?"

Jack sighed and continued, "There's also evidence that
Weston Whitset killed his elementary school teacher when he
was seven years old. After that, he was committed to a state

institution for the criminally insane. Anyway, Weston assumed the identity of his brother, Lester, about twenty years ago. Lester was a hospital administrator in the British West Indies and died there rather unexpectedly. As a matter of fact, he died during a visit from Weston. Weston Whitset had been released earlier from a forensics unit and had gone there to visit. Apparently, Lester Whitset's death was never reported in the United States, but Weston Whitset's was." Jack looked around at the incredulous stares of the group.

The commander continued, "Therefore, the psych hospital wrote him off and never expected him back for follow-up. There was some speculation of foul play in Lester's death, but the evidence against Weston was inconclusive. After a year or so, Weston Whitset reappeared in the United States as Lester Whitset and assumed his brother's identity and occupation."

Alex moaned and said, "Oh, my God, this is unbelievable!"

Françoise agreed, "Yes, unbelievable, but true. Anyway, the records at the Pennsylvania psychiatric hospital noted that Lester Whitset had called from the West Indies, shortly before his death, and expressed concern because his brother had stopped taking his medicine and was acting strangely. Shortly after that, the hospital received notice of Weston Whitset's death, so they closed their case."

Robert interrupted, "So, was it proven that Whitset killed his brother?"

"No," Jack said. "Lester Whitset apparently drowned while sailing. An autopsy revealed he had been taking illegal drugs – a real surprise to everyone. Anyhow, the investigation and evidence against Weston was inconclusive. It's an incredible story!" Jack lamented, as he shook his head.

"What was Whitset's psychiatric diagnosis?" Robert asked.

Jack shook his head and said, "I'll try to explain, but it's hard. He was diagnosed with autism when he was little and then as a paranoid schizophrenic. He was dangerous and violent. I'll never understand why they let him travel out of the United States." Françoise shook his head disgustedly.

Alex remembered back when psychiatric hospitals had emptied their patients into society. The timing was about right, the late 1960s and early 1970s. "Not so surprising, really. Has anyone in psychiatry reviewed Whitset's records from Pennsylvania?"

Commander Françoise smiled at her. "Funny you should mention that, Alex. Our state forensic psychiatrist called me an hour ago. He said that, based on his review of Whitset's records, he would diagnose him as having delusional misidentification syndrome."

"What! What in the heck is that? I've never heard of it. Delusional misidentification syndrome. Is that for real?" Robert asked.

"It's apparently a syndrome in which the affected patient believes that people in his environment experience radical changes in their psychological identity without a change in their physical appearance. In this case, the forensic expert said he based his opinion on the fact that Whitset was actually suffering from Fregoli Syndrome. Fregoli's occurs when the patient has the delusion that others exhibit radical changes in their physical identity without changing their behavior."

"Huh? Say that again, Jack. I want to be sure I understand," Nadine said. The others nodded their heads in agreement.

"I wish Monique was here to explain it. I really can't. Interestingly enough, she had suspected it and had noted that as a potential diagnosis in his file in her office. Let me try to tell you what I can." Jack looked so tired and sad that Alex was alarmed for him.

Jack repeated the definition of misidentification syndrome and continued, "Whitset's records say that he reported his schoolteacher turned into plastic before he killed her. He said she was a plastic person, an imposter, and he had to kill her because his voices told him to. He referred to these plastic people as imposters all the way through his medical records. The forensic psychiatrist thinks that is why Whitset tried to destroy and eradicate the faces of Angie, Monique, and Mrs. Smithson. The shrink thinks Whitset saw them as plastic people. Apparently, it's written all through his medical records that his job was to kill imposters!"

Noting the confusion on the faces of his colleagues, Jack tried again, "In other words, Monique, Angela, and Mrs. Smithson turned to plastic in front of him. A delusion, I guess. Anyway, whenever Whitset got angry with them, they appeared plastic to him. They were physically, in his mind, the same people with plastic faces. They were the same people with the same behavior, but, Whitset, the wacko, considered them imposters and his enemies. Since his voices told him to destroy imposters, he went about his mission."

Alex felt sick to her stomach. "This is hideous, just grotesque. It sounds like the plot for a horror movie. I can't believe it happened here at Crescent City!"

Nadine nodded her head in agreement with Alex and said, "Yeah, it's a ghastly story. Isn't it ironic that it was Whitset who was actually the imposter? Do these types of patients usually commit rape, Jack?"

Jack shrugged his shoulders and said, "I don't know, Nadine. The state guy didn't say. There is no evidence to suggest they do. I forgot to ask, I was so appalled at the story. Anyway, Whitset did have an aberrant sexual history. There were several sexual situations when he was hospitalized, so I guess it's hard to say. We do know that Whitset raped people."

342

"I guess Whitset planted the evidence to try to implicate Jim McMurdie, didn't he?" Alex asked.

Jack answered affirmatively. "Yep, and almost got away with it too. I think he knew Monique was on to him. I think that's why he went after her. Just like Whitset's schoolteacher, Angie, and Mrs. Smithson, I suppose Monique turned to plastic and appeared as an imposter in Whitset's sick, whacked out mind." Jack's voice was sad and forlorn. "I hate crazies," he added.

There was a long silence as each of them considered Jack's story. It was a lot to take in and understand.

Finally, in a quavering voice, Alex asked, "Jack, do you have the results of my rape tests?"

The commander looked at her gently and said, "Yes, I do, Alex. The tests are inconclusive. Whitset was a non-secretor and ..."

Alex felt her heart sink. *Now I'll never know*, she thought to herself.

Jack interrupted her thoughts and said, "However, the other tests were conclusive. The physician reported no evidence of penetration or any other physical evidence that would support an actual physical rape."

Alex felt optimistic for a moment, until Nadine's sharp voice interrupted her.

"You still encountered a psychological rape, so you'll have to be prepared to work through the trauma. The emotional piece is unchanged. You do understand that, don't you, Alex?"

Alex nodded and said, "Of course I do. Thank heavens that Josh Martin arrived when he did. I'll be thankful for that for the rest of my life." In her heart, Alex knew that she hadn't been raped by Whitset. For some reason, that gave her comfort and she was ready to move on.

Robert took her hand and smiled at her.

Alex resisted the urge to jerk it away from him, not quite understanding why she was having such a negative reaction to Robert. He had been just great, wonderful to her in fact. *What the hell was wrong with her?*

Just at that moment, Mona appeared at the door, breathless, and said, "Commander, Commander, the nurse in neurosurgery is on the phone. She has news for you. The phone in here should ring in just a moment."

Jack jumped up and grabbed the conference phone.

Alex, Robert, and Nadine looked at him expectantly, hope on each of their faces.

Jack broke out into a gleeful laugh, saying, "I'll be right up." He turned to his friends, "She's awake, she's awake! She asked for me! I'll see you yo-yo's later."

Jack hugged Alex, Nadine, and Robert all at the same time and then literally danced out of Alex's conference room.

"Think he'll take the elevator?" Alex quipped.

"Nah," said Robert. "He'll run up the four flights of stairs! I'd better arrange for a crash cart by the elevator."

They all burst out laughing, all aware of Jack's elevator phobia. Life was good after all.

Chapter 44

Later that evening, Alex and Robert were finishing dinner at Café Dégas, one of Alex's favorite neighborhood restaurants. The mood had been light and joyful. Now, as Alex looked around the restaurant, she found herself a little depressed. Café Dégas had been Mitch's favorite restaurant and they had dined there often. Her thoughts returned to Mitch and how much she had loved him – or, *at least, thought she had.*

Robert leaned forward and asked in his deep, beautiful voice, "Why so pensive, Alex? We're having a wonderful time! We have so much to be thankful for."

Alex looked at him, smiled lightly, and said, "Yes, we do, but I need to tell you something, Robert."

Robert felt the walls crashing in. He knew it was his depression returning. "Yes," he said hesitantly, afraid of what she would say and knowing he didn't want to hear it.

"I'm going to Virginia for a few weeks. You know how I go back home for renewal. I need to see Dundee and ride her through the woods. I need some time away. I also need to check on Grand and Granddad."

"Yes, I know that," Robert said, his voice anxious, hoping that Alex would invite him as she had in February.

Alex knew what he was thinking, but she also knew she needed time alone. She continued, "I need some time to myself. So much has happened. I'd like to spend some time in friendly, familiar surroundings."

"I understand. I'll be here when you get back. You know that." His voice was low and gentle, his French accent subtle, refined, and cultured.

Alex was trying to choose her words carefully. She knew Robert loved her and she didn't want to hurt him any more than she had to.

She continued, "When I return from Virginia, I think I'm going to consider an opportunity in San Francisco. They're looking for an attorney to set up a legal department in a new managed care organization. I've gotten several letters from them and I..."

Robert felt like something was grabbing his heart. He looked at her sadly and said tenderly, "I understand, Alex. I want you to do what's best for you. I have always wanted that." His eyes were sad.

"I'm not planning to leave forever. I'm only going to take a sabbatical. Maybe a year or so, just to get this legal department up and running. I will come back to New Orleans. You know my grandfather would just die if I moved to San Francisco permanently. He's half dead now because I'm living here."

Robert nodded and smiled. "Yes, I know very well. I am well aware," Robert said, trying to make light of the situation.

"Anyway, he's convinced it's past time for California to fall into the ocean. It's just that ... I need time to think things out and recover from this year. So much has happened ..." Her voice faltered.

"You don't need to explain, Alex. I know you need time. I'll be here when you get back. I'll take care of things here – Monique and Jack, and the like. And I'll clean this place up while you're gone. I'll be sure Farve is gone when you return, and will work hard on getting Montgomery out of here too." Robert's voice was strong.

"Thank you, Robert. Thank you for loving me enough to let me go." She looked at him sadly.

"I do, Al, and I will." He leaned across the table and gently kissed her. In his heart, he believed he had lost her.

346

But, he could still hope, right? He could wait for her forever ... and then some.

Epilogue

Jack Françoise sat back in the recliner in his office on Royal Street, his door shut tightly against the noise of the bullpen, his eyes closed tightly as they oozed silent tears. He had been motionless for hours, battling emotions he never knew he had. For the first time in his life, Jack felt hopeless, useless, and drained of everything that was good in life.

He had returned from CCMC late in the afternoon where Monique, who had been doing well since she had awakened several days ago, had once again lapsed into a deep coma. Her neurosurgeon was an asshole and was not hopeful that she would awaken again. Of course, the jackass doctor had never thought she would wake up to begin with. Robert encouraged Jack to be hopeful, but of course, Robert was of no use because he was devastated over Alex's plans to leave CCMC for a year in San Francisco, pending Don's approval of course. Robert viewed her exodus as a direct rejection of him and their future. Unfortunately, his therapist was in a coma and unable to help. *Things really suck around here,* Jack thought to himself.

To make matters worse, his nemesis, the mayor had called the commander to City Hall and berated him for not finding the killer of Senator Beau LaMont and DNC Hayes Hunter. Jack figured the governor was giving the mayor grief and since shit flowed downward, it was now his turn. The mayor didn't give a damn about the two kids who had been murdered on the same day. What a surprise! Jack knew that Dr. Madeline Jeanfreau had connected the political killings with the murder of the kids, but he hadn't had time to meet with her to examine the evidence. There was never enough time and never enough energy to get things done.

Jack sighed to himself as the tears began to cease. He felt his weariness subside and despondency decrease. Tomorrow was another day. Hopefully, it would be a better day. Perhaps, Monique would squeeze his hand, and he could focus once again on finding St. Germaine.

After a short nap, Jack took a deep breath, rose from his recliner, swung open his office door, and roared greetings to his nightshift. They rallied around him in support. The NOPD of the 8th Police District loved and respected their leader. Jack felt his vigor and energy return. He *would* make it and so would Monique, Alex, and Robert. He was confidant again. Life was good.

The End

To be continued in Viral Intent

The Imposter

Thank you for reading *The Imposter*, the second Alexandra Destephano Medical Thriller. I hope you enjoyed it. Alex's story continues in five more fast-paced medical thrillers that will take you into the deep, often complex world of medical, hospital and organized crime.

Read More About Alex in Viral Intent

Book 3, **Viral Intent** opens with the outbreak of an unidentified killer virus in the Crescent City Medical Emergency department. The first victim is a Secret Service Agent who is in New Orleans providing upfront security for the President of the United States who arrives the next day. **Get Your Copy Now!**

Viral Intent

Book Three of the Alexandra Destephano Series

Chapter 1

"Sandy! Sandy! You have got to come here right away! Something horrible is happening to the guy in bed 3! I have no idea what's up with him, but I think he's going to die!" Kelsey Saunders voice was shrill with anxiety.

Sandy Pilsner, nurse manager of the newly-named Crescent City Health Sciences Center looked up from the nurses' station and said, "What's up, Kelsey? I just saw him twenty minutes ago when I was making rounds."

Kelsey's face was white with fear. "It's awful. He has blood coming out of his eyes and his blood pressure is really low. He's also shaking all over. I don't know if it is a seizure or his fever. Trouble breathing too. "

Sandy Pilsner, rose from her seat and looked into the eyes of the almost hysterical Kelsey, her new nursing graduate intern from LSU. She said gently, "Kelsey, it's okay. I just checked on him a few minutes ago. He seemed fine

352

except for his fever and the fact that his blood work is really screwed up and he has scant urine output."

"I know, I know I know, but I am telling you that things have changed quickly. Hurry up! I am sure he is going to die in a few minutes. There is just something wrong. He is totally going bad." Kelsey brown eyes were huge and Sandy could see anxiety and worry reflected in them.

"All right, let's go and check him out," Sandy suggested as she thought of the ideal teaching moment they would have when suddenly a harsh voice barked CODE BLUE, CODE BLUE, ED, Bed 3 over the hospital voice system.

Sandy grimaced. "Well, Kelsey, you called that one right! Let's see what we can do," as two nurses rushed towards the opposite end of the ED, one pulling an extra crash cart in case it was needed.

The Code team was in action and two amps of bicarb had already been administered when Sandy and Kelsey reached Bed 3. The patient's lips were blue from circumoral cyanosis . His nails looked as though someone had painted them with a pearly blue nail polish. His eyes, which were open and staring were blood red from petechiae and broken blood vessels. There was bloody drainage from the right orbit staining his cheek. Sandy noticed the flat, and raised maculopapular rash on his chest. She could swear he hadn't had that rash thirty minutes ago.

The ED doc in charge, Dr. Fred Patterson, saw Sandy and hollered, "What the hell does this guy have? He's bleeding from everywhere and I have no idea what is wrong with him! Give me a history and for God's sake, get us some protective gear in here."

Sandy stood quietly, transfixed. She had never seen Dr. Patterson anxious or even tense. She panicked for a moment but didn't know why.

Dr. Patterson glared at her. "Give me a history. He's bleeding out, for God's sake, Sandy, and I don't know why. This is at the very least malaria or typhoid or perhaps something worse. Holy Shit, I don't like this! Get us some protective gear, NOW." Sandy's stress soared exponentially. Fred Patterson was their calmest ED doc and he was freaked.

She grabbed the chart from the medication nurse and said, "Fred, not much to tell. The guy came in several hours ago; he was staying at the Burgundy Hotel in the Quarter. He's part of the staff for the Democratic Caucus that starts tomorrow. His friend who bought him here said he started feeling sick last night, had some nausea, vomiting and a sore throat. Then this morning his temp got higher and he couldn't stop vomiting so they brought him in. We started some IV fluids and gave him from nausea medicine. He was okay thirty minutes ago.

"Well, he sure as hell isn't okay now! I'm sure he is in liver failure at least and probably multi-system failure. Any recent blood work? Does he have any friends or family here? Any idea where he's been? Do you know if he has been traveling?" Fred was barking the questions at Sandy nonstop.

Sandy shrugged her shoulders as she and Fred watched as the Code team continued and respiratory intubated the patient. There was no cardiac response at all. Flat line. A nurse rolled the defibrillator closer.

"I've no idea," replied Sandy. "His friend stayed about thirty minutes and took off. Said he had a bunch of stuff to do. You know the politicians are here for the next few days, right? They are trying to clean up their act in the Washington."

"Yeah, goody, goody and the President is coming over the weekend, right?

Sandy could detect the sarcasm in Fred's voice. She really couldn't blame him for his jaded and sarcastic nature. Just this year, his twin brother, Ron, also at ED doc for CCHSC had died working in the ED. No one had recovered from it and most assuredly, Fred had not. Nevertheless, he was a great ED doc and he knew his stuff. Besides, almost everyone in America had lost respect for the politicians in Washington D.C. and Fred wasn't any different.

"Yep, that's what the papers say. I think a food service worker from the hotel was admitted earlier. I'll need to check." Sandy's voice was casual. She didn't want to upset Fred anymore then he already was.

"Find out where he's been from his friend that brought him in. Call the hotel. I think he has some kind of really bad virus. Get the infectious disease people in here too. I'm bringing in Tim Smith in Tropical Medicine over at Tulane as well."

Sandy could hear the tension in Fred's voice and paused for a second to respond, but Fred Patterson glared at her and said, "STAT, Sandy, we need to know what we are dealing with. If it's bad, we need to contain it. Be sure we have gathered all available blood samples for diagnostic testing. Get a tube for everything."

Sandy, an old hat ED nurse who thought she had seen everything working in New Orleans, was disturbed by Fred's behavior and the wild look in his eyes. She could feel herself becoming anxious, something she hardly ever did as an expert practitioner. She replied calmly "Got it, Fred, I'll take care of it," she said, pushing a reluctant Kelsey forward so they could get to work. Sandy could feel the slow but increasing thud of her heart. *Oh my God* she thought to herself, *suppose we have an outbreak of Ebola or some unknown hemorrhagic virus.*

Sandy looked at Kelsey who was even whiter than she was before. "Kelsey, have central supply bring in full gowns, masks and booties for all staff in the ED. Face shields as well. We need to start isolation on all patients and close the ED to further traffic. We must close down and transfer out the patients we can and divert potential admissions to other local EDs. I'll call and let administration know. This could be bad. We don't know what the guy's got."

Kelsey was onboard and quick to respond. "I'll take care of it, Sandy. I'll get the gear and report back to you. I'll call CCHSC infectious disease docs in here too if you want.

"Thanks, Kel. I'll call the infectious disease people. You're the best," Sandy patted her shoulder as she rushed towards her office to call administration and report a potentially serious biological threat to the health sciences center. She almost collided with Dr. Robert Bonnet, the interim chief of medicine at CCHSC.

Robert smiled brightly at Sandy, "Whoa! What's up, Sandy! Why are you hurrying so fast? I heard the CODE BLUE so I came down. What's going on?

"Come into my office, Robert. We need to talk for a moment. We have a guy, the Code actually, which I am sure they will call if they haven't already, who looks like he has some type of really weird virus. Fred said typhoid or malaria at the best and perhaps something else. Maybe even a really bad virus of some kind. The patient works for the Democratic Party. He was bleeding out, has a significant trunk rash and high fever. Also, his kidneys and liver have shut down. Bad rash over his trunk area too."

Robert's smile disappeared as he analyzed the info Sandy gave him. "This could be bad. Get Dave Brodrick, our head of infectious disease here at CCHSC and get him over here. If it looks like a hemorrhagic fever, we will need to call the CDC as well. Has anyone else been admitted with similar symptoms?"

'Yeah, but he was transferred to Intensive Care where this guy was headed before he coded. I think the guy in the ICU is South African and I believe he is food service staff at the Hotel Burgundy . He had a temp of 105.2 as well as nausea and vomiting. His platelets were whacked and WBCs

358

were way up. Short of breath too, but we treated him symptomatically. He was just like the guy who coded, but the South African guy stabilized and was transferred to ICU an hour or so ago." Their symptoms were almost identical at admission.

"Find out how he is and call me. I think we have a serious situation, at the very least a viral outbreak." Sandy noted the etched lines of concern on Robert's handsome face as he left her office and started down the hall.

*Damn, that man is hot....if I were a few years younger.....*Sandy thought admiring Robert's retreating figure as she picked up her phone. She had just completed her call to infectious disease when Robert returned, framed her doorway and asked, "Sandy, when does the political convention start? Do you know?"

Sandy shrugged her shoulders and said, "I don't know, sometime this weekend. Today is Thursday, right? I think it is Saturday morning, but I'm not positive." She gave him a reproachful look and teasingly added, "Really, Dr. Bonnet, you should know. You father is a senator!"

Robert cracked a half smile. "Find out," he said as he stared at her steadily, his eyes unwavering and holding hers.

After several seconds, Sandy got the message and asked, "Dr. Bonnet, you don't think someone is—"

Robert interrupted her, "I don't know, Sandy, but we have to think proactively. There're gonna be a lot of very powerful people in the city this weekend. We've got to consider it.

"Oh my God, Robert. We've had enough this year, please not this." Sandy's voice was shrill with fear.

"Yes, we have, but I have a bad feeling that this could be the worst. Close the ED to further traffic, have everyone wear full protective garb and for God's sake, no one is allowed to leave until we figure out what we are dealing with. Implement our full biocontainment protocol and only accept patients with flu-like symptoms into the ED. It's better to be safe than sorry.

Sandy stared at him, her eyes wide with amazement as she nodded and said, "I've already closed the ED and we are transferring everyone out we can. I just need to contact administration."

Robert smiled and said, "You have. These days I am administration. I'll talk to Alexandra. We're the administrators in charge. Keep this viral thing under your hat. It may be nothing but a bad bug but just to be safe, I'm calling CDC."

Sandy watched Robert leave for the second time as a dark, ominous feeling of dread permeated her body. *Oh my God, what are we in for,* she thought as she wiped the chill bumps from her arms.

Chapter 2

In the back of a deep warehouse off of Chartes Street in the Quarter, Ali, a thin, frail twenty-three-year-old Muslim stared at his older brother, thirty-one-year-old Nazir and said, "Nazir, are you sure we know what we are doing? I don't trust Vadim at all. Every since I hacked into his email and saw the exit plans he sent to his comrades in Russia, I have been suspicious. Maybe we should abort this mission. At least postpone it." Ali's young face looked scared and uncertain.

Nazir's face remained unchanged and he rolled his eyes and looked at his little brother condescendingly. "Ali, stop it. I thought you were ready for this. I thought I could trust you to be okay. We are doing the work of Allah." Ali seemed to shrink in stature at his brother's criticism and impatience. He seemed to retreat into his skin."

"I am ready, I really am," Ali replied with bravado in his voice. "I just don't like working with others, those that are not dedicated to our cause.

Nazir's impatience continued. "You have been training for over three years and I have been planning for a mission such as this for many years. Sometimes in order to do Allah's work, we have to work with others. This is one of those times."

Ali still looked doubtful, uncertain. His brother's words did not sway him.

Nazir moved over and put his arm around his little brother. Ali certainly wasn't a warrior, but he was a brilliant scientist and computer genius. He said gently, "Vadim is okay. He's just different from us. He is Russian and they do things differently. But he is a Muslim and worships as we do. He is one of the leaders in the Red Jihad movement at home in Eastern Europe."

Ali nodded as Nazir continued, "Remember, we needed Vadim and his connections to get us the virus. The Russians have been holding that strain since the Cold War. It would have taken us years to produce a similar strain. You more than anyone know we haven't been able to produce the more virulent strain in our laboratories." Nazir eyed him reprovingly.

"I know, I know," lamented his brother. "But we were very close. If you had just given me six more months I could have had the very same thing or perhaps something even better with a higher kill rate. Maybe even a virus that would be even harder to detect. Nazir, you have to understand that these things take time, believe me. I haven't been doddering." Ali's dark eyes were brooding and angry.

"No, my little brother. I certainly don't think that at all." Nazir continued to talk softly and reassure his brother how much he and the local jihad cell appreciated his talents and contributions. "I know that, I know that, little one. But you know how the Americans are. Very seldom are there so many of them from all parts of their leadership gathered together in such an iconic, filterable city such as New Orleans. Washington is just too difficult to attack. It is a fortress. But New Orleans.... What can I say? This is a perfect place for an attack. Ali, the place is half underwater and a sewer. It cannot be secured. Besides, they'll have a hard time figuring out if the virus is endemic to New Orleans. Nazir smirked to himself and continued, "They have so much stuff growing over there in Tulane's lab not even to mention all that stuff they're growing since Katrina. Besides, we have hundreds of places we can hide. We can hide here for years if we need. The time is right and the time is perfect. Besides, it will cause terror and fear in the hearts of Americans if we are successful so soon after Boston."

Ali was being stubborn. "I like New Orleans. I like all of our friends and where we live. I have fun here. I am happier than I have been in anywhere since we left home after our parents died. I like going to school at Tulane too and studying with Dr. Smith. I like being his lab rat and he says he can get me financing for my PhD if I decide to get it. He's taught me a lot, and in some ways he has been helpful to our cause."

Nazir's face had darkened and he shook his younger brother violently until Ali's teeth chattered. He gritted his teeth and barked at the slightly build young man in a hoarse voice, "Ali, for the last time. Don't you *remember* the Americans killed our parents? It was their drone that killed them. *These* people are our enemies. We are here to KILL them, not become their friends and help them in their labs. Do you get it or do you need to go back to Yemen?"

Ali was shocked at his brother's words. "I get it, I get it, Nazir. I am sorry. Now let me go. I must get to work. My shift starts in less than an hour," Ali shuffled out of his brother's arms, terrified but trying hard not to show it. He left the warehouse quickly walking quickly towards Canal Street and Tulane Medical Center.

Ali's heart was heavy on his way to work. He didn't like the business of hurting others, even though his parents had been killed. Hadn't the Taliban killed the parents of many American children during 9/11? Wasn't jihad just as destructive as the Americans had been over the years? He guessed his western education had made him question his supposed "mission". He was startled when his phone alarm sounded signaling a text. The text was from Dr. Smith that said,

ALI, CAN YOU COME ASAP? WE HAVE A VIRAL OUTBREAK IN ONE OF THE HOSPITALS. Tim.

He quickly texted back and said, I AM ON MY WAY. Ali. He didn't feel good about this at all. There was nothing good about a viral outbreak that could be good for him and Nazir or Vadim even, for that matter. At least not today. He wondered what was up. His heart began to thud with anxiety. Things were just not right and that bothered him. It bothered him a lot.

Finish Reading Viral Intent

The Alexandra Destephano Novels

Chaos at Crescent City Medical Center

The Imposter

Viral Intent

Toxic New Year

Evil: Finding St. Germaine

RUN For Your Life

Demons Among Us